"I'm all Cade

"You've got your fa

"Yes, but—" Panic reared and bucked in Seth's chest. "Luke and Tracy left me the Hollister ranch, as well. It's Caden's legacy. But I don't know the first thing about running a cattle business. I can't *do* this. I can't be Caden's daddy. I don't know how."

"Stand up," Rachel said, moving to his side. Her voice was strong and determined. "Now, take the baby in your arms."

Seth swallowed hard but tucked a sleeping Caden against his shoulder. The boy seemed to curve right into Seth. The gentle rhythm of the child's breath against his neck somehow soothed Seth.

"What are you feeling?" Rachel asked gently.

How *did* he feel?

Nervous. Overwhelmed. Panicked. Devastated. And yet, there was something more hovering just below the surface.

He was responsible for this little human being. And even though it meant his entire life had just been turned upside down and backward, there was something somehow…*right* about holding Caden in his arms.

A *Publishers Weekly* bestselling and award-winning author with over 1.5 million books in print, **Deb Kastner** writes stories of faith, family and community in a small-town Western setting. She lives in Colorado with her husband and a pack of miscreant mutts, and is blessed with three daughters and two grandchildren. She enjoys spoiling her grandkids, movies, music (The Texas Tenors!), singing in the church choir and exploring Colorado on horseback.

A sixth generation Texan, award-winning author **Debra Clopton** and her husband, Chuck, live on a ranch in Texas. She loves to travel and spend time with her family and watch NASCAR whenever time allows. She is surrounded by cows, dogs and even renegade donkey herds that keep her writing authentic and often find their way into her stories. She loves helping people smile with her fun, fast-paced stories.

The Cowboy's Baby Blessing

Deb Kastner

&

Her Unexpected Cowboy

Debra Clopton

LOVE INSPIRED
INSPIRATIONAL ROMANCE

LOVE INSPIRED®

INSPIRATIONAL ROMANCE

Recycling programs
for this product may
not exist in your area.

ISBN-13: 978-1-335-45615-1

The Cowboy's Baby Blessing &
Her Unexpected Cowboy

Copyright © 2020 by Harlequin Books S.A.

The Cowboy's Baby Blessing
First published in 2017. This edition published in 2020.
Copyright © 2017 by Debra Kastner

Her Unexpected Cowboy
First published in 2014. This edition published in 2020.
Copyright © 2014 by Debra Clopton

This edition published by arrangement with Harlequin Books S.A.

For questions and comments about the quality of this book,
please contact us at CustomerService@Harlequin.com.

Love Inspired
22 Adelaide St. West, 40th Floor
Toronto, Ontario M5H 4E3, Canada
www.Harlequin.com

Printed in U.S.A.

CONTENTS

THE COWBOY'S BABY BLESSING

Deb Kastner

To my forever sweetheart, Joe.
We've been through a lot, you and I,
and I wouldn't trade any of it for the world. Every
day with you is a great joy, and I'm so blessed by
our thirty years together. Here's to thirty more.

The Lord is near to all who call upon Him,
To all who call upon Him in truth.
—*Psalms* 145:18

Chapter One

Rachel Perez was looking for a man, not a monkey.

And she was most definitely *not* looking for a date, unlike many of the other single ladies scattered across the lawn at the First Annual Bachelors and Baskets Auction in Serendipity, Texas. What better way to nab themselves a bachelor for romantic reasons than a bachelor auction?

But that was *so* not Rachel.

No, not even close.

Rachel was in the market for a guy who was handy at fixing things—and she needed him, like, yesterday. She needed someone to tear down the well-used play set in her backyard and replace it with something new and to government specifications. The recertification status of the day care she ran out of her home depended on picking the right man for the job.

That was why she was glad that her town had chosen this particular type of "bachelor" auction to raise funds to build a senior center for the town—an auction that wasn't actually about getting dates with bachelors at all.

The Bachelors and Baskets Auction had started out

with the idea of hosting only true bachelors, but because the auction was for such an important cause, married men had jumped on the bandwagon, as well. Every man had his own unique skill set to offer to the crowd.

Making the auction a full-town event had also opened the bidding to a wider range of individuals. Single and married women alike were encouraged to bid on the men of their choice to help them with whatever projects needed doing around their homes and ranches.

Rachel suspected there would be a lot of husbands washing dishes and folding many loads of laundry before this day was done.

And determined not to be outdone by the men, the ladies in Serendipity had soon added their own contributions to the auction—loaded picnic baskets as a prize for the fellows they won. Virtually everyone in town was involved at some level. That was just the way the folks in Serendipity were—generous to a fault and ready with any excuse to get together and have a celebration. And willing to buckle down and put in good work, too, when it was needed. Surely there'd be someone perfect for the job of fixing up her outdoor play area for the kids in her care.

She intended to be picky about her choice. Someone older with lots of experience.

Even so, she had to admit she was amused by former army corporal Seth Howell's grand entrance. He might be too young and flighty to fulfill her requirements, but he was admittedly fun to watch.

At a full run, Seth banked his feet off one tree trunk before swinging from the branches of another. He hurdled over a bench and backflipped onto the platform where the auction was being held.

Jo Spencer, the redheaded owner of Cup O' Jo's Café, second mother to most of the town, as well as self-appointed auctioneer of this event, cackled with delight at his antics. She put a hammer in his grasp so he could continue to entertain the audience by displaying his abilities and showmanship.

He swung it around in circles and jabbed it a couple of times like a rapier, then posed like a well-built statue of a carpenter, showing off the sinews of his muscular biceps. Seth was shorter and leaner than some of the other cowboys Rachel had seen auctioned off so far—like the gigantic McKenna brothers, who towered over most of the crowd, but Seth was clearly in prime shape.

"Now, you can see for yourself, folks, what a unique specimen we have right here," Jo began. "He is ready and willing to help you with whatever odd jobs you've got planned for him, and you can be certain he will be adding his own brand of fun to the mix.

"Doesn't that sound lovely? Now, don't be deceived by his incredible physical prowess. Seth is not just a good-looking hunk of a man—he has a brain, to boot. You may not know this, but Seth is the fellow who single-handedly designed and built the new playground in the park. The man has *skillzzz*."

"Jo's right." Lizzie Emerson, Rachel's best friend, elbowed her in the ribs and grinned like she'd just pulled off a major prank. "That guy is cute *and* talented. And he couldn't be more perfect. He made the play set at the park. You need a play set built. He can do that—and so much more. Maybe one of your *odd jobs* could be for him to take you out for dinner."

Rachel locked gazes with her sixteen-year-old daughter, Zooey, and rolled her eyes. "For someone else, maybe, but I'm not looking for a date. You know perfectly well that all I'm looking for is a handyman to help bring my day care up to snuff before the next inspection. I don't have time for a romantic relationship even if I wanted one. Which I don't," she added when Lizzie's eyes glowed with mischief. "Even if I was looking for a date, I wouldn't try to find him at a bachelor auction. No—he's not the one for me."

Which was too bad, really. With what she now knew of Seth's background, she might have considered bidding on him, even if she had to put up with an occasional goofy antic. She'd seen the amazing wood-and-pipe structures he'd built for the kids in the park. She could easily imagine a similar structure gracing her backyard and replacing the well-worn swing set and climbing tower she now possessed.

But thanks to Lizzie and Zooey, bidding on Seth was out of the question, with the pressure she'd be under to make her work with him some kind of romantic rendezvous. The new playground in the park was nice, but under the circumstances, it was not enough to tempt her to make an offer on him.

Too much trouble, with a capital *T*.

"Which one of you pretty ladies is going to open the bidding on this handsome fellow?" Jo called, looking out into the audience. "Grab those pocketbooks and bid as generously as you can. Our senior center is just awaitin' to be built with the money we raise here today, and Seth's worth every dime you spend, don't you think?"

Zooey laughed and snatched the three crisp one-hundred-dollar bills Rachel had tucked in her hand, waving one of them in the air so Jo would see.

"One hundred dollars!"

"*What* do you think you are doing?" Rachel snapped, enunciating every word as she frantically reached for her daughter's wrist.

Zooey danced away, laughing in delight.

Lizzie offered a complicit grin. "We are buying you a bachelor. Which you desperately need, by the way. You need a *man* in your life, at least as much as you need a handyman. We know it, and so do you, if you're being honest with yourself."

"Oh, for crying out loud, you two. Didn't you listen to what I just said?" She was relieved when elsewhere on the lawn someone bumped the bid up to $125.

"Seth is the best of both worlds," Zooey pointed out. "You aren't going to find a better handyman out there when it comes to building playhouses."

Her statement might be valid, but Rachel wasn't about to concede. Not since the whole *both worlds* thing came into play with them. Dealing with a pair of matchmakers could lead only to embarrassment, for her and for Seth. She needed to nip this in the bud, right now. She scurried to make a mental list of reasons Seth wouldn't work out for her.

She wasn't coming up with much.

"I don't want—" she started to say, but her daughter interrupted her.

"Seth will be good for you, and he's the exact right fit for repairing your play equipment at the day care. No more arguments."

At the moment Rachel couldn't think of any, other than that Zooey's idea of the perfect candidate and hers were as different as night from day. As with so many things lately, this was just going to have to be another topic on which they couldn't seem to see eye to eye.

"One fifty for Seth!" Zooey shouted, squealing in delight when Jo pointed to her and acknowledged her bid.

"Zooey Maria Josephina Perez. Stop bidding and give me back my money this instant."

"I always know I'm in trouble when my mom uses my full name," she told Lizzie. "I think that's how she decided what my name would be when I was born."

"Zooey Maria Josephina Perez, get out of that tree before you fall and break your neck!" Zooey quipped.

Rachel sighed inwardly. If only it were that simple. Raising a teenager was much more difficult than having a good name to scold them with. For the scolding to work, the teenager first needed to be willing to listen to what the mother had to say.

Zooey's words were meant as a joke, but Rachel's heart tightened just a little. She loved seeing Zooey happy and carefree as she was acting today, focused on something that she genuinely seemed to believe would make her mother happy, but lately that had been the exception to the rule. It wasn't even funny to *jest* about Zooey getting into trouble—not when it was happening in fact, and all too often lately. And though they'd always been close, nothing Rachel said to her daughter seemed to get through to her at all anymore.

"It's for a good cause," Lizzie reminded Rachel, redirecting her attention to the stage.

"Yes, of course it is. To raise funds to build the senior center. I'm aware of that, as is everyone else who has come out today."

"No," Lizzie replied tartly. "The senior center is important, of course, but I was referring to finding you a single guy who is as good for your social life as he is for your day care. It could happen."

Rachel opened her mouth to protest once again, but Lizzie held up her hands to stop her.

"You heard Jo. Seth built the new playground in the park. You're looking for a man to spiff up your playhouse and swing set. Face it, girl. Seth Howell is exactly the man you need for the job. That he's nice on the eyes is purely going to be a side benefit."

Maybe he was the best man for the playhouse job, and he was rather handsome, but Rachel wasn't going to dig herself any deeper by admitting she privately agreed with her friend.

The guy was good-looking. If he was hoping to get a date out of this, he deserved to have that chance—but not with her. She would not embarrass Seth by being the high bidder when clearly there were any number of pretty young ladies spread out over the green seeking his undivided attention in far more interesting ways than anything she could offer.

She was confident he wouldn't want to be stuck with a woman who had long since exited the dating scene and who had nothing more on her mind than getting her play equipment recertification-ready.

The bidding war on Seth, who had passed the hammer back to Jo and was currently amusing the crowd by walking on his hands, was inching up in twenty-five-dollar increments. Her daughter had, thankfully, stopped participating in the back-and-forth volley, letting the younger women who *really* wanted social time with Seth fight it out between them. Rachel had brought her hard-earned cash with the intent to bid on one of Serendipity's best handymen or weekend do-it-yourselfers, most of whom were old or married or both, and she was fine with that. Better than fine—even if none of them had been the one who'd built the playground in the park. She *definitely* didn't care that none of them could hold a candle to Seth's youthful good looks, even an upside-down Seth whose blood was rushing to his face.

When the bidding finally passed the $300 mark, the knots in Rachel's shoulders relaxed. He was officially out of her budget now, so there'd be no more nonsense about Seth Howell. She would wait and bid on another man who would be willing and able help her spiff up her day care without putting crazy romantic ideas into her daughter's and best friend's heads.

Now that she was legitimately out of the running for Seth, she was beginning to enjoy watching the excitement the young, eager women were currently bringing to the auction. It was kind of cute, actually, seeing the hope and excitement in their expressions as they bid.

Eventually, the bidding stalled at $375. A happy seventy-five dollars more than Rachel could afford, thankfully.

"Going once," Jo announced. She bobbed her head so her red curls bounced and hovered her gavel over the makeshift podium. "Going twice."

Jo paused, her gaze spanning the green. She had just raised her gavel for the crack of a sale when Zooey spoke up.

"Four hundred," she announced brightly.

"Wait, what?" Rachel said aloud.

Zooey knew perfectly well how hard Rachel had had to scrape the bottom of the barrel for the $300 she'd collected to bid, and even then only because the need for a senior center was so great and because she could justify the remodeling work as a business expense.

And now she was going to be out another hundred?

She didn't want to be stingy when the money was going to such a good cause, but she was on a tight budget.

Her home day care kept a roof over her and Zooey's heads and food on the table, but there wasn't a lot of wiggle room for extras—like bidding on a goofy young man doing flips and handstands just because he was *cute*.

"Sold, to—" Jo paused as Zooey pointed both hands toward Rachel "—Rachel Perez."

Even with everyone's eyes on her, Rachel balked for a moment and then caught her daughter's elbow. "That hundred dollars is going to come out of your allowance."

Thankfully, Rachel had enough spare cash in her wallet to cover the difference, but that wasn't the point. Her daughter had taken her decision right out of her hands.

"I know it will," Zooey agreed cheerfully. She reached into the pocket of her blue jeans and withdrew a wad of five crumpled twenty-dollar bills. "Don't worry. I've got it covered. I've been saving up. You don't even need to worry about paying me back. Now take the money and go up there and rope yourself a Cowboy Charming."

Rachel momentarily considered withdrawing the bid, but she didn't want to humiliate herself—or Seth—in a public venue.

How would it look if she backed out now? Would everyone think she was too flighty to know her own mind? Or that she didn't think Seth was good enough?

At least he had the *skillzzz*, as Jo had phrased it, to repair the playground equipment for the day care, which, at the end of the day, was all that really mattered.

She could deal. She *would* deal.

She huffed and snatched the money from her daughter's grasp, then threaded her way through the crowd to the staging area. She was well aware of what she would be required to do as the winning bidder and her face flushed with heat as she handed off the cash in exchange for a lariat.

Lovely. Now all she had to do to get this over and done with was make a public spectacle of herself, thanks to her incorrigible daughter and her best friend. She supposed she would have ended up on the platform being required to throw a lasso to "rope" the man she'd won either way, but she doubted that with all the silly antics Seth had demonstrated, he would make this easy for her.

Not to mention the fact that she'd never thrown a rope before. Despite that she lived square in the middle of the country, she'd never even visited a ranch or ridden a horse, much less roped a cow.

How was she supposed to lasso a guy who couldn't stand still for more than one second at a time?

Yeah, that was *so* not going to happen.

Seth's bright blue eyes met hers, full of impetuousness and humor. It took her aback for a moment. She'd forgotten what it felt like to be that lighthearted and carefree.

Maybe she'd never been.

"You've got this," Seth assured her, gesturing for her to throw the rope. Despite his grandstanding before, he was ignoring the audience now to smile supportively at her—a purely kind gesture that left her feeling a bit flustered.

"I wouldn't be so sure about that."

Seth's smile turned into a toothy grin. "Why don't you toss that thing and we'll see?"

Good grief. It was probably better for her to throw the rope and be done with it. She had no idea what she was supposed to do when she missed, because up until this point in the auction, all the men had been successfully roped, one way or another. Sometimes the cowboys had to be artful in getting that rope around them, but so far every single one of them had managed.

Rachel was bound to disappoint everyone with her pathetic attempt at lassoing Seth. Hopefully, the crowd would just let her retreat gracefully off the stage with her "prize" when she failed.

Releasing her breath on a sigh, she aimed the loop like a Frisbee and threw her lariat in Seth's general direction.

As she knew it would, it didn't even come close to flying over his head.

More like waist high.

How humiliating.

But before she could so much as blink, Seth dived forward, over and into the lariat, rather than under it. She gasped in surprise as he tucked his body and somersaulted to his feet, the lariat successfully tightened around his waist.

He offered his hand and gestured toward the platform stairs with another cheeky grin.

"Ready for lunch?"

Rachel couldn't find her voice, so she merely nodded as the crowd applauded them both.

Great. Her first thought of Seth being half man, half monkey was apparently not that far off the mark.

He might be well able to come to her rescue where repairing the playhouse was concerned, but she had major doubts about how easy he would be to work with. He seemed like a nice enough man, but he didn't appear to take anything too seriously.

Would he go off swinging through the trees when he was supposed to be building playground equipment?

She glanced over to Zooey and Lizzie, expecting to see smug looks on their faces, but they'd already lost interest in her and now stood with their heads together, no doubt debating the pros and cons of the next bachelor on the docket. Lizzie hadn't put in her bid yet—and she *was* looking for a bachelor, someone she could eventually call her sweetheart.

Rachel considered rejoining them and then discarded the idea. Her impish daughter and equally mischievous best friend were bound to embarrass her—and worse, Seth—and she'd just as soon wait as long as possible before that eventuality.

Besides, Seth was probably hungry from all that back-flipping and handstanding he'd done. At least if she had Seth to herself, she would be able to find out when and how she could avail him of his talents—those of the non-branch-swinging variety.

She led him across the community green to where she'd left her picnic basket under the cool shade of an old oak tree. She'd had the toddlers in her day care decorate the basket as part of arts-and-crafts time. It was now threaded with multicolored ribbons and randomly dotted with finger paint. Rachel was proud of the creation, and especially of her kids.

"Your basket looks awesome," Seth complimented.

She turned and met his gaze, half expecting to find mockery in his eyes, but he was totally earnest, insofar as she could tell. His smile looked sincere.

"Thank you. My day-care kids made it for me."

"I can tell it was created with love," he said, sinking down onto the checked wool blanket she'd spread on the ground before him.

She smiled, pleased by his thoughtfulness. He was

clearly a nice guy. Maybe this experience wouldn't be a total disaster after all. She smiled appreciatively and laid out the classic country picnic fare of fried chicken, macaroni salad and baked beans, with chocolate cupcakes for dessert.

Seth opened the water she offered him and downed the entire bottle without taking a breath. Wordlessly, she handed him a second bottle.

"Thirsty much?" she asked when he took another long drink.

He grinned. "Just rehydrating. Wait until you see my appetite."

She gestured to the food. "It's all yours."

Although technically, it wasn't. She couldn't forget that Zooey would be around before long with her own healthy appetite. Rachel had packed some of Zooey's favorites.

In preparation, Rachel fixed her daughter a plate and set it aside, then filled a plate for herself.

"Eating for two?" he teased.

For the briefest moment Seth's words took on an ugly context, one she'd long ago fought and overcome. She wasn't reed thin like Lizzie and even Zooey, and she accepted now that she never would be.

As a child, she'd been bullied. Worse than that, even, when she'd become a teenager.

But the glimmer in Seth's eyes wasn't cruel. He was joshing her about the two plates she'd fixed. She wasn't going to make it a sore point just because at one time in her life she'd had low self-esteem because of her weight.

She laughed and casually leaned back on her palms, crossing her feet at the ankles.

"This extra one is for my daughter, Zooey. She's still

following the auction, helping my best friend, Lizzie, pick out the perfect handsome bachelor for a date, but I imagine she'll be around as soon as she gets hungry."

"Was that your daughter I saw bidding on your behalf?"

Rachel nodded and shifted her gaze away from him, suddenly uncomfortable and embarrassed that he'd noticed that she hadn't been doing her own bidding. She also worried that he might have misconstrued her words.

If Lizzie was looking for a handsome bachelor to date, it stood to reason that Rachel had been looking for the same exact thing. And that Seth might think that bachelor was him.

Oh dear.

"Yes, that's Zooey," she cut in quickly, before he had too much time to think about what she'd said previously. "She's sixteen. To be perfectly honest with you, she had an entirely different idea than me on what I was looking for. She took over my bidding completely without my consent." Suddenly realizing how insulting that might sound, she scrambled to backpedal. "I didn't— That is— I wouldn't—"

When she stammered to a halt and heat rushed to her face, he finished her sentence for her.

"You wouldn't have chosen to bid on me."

No big deal, he told himself, but knowing that Rachel hadn't really wanted to win him still pricked at his pride.

Rachel met his gaze, her deep brown eyes thoughtful and expressive.

"No. To be honest, I probably wouldn't have. That is, originally, I *would* have considered you, especially regarding the particular tasks I have in mind for you to do for me." She took a great gulp of air. "But then Lizzie and my daughter got it in their minds to—"

She stammered to a halt. Inhaled another ragged breath. Exhaled on a deep sigh. Seth wanted to say something to make her feel better, but he honestly had no clue what he could offer. Frankly, it was strange to him to see her this flustered. He knew her only in passing, but she'd always given off this air of calm competence that he admired, seeming sure of herself in every situation.

Well, apparently not this one.

"I'm afraid all I will be able to offer you is some general fix-it work on the play yard of my in-home day care," she said at last.

He took a sip of cold water and gestured with his hand. "As opposed to…?"

Her cheeks, which were already flushed a pretty pink, now turned bright red, and she broke her gaze away from his.

"Okay," she muttered under her breath. "I'm just going to say it."

She paused dramatically. "As opposed to a date. I feel like I cheated you out of something special. You know, something more, er, romantic. You would have been better off with one of the beautiful younger ladies who were bidding on you for your—" her voice tightened and she squinted as she choked out the last part of her sentence "—good looks."

He sat up straighter as his wilted ego reinflated faster than a balloon on a helium pump.

"No worries on that front," he assured her with a grin. "I'm glad you won the bid on me. Relieved, even. You just saved me from what could have been an awkward situation. I assure you I'm not looking for a girlfriend, not even a casual one. That wouldn't be fair to her. I'm only home for a few weeks before I'm heading off to college."

"That's exciting. I never made it to college. Have you picked a school yet?"

"Texas State University. I'm a little nervous about it," he admitted. "I've never been a great student, and it's not like I'm right out of high school, so I'll probably stick out like a sore thumb."

"Oh, I wouldn't worry too much about that. It's not like you're over-the-hill, and many adults these days are choosing to go back to school after they've been out in the real world for a while."

A brief cloud of sadness crossed over his heart. "That, I've done. Seen the real world, I mean, in the army. I'm looking forward to putting my full focus on my academics."

And keep his mind off everything he'd experienced while on tour. He was haunted by questions and guilt that wouldn't leave him alone. He was hoping he'd be so busy studying that he wouldn't have time for reflection on just how cruel he'd seen the "real world" be.

It couldn't get much more real than watching his best friend, Luke, being gunned down right in front of him, hit by a sniper who barely missed Seth, but that wasn't something he wanted to share with a woman he'd barely met.

He didn't even like to think about it, much less talk about it.

"I'm so sorry. I know you were in the army. I didn't mean to remind you of hard times."

He shrugged. "Life is what it is. I've learned that I

have to accept it and move forward. The key is to watch my attitude. I've chosen to remain positive."

"That's a wonderful outlook, and one I try to follow myself, although I'm not always successful at it. Sometimes it's easier to see the glass as half-empty."

Her gaze dropped and she blew out a breath. He waited for her to finish her thought, but she remained quiet. He knew what she wanted to say but couldn't.

Easier, but not better.

"I'm majoring in athletic training," he said to fill the silence.

"Based on your demonstration before, I'd say that ought to be right up your alley." She snapped back to the present and smiled at him, although he could see it was forced. "What do you plan to do when you graduate? Coach high school sports?"

He shrugged. He wasn't much of a planner and never had been. He only vaguely pictured his future beyond the challenge of four years of hitting the books. He knew from experience that too much could change between now and then. What was the point of making all these grandiose plans only to discover life is nothing like you expect it to be?

"I don't know yet. I think it'd be cool to work with a pro sports team. Football or baseball, maybe, or even basketball. That'd give me the opportunity to travel the country, which I'd like to do. Or if not that, then maybe I could work with a college sports program. I'd like to think I could make a difference with the kids coming through the ranks."

"I suspect you'd be very good at that, given the *skillzzz* I saw you display today."

He laughed at her exact replication of Jo's word, all

the way down to the crackly tone of voice that the old redhead had used.

"I'm probably just kidding myself thinking I can get into the big leagues, but I figure I might as well reach for the sky, right?"

"Or swing for it." She laughed. "What's that called, anyway? That thing you were doing earlier with the swinging and jumping and backflips?"

His smile widened. "Parkour. It's basically focusing your mind with the intent of seeing and interacting with your environment in a different way. It puts everything into perspective. You should try it sometime. I could give you a lesson or two."

Her eyes widened in surprise and then she burst out laughing.

"With this body?" She gestured at herself from head to toe. "I don't think so."

He didn't see anything wrong with her body. She was full figured, but in a healthy way. Besides, parkour was a mental exercise as much as a physical one.

"You shouldn't limit yourself, Rachel. Parkour isn't about what you can't do—it's about what you *can*."

"I believe I'll stick to working out in my living room to my exercise dance DVDs, thank you very much. Somewhere no one can see how awkward I look when I move."

He wanted to press her but sensed this wasn't the time. Plus, this was the first time he'd really spoken to her—brief chitchat at church or his family's grocery store didn't count—and he didn't want to give her the wrong impression about parkour. Or about *him*.

"What about your daughter? Do you think she might enjoy parkour?"

Rachel voraciously shook her head, her dark hair flipping over one shoulder.

"Oh, no. She needs to concentrate on her academics right now if she's going to get into a good college. She didn't pass two of her classes last year and consequently is in summer school right now. It's not that she's not smart," she modified. "She just hasn't been applying herself lately. I'm trying to encourage her to do better in summer school. Anyway, sports aren't really Zooey's thing."

"Did I hear my name?" Seth's gaze shifted to the teenager who'd jogged up to Rachel. Zooey was a pretty, dark-haired, dark-eyed teenager who looked a lot like her mother. The girl dropped onto her knees next to the picnic basket and flashed a friendly smile at Seth.

"I was telling Seth here what a pickle you are, taking over the bidding on my behalf."

Zooey stuck out her tongue at Rachel and reached for the plate Rachel handed her. "Someone had to do it. You don't mind, do you, Seth?"

He chuckled. "No, of course not. In fact, I'm thinking this day turned out rather well."

"Ha. Told you, Mom." She picked up a chicken drumstick, took a bite and pointed it toward Seth.

"Have you tried your chicken yet? My mom makes the best fried chicken ever."

"Don't talk with your mouth full," Rachel admonished. "And we haven't said grace yet."

Seth had been reaching for his chicken breast, but he stopped midmovement at Rachel's reminder that they needed to pray before their meal.

It wasn't something he was used to doing—not since his youth when he lived with his parents. He was used to diving straight into his meal, and this meal definitely seemed worth diving into. His stomach growled when the delectable, greasy smell of fried chicken reached his nose, and his mouth watered in anticipation. He usually limited himself to grilled meat served with lots of fresh fruits and vegetables, but he wasn't about to pass up homemade fried chicken.

This was a special occasion, right?

It was all he could do not to take a bite of his chicken, but he restrained himself and politely bowed his head.

"Would you like to say grace?"

With his eyes closed, he didn't immediately realize Rachel was speaking to him.

"Seth?"

His eyes popped open to find Rachel and Zooey both staring at him.

"I—er—I'm more of a Christmas and Easter kind of man. So I— Well, I'm out of practice. You go ahead." His voice sounded stilted and awkward, even to him.

"I'm sorry. I just assumed— I see your parents and sister at church every Sunday. I didn't mean to make you feel uncomfortable."

"You didn't," he assured her, even though he was itching in his skin.

He searched his mind for a way to describe his current relationship with the Lord, but nothing sounded right. It was too complicated for casual conversation. He believed in God, but God hadn't always been there for him.

Certainly not lately. Not when it really counted.

He was relieved when she spoke, removing the need for a coherent explanation.

"Let's thank the Lord for our food."

Quietly and with gentle reverence, she offered heart-felt gratitude for the food, the day and the company.

Seth shifted uncomfortably. He'd been raised in a Christian home and, since he'd returned from the army, occasionally attended church services with his family, but religion didn't play a big part in his life anymore.

He cracked his eyes open to watch Rachel pray and noticed he wasn't the only one feeling uncomfortable. Zooey's eyes were also open, her gaze on her folded hands. Or rather, she was frowning at her clenched hands. He was surprised she didn't seem tapped into faith. He certainly had been at her age, with his family's example all around him, and from the way that Rachel prayed, it was clear that faith was important to her and played a big role in her home.

Rachel's grace wasn't dry or bottled, but rather she spoke from her heart, which Seth admired and, if he was being honest, envied. He missed the innocence of his youth, of a faith that transcended the trials of daily life, but he'd seen far too much of the world not to question what he believed.

Still, he echoed her *amen.*

Zooey scooped a forkful of macaroni salad into her mouth and chewed slowly. A group of young men Seth guessed to be around Zooey's age walked by, jostling and shoving and trying to talk over each other. Zooey didn't turn her head, but her gaze trailed after the guys.

Rachel must have seen that, as well.

"It's a good thing they didn't allow the teenage guys to participate in the auction," she said after swallowing her bite of baked beans.

The boys had moved out of hearing distance, but that didn't stop the blush that rose to the teenager's cheeks.

"Mom," she whispered harshly. "That is so uncool. They could have heard you."

A little adolescent and overdramatic for Seth's taste, but it was an amusing scene, at least until Zooey tossed down her plate and popped to her feet.

"I am *so* out of here."

"Sit down and finish eating." Rachel's voice was low and even, but Seth could hear the barely contained tension coating her voice. Her daughter seemed all too willing to ignore it.

"Zooey," Rachel called after her, but the teenager loped away as if she hadn't heard, joining a group of friends on the other side of the green.

Rachel sighed and rested her forehead against her palm. "I'm getting a migraine. Sometimes I really don't know what to do with that girl."

Seth chuckled. "She's a teenager. Most of the time, rebellion is written in their DNA. Are you going to tell me you didn't get into a few scrapes and give your mom a hassle when you were sixteen?"

She scoffed. "I had a newborn baby when I was sixteen. My mother didn't care for the idea of becoming a grandmother at such a young age and she threw me out of the house."

Seth's gut tightened. "Are you serious?"

"Unfortunately, yes. My mom and dad are fairly well-to-do and their unmarried teenage daughter becoming pregnant didn't go down well in their social circles. It was better if I just disappeared before anyone found out. I would have been interested to hear their explanation for why I dropped out of school and off the map, but I never got a chance to hear it. I haven't seen them since that day, nor do I want to. I've forgiven them for what they did to me and Zooey, but they're not part of our lives."

"They sent you away?" Seth almost couldn't believe what he was hearing. What kind of parents did that to their child? He had made more than his share of mistakes in his life, but he knew beyond a doubt that his mom and dad would never turn their backs on him, no matter what he did. It was almost inconceivable to even think about. "What did you do?"

"Given that I had no money and nowhere to turn, I am one of the blessed ones. I didn't end up on the street. Instead, I was taken in by a church-run home for teenage mothers. They taught me how to care for my daughter and helped me finish high school and get on my feet. They gave me real-world skills I could use to provide for Zooey and myself. When I was eighteen, I moved to Serendipity, set up shop as an in-home day-care provider, and the rest, as they say, is history."

"Wow. That must have been tough, especially at such a young age. I admire and applaud you for your courage."

Rachel shook her head. "It wasn't courage. I was scared to death. But I had a lot of support. And though Zooey wasn't conceived in an ideal situation, I loved her from the first moment I discovered I was carrying her in my womb. I did what I had to."

"My buddy Luke used to tell me that courage wasn't the lack of fear. It was being afraid and going forward anyway. That's what you did. I call it courage."

Rachel nibbled at her chicken, chewing thoughtfully, her gaze distant. Then, with effort, she seemed to set her emotions aside.

"But enough about me. Tell me about you. Did you

join the army right out of high school? Thank you for your service, by the way."

He gave her a clipped nod. He didn't really want to talk about his time in the military, and though appreciative of their acknowledgment, he never knew what to say when people thanked him for serving.

"Like many little boys, I dreamed about becoming a soldier when I grew up," he said. "But I followed through with it and, along with my best friend, Luke Hollister, enlisted before I even finished high school. We were off to boot camp right after we graduated. At the time, I intended to make the army my career. Twenty years and a decent pension sounded good to me. And I really loved serving in the army."

"What happened?" she asked softly.

Seth blew out a breath. "Luke was killed in a firefight. I was right there next to him and—" He swallowed hard to dislodge the memory. "And then a sniper got him. The bullet whizzed right by my ear and hit Luke."

He frowned. It was hard to get the words out.

"That day haunts me. I'll never understand why God let things go down the way they did. I'm a bachelor and yet I was the one who dodged the bullet. Luke left behind his pregnant wife, Tracy, and their ranch land, which has been in the Hollister family for generations."

"It must have been very rough for her," Rachel said. "I remember the prayers that were said for her in church. Such a sad situation. I know what it's like to be pregnant and on your own, but I can't even imagine dealing with the grief she must have felt, on top of having to run the ranch by herself."

Seth nodded his agreement. "Thankfully, Tracy was born and raised on a ranch, so she gradually adapted to becoming the sole owner. I admire her courage so much. She's one of the strongest women I know."

"At least she had her child to look forward to. She had a boy, right?"

"That's right. Little Caden is almost three years old now. I promised Luke I'd watch over Caden and Tracy if anything ever happened to him, which is a big part of the reason I came back to Serendipity before heading off to college. I wanted to check in on them and make sure everything was as okay as Tracy tried to make it sound whenever I spoke to her on the phone. I needed to see her with my own eyes."

"And how is she doing?"

"She appears to be making a success of it, although honestly, I can't even imagine how she does it. She told me straight to my face that she was fine and she didn't need my help, that I should worry about getting my own life in order. I realized then that I didn't want my life to go the same way as Luke's. I didn't re-up in the army, because my heart wasn't in it anymore. I knew I had to do something different."

"I imagine so," Rachel said, sympathy evident in the tone of her voice.

"The truth is, I just want to get away from responsibility for a while. I want to be *me*—to find out who I am outside of the military. I've always had someone else in charge of where I go and what I do in my life. I didn't even take the summer off after high school. Straight from my parents' house into the army, where I was under orders for everything, even eating and sleeping. Right now all I have on my mind is doing my own thing for a change. Make my own decisions without regard to anyone but myself. No strings attached. Saying that aloud makes me sound like a selfish lout, doesn't it?"

"Not at all."

She was generous to say so.

"When I go to college, all I want to worry about is keeping my grades up. That will take some doing. Like I said, I wasn't the best student, but I'm not sure if it's so much that I wasn't good at school as that I didn't really apply myself. I only worked hard enough to keep my grades high enough for sports." He could feel himself flushing with embarrassment. "Aw, man. I sound like a regular slacker. Don't worry—I promise I won't rub off on Zooey."

Rachel laughed. "She could use a little of your good attitude. You certainly sound ready to buckle down and work hard now. So after college, some kind of big-league sports work, and then what?"

"I imagine I'll probably want to settle down at some point—you know, get married and have children. But that is *way* down the road from now, though."

He pressed his lips together. He wasn't even close to being ready for a family of his own. He wasn't financially prepared to support anyone—and frankly, after losing his best friend, he wasn't ready for any relationship that would leave his heart open to getting hurt again.

"But," he continued, forcing the corners of his mouth to curve upward, if only barely, for Rachel's sake, "in other news, I am now the awesome godfather of the cutest baby ever, Luke and Tracy's two-year-old son, Caden. And thanks to my sister and brother-in-law, I'm also the proud uncle of an adorable seven-year-old niece and a feisty pair of twins—one boy and one girl. Samantha and Will's kiddos keep them good and busy."

"So you're the fun uncle, huh?"

He flashed his most charming smile. "Exactly. And that's how I intend to keep things."

"Chief tickler and bogeyman storyteller. The children will look forward to you coming home to visit when you're on breaks at school or the football season is over."

Considering how little they knew of each other, Rachel had just nailed it.

That was the man he wanted to be. The fun uncle who could come and go as he pleased. He was happy to have found someone who seemed to understand where he was at in his life—and why he would soon be leaving town for greener pastures.

Chapter Two

Sunday was usually Rachel's favorite day of the week. It was the only day out of seven that she allowed herself the opportunity to worship, relax and just *be*, after a frantically busy week filled to the brim with toddlers followed by a Saturday crammed with a week's worth of leftover chores and errands.

After Sunday services, she could read or binge on a television series or just nap, which was her favorite way to spend a quiet Sunday afternoon. But today her usual sense of peace had been replaced by a nagging sense of worry.

This morning, she'd watched for Seth at the small church that was home to Serendipity's community of faith. On the day of the auction, they'd agreed to meet after the Sunday service to go over the specific details of when and how he'd work off her auction win, but he hadn't shown up. In fact, none of the Howells had been present, which was unusual, since Seth's parents—Samuel and Amanda—along with Will and Samantha Davenport and their brood usually took up an entire pew.

She'd have to make time to seek Seth out sometime

during the week, as soon as possible. Or maybe she could get his cell number from Samantha. She needed the work done without delay. Her day-care recertification was close on the horizon, and from what she'd heard, many of her friends' in-home day cares were failing in favor of corporate-run day cares because of tightening restrictions.

She couldn't afford to fail.

Her business was her lifeline—hers and Zooey's. She couldn't even imagine what she'd do if she lost the ability to take care of the children. It was the only job she'd ever had, the one thing she felt capable of and qualified for.

Rachel didn't regret having Zooey, not for one second, but it *had* put a halt on her college plans and the dreams she'd had for her future. She'd intended to pursue a degree in early childhood education and get her teaching degree.

She'd adapted those dreams into running an in-home day care. Maybe she didn't have the degree behind her name, but she knew she was a good teacher, and the best part of her day was sitting with the kids, reading to them and teaching them letters and numbers.

Every so often she had to pass a government inspection like the one that was coming up in a few weeks. She kept her day care strictly by the code, but the inspectors were becoming more nitpicky.

She had to keep hold of this job, not only because she loved it, but because it paid her bills and she was able to save a little toward her daughter's future.

Zooey came first, and she always would. And that was tied to the other frustration in her life—that her daughter, whom she loved more than anything, was pulling away from her. And the situation kept getting worse.

This morning, Zooey had once again pleaded that she was too sick to go to church, when the truth was she was just trying to get out of going to the Sunday service. It had been happening far too often lately. Usually, Rachel insisted that her daughter accompany her, but she was beyond tired of arguing all the time, so this Sunday she'd given in and allowed Zooey to stay home and sleep in.

As soon as Rachel had walked through the doors of the church, guilt had crushed her. She was the parent in this situation. She needed to be the strong one, no matter how hard Zooey pushed back. She should have required that Zooey come with her—no matter what her flimsy excuses might be.

She wouldn't let it happen again. It didn't matter how tired Rachel was or how much stress she was under, she couldn't shirk her responsibility as a parent. As long as her daughter lived under her roof and ate her food, she was going to go to church on Sundays.

Period.

It wasn't a huge shock to Rachel when she walked in the front door of her modest two-bedroom house and found her daughter playing a video game and talking to someone through her headset. Unfortunately, Rachel had expected it. Zooey didn't even look up—not until Rachel loomed over her with her arms akimbo and a frown on her face.

At least Myst, a black cat with the most extraordinary emerald-green eyes, appeared happy to see her. He threaded in and out of her legs as she stood waiting for Zooey to acknowledge her, his purr sounding like a truck engine.

"I thought you were too sick to go to church," Rachel

reprimanded. "And you know you're not allowed to play video games on Sunday."

Even though their family unit was small, Rachel had always tried to make it clear that family time was a priority. In particular, she went out of her way to make Sundays special, a quiet time to spend with her daughter away from the technology that so often drew them apart. She stayed off her phone and computer and she expected Zooey to do the same.

"Sorry, James. I have to go," Zooey said into the headset. "My mom's bugging me."

Rachel stood silently as her daughter turned off her video game, unsure of which part of Zooey's statement she should address first.

The teenager's disrespectful words and behavior or the boy?

"Who is James?" She forced herself to remain calm and not sound accusatory.

"He's just a guy, Mom." She used to know all of Zooey's friends. Though Rachel treasured the time she could spend one-on-one with her little girl, she had always been pleased to welcome any friend who wanted to come over for dinner or join them while they went shopping or to the movies. She'd willingly hosted birthday parties and slumber parties and had enjoyed seeing her happy, social daughter having fun with her friends.

It was only in the past year or so that Zooey had become secretive over what went on in her life. Her longtime friends rarely came over anymore—she seemed to have taken up with a new crowd that Rachel hadn't met. Meanwhile, her grades had dropped to the point where she had to attend summer school. If Zooey had legitimately had problems with a subject, Rachel would have understood, but Zooey had simply not turned in assignments and, worse, had cut class on more than one occasion.

Though Rachel didn't like to judge, she was responsible for Zooey's safety, and in her opinion, some of her daughter's current friends were questionable at best.

That was what had Rachel worried. She'd raised Zooey to be street-smart as well as book-smart, but she was only sixteen and, whether she wanted to admit it or not, was innocent and vulnerable. Those traits left a girl open to all sorts of predators wanting to take advantage, as Rachel knew all too well.

After all, Rachel's life had drastically changed when *she* was sixteen. She wanted so much more for her own daughter.

"And how do you know this James?" Rachel knew her suspicion was creeping out in her tone. She had heard too many horror stories about creepy men stalking girls online not to worry or to ask questions. She wasn't exactly sure how the game console worked, but she suspected it might be similar to a computer in the ability to connect with strangers. Zooey had been speaking in real time to whoever this James person was. For all Rachel knew, it could be a grown man on the lookout for a girl he could manipulate.

Zooey scowled and defiantly tipped up her chin.

"Check the attitude," Rachel warned.

"He's just a friend. My best friend Lori's boyfriend. Nobody to worry about."

"So you've met him before, then? He's your age? You've seen him face-to-face?"

Zooey sighed overdramatically. "Yes, Mom. He's in summer school with me."

Not so long ago, her daughter had been a sweet little infant curled in her arms. It had been easy to protect and care for her then.

Where had the years gone?

Zooey was old enough to date, although up to this point she'd shown little interest in any particular guy, at least as far as Rachel knew.

Zooey used to talk to her about these things, but lately, not so much. The thought of Zooey dating frightened Rachel more than she could say. She knew it wasn't fair to project her own teenage inadequacies on her daughter, but she couldn't seem to help herself.

Zooey was a different girl from the teenager Rachel had been at her age. Zooey was smart. Confident. Beautiful. Maybe too much so. There was no doubt she would be catching the eyes of Serendipity's young men. And all it would take was one bad decision, one mistake, one misjudgment.

Life could change in an instant. She knew that from her own life and had been reminded of it when she'd been talking with Seth at the auction. Rachel wanted her daughter to be able to be free to chase her dreams, something Rachel had never been able to do, but in order to do that, she had a lot of hurdles to jump.

Rachel had been insecure as a teenager and peer pressure had overwhelmed her. She'd had body-type issues and high school bullies had sometimes fat-shamed her into doing things she would not otherwise have done.

That was how she'd gotten pregnant with Zooey— trying to find someone who would love her for who she was. But the boy had dumped her the moment he found out she was pregnant, accusing her of sleeping around and denying that he was even the father of her child.

He'd never loved her. Looking back, she was pretty sure he'd never even *liked* her. Rachel had found out the truth the hard way.

She didn't want that for her daughter. But she couldn't seem to find a way to express her concerns without sending Zooey on another rant, angry that her mother didn't trust her.

Rachel didn't know how to bridge the gap that was growing between them, but she had to try.

She sat down on the couch, curling one leg underneath her and turning toward her daughter. "I was thinking maybe if you got more involved in church activities, you wouldn't feel so inclined to skip Sunday services."

Zooey twirled a lock of her dark brown hair around her finger and didn't say a word.

"You're really good with my day-care kiddos," Rachel continued. "Maybe you could teach Sunday school when fall comes. The preschoolers would love you. And I'd like to see you go back to youth group this summer. Didn't you used to have a lot of friends there?"

Zooey wouldn't meet her eyes.

She looked—*what*?

Frustrated? Upset? Stricken?

"Zooey?" she prompted when the girl did not speak. "What are you thinking? You can be honest with me."

"I don't want to hurt your feelings," she mumbled.

"This isn't about my feelings. It's about trying to figure out some solutions that will work for both of us."

"Well, I don't want to go to youth group anymore. None of my friends go to church. They think it's stupid."

Rachel felt like someone had slapped her. This was one battle she really didn't want to lose, watching her daughter walk away from the faith she'd been brought up in. But how could she stop Zooey from sliding down that slippery slope?

She pinched the bridge of her nose where another headache was developing.

Peer pressure.

Rachel's breath snagged in her throat. She knew all about peer pressure.

Lord, help me reach my daughter.

"Which friends are those, exactly?" she asked through a tight jaw, barely restraining herself from adding that those friends probably weren't real friends at all if they led her away from church.

"Lori and James. We want to hang out at the community pool and get a good tan once summer school is over. That's where all the cool kids go."

"I see."

She saw all too well. But she didn't know what to do about it.

Push her? Back off?

At least it was just suntanning at the pool.

For now.

"I'm not going to force you to go to youth group, if that's what you're worried about. But you should have been honest with me earlier and told me that you didn't want to go rather than lying about being sick. You don't want to participate? Then don't. But please, be honest with me either way. And don't make your decision based on what your friends think. I've taught you better than that."

Zooey stared at her a moment without speaking. Rachel held her breath, praying she'd gotten through to the rebellious teenager. But when her daughter picked up the headset to the video game console, intending to hook it back up to the system, Rachel felt a sinking certainty that her words hadn't had any impact at all. Reaching out to her daughter wasn't going to work this time. So instead, she'd have to try standing firm. She stopped Zooey with a hand on her arm.

"You may be your own person, but you are sixteen years old and you are living in my house, so I make the rules. No video games on Sunday."

Zooey's face turned red and she dropped the headset onto the coffee table, where it bounced and then clattered onto the wood floor.

"I've had enough of your attitude, young lady."

"Fine." Zooey scowled and then marched straight out the front door.

"Where do you think you are going?" In her frustration, Rachel enunciated every word.

"Out. I'm going out. I can't stand this. I don't want to be around you right now."

"Zooey, stop." It wasn't a suggestion, but the teenager ignored it anyway and shot off down the street on foot, not even bothering to look back.

Rachel huffed out an irritated breath and made to follow her, but just as she was leaving, Seth pulled into her driveway and exited his car—

With a baby in his arms.

Seth's knees were weak and his gut clenched into knots in an excruciatingly uneven rhythm. His vision felt fuzzy and it was all he could do to plant his feet on the ground, step by agonizing step. The only thing that was keeping him upright was the fact that he was carrying a two-year-old baby in his arms, curled up against his shoulder and sound asleep.

The baby he had vowed to protect, never realizing that one day he would be called to do just that.

Grief sucker punched him, but he willed it back. He had to stay strong for Caden's sake.

"I saw Zooey fly out of here," he said, rocking back and forth on his heels and patting Caden's back. "Is everything all right?"

Rachel nodded, tight-lipped. Her face was flushed red and marked with lines of strain. She didn't look much better than he felt.

"Well…good."

He hesitated. Obviously this wasn't a good time for Rachel. He wasn't even positive why he was here, except for a niggling sensation in the back of his mind that Rachel might be the one person in Serendipity most able to understand what he was going through right now.

She narrowed her gaze on him, studying him intently. "You don't look so good. Would you like to come in?"

"Um, yeah. Thanks."

He followed her through the door and took a seat on the plush armchair. Thankfully, the baby was still sound asleep on his shoulder. Seth hadn't been able to get Caden to stop crying earlier in the day.

He'd tried everything to no avail—changing, feeding, rocking. Nothing had worked until the little tyke had finally worn himself out.

It was only one of many new challenges he was about to face. Despite the way his family had rallied around him, he'd never felt so alone in his life.

"Would you like some coffee? It'll only take me a minute to make us a pot."

"No, thank you."

She gestured to Caden. "I see you've got Caden with

you. I love that he has Luke's blond hair. He's such a sweetheart. Are you babysitting for Tracy today?"

This time he couldn't hold his grief back. It burned like molten lava from his gut to his throat and he had to swallow hard just to speak.

"Tracy's dead."

Rachel's eyes widened and she grasped for the arm of the sofa, shakily seating herself.

"I'm so sorry. I hadn't heard."

"To tell you the truth, I feel numb, like I'm in the twilight zone or something. Yesterday afternoon, she dropped Caden off at my house, saying she had a bad headache. She asked me to watch him. I thought I would only be babysitting for a couple hours."

He blinked hard several times to erase the moisture forming in his eyes.

"Tracy…she…she passed away last night. She didn't just have a headache. She had a brain aneurysm. One second she was here and then she was gone. I've been with my family since yesterday trying to process everything."

"Lord, have mercy." Rachel whispered the prayer. "Poor Tracy. Poor Caden."

Rachel's gaze was full of compassion, but she didn't speak further, as if she somehow knew he needed to get it all out at once.

"May I?" She stood and held out her arms for Caden, who had awoken and was making tiny sounds of distress.

As soon as Caden was in Rachel's arms, his crying abated. To say the woman was naturally gifted with children would be an understatement. Caden was responding to Rachel way better than he had to Seth or even to Seth's mother or sister throughout the long, grief-filled day.

This was so hard to talk about, or even to think about. The circumstances were surreal.

He felt more helpless at this moment than he had even when he'd seen his best friend gunned down right in front of his eyes.

"You know how the Bible says God won't give you more than you can bear?" he asked, his voice cracking with strain.

She nodded and ran her palm over Caden's silky hair, quietly shushing the baby.

"I don't think that verse is true. I think God has just given me way more than I can handle."

He pulled in a deep breath and continued. "The reading of the will is going to happen directly after the funeral. I already know what's in it. Luke and Tracy appointed me as Caden's guardian should anything ever happen to them, but— I don't know. I never thought it would actually play out this way. After Luke's death… well, I should have realized whole lives can change in a split second. But it's just not something that I wanted to think about, so I put it out of my mind."

"There's no one in Caden's extended family who might be able to take him?"

"No, Luke told me that wasn't an option back when he asked me to be godfather. Luke's parents died in a car crash a few years ago. His grandparents are in an assisted-living facility. Tracy's dad is disabled from a stroke and needs constant care from her mother. They're in no position to raise a child, even their own grandson. Tracy has a sister, Trish, but I've never met her. Luke told me she took off for New York the moment she graduated high school and never looked back. She wasn't at the wedding, and she's never even met Caden, to my knowledge."

He set his jaw to clamp down the emotions roiling through him. "I'm all Caden's got."

"You've got your family to support you."

"Yes, but—" Panic reared and bucked in his chest like a wild stallion. "Luke and Tracy left me the Hollister ranch, as well. It's been in the family for generations. It's Caden's legacy. But I'm not a rancher, Rachel. I hardly even know how to ride a horse, and I don't know the first thing about running a cattle business. I can't *do* this."

Rachel was silent for a moment.

"Of course you can," she said at last.

"No. I… I had plans. I wasn't going to stick around Serendipity. I've already got college lined up, although obviously now there's no way I'm going to go."

His panic was rising steadily in his chest. "I can't be Caden's daddy. I don't know how."

She chuckled mildly. It wasn't a happy sound, but her expression radiated empathy. "Not to quote clichés at you, but you know what they say about the best-laid plans. You'll find a way—a way to take care of Caden and to get your education if you want."

"But a *baby.*"

She nodded. "I understand. That's why you've come to me seeking advice. I can empathize with you because I've been there myself. It's mighty intimidating thinking about raising a child on your own. An unplanned pregnancy really threw my life into turmoil, and I was just a kid myself."

Yes.

He'd come here thinking he needed to ask Rachel's help in caring for Caden.

Of course, he needed to get Caden set up in day care so he could spend his days trying to figure out what he was going to do about the ranch. But now he realized it was more than that.

Because she really *did* know what he was going through, the outrageous cyclone of emotions that swirled through him, threatening to blow him away.

He looked her right in the eye. Her gaze was shiny, too, as he expected his own was.

"I am not responsible enough to raise a child," he told her. "I'm only twenty-six myself."

She reached out and touched his arm. The contact somehow grounded him.

Human-to-human.

"I was ten years younger than that when I had Zooey. And I really was all alone. You have your family—and me, if you need me, to help you get your bearings. God brought Caden into your life. He will see you through. It'll take a while, but you'll work this out. For Caden's sake, you have to."

He jerked his chin in a brief nod. He was glad she was straightforward with him instead of couching everything she said in softer language. He desperately needed to be told exactly what to do.

"How?" he asked gravely.

"By taking it one day at a time."

"Sage advice."

But not nearly enough.

"For starters," she continued, "where is Caden sleeping tonight?"

"My place, I guess. I'm staying in one of my mom and dad's cabins. I suppose I'll have to move into the ranch house eventually, but right now, I just can't be there. The memories are too fresh. They hurt too much." He picked off his cowboy hat and threaded his fingers through his hair. "I hadn't really thought about it. I can't seem to think beyond minute to minute, much less one day at a time. How am I going to do this?"

"Stand up," Rachel said, moving to his side. Her voice was strong and determined, as if she were giving him an order. "Now take the baby in your arms."

Seth swallowed hard but did as Rachel bid, tucking a once-again-sleeping Caden against his shoulder. The boy was all toddler, with chubby cheeks and with thick arms and legs, and yet he was so light he seemed to curve right into Seth as he shifted his weight side to side in a rocking motion. The gentle rhythm of the child's breath against his neck soothed Seth as much as the rocking did Caden.

"What are you feeling?" Rachel asked gently.

Seth closed his eyes and breathed in Caden's little-boy scent.

How *did* he feel?

Nervous. Overwhelmed. Panicked. Devastated. And yet there was something more, something indefinable, hovering just below the surface.

He was responsible for this little human being. And even though it meant his entire life had just been turned upside down and backward, there was something somehow…*right*…about holding Caden in his arms. He couldn't name the emotions, but they were there, cresting in his chest.

"See?" Rachel murmured, even though Seth hadn't answered her question aloud. "Pretty special, isn't it?"

"Mmm," Seth agreed softly, afraid to put his emotions into words.

"I have a mobile playpen that you can use until you

have time to outfit yourself better. Caden will be able to eat finger food and finely cut meats, fruits and vegetables. I don't even have to ask if you're a healthy eater, so I imagine you'll have everything you need already stocked in your refrigerator. Do you know how to change a diaper?"

"Caden is in those pull-up ones. My mom showed me how to work them. Although those dirty diapers are going to take some getting used to." He wrinkled his nose at the thought.

"Since you've got the Hollister ranch to worry about, you're probably going to need someone to watch him during the day. Or is your family on that?"

"That's actually why I originally came over. It wasn't to break down on you, I promise."

She laid a reassuring hand on his arm. "I know. It just so happens that I have an opening in my day care, so you can bring Caden over in the morning while you take care of whatever needs doing at the ranch. No charge for the first week while you get on your feet and find the lay of the land. No pun intended."

Her joke drew a slight smile from him. "I can't ask you to do that."

"You didn't ask. I offered. Honestly, things are going to work out. You may not be able to see it now, but God's got it all in His capable hands. Start walking the path, step-by-step, even if you can't see a single thing in front of you. Trust Him to show you the way."

"Mmm," Seth said again. He wasn't sure he believed what Rachel was saying, or even understood all of it, but *she* did, and he didn't want to contradict her when she was doing so much for him.

"You'll have to baby-proof your house right away.

Toddlers have the tendency to get into everything and climb on everything. Caden will bump his head and fall to the floor more times than you'll be able to count. But we can at least make the bumps less bumpy and the falls less painful."

We?

Had he really come over only to find day care for Caden, or had God led him over here for more than that? He knew what Rachel would say if he voiced the question aloud. He appreciated her so much for offering her advice and assistance, but again he had trouble forming the words to express his gratitude.

"I know a little bit about baby-proofing. My sister gave me some extra hardware they had left over after putting their own house in order for the twins, but I'm not sure where everything goes or how it works. Samantha or Will can probably help me, but they're busy with the store, so it may be a few days."

"I'm sure they have their hands full with the grocery and their own kids. I'm free after work tomorrow. I could come over and help you set everything up," she offered.

Caden started hiccuping in his sleep, and Seth and Rachel chuckled softly together.

"I guess this will be an adventure," he admitted. He'd always been one to chase adventure…though he'd never expected to face one quite this huge. There was a big, wide ocean in front of him and he didn't even know how to trim the sails.

But he could learn. And whether it was God or circumstance or whatever, he was grateful for all the support he was receiving. From his family…and from Rachel. What if she hadn't been the one to win him at the auction, telling him her story and putting her in his head as someone he could turn to in this situation? He didn't even want to think about that.

"Adventure is a good way to look at it," she said. "You and Caden are a team."

He looked down at the still-hiccuping but soundly sleeping little boy in his arms and his heart welled.

He wouldn't let Caden down, no matter what.

He was Caden's permanent legal guardian and would be the only parent the boy would ever know.

It was what Luke and Tracy would have wanted. It was what Caden needed. And it was what Seth was determined to be.

A father.

Chapter Three

One day at a time.

Rachel was great at doling out counsel but not so much at putting it to use in her own life.

Seth was trying to figure out how to parent Caden—and he was looking to *her* for advice?

She felt as if someone had stamped a giant fail sign on her forehead. What use was she going to be to Seth—or Caden—when she didn't have her own house in order?

Actually, helping Seth was a good way to get out of her own head for a while, to forget the constant bickering that had taken over her relationship with Zooey. At least she knew what to do with Caden.

She had to admit she was looking forward to Seth bringing sweet Caden over for day care. Rachel loved children of all ages, but there was something about a pudgy toddler, just learning to strike out on his own and explore the world, that really captured Rachel's heart.

And Caden would need all the extra love and attention she could give him. He was fortunate to have such a dedicated guardian in Seth, and he had Seth's extended family to offer strength and support. He was going to be okay, but Rachel still grieved over the circumstances that had left this boy without his mother and father.

And yet she saw something in Seth—his dedication and determination—that made her think he would turn out to be a fine father for Caden in the long run.

Seth had entrusted her with Caden's day care, and she was resolved to do everything she could to make Seth's transition from *footloose and fancy-free* to *father and rancher* as streamlined and painless as possible.

In some ways it would be easier for Caden than for Seth. Caden would adapt quickly. Poor Seth knew next to nothing about child care and had admitted he understood little about ranching, either.

And now, in the space of one day, he had a child and owned a ranch.

Talk about a learning curve.

Rachel poured herself a cup of coffee and went out to sit on the front porch and enjoy the early morning. Seth would be coming a bit earlier than the other parents so he and Caden would have more time to adjust to their first day.

Most of the time it was harder on the parents than it was on the children to let go that first day. Given Seth's peculiar situation, she suspected it might be even more difficult for him. His life had undergone so many changes so quickly he probably didn't know which way was up anymore.

Putting everything else aside, she felt sure he was mourning the loss of a sweet, lovely woman who had died far too soon. It was clear Seth had considered Tracy a friend, and her death would have been a shock to him even if Caden hadn't been in the picture, especially on top of the grief he still experienced over Luke's death. Caden was all Seth had left of his friends to hold on to. Rachel wondered if it would be difficult for him to let the boy go, even for just a few hours.

As for Caden, he might be too young to understand the whole truth of what had happened, but in his own way, he had to be wondering where his mama had gone and why she wasn't coming back to get him. Rachel was certain he must be missing her terribly.

She fought back the tears that sprang to her eyes. She needed to be strong for both Caden and Seth.

Her cat, Myst, diverted her attention when he appeared and flopped by her side, his purr like the deep revving of an engine as he groomed himself. Myst would make himself scarce for the rest of the day, having learned the hard way to avoid overexcited toddlers with grabby hands. He was a typical feline, antisocial to most humans except when he wanted to be snuggled and petted on his own terms, and even then he graced only Rachel and Zooey with that honor.

Mr. Picky was his nickname.

Rachel had just finished her coffee when Seth pulled his car into her driveway. She stepped forward to help him release Caden from his car seat. She laughed, her heart welling, when the little boy wrapped his arms around her neck and squeezed tightly.

"This ridiculous thing is more complicated than it looks," Seth said of the five-point buckle. "It took me forever to figure it out the first time."

"Car seats are one of my many areas of expertise," she teased, but Seth nodded solemnly.

"I imagine so."

A lump burned hot in her throat. It didn't take a genius to realize he was thinking about all the things he *didn't* know about raising a child, and Rachel mentally kicked herself for her insensitivity.

She was relieved when he changed the subject.

"If you have a moment, would it be okay for me to take a look at your backyard and the play equipment you currently have?" he asked, leaning down to scoop Myst into his arms. He stroked the cat, who in turn nuzzled under his chin, demanding his complete devotion and attention. "We can discuss your needs and then I will draw up some preliminary suggestions on how best to make this work."

"How did you do that?" she asked, so stunned she forgot to answer his question.

"Do what?"

"Myst doesn't like anybody, especially men."

He scratched the cat's ears and chuckled. "Cats like me. I don't know why. I've never had one of my own. Hopefully, I have the same effect on horses and cows."

Seth was such a charmer that Rachel suspected he might have that effect on every living creature he came in contact with, including every pretty young lady who crossed his path, and most of the older ones, too. Cats were especially intuitive, and Myst obviously thought highly of Seth.

But as far as the play yard went—

"Don't worry about building anything for me. I'm officially absolving you of any obligation. You have way too much going for you to be concerned about my needs."

She was worried about what she'd be able to do, with the recertification coming up so rapidly, but it wasn't fair to bring Seth in on it. He'd just landed himself a baby. That took precedence over any problems she was experiencing.

She'd just have to figure out how to handle this herself. The most logical thing to do would be to break down the old play equipment on her own and rent a trash bin one weekend to get rid of all the pieces. She could clean up the backyard well enough to pass the inspection. New equipment would have to wait.

"No, Rachel. Let me do this for you. You're helping me out so much by caring for Caden and with all the instructions you've given me."

He made it sound as if she were a how-to manual. The thought made her smile.

"You'll be paying me for the day care, remember? Although like I said earlier, don't forget that the first week is on the house."

"And you paid for *me* at the auction," he shot back. He gestured toward the door. "I mean it. I don't mind building you a new play yard. I know you said you have someone coming to assess the day care soon for recertification. This is important to you—and honestly, I think it will be good for me. Building a project like a playhouse that I know I'll excel in will take my mind off all the stuff I *don't* know how to do. So you see, you're doing me a favor."

She didn't see how he could possibly smile after all he'd been through in the past twenty-four hours, but the toothy grin he flashed her worked its charm.

She was not immune.

How could she say no?

With Caden still in her arms, she led Seth out to the backyard and then let the toddler down to play while she talked to his new guardian.

She gestured to her current play equipment, a combination of wood, pipes and canvas that included a tent, a slide and a couple of swings.

"I've been told I have to remove or replace it by the beginning of July. At this point I'm thinking that removing it is going to be challenge enough in itself."

"I can probably hack it down in half a day," Seth said, setting Myst on the ground at his feet. The cat wound in a figure eight around his legs, his tail curling around his black cowboy boots in a ploy for more attention. "And then, once we've settled on something you like, it's just a matter of ordering in the materials. I can probably build something new in a weekend—if you're willing to watch Caden for me, that is."

"That's a given," she assured him, pointing to where Caden was scaling a kid-sized slanted climbing wall. "Look at that little boy crawl. If I didn't know better— It's almost as if he's related to you."

Seth's brow lowered and his lips tightened, but his smile remained. "Yeah. Well, I guess Caden is related, kind of, or at least he will be when I formally adopt him."

"That's for sure the direction you're going, then?"

He nodded. "It's what Luke and Tracy would have wanted. And it's what I want to do."

"You're a good friend. And you'll be a great father."

"Your lips to God's ears," he murmured.

Seth had formed a plan, kind of. He could see no way around it but that he accept that he was Caden's permanent legal guardian. He needed to adopt Caden as his own and be his *father*—and then somehow he had to keep the Hollister ranch up and running for Caden's legacy.

He'd considered every other possibility and had come up with nothing. As he'd told Rachel, adopting Caden was what Luke and Tracy would have wanted.

How could he do less?

So much for the carefree days of being his own man. He knew it was not only immature but irresponsible even harboring that moment of regret, but there it was. He let it flow through him…and then he let it go.

Making decisions with only his own happiness in mind was a thing of the past. Period. Now his life belonged to Caden, and under the circumstances, that was exactly as it should be.

He would do everything in his power to be the father Caden needed him to be, despite that the thought sent shivers down his spine and he was looking at a learning curve that was a series of hairpin turns down a steep mountain road.

The more time he spent with Caden, the more he admired Rachel for the success she'd made out of her life. A bright, intelligent daughter. A thriving business that she loved.

Before having a toddler of his own to take care of, he never would have comprehended all of the sacrifices Rachel, as a single mother, had made—and continued to make—for Zooey's sake.

Big things like not going to college. Little everyday things like cooking meals and playing blocks with her on the carpet.

Now that he was in a similar situation, he'd become minutely aware of just how much parents, especially single parents, acted and sacrificed for their children's sake on a constant, daily basis. It didn't matter if the child was two or twenty. A parent would always be a parent.

He would always be Caden's dad. It still sounded odd to think of himself that way, but there it was.

Friday of the first week had finally come, and Caden's introduction to day care had gone well. Rachel had reported that he had no trouble fitting in with the other children. He was a social child and especially enjoyed snack time. And to Seth's amazement, Caden always appeared as happy to see him at the end of the day as Seth was to see Caden. The baby still had moments when he'd cry uncontrollably. Seth thought he must be missing his mama. But they were coping, he and Caden, moving forward together, step by step.

Seth was anxious for this particular workday on the ranch to end. He'd thought he was in good physical shape before all these new challenges in his life began, but at the moment he was sore head to toe from all his hours on horseback, and his brain was aching from the amount of new information he was trying to consume all at once.

Who knew that running a ranch would be so complicated?

Though he'd grown up in a ranching community, he hadn't ever been so much as a weekend cowboy, and aside from half listening to the complaints of friends in school, he'd never thought about cows.

All he knew was that ranchers roamed the range herding cattle to new pastures as the old grass got eaten up.

His learning curve with the ranch was nearly as complex as the one with Caden. Thankfully, Tracy's foreman, Wes Gorman, was a kind, knowledgeable older man who'd spent his entire life as a working cowboy and who was willing to keep things running while he taught Seth the ropes of the business.

Seth would have laughed at his unintended pun except his backside was so saddle sore he wasn't sure he could conjure a smile. He'd be sitting on ice for a week.

He felt like a fraud in his hat and boots, although he'd worn both from the time he hit high school. Nearly all the men in Serendipity wore cowboy hats. But then again, nearly all of them were ranchers.

He'd sometimes ridden the range with Luke when they were boys, but they'd never done much real ranch work. They'd always been too busy goofing around. He vaguely remembered the freedom he'd felt when he'd galloped across the meadow back when he was a teenager, but he hadn't been anywhere near a horse in a decade.

He was more cautious now than he was when he was a hormone-ridden high schooler. He wasn't about to gallop anywhere and risk breaking his neck, thank you.

Still, he was determined to learn everything there was to know about the Hollister family's ranch, Bar H, and that started with hands-on experience at everything from riding out and evaluating the herd to mucking out the horse stalls.

He was proud of his progress so far. He hadn't lost his seat in the saddle—*yet*—although he was careful to keep his mount, Luke's old chestnut gelding, Windsong, from moving any faster than a trot. He had spent the first couple of days surveying the Bar H holdings and becoming acquainted with both horses and cattle. Wes had explained to him about rotating the grazing stock among the fields and pastures and that the cattle were beef cows.

He had yet to learn how to balance the books, which was on the docket for the weekend, but at least that could be done from a desk. He would be glad to be seated on something that didn't move, for a change.

He wasn't looking forward to wrestling with numbers. Math had been a weak spot in school. But if he was going to run the Bar H property right, he was going to have to understand the financial status of the ranch.

When he pulled Windsong up to the old barn, exhausted and ready to slip out of the saddle and take a long, hot shower to soothe his weary muscles, he was surprised to find Rachel already there waiting for him.

She had agreed to bring Caden to him today rather than him picking the boy up, but he hadn't intended for her to meet him at the stable. No sense everyone getting dusty and mud caked. They had planned to meet later at Seth's house so she could help him finish baby-proofing, and he was stoked to show her the designs he'd drawn up for her new play equipment.

She didn't immediately see him approach and he reined to a halt, watching the interplay between woman and toddler with interest. She was holding Caden by the hands as he hopped on and off a square bale of hay. Rachel displayed unending patience as Caden wanted to jump again and again. They were both giggling as she picked him up, twirled him around in circles and tickled his tummy.

The stress lines usually so prominent around her eyes and mouth eased as she played with Caden. Seth had always thought Rachel was pretty, but she simply lit up like an evergreen at Christmas when she was around children, especially Caden.

She had a special gift, and he was beyond grateful she had won him at the auction. *Someone* was watching out for him, and in the deep confines of his heart he knew it was the Lord.

How else could he explain having been so fortunate? Rachel was giving Seth back at least as much as he would be able to do for her in building her new playhouse, and she'd spent money for his efforts.

What she did for him, and for Caden, she did out of the kindness of her heart and nothing more.

Rachel caught sight of him and stopped twirling around, settling Caden on her hip and pointing to Seth, who was still on board Windsong.

"Look who just rode in, Caden."

Seth grinned and tipped his hat to her.

"It's your cowboy father. Er…is that what you're going to have him call you? Father?"

His gaze widened, the burden of responsibility weighing even more heavily on his shoulders as he realized that was just one more decision he had to make, out of the hundreds he'd already made and the millions more ahead of him.

"I haven't even had a chance to really think about it. I've been talking to my lawyer about the steps I'll need to take to legally adopt him as my son, so I guess that would be an important step."

"And probably the sooner, the better, so Caden can get used to it. What do you think? *Father? Dad? Daddy? Pop?*"

"I called my own father *Daddy*, at least when I was a little tyke like Caden. I'd feel honored to follow in my father's footsteps—and hope to be able to do half as good a job as he did parenting Samantha and me. We were a handful."

"Did you hear that, Caden?" Rachel raised the toddler from her hip to seat him in the saddle in front of Seth. "Do you want your *daddy* to take you on a horsey ride?"

Caden squealed with delight and pumped his arms and legs with such joyful abandon that Seth could barely contain him in the saddle, never mind keep Windsong steady. Fortunately, the horse was calm and patient. Seth wasn't a great horseman yet, but somehow he managed to walk the horse around the corral a couple of times.

He couldn't contain the smile that split his face. He knew Caden's excitement was over being on a large animal well off the ground, but his own heart was internally performing the same squealing pump-and-wiggle dance.

Daddy.

So *this* was what it was like to care for another person more than he cared for himself. A peculiar array of emotions slammed into him so suddenly and so intensely that it was all he could do to keep his back straight and his boots in the stirrups as he continued to lead Windsong around the corral with Caden propped securely just behind the saddle horn.

Despite the tragedy that had put them here, he and Caden were now a family. He would love and cherish this little piece of humanity with everything in him.

All of a sudden, Caden wasn't a burden.

He was a blessing.

"Say *horsey*," Rachel said, waving to get Caden's attention as she snapped a picture with her cell phone. She held it up so Seth could see what she'd taken.

"There you go, you two. Your first family photo."

Chapter Four

"Has Seth asked you out on a date yet?" Zooey teased as she helped Rachel unhook the swings from the old swing set in anticipation of tearing the entire thing down.

It had been a crazy week with Seth learning to be a new father. Rachel had spent several evenings with him, sometimes working on modifying his apartment, other times simply enjoying playing with the toddler.

She'd told him multiple times that he didn't need to worry about her backyard plans, that she'd find another way to get the work done on her play set, but he'd insisted on starting on his project on this bright Saturday morning in June.

To Rachel's relief, Zooey was in a good mood for a change and had even offered to help break down all of the day care's old playground equipment. Rachel suspected that Zooey's good mood had more to do with the fact that Seth and Caden were on their way than any genuine desire to help her mother.

But at this point Rachel was grasping at straws with the girl and would take whatever pleasant interaction she could get, even with strings attached. Zooey had really taken to Caden in the past week, giving the toddler extra attention when she wasn't attending summer school. If Rachel had to use Seth and Caden as bait in order to spend more time with her daughter without it turning into an argument, so be it.

"No," Rachel answered, using a hand drill to remove some of the screws that held the play set together. She was both systematic and judicious, not wanting the whole set to collapse on top of her before Seth arrived to direct the project. "Seth has *not* asked me out. And he's not going to. I would appreciate it if you wouldn't mention the harebrained scheme you and Lizzie came up with at the auction. I already came clean with him and told him all about it, so there's no sense bringing it up again and putting him—well, everyone, really—in an awkward position, right?"

Zooey shrugged. "I don't see how you two going out on a date would be awkward. It might just be nice, you know. Dinner and a movie? How long has it been, Mom, since you've been in a relationship? I mean, really."

Too long.

Rachel wouldn't even know what to do on a date or how to act. She felt certain it would be *beyond* awkward.

Especially if her date was Seth.

"Give the poor man a break. He just found out he's going to be an adoptive father. He doesn't have time to be asking women out on dates."

"But that's what makes you two a perfect match. Single mom. Single dad. Totally gorgeous guy. Pretty woman. Mom, really. What more could you ask for?"

"For you to keep your nose out of my business," Rachel replied promptly, wrinkling her nose at her daughter.

Zooey sputtered out a laugh, knowing Rachel was teasing. She didn't sound at all convinced.

"I'm not looking for a relationship right now, and he's definitely not. He's barely keeping his head above water with all that has just gotten dumped on him."

"Then he needs a woman's help now more than ever. You'd be great for him, Mom. I know you would." She paused and frowned, her forehead wrinkling as if she were pondering some great thought. "You should be in the market for a husband, or at least a boyfriend. Why aren't you?"

"In a relationship? When would I have time to date? Between operating my day care and raising you—"

"Mom," Zooey protested, the word sharp and piercing. "I'm sixteen."

Precisely the point, Rachel thought but didn't dare say aloud.

Boys. Dating. Parties. Peer pressure. She needed to keep a closer eye on her daughter than ever.

"I know you don't want to think about it, but I'm not going to be around forever," Zooey continued. "College is only a couple of years away and then I'll be off living my own life. What are you going to do then?"

Zooey's words jabbed Rachel's heart. She knew them to be true and right—the way life should be—but that didn't make it any easier. She'd spent half her life caring for her daughter. What would it be like when she was gone?

Lonely.

For the single mother, it was the empty-nest syndrome in spades.

She didn't know what to say to Zooey. She didn't

want her daughter to worry about her when she should be thinking about her future.

Relief rushed through her when Seth let himself into the backyard through the side gate she'd unlocked for him.

"Good morning, pretty ladies," he called.

Whew. Saved by the bell—or rather, the handsome man. Now she wouldn't have to continue with the excruciating task of answering Zooey's question—especially because she had no idea *what* her future would look like when Zooey struck out on a life of her own. She'd been so focused on securing Zooey's future that she had neglected her own.

It was a sobering thought, but one she couldn't dwell on. Not with Seth here.

Seth would have caught any woman's eye this morning, not just Rachel's. He had changed up his look, favoring a black T-shirt that hugged his muscular frame and a Texas Rangers baseball cap, along with bright blue running shoes rather than his usual cowboy hat and boots.

He was holding a squirming Caden under his arm like a football, just above the tool belt strapped around his waist. Rachel's first and natural instinct was to dash forward and correct Seth for the way he held the boy, but then she realized both he and the toddler were making zooming noises while Caden stretched his arms out like the wings of an airplane.

It was a very guy kind of thing to do, and it warmed her heart to see the way the handsome suddenly-a-cowboy-daddy and Caden were bonding.

"Not a word to Seth about what we've been talking about," Rachel cautioned Zooey from under her breath as Seth put the little boy on the ground. Rachel cast a sidelong look at her daughter to make sure she'd been listening.

If she saw so much as a mischievous sparkle in Zooey's eyes, she was immediately going to send her on an errand to pick up...*something*...she needed right away.

From Australia.

As it turned out, Rachel needn't have worried. The moment Zooey spotted Caden, she rushed forward and swept the toddler into her arms, asking him if he wanted to dig in the sand with her.

The oversize sandbox contained not only shovels and pails but a large collection of toy dump trucks, bulldozers and a toddler-sized backhoe to scoop the sand up and into the backs of the trucks.

Zooey wasn't the type of teen to worry too much about fashion or invest in clothes that had to be kept immaculate. Dressed in jeans and a baggy bright green T-shirt, she sank on her knees into the sand and pulled Caden onto her lap, showing him how to use a bulldozer to push the sand into a pile and then scoop it up with the backhoe and haul it around with a dump truck. To Caden's delight, she even made truck noises to go along with the various movements.

Rachel shook her head at the incredible sight.

If she didn't know better, she would never have guessed that Zooey was an only child with no brothers and sisters to play in the sandbox with. She'd always interacted regularly with Rachel's day-care children, but the scene playing out before her somehow went beyond anything in Zooey's past.

She and Caden almost appeared to be brother and sister, even with the age gap between them. Zooey was clearly taken with Caden, and the little boy was smitten with her, as well. It was the cutest thing to watch, and Rachel's heart warmed.

After a brief discussion with Seth, she waved at Zooey. "Seth and I are going to unload some more tools from the back of his truck. Are you going to be okay with Caden for a few more minutes?"

Zooey grinned, her face beaming with delight. "We're fine right here, aren't we, Caden?"

Caden giggled and tossed a handful of sand into a nearby bucket.

Rachel's throat pinched and she snagged in a breath. It was a poignant moment, watching Zooey and the toddler having fun together.

"Wow," Seth said with a low whistle as he and Rachel headed out front. "Like mother, like daughter, huh? She definitely picked up your nurturing genes. Look how great she's doing with Caden. She's a real natural at this. You can tell Caden already loves her."

"I agree," Rachel said. "She's always had a special gift for children."

Her memories were bittersweet.

"From the time she was about four years old, she started helping me out in my day care. At first she'd just play with the kids, but as she got older, she'd read to them, feed them snacks, give them hugs if they fell down and scraped their knees. She'd bandage them up and kiss all their owies away."

"Sounds like maybe she'd make a good doctor," he commented as he sorted through some of his tools.

Rachel sighed. "I used to think so, too, until she hit Algebra II and didn't pass the course. I'm not sure if it's because math is not her thing, or if she just wasn't applying herself. I believe that part of it is that she lost interest in doing well in school."

And she started hanging out with a questionable group of friends who influenced her in a bad way, but Rachel wasn't about to admit that aloud.

"I guess who can really blame her, right?" Seth said, chuckling. "Algebra II is when they start you on imaginary and irrational numbers, isn't it? Why in the world would you want to work with irrational numbers? And don't even get me started on imaginary. If they aren't real, why would you want to do equations with them?"

"I excelled in language arts and literature when I was in school," she agreed. "*Irrational* and *imaginary* apparently have entirely different definitions to science nerds."

Seth belted out a laugh. "Good point."

He grabbed a couple of sawhorses and leaned them against the truck, then handed her a circular saw.

"Careful. It's a little heavy," he warned her as he picked up the sawhorses and carried them, one under each arm.

The saw *was* heavy and was awkward in her grasp, much like how her emotions played out nearly every time Seth was in her presence.

Heavy and awkward.

She liked him, and she liked being around him. Most of the time she felt comfortable with him, but she couldn't always account for her feelings when their eyes met and her stomach flipped or a spark of electricity zapped through her.

That, she was keeping a major secret. If Zooey ever even suspected Seth had a crazy effect on her, she would never hear the end of it. Besides, it wasn't like it was a big deal. He was an attractive man. There was nothing strange or unusual in noticing that, particularly when she had no intention of doing anything about it.

"I don't know that I had a favorite subject in high school, but I did enjoy playing sports."

"Which one?"

He chuckled. "Oh, all of them. I especially liked track and soccer. I hadn't grown into my full height yet, so football was something of a challenge for me. My smaller frame had its advantages, though. I was a decent running back, and I could slip through the lines because of my size. I would pretty much do anything as long as I was outside running in the fresh air and not cooped up in a stale classroom."

She could easily imagine Seth as a youth, antsy and squirrelly and not wanting to feel boxed in by four walls. Maybe that was why parkour appealed to him so much. He could jump on the walls rather than be smothered by them.

"I don't know why the school system thinks it needs to torture every one of its students with upper-level math. Who actually uses that stuff?"

"Right?" he agreed, shaking his head. "I mean, I suppose if you want to be a chemist or a rocket scientist, you need to know equations and formulas and Xs and Os."

She laughed at his misuse of algebraic formulas. She'd never seen an equation with XO before.

"I don't believe I've ever seen an O in a mathematical formula, though I have seen some at the bottom of a love letter." She blushed. "On television, I mean."

She sped forward so as to cover her own embarrassment. She'd never received a love letter in her life.

"Honestly, I've never used algebra at all," she said, "other than solving for a single X, which comes in handy when I'm missing one variable of a real-life equation. Otherwise, I don't use upper math. Ever."

"Me neither. I've got to say, I am freaking out about keeping the books at the Bar H ranch. I'm not sure I can afford to hire a regular accountant, but I don't know how I am going to be able to get along without one."

"Let me help you," Rachel offered. "I've always done my own books for the day care. I can show you how to use the spreadsheets you'll need for taxes and work with you until you're comfortable doing it on your own."

"I can't ask you to do that."

"You didn't. I offered. And it's no big deal, especially after all you're doing for me with the playhouse. Just let me know when it's convenient for you and we'll take a look at your ledgers together. I'm not familiar with the business side of ranching, but tallying income and expenses is the same no matter what kind of business you're running."

"It's not paper ledgers. It's some computer program that's supposed to make things easier. So far I haven't found that to be the case. It may as well all be written in Greek for all the good it does me."

"Trust me. Once you learn the program, entering or scanning your numbers into the computer is *way* easier than using a paper ledger, like I had to do when I first started my day care. The computer does all the hard calculations for you."

"If you say so."

She didn't know how the conversation had gone from Zooey and Caden to accounting, but after seeing Seth's relieved expression when she said she would assist him, she was glad they'd set off on that particular bunny trail.

She wanted to help him, however she could, and it

wasn't just because he was helping her prepare her day care to pass inspection.

His success was Caden's success, and that little boy deserved the best.

"If you ever find a use for upper arithmetic, be sure to let me know," she teased. "I've been around longer than you and I've never seen it."

"You make it sound like you're ancient. You're not exactly an old lady. What are you, maybe—"

"Stop right there, mister." She nearly dropped the circular saw in order to hold up a hand. "Haven't you ever been told not to guess at a woman's age?"

He shrugged. "I'm just telling it how I see it."

"Let's just say I'm older than you. And I've seen a lot in my...*years*."

Rachel didn't miss the flash of sorrow and grief that crossed Seth's gaze and immediately began to apologize.

"I'm so sorry. That was a thoughtless remark for me to make. You may be a few years younger than me, but I know you've seen and experienced the world in ways I never have. It's not like you're fresh out of high school. I imagine two tours in the military made you grow up pretty fast."

She didn't mention Luke's and Tracy's deaths, but she knew they were heavy on Seth's heart.

With effort, he turned his frown into a smile. "Yeah. Well, that may be true. I have seen a lot, and not all of it good. But I don't like to think about those times, much less talk about them. Anyway, my biggest challenge ever is right in front of me, hanging out in the sandbox getting ready to—"

With a choked squeak, he dropped the sawhorses with

a clatter and dashed toward Caden, who was pumping his arms, clumps of sand in both tiny fists.

Seth snatched Caden from the sandbox and brushed the sand from his fists.

"No, Caden. We don't eat sand." His voice sounded hoarse and frantic.

Zooey giggled. "I don't think he was going to eat it. Throw it at me, maybe. I've been trying to teach him not to do that. But don't worry. I've been keeping a close eye on him. He hasn't put any sand in his mouth."

Blowing out a breath in relief, Seth shifted Caden to one arm and picked off his ball cap, then scrubbed his fingers through his dark hair, leaving the tips in jagged peaks. He groaned in exasperation, seemingly more at himself than at Caden or Zooey.

"No, I know. You have a lot more experience with toddlers than I do, Zooey. Sorry. I shouldn't have freaked out on you. It was a gut reaction. And not a very good one."

"He'll get more sand in his shoes than in his mouth, I assure you," Rachel teased, amused by the look of sheer horror that crossed Seth's face.

"I'm kidding." She set the circular saw down in a safe corner next to the playhouse and away from the sandbox and laid a reassuring hand on his arm. "Well, I'm half kidding, anyway. I highly suggest you make a habit of removing his shoes or boots over a trash can whenever you leave a sandpit."

She chuckled. "I learned the hard way the first time I took Zooey's shoes off after a jaunt on the playground. She was lying across my bed. I had to wash the comforter twice to get all the sand out of it."

"Right. Empty his shoes over the trash can. Don't

get sand on the bed. Got it." He sounded as if he was adding her latest words of guidance to an already-enormous mental list. "Any other sage advice you want to give me?"

"Only one thing."

"And what is that?" His brow furrowed in concentration. She knew a grown man wouldn't want to be thought of as adorable, but that was exactly the adjective that flashed across Rachel's mind at his determined expression.

"Relax. Take a breath. You're going to be okay. Caden is going to be okay. Of course, there will be bumps and bruises along the road. Trips and falls. No one is a perfect parent, Seth, so don't beat yourself up when things don't go quite as you anticipated. You'll make mistakes. Caden will take a spill and scrape his knees, and you'll be there to pick him up, clean him off, put a bandage on his owie and kiss it better. And then life will go on."

"But what if—" He put his ball cap back on his head, with the brim facing backward this time. He released a breath and groaned. "This is hard."

Rachel nodded. She wanted to chuckle but resisted, knowing how serious Seth was at this moment.

"Yes, it is. Parenting is the toughest job ever, but it is one of the most rewarding things you'll ever do. Zooey is the light of my life."

She spoke loud enough for Zooey to hear the compliment, but her daughter suddenly appeared more interested in bulldozing sand toward Caden's dump truck. Rachel hoped Zooey knew she meant what she said.

Rachel envied Seth the toddler years. Toddlers, she could handle. Zooey had never gone through the terrible-twos stage. Rachel might have had to struggle to make ends meet, but she'd never had any issues with Zooey acting up. As she'd told Seth, Zooey was her biggest blessing. Motherhood was hard, but even as a baby, Zooey had been an endless source of joy that made all the work so very worth it.

Teenage years, on the other hand—she was *so* out of her depth there.

But it was Seth's relationship with Caden they were discussing.

"One more thing."

"Yeah? What's that?" He was busy brushing granules of sand from the spaces between Caden's fingers and didn't glance up at her.

"Don't worry if a little sand makes it into Caden's mouth from time to time. He'll learn fairly quickly that it doesn't taste good. Right now he's just exploring his world with all of his senses."

Which was much less complicated than watching a vulnerable teenager who thought she already knew everything explore hers. If only sand in the mouth was Rachel's largest concern.

"Right," Seth agreed, plunking Caden back down in the sandbox. "Don't worry so much. Got it."

He trusted her judgment. That meant a lot.

He bent down to retrieve the sawhorses he'd dropped earlier and set them up, then surveyed the old play set with a practiced eye.

"Why don't you start removing all the plastic pieces— the slides and climbing ladders," he suggested. "I'll work on the wood. We may be able to salvage some of this stuff to share with others for their woodstoves. It's not cold now, of course, but once the chill of winter sets in, folks will be glad to have a little extra wood on their piles. I don't know exactly what would be the best way to distribute it, but I'm sure we can come up with something."

She flashed him a warm smile. There was nothing more attractive in a man than a heart for serving others—friends and neighbors, and especially the baby that had been given into his care.

Warning sirens were blaring; lights were flashing in vivid colors.

Warning. Warning. Attraction alert.

She scrambled back to the subject at hand.

"What a great idea. I suggest we stack the scrap pieces just outside of the church for people to take as they have need for them."

His gaze widened. "I hadn't thought of the church. It makes sense, though, since nearly everyone in town attends Sunday services. And we can have Jo put the word out about where to find the wood for those that don't regularly visit the chapel."

Good idea, particularly because she knew that Seth had been one of those Christmas and Easter Christians who rarely darkened the door of the little community church for the past several years. Now, after losing his friends, faith might be even more of a struggle for him. She prayed God would work on Seth's heart through everything he'd experienced and not have him turn away based on what he'd seen and gone through.

She couldn't even begin to imagine having to deal with everything that had happened to him. All she knew was that God's light had found her during her darkest moments, and He could do the same for Seth.

In the meantime, she would strive to be a living witness of God's love for him.

"You know, Rachel," Seth said, breaking into her thoughts, "there's one thing you said to me this morning that's still eating at me."

"What's that?"

She tensed. His tone made it sound as if she'd said something wrong. She hoped she hadn't said anything that would lead him off the path of grace.

"You said you felt like an old lady." He frowned and shook his head. "As if."

"Believe me, I do."

Ancient.

Prehistoric, even.

Seth gave her a slow and thorough once-over, head to toe and then back again—a very *masculine* and appreciative examination. His midnight-blue eyes blazed into hers and a half smile curved slowly up one side of his lips.

A shiver ran down her spine, and while it felt unfamiliar to her, it was not altogether unpleasant. Those warning sirens in her head weren't sounding loud enough to stop these feelings or even slow them down.

She was in trouble.

"Trust me," he said, his voice dipping to a lower octave. "You are *so* not over the hill. Not that you really could be at—what?—twenty-nine?"

"I thought we'd already covered this ground. It is rude to ask a woman's age or even to guess at it."

He barked out a laugh. "I'm not asking. Just sayin'. From my viewpoint, you've got a good long way before you reach old anything."

She didn't know how to respond to the glittering look in Seth's eyes, never mind the admiration he'd verbally heaped on her.

This—the slightest hint of *this*—wasn't supposed to be happening. She shouldn't be thinking about Seth as a...well, as a *man*...much less reacting to him as a woman. Years earlier, after a few disastrous attempts to try dating as a single mom, she'd made the decision to focus on her daughter, her work and her church. Those were her priorities, and dating had no place in them. Zooey and Lizzie had put silly ideas into her head and now she was imagining all kinds of things that didn't exist, thoughts that shouldn't be so much as flashing through her mind, never mind lodging there.

Get ahold of yourself, Rachel, she mentally coached herself. *Get off this slippery slope before someone gets hurt. Before* you *get hurt*.

She could make a mile-long list of the reasons she shouldn't be attracted to Seth and why she was all wrong for him even if there was a certain physical and emotional chemistry between them.

They were opposites in every conceivable way. He swung from the trees and somersaulted over benches. She was lucky if she could make it through a round of push-ups and sit-ups while she worked out with her in-home DVDs. A couple of flights of stairs winded her. Seth could probably climb Mount Everest.

His life was all about health and fitness, whereas hers...*wasn't*.

He'd seen the horrors of war in the worst way, with his best friend being shot down right in front of him, and yet he made it a habit to build his world on the positive, the cup half-full. She had to be careful not to get down on herself and view the world under a gray and miserable thundercloud.

Seth sometimes acted immature for his age. Rachel

acted too old for hers. The six-year gap between them might as well be a chasm without a bridge, one that was impossible to cross.

Most important, Seth had recently inherited both a baby and a ranch. It was all he could do just to adapt to his new roles, though he was nothing if not determined.

She couldn't help thinking of the way he panicked when he thought Caden might be in danger of eating sand and somehow hurting himself with it. How he proudly rode his soon-to-be-officially-adopted son around on his horse. The picture of him cradling Caden in his strong arms with such tenderness that even now, at the mere thought of it, tears pricked in Rachel's eyes.

Seth's plate was full to overflowing, and that was the biggest hurdle of all that separated them—one that, if it had not already been intact, Rachel would have mentally placed between them for her own sanity.

Because really, was there anything in this world quite as attractive as a cowboy daddy?

It took all day Saturday to disassemble the play set and saw the wood into pieces small enough to fit into woodstoves.

Seth felt great about the fact that he was doing double duty with his charity—working off the auction bid for the senior center and providing folks with wood to heat their homes through the winter cold—although right now, near the beginning of June, he was working up a good sweat under the sun's hot rays.

Seth had thought the project would take only a couple of weekends once the materials were delivered, but Rachel didn't want to work Sundays, and he respected that. And if he was being honest with himself, he wasn't exactly in a hurry to rush the job. He enjoyed hanging around Rachel, and Zooey and Caden really seemed to have hit it off, almost like an older sister with her baby brother. She had even offered to babysit while Seth and Rachel took the wood over to the community church for distribution.

As the sun started to disappear over the horizon, Seth and Rachel had finally loaded all the wood in the back of Seth's truck and had taken it to the church, where Pastor Shawn gave them a cheerful welcome.

"Good to see you, Seth," the pastor said, shaking Seth's hand before filling his arms with wood pieces. "Let's stack the wood on the south side and I'll put a tarp over it to keep it clean and dry until people need it."

While the three of them unloaded and piled the wood, Shawn and Rachel conversed easily with each other, catching up on the week's events and talking about who was ill, who'd been promoted and how excited Shawn was for the Vacation Bible School program this year.

Seth knew they didn't purposefully exclude him from the conversation, but that didn't stop him from feeling like the odd man out.

The third wheel.

He didn't know a lot about the pastor, since Shawn, who wasn't originally from Serendipity, had been received into the community church after Seth had enlisted in the army.

Shawn had officiated at Tracy's funeral, but Seth had been too full of grief, and too overwhelmed by his new role as Caden's guardian, to really pay much attention to him then.

It had never bothered Seth before that he usually skipped Sunday services. He knew his parents were probably disappointed that he didn't attend more often. They had diligently raised him and his sister, Samantha, in the Christian faith, and they rarely missed a Sunday themselves.

But he just wasn't ready.

Anyway, he had a full life and a busy schedule to keep—especially now that he was learning parenthood and ranching all at once. He didn't like feeling cooped up by four walls while he listened to a preacher drone on for half an hour.

God was everywhere, wasn't He? Seth didn't need to be caught up in a stained-glass-windowed establishment, sitting on a hard pew and using kneelers every Sunday morning, to pray and stuff.

Did he?

As Shawn and Rachel talked about various parishioners, Seth began to see what he was missing. It felt a little bit like what he heard when he visited Cup O' Jo's Café, which was the best place in town to catch up on all the latest goings-on.

Everybody knew everybody here, and Jo Spencer, the queen bee of the gossip hive from her prime position as proprietor and waitress in the café named after her, had the lowdown on everyone and loved to share it. She considered herself most folks' second mother, Seth included, and she always made people feel like they were at home.

He knew all the people Shawn and Rachel were discussing—Serendipity was a small town with one Main Street and a single three-way stoplight.

This felt different, though.

Not gossip. Not news.

Something deeper.

It wasn't just what was happening and to whom, but

who was going through current trials and how they could help people get back on their feet. He listened as they planned to provide meals to the sick or transportation for the housebound. Visit shut-ins and those laid up in the hospital.

Practical, useful stuff.

Though it had originally been his idea to give away the planks from the playhouse to use as firewood, Rachel's suggestion to donate the lot to the chapel to help parishioners stay warm seemed to fit right into the church's mission. It was summer now, but it wouldn't be long before the nights became cooler and fall approached, and it was good to plan ahead for how to help.

This was community.

And Seth, who'd been born and raised here, suddenly felt like somehow he was missing out.

Which made him even more uncomfortable. The sooner they got the wood unloaded and got out of there, the better.

Just as Seth was grabbing the last of the wood and stacking it against the side of the church, the pastor clapped him on the shoulder.

"This is a good thing you're doing here," he said, opening a tarp he'd brought out to cover the pile.

"Bringing the wood in, you mean?"

"Helping Rachel."

Seth barked out a laugh. "She bought me at the Bachelors and Baskets Auction. I'm working off my time by building a new play set for her day care."

"That's not the way I heard it."

Shawn chuckled. "No?"

"It sounds like there's been a lot of upheaval in your life recently. Tracy's death. Accepting Caden's guardianship. It says a lot about a man that he fulfills his obligations even under duress."

"I wouldn't call it duress." Seth frowned. He wasn't caring for Caden under any kind of compulsion. Caden wasn't just his responsibility—he was his family now.

He shrugged but didn't elaborate. Was this going to be the beginning of a sermon? He hoped not. That was the last thing he needed right now.

"Rachel said she tried to absolve you of your obligation to her, but you refused."

Again, Seth shrugged. "I'm not the kind of man to renege on a promise. Besides, I like to build things. It's kind of a hobby for me."

Shawn nodded, his gaze full of respect. "So you're building something as intricate as a play set, even though you've suddenly found yourself the adoptive father of a baby and have a ranch to run. That can't be easy."

"The gossip hive must be buzzing overtime," Seth muttered irritably, stooping to rearrange the woodpile rather than continuing to make eye contact with the pastor.

"People are concerned about you and Caden, and they want to help," Rachel said, laying a reassuring hand on his arm. He hadn't heard her come up beside him and her touch was like a zap of electricity bolting through him.

"No one needs to worry about me. I'm handling it."

He didn't know why he'd said that, especially with a resentful tone to his voice that even he could discern.

For one thing, Rachel knew exactly how well he was *not* handling it. And for another, even he could see that he was letting his pride and male ego get in his way.

For Caden's sake, he needed to take all the help he could get and be grateful for it. But it wouldn't be easy.

He wasn't good at being humble. He didn't like accepting things when he'd rather be giving them.

And he especially wasn't thrilled about the idea of all of the people in church watching him and finding him wanting in any way.

Were they *concerned* that he wouldn't be good enough for Caden? Did they think the baby deserved better?

He could hardly blame them if they did. There wasn't a moment that had passed since he'd been given the guardianship of Caden that he hadn't wondered the same thing himself. He'd measured himself often—had he come up wanting?

Where had the stubborn streak suddenly come from? If he looked foolish, it was no one's fault but his own.

"I appreciate your concern," he said, relaxing his shoulders as he allowed his resentment and stubborn ego to flow out of him.

"As Rachel well knows, raising a baby on your own is no easy task," Pastor Shawn said. "But when it comes at you with no warning— Well, I remember how difficult the first few weeks were."

Pastor Shawn *remembered*? What did that mean?

"You have a baby?"

Shawn nodded. "A little girl. Noelle. She was abandoned in my church on Christmas Eve a year and a half ago. I found her tucked into the hay in the manger the kids used for the Christmas pageant. I was just getting ready to leave after the late service when I heard a strange sound. You can imagine my surprise when I found a live baby in the manger."

Seth was stunned. As unusual as his situation was, it wasn't completely unheard of for someone to gain custody of a godchild if something happened to the parents, and he'd given Luke and Tracy his consent when they were amending their will, so it wasn't as if he'd never considered the possibility. He'd just never thought it would happen.

Shawn's circumstances beat his by miles.

What a story.

"I kept her at my place for the weekend due to it being the Christmas holidays and all. And then…well, I just plain fell in love with the sweet little thing."

"So you adopted her?" Seth asked, running a hand across his jaw.

Shawn laughed. "It wasn't quite that simple, but eventually, yes. First I applied to be her foster father. Even that is a pretty far stretch from the norm—a single man wanting to foster a baby girl. I probably wouldn't have been able to keep her were it not for Heather. She had three foster kids of her own, so she knew how the system worked. She guided me through it from start to finish or I would never have made it. *And* she knew all about child care, which I think was my biggest learning curve. Dirty diapers." He grinned and shivered dramatically.

Seth groaned. He had a learning curve not only with Caden—and dirty diapers—but also with the Bar H ranch. At least Luke and Tracy's will clearly stated that he was Caden's legal guardian, so he didn't have to worry about someone trying to take him away.

When the time came, which would be as soon as he was able to file the papers, he'd fully adopt Caden as his son.

No question about it.

"I thank God every day that he brought Heather, her children and baby Noelle into my life. They are my biggest blessings and have filled my world with joy."

He clapped Seth on the back. "Let me give you some advice, son. Not as a pastor, but as a man. You hold on tight to this one," Shawn said, nodding toward Rachel. "You'll find she'll be an invaluable resource to you, just as Heather was, and is, to me."

Rachel's face reddened under the pastor's praise, but this was one situation where Seth agreed with Shawn. After his family, Rachel had been the first person Seth had turned to after he had become Caden's legal guardian. And what had started as a desperate cry for help had only grown from there. It seemed he and Rachel were spending more and more time together, and he wasn't about to complain.

When he had questions about Caden's care—which was often—she had answers. She'd encouraged him to call at any time of day or night. And sometimes he did.

But it was more than just getting answers to the billions of issues that cropped up.

It was Rachel's own brand of *encouragement* that she gave him—which was probably what he needed most of all right now.

"Oh, I'm not letting her go anywhere," Seth assured Shawn. "Believe me, I know what a blessing I have in her, and in her daughter, Zooey, who is babysitting Caden as we speak. I'm probably driving Rachel crazy with all my questions and concerns, but she has unending patience."

"No, not at all." Rachel didn't waste a moment in responding. "You're not a bother."

"I felt the same way about Heather. I figured with the way I was hounding her, I would chase her away. Thankfully, she doesn't scare easily. I still have new questions all the time, even though Noelle is now a toddler like

Caden. I guess we both ought to be thankful that the Lord made ladies of sterner stuff than us, huh?"

"You're still friends with Heather?" For some reason the answer to that question was inordinately important to Seth and he held his breath waiting for the answer.

"Oh, yes. Best friends." Shawn grinned.

Rachel sputtered.

Seth looked from Shawn to Rachel and back again, feeling like he'd missed something important.

"We are best friends," Shawn repeated. "And so much more than that. I was slow at figuring out my emotions at first, but I'm no fool. I made that woman my wife."

If a smile on a man of God could be called wily, then that was absolutely the right adjective for Shawn's toothy grin, and it was followed by a knowing wink in Rachel's direction, making Seth's skin itch all over.

A pastor winking at one of his parishioners. Wasn't there a rule against that?

"You never know about these things," Shawn continued. "The right people come into your life when you least expect it. As they say, the Lord works in mysterious ways."

Chapter Five

Rachel didn't know who *they* were—the ones who were spouting off nonsense about the Lord working in mysterious ways. If it was in the Bible, Rachel didn't know where, but then again, the proverb had come from Pastor Shawn's lips, and he was definitely the one who would have the most insight on the ins and outs of the way the Lord worked, wasn't he?

She was certainly no expert, despite that she read her Bible, prayed daily and went to Sunday services. Her faith had rescued her many a time, and yet she made no bones of the fact that she didn't always understand why things happened the way they did. She just held on to faith that the Lord had it all in hand.

But in this instance the pastor was mistaken. However the Lord was working, mysterious or otherwise, He was not interested in the romantic prospects of Seth and Rachel as a couple. They both had far too much on their plates to so much as consider a relationship with each other. Put it together and there would be an enormous explosion—and that was without the dozens of reasons she'd given Zooey and Lizzie for why such a relationship could not and would not ever exist.

Though if there was one really good thing to come out of this whirlwind of change—besides sweet Caden—it was that Zooey's attitude had appeared to have calmed down a bit. She'd attended summer school that week without a single protest, and on time, and had completed all her homework without having to be nagged—er, *reminded*.

She'd even offered to accompany Rachel to Seth's ranch so she could play with Caden while Rachel figured out the bookkeeping software with Seth at the end of the next week. After moving into the Bar H ranch house, Seth had spent his evenings during the week building her new play set, and she was anxious to return the favor.

When they arrived at the ranch, it was to find a beaming Seth bouncing on his toes with excitement as Caden toddled around the paddock area.

Curious. Smiling and abounding with energy wasn't quite the reception Rachel had been anticipating from Seth, given his aversion to all things numerical.

"Watch this," Seth exclaimed as soon as Rachel and Zooey had exited her sedan. "Come here, Caden, and show Zooey and Miss Rachel what you can do."

Caden giggled and immediately responded to Seth's open arms, reaching his chubby little hands up to grasp Seth's thumbs.

"Prepare to be amazed."

Seth's grin widened even more, if that was possible, and Rachel couldn't help but smile herself.

"All right, little man, let's show off your trick for the ladies."

Seth crouched slightly, and with his encouragement,

Caden stepped one foot onto Seth's knee, then the other, and as Seth slowly straightened, Caden continued to walk up his body. Seth remained steady with a good grip on the toddler's hands as the little guy's feet stepped on his chest.

Then, with a delighted squeal, Caden pushed off and flipped backward. With a whoop of excitement of his own, Seth skillfully set Caden on his feet for a perfect landing.

"Again. Again," Caden pleaded.

"Is that not the most incredible thing you've ever seen?" Seth crowed, scrubbing an affectionate hand through Caden's hair.

Rachel didn't know whether to be appalled or impressed. She was a little of both, she supposed. Two years old was a little young for backflips, in her opinion, but Seth had him completely under control every movement of the execution. Most interesting of all, Seth appeared just as excited about what Caden had done as if he and the boy were blood relatives.

And from what she'd just seen Caden do, they almost might have been.

"Awesomesauce," she said, clapping.

Zooey groaned. "Mo-om," she wailed, stretching out the word. "No one says *awesomesauce* anymore."

"'Sauce," Caden repeated, jumping and grinning and patting his tummy.

"Caden does. See?" Rachel laughed. "I have been vindicated—by a two-year-old."

Seth chuckled. "Not to burst your bubble or anything, but I'm pretty sure Caden thinks you were referring to *applesauce*, which is one of his favorite foods."

Zooey snorted and Rachel narrowed her eyes on her and pursed her lips.

"Just go ahead and laugh at your mother, Miss Too-Cool-for-Words."

Zooey's eyes twinkled and she pressed her lips together, but a giggle escaped her nonetheless.

"Looks like you're one proud papa, with what Caden just did," Rachel said, shifting her attention to Seth and away from her rascally daughter.

"Right?" He pumped his fist in the air. "Two years old and I have just taught him his first parkour trick. He may have set a world record or something."

"I don't know about a world record, but definitely like father, like son," she agreed.

His smile wavered. "That still sounds so strange to me. I mean, there's no question that I'm going to legally adopt him, or that I am a proud parent. But do you think I'll ever get used to being called Daddy?"

"It'll take a while. Most parents have nine months to prepare themselves to be called Mommy or Daddy, and it still sounds odd at first, even after the baby is born. Don't worry about it, though. After a while it'll sound natural."

"Can you teach me some of those moves, like you did with Caden?" Zooey asked, excitement crackling in the tone of her voice.

Zooey wanted to learn parkour?

What was that about?

"You are much too tall to walk up Seth's chest and do a backflip," Rachel pointed out, thinking that was the end of that.

"Well, no," Seth concurred. "It won't work that way. But if you're up for it, I think I can teach you how to take a running start at a hay bale, then bank off it and do a pretty nifty backflip."

"Cool beans," Zooey exclaimed.

"Oh, I see. So it's okay for you to say *cool beans*, but *awesomesauce* is out of the question?"

"'Sauce," Caden repeated.

"I think he's hungry," said Seth, and the three of them laughed over it. "I'll give him a snack while we work on the computer."

"Which we probably ought to be doing right now," Rachel said, hoping all this nonsense about Zooey attempting parkour moves would blow over. Rachel had never known Zooey to be the least bit interested in athletic endeavors in the past. She regularly complained about the running she had to do in gym class. Since Zooey was healthy and got plenty of activity walking around town, Rachel had never kicked up a fuss about trying to get her involved in sports.

She certainly never would have expected her daughter to sound so enthusiastic about parkour. If she had to have a sudden athletic interest, couldn't she have gotten fired up about swim team? Or soccer? Or something else that seemed less likely to end in a broken neck?

Rachel wished they could skip the parkour and go straight to the software.

But given the circumstances, she preferred to spar with her daughter over expressions like *awesomesauce* and *cool beans* than ponder the disaster that was no doubt coming next.

"It'll only take a moment for me to show Zooey the move," Seth said. "Ready, Zooey?"

Zooey nodded eagerly.

Rachel scooped Caden into her arms and patted his back, reassuring herself as much as him.

"You're going to approach the hay bale at a jog," Seth explained. "Then you're going to plant your feet against the top edge of the bale and push yourself upward and backward. Like this."

He demonstrated, making the entire move look fluid and ridiculously simple.

Rachel knew what would happen were *she* to try such a trick. She'd trip right over the hay bale and take a nose-dive that would leave her scratched up for weeks. And that was to say nothing of her dignity.

She only hoped her daughter would be able to keep *her* dignity intact—along with all of her bones. That backflip looked like it could go wrong all too easily.

"Ready to try it?" he asked Zooey. "Don't worry. I'll be right here to spot you."

Rachel kissed Caden's soft cheek and whispered, "If you ask me, this is a very bad idea. Don't tell your daddy, though. I wouldn't want him to think I'm not support-ing him."

She held her breath as Zooey broke into a jog, her jaw set with determination. It looked as if she was going to successfully bank the hay bale, but at the last moment she tensed and skidded to a halt just short of it.

"Sorry," she murmured, looking crestfallen.

"No problem," Seth reassured her. "Sometimes it takes me many tries before I finally get a move right. Do you want to give it another go?"

No, she does not, Rachel thought.

But Zooey said, "Yeah. I think I just psyched myself out there for a moment. I can do this."

"It's all in your mind," Seth said. "If you believe you

can do it, your body will follow your mind's lead, even if you have to work on it. You'll find that after a while, flipping is the easy part."

Rachel couldn't have disagreed more. Doing a backflip by banking off a hay bale was most definitely not something one did all in one's head, but before Rachel could voice her concerns, Zooey was already racing toward the hay bale.

With a whoop, she planted her feet right where Seth had indicated and, with just the slightest bit of assistance on Seth's part in order to help her to get all the way over, she completed a backflip and landed on her feet.

"I did it. Did you see that, Mom? Woo-hoo!"

Zooey's whole body was pulsing with energy and her expression was a match for how she used to look on Christmas mornings when she was a tiny tot.

"That was great, honey."

Rachel relaxed some after she'd observed the careful way Seth had confidently and knowledgeably spotted her daughter through the entire flip.

There was no way Zooey could have fallen. Not in Seth's capable hands.

"Can we do it again?" Zooey's enthusiasm was catching, and Rachel even caught herself smiling. Caden had been asking the very same thing only minutes earlier.

"One more time, and then Seth and I need to work on the ranch's books."

"Parkour's more fun," Seth muttered under his breath, frowning like a little boy who'd just had his favorite toy taken away from him.

"That may well be," Rachel said, though she didn't exactly agree. "But sometimes we've got no choice except to *adult*, like it or not."

Seth screwed up his face at Zooey and cringed like he'd just sucked a lemon. "Take my advice and don't grow up."

Zooey laughed, as did Rachel. She was amazed by the way Seth so effortlessly appeared to reach her daughter.

Seth spotted Zooey through a second banking backflip. Rachel couldn't help but be impressed. He had a gift, not only of performing parkour himself but of teaching it to a two-year-old and a sixteen-year-old.

As she well knew, not everyone was good at working with children, especially over such an expansive age range.

She was surprised at how vigorously Zooey was taking to the sport. Now she was talking about backflips and learning how to walk up walls and leap benches in a single bound, superhero-style. Strange words coming from a teenager who'd never before been remotely interested in gymnastics, dance or even running.

"Back to being a cowboy," Seth said with a sigh. "Putting on my big-boy hat now."

He sounded miserable, and the joy that had lit his face only moments before was doused out.

"If it's any consolation, you look fantastic in a cowboy hat."

As soon as the words were out of her mouth, heat rushed to her face. She sounded as if she was flirting with him.

Which she wasn't.

Much.

He straightened and his smile returned. Maybe the compliment *had* done him some good.

"I got one for Caden, too. A white hat, 'cause he's one of the good guys. And boots so he really looks the part.

He's already a serious lady-killer. Those little girls in your day care had better watch out or he'll knock their socks right off their feet."

Rachel grinned. That much was true.

"Like father, like son."

Seth led everyone into Tracy's old office, which was little more than an offshoot built onto one side of the stable. The front room held a desk with an ancient computer monitor. The back room contained the printer and a couple of metal filing cabinets. Zooey laid down a blanket for Caden in the back room and pulled a few books out of her backpack to read to him.

"Here's Tracy's old work computer."

The smell of old leather and fresh horse assaulted his nostrils, as it did every time he entered the stable. He was slowly getting used to it.

Old tack, mostly bridles and neck yokes used for pulling wagons, decorated one wall, featuring an antique wooden wagon wheel as a centerpiece. The opposite wall sported a large display of spurs, some polished to a high shine and others rusty with wear. Seth suspected some of them might even go back a hundred years or more.

There was some serious history in this building.

Including the computer.

The monitor was a gigantic box type that reminded Seth of an old-time television set. Seriously. How long ago had the flat screen been invented?

Apparently, Luke and Tracy hadn't been interested in upgrading to anything made in this century.

"Do you see what I'm working with here?" he complained. "I know how to use a computer, obviously, and

I enjoy playing games on my console—but this? This is one intimidating piece of software."

"Hardware, actually. The software is the program we'll use to help with the accounting."

His face heated. He was a soldier. He didn't like exposing his weaknesses.

"But this monitor?" she said, smiling to cover his faux pas. "Yes, it's a dinosaur, all right."

"Yeah. A T. rex."

"Let's conquer this thing, shall we?"

He pulled back the office chair for her, then pushed a second chair up beside her. She turned on the computer and the monitor snapped and crackled to life.

"Fortunately, it looks like the CPU itself is a relatively new model," she explained, "one that can easily host an up-to-date accounting software."

"And that's a good thing?"

"That's a great thing." She held up the finance CD lying on the desktop and waved it at him. "I use this very same program with my day care. This little guy here is going to make your life considerably easier."

"I hope so," he muttered, but didn't really believe it would help him much.

Any math was too much math in his book.

Rachel sifted through the piles of invoices, separating those that had been paid from those yet due, as well as taking a quick gander at the bookkeeping program's spreadsheets to look at the accounts payable and receivable, as well as the payroll.

"Since the printer has a scanning feature, we'll start by scanning all of these documents into the computer. The software will automatically sort your receipts into categories, and by the time we're finished, we'll have most of the documents you'll need to give your tax accountant—profit and loss, balance sheets and detailed lists of receivables and payables."

"What I've learned so far is that ranching is a long game. Cows are bred in the spring and fall and delivered eight months later. When the calves get weaned, we sell them. The rest of the year we're working with that profit."

Even though he'd managed to learn that much, Seth's head was still spinning. As a soldier, he'd been kept comfortably fed and bedded, or as much as possible for a man on tour to the Middle East. He hadn't had much reason, or opportunity, to use the money he was accruing, so most of what he'd made had gone straight into his savings accounts. He wouldn't know a financial balance sheet if it bit him in the nose.

Rachel was staring at him curiously. "You look green around the gills."

Great. Wonderful. So he looked as bad as he felt.

And of course Rachel had noticed.

"I'm good." He straightened his shoulders and made direct eye contact with her. His stomach might be lurching, but that was his business and his alone.

"Like I said, the software does most of the work for you. Once you get familiar with the categories Luke and Tracy set up to run the ranch, the bookkeeping shouldn't take much more than a couple of hours a week, max."

"That's better than the entire day I spent last Wednesday. As you can see, I didn't make a dent in it at all. The only thing I got was a headache."

Her head tilted in concern as she observed him. "You don't have to learn this. You could hire someone to come in and keep the books for you."

Seth shook his head. "No way. Tracy always did this on her own. She said it was the best way to know what was really going on with the ranch. I'm not going to pass that baton just because it's a little confusing. If I'm going to do this thing, I'm in it for all or nothing."

"Good for you." She laid a hand on his shoulder and smiled up at him. "You're just psyching yourself out. It's like you said to Zooey about parkour. Accounting is really not as hard as it looks. You'll get the hang of it. Most of what's holding you back is in your mind."

"Yeah, but I've never been good at math."

He was itching in discomfort. She must think he was a dumb jock, able to swing through trees but not add two plus two together.

Her gaze met his, and to his amazement, he didn't see a trace of ridicule or disdain in its depths. Only encouragement and reassurance.

"Keep in mind that Zooey has never done a backflip in her life. Yet with your help, she did it today. Twice. Think of this software as your backflip. I'm going to help you get through it."

Seth lowered his brow in concentration. "You're saying I need to explore new ways to see the obstacles in my world."

"Precisely. Now, as I was saying, one very nice feature of this particular software is its ability to read and organize scanned documents. Back before the advent of the computer, everything had to be written into paper ledgers. When computers came on the scene, those numbers could be manually entered into an accounting software program. That was definitely less of a hassle than scribbling on paper and easier to keep organized, but it still took a fairly significant amount of time. Now we just stack—" she demonstrated by straightening the pile of invoices in front of her "—and scan. The software sorts and categorizes line items into categories for you."

"Awesomesauce," Seth said drily. "Which reminds me. I'm getting hungry. I have veggies all cut up and ready to eat back at the ranch house. Aren't you ready for a snack?"

"No, and neither are you, at least until you get a feel for the categories Luke and Tracy used. Stop dangling carrots in front of me," she teased. "Now, if we also take a quick look at how they had their personal accounts organized, we will have a clearer picture of what was important to them, both in the short-term and in the long-term. You'll be able to discover not only how they wanted their ranch to be run but also what they considered the most important investments.

"You can see here where they set aside the money for Caden's college trust fund and how they funneled money into it on a regular basis. And hey, look here."

Rachel sounded excited, and Seth leaned in over her shoulder, his palm on the desk next to hers, so he could see what she was pointing at.

A sweet scent wafted across his senses, clouding his mind. It was her shampoo, he realized, and it smelled a great deal better than the office around them.

Coconut.

He liked coconut.

It was all he could do not to lean in closer, just to get another whiff.

"See here?" She pointed at a line item.

"'Caden's horse.'" Seth's throat tightened and he had to clear it in order to speak. "They were saving to buy him his first horse."

"Looks like."

"But why? There are more than a half-dozen horses in the stable already."

"Yes, but they're used by the wranglers who work your cattle, aren't they? Did any of them even belong to Luke and Tracy? And even if some of them do, Caden's horse would have to be especially gentle when he was first learning to ride. Maybe they were looking for something special, just for him."

Seth shrugged. She had a point. He lifted his hat by the crown and tossed it onto the side of the desk, then jammed his fingers through the thick ends of his hair, which was only just beginning to grow out to where he liked it, now that he was no longer in the military.

He blew out a breath. It seemed like every time he turned around, he found out something else he didn't know, and he was getting weary of it.

"I haven't been able to work all that out yet," he admitted. "The horses, the cattle. Pigs. Chickens. I really don't know what I'm supposed to do with it all. I do know that at least a couple of the horses stabled now are—*were*—Luke and Tracy's personal mounts. I've been riding Luke's horse, Windsong. I'll have to check on the rest, whether the ranch owns them or if they are the wranglers' personal mounts."

"We can get those details later. I think for right now it's enough to be aware that the Hollisters wanted Caden to have a horse in his future. Maybe somewhere around his third birthday next month. Unless you'd rather start looking now."

"Isn't Caden a little young for a horse?"

Rachel laughed. "I'm no expert, of course, having never ridden myself, but Caden is likely to grow up to be a rancher, after all, since this land is his legacy. I think most of the children in Serendipity start out riding fairly young."

"I'll ask Wes," he said, referring to the ranch manager who'd been patiently walking him through all the many facets of owning a ranch. "He'll know when will be the right time for us to start looking for a gentle horse, and more important, where to find one, because I haven't got a clue."

"That sounds like a reasonable plan."

He felt as if his head was going to burst.

"Would it be too much for me to ask you to accompany me when the time comes?"

Her beautiful brown eyes widened. "I'd be happy to go with you, but I don't know what kind of help I can give you. I know less about horses than you do."

"True, you may not know anything about horses, but you do know children. I think you'd be better able to recognize a bond between Caden and his potential horse than I would."

That was the rational reason, if a little flimsy, and it was the only one he was going to admit to.

"Do you mind if I make a suggestion?" She turned slightly in her chair so she was looking up at him and she rested her palm over the top of his hand on the desk.

Her expression exuded empathy and her touch somehow calmed him as much as her gaze did. The tension in his shoulders eased and the pounding in his head decreased until it was down to a dull roar.

"Please do."

"Start making lists of things you plan to do. Write stuff down. Don't try to keep it all straight in your head.

There's too much for you to remember and you're getting overwhelmed."

"I'm way past overwhelmed. But I have been making lists."

She smiled softly and tapped his temple with the tip of her finger. "Yes, I know. Up here, right?"

Was that why his head always felt ready to explode?

"Use your cell phone. I've got a good app I can show you how to use. You can divide your projects into categories so you don't forget anything and tick items off as you go."

"And psychologically make myself feel as if I'm accomplishing something."

"Exactly." She grinned, and he chuckled.

He'd had enough of standing and staring at numbers. He wanted to climb on something, stretch his back and legs and work out the kinks in his muscles.

But because he was stuck in a musty old office that smelled of horsehair and leather, he did the next best thing.

He reached for Rachel's hands, drew her to her feet and twirled her around until they were both laughing and out of breath.

"What would I do without you?" he asked, hoping he never had to find out. At least, not for a long time to come. At the moment he couldn't imagine being able to conquer all those *lists* without her. She was his number one go-to person where Caden was concerned. "You've got my six, and I really appreciate it."

She squeezed his hands.

"No worries there. I'll be around to help you as long as you need me."

She winked and Seth's breath caught in his throat.

He'd known Rachel long enough to be sure she wasn't the flirtatious type, and they'd both established that they weren't in the market for a relationship.

But right this second, he couldn't seem to remember any of the reasons why. She touched his heart in a way no other woman ever had.

Granted, he hadn't had many relationships in his adult life, since he'd enlisted in the army straight out of high school and had served two tours overseas. He wasn't sure if he'd know true feelings if he tripped over them.

But this thing with Rachel? It felt real.

She must have read his thoughts in his expression. Her face pinkened and she pulled her hands away.

He cleared his throat. "We…uh…probably ought to go check on Zooey and Caden. They must be getting hungry for a snack. I know I am."

"Sure," Rachel agreed, her eyes glowing. She'd recovered quicker than he had. He couldn't even tell she'd been flustered only moments earlier. "I'll let you off the hook this time. But next time we're going to go over your balance sheet."

One more reason to like her. She knew when to push him and when to back off, and she wasn't afraid to do either.

He suspected they would be friends long after he'd straightened out this mess with the ranch, and even when he was more confident in raising Caden.

As if she guessed what he was thinking, she grabbed his cowboy hat from the edge of the desk and reached on tiptoe to plant it on his head, tilting her chin and appraising him before giving the brim of his hat a little tug.

"There," she said, sounding pleased with herself. "You have the looks, and soon you'll have the know-how. We'll make a cowboy out of you yet."

Chapter Six

Exactly one week and one day later, Rachel sifted through her blouses on the hangers in her closet, looking for the perfect shirt for the day ahead. Ultimately, she settled on a soft-pink cotton pullover. She needed something to match her oldest pair of jeans and the brand-spanking-new pair of burgundy-colored riding boots she'd purchased from Emerson's Hardware earlier in the week.

She had no intention whatsoever of actually riding a horse, but since she was spending an increasing amount of time on the Bar H ranch with Seth, it only made sense to dress like the ranchers did. She didn't want to ruin her good running shoes trudging through mud and cow pies.

So now she had a pair of riding boots she'd never use to ride a horse and a pair of running shoes that would never see so much as a single run.

Irony was her middle name.

"I'm going out," she told Zooey, who was lying across the couch with her feet propped up higher than her head, chatting away on her cell phone to one of her friends about a new boy in town named Dawson.

Rachel wasn't trying to eavesdrop, exactly, but it was hard to miss Zooey's excited giggle when she exclaimed how cute he was and asked her friend if he would be at the party.

Typical teenage conversation.

Nothing to be concerned about. As much as she wanted to put a large rock on Zooey's head to keep her from growing up, it was happening whether she liked it or not.

In two years Zooey would be off to college and Rachel would still be here. Only, in the evenings, the house would be too quiet.

She would be alone.

If she didn't think about it, would it go away?

She wished that she had more time, that she could do it all over again. But this was the way the Lord had made the relationship between parents and their children. Parents nurtured their kids into adulthood. And the older the kids got, the less they needed their moms.

Or in Seth's case, dad. In some ways she envied Seth, being able to cuddle little Caden in his arms whenever he wanted to, having so many more years ahead of them before Caden, too, was grown and gone.

Zooey was long past the cuddling stage. Once in a great while she still wanted or needed a hug from her mom, but that was happening less often, especially after she'd started hanging out with that questionable group of friends.

She'd been doing better for the past few weeks, putting effort into summer school and spending more time playing with Caden than she did out by the pool.

Rachel wondered if that was one of those friends she was speaking to now. And what was that about a party?

Rachel waved to get Zooey's attention and indicated for her to put the phone on mute. Instead, she surprised Rachel by telling her friend she'd talk to her later and hanging up, giving Rachel her full attention.

"Seth's picking me up in a minute. We're going out to the McKenna ranch to see about getting Caden a horse. According to Seth's foreman, the earlier a future rancher learns to ride, the better. Make sure you get your homework done. You know I don't like it if you have to study on a Sunday."

"Yeah. I know. I finished my homework last night. Can I come along with you to see the horses?"

"I'll have to ask Seth, but I don't see why not. We can probably use the help with Caden."

"Awesomesauce," Zooey replied, flashing Rachel a sassy grin.

"It's not that bad."

"No," Zooey agreed. "In fact, I think it will go viral. I'll make a video. 'Moms Using Out-of-Date Vernacular.' Pretty soon everybody's mom will want to make a video and upload it online."

"Hey, watch yourself, Miss Cool Beans." She gestured toward the phone. "Who was that, by the way?"

"Just Abby."

"Abby? I don't think I've heard that name before."

"You should have. Abigail Carter. She's in my class at school, and she was in your day care when she was a toddler. We used to play in the sandbox together."

"Oh, that Abby. I know you used to be friends, way back when, but I haven't heard her name mentioned in years. What happened?"

"I dunno. Different paths, different interests. But we've kind of reconnected lately."

"Over *Dawson*?" Rachel was only half teasing.

Zooey's face turned a vibrant red and she rolled to her feet.

"Mom," she wailed. "My phone conversations are supposed to be private."

"Can I help it if you talk loud? I could hear you all the way down the hallway in my bedroom. I would have had to shut my door and put in earplugs not to hear every word you said."

"Please, please don't embarrass me by mentioning this to anyone?"

Rachel flashed an impish smile. "Why would I do that?"

She wouldn't, of course, but it was too funny to see Zooey squirm.

"What party, by the way?"

"Mom," Zooey protested again.

"Will there be an adult chaperone? I'd like a phone number so I can check out the details."

Zooey crossed her arms and frowned. "Check up on me, you mean."

"I'm just doing what any responsible parent would do. It's not that I don't trust you, but I do want you to be safe. So sue me."

She did trust Zooey, although in recent months, that trust had been sorely tested.

"But there's no reason not to share that information with me, right? If everything is on the up-and-up, which I'm sure it is, and you've got nothing to hide, then there should be no problem."

"There is no problem." Zooey rolled her eyes and sighed. "If you insist. The chaperone's name is Pastor Shawn, and I'm fairly certain you already have the church's number stored on your cell phone."

"Pastor Shawn?" Rachel repeated, dumbfounded.

"The youth lock-in the weekend after next. I thought I'd go check it out. I thought maybe they were lame, but Abby says they're pretty fun." Zooey tried to make her voice sound casual, but Rachel could see right through the facade.

She wanted to jump for joy and pump her fists in the air. This was exactly what she'd been praying about for months. Zooey coming back to church? It was exactly the news she'd wanted to hear. And she definitely wanted Zooey to know she was pleased.

But fist pumping?

Somehow Rachel didn't think that would go over so well with her daughter.

Besides, there was one other thing.

"Don't take this the wrong way, honey. I'm thrilled that you're interested in attending a youth-group event, and I really like Abby, but I have to ask—does this sudden interest in youth group have anything to do with that Dawson boy?"

"No," Zooey exclaimed, the color in her face heightening once again. "Well, yes. I mean, he'll be there, but that's not why I'm going."

"Then why…?"

Zooey frowned and dropped her gaze, shoving her hands in the front pockets of her jeans. "I didn't want to have to tell you. I knew you'd be so ashamed of me for being so gullible. It's Lori and James. I found out they were getting into drugs." Her eyes filled with tears. "I can't believe I ever—"

Rachel opened her arms and Zooey ran into them. She

brushed the hair off her daughter's forehead and held her while she cried—for the loss of her friends, the loss of innocence and the vulnerability that had nearly landed Zooey in a situation beyond her control.

Rachel silently thanked God for taking care of her little girl.

Maybe Zooey no longer needed to snuggle like Caden, but in many ways a daughter would always need her mother, and right now, at this moment, holding Zooey and reassuring her that she would always be there for her was the most important thing in the world.

The sound of a truck's horn pulled them apart. Zooey sniffed and wiped her face on her sleeve, and Rachel found her eyes were also wet with tears. She reached for a tissue and dabbed at her eyelashes, hoping her mascara wouldn't leave any telltale signs that she'd been crying. She didn't want to embarrass Zooey by making this a public event.

"Shall I ask Seth if you can tag along?" Rachel asked, a little too brightly.

"Yeah. I'd like that."

Rachel dashed out to speak to Seth and returned a minute later with a broad smile on her face.

"Seth said he was hoping you'd want to come. He said he could use an extra opinion about which horse he should buy for Caden."

"He's probably just being nice to me because...well... I'm your daughter, and you know why he asked *you* to go, don't you?"

Zooey seemed to find something amusing in the question, for a reason Rachel didn't quite understand.

Rachel shot her a surprised look.

"Is this a trick question?"

"Do you think it's because you're such an expert on horses?" Zooey teased mercilessly. "I'm sure that's gotta be the reason."

"If you must know, he wants me to accompany him because I'm an expert on *children*. He thought I might have some insight and be able to discern whether Caden liked a particular horse or not."

"Good cover story."

"And what's that supposed to mean?" Rachel planted her fists on her hips and raised her eyebrows. "Be careful, missy. You're treading on thin ice here."

"All I'm saying," she said with a shrug that told Rachel she wasn't the least bit worried about her mother's threat, "is that if you can't figure out why Seth keeps asking you to do things with him, you're more hopeless than me."

"Seth and I are friends." Rachel didn't like the defensive note that had stolen into her voice.

Zooey just laughed.

"Right, Mom. You keep telling yourself that. I'll tell you this, though. Now that I'm hanging out with new peeps, I could sure use a 'friend' like that for myself."

The McKenna spread was much larger than the Bar H ranch. Two of the three McKenna brothers, along with their mother, Alice, still lived on the land. Alice lived in the main house, and Nick and Jax in separate cabins. Nick ran the cattle side of the operation, while Jax trained some of the finest horses around.

It was Jax they'd come to see. Wes had told Seth there was no one else like him in the county, maybe even the state. Jax knew horses like nobody's business, and if anyone could pick out the perfect horse for Caden, it was Jax.

Jax greeted the small gathering with a wave and a smile. He had already saddled three horses and had them hitched to the corral fence.

To Seth's untrained eye, he couldn't see why Jax would choose these animals over others. He had expected them to be smaller, for one thing, and maybe older. Preferably so old that the horse couldn't move beyond a walk if it had a bear chasing it.

That was Seth's idea of the perfect horse for Caden. But Jax was the expert, so he held his tongue.

"Oh, what beautiful horses," Rachel exclaimed, putting her hand in Seth's. He glanced down at her and she smiled, her eyes brimming with encouragement. Obviously, she'd seen the doubt he was feeling and wanted to reassure him.

He only hoped Jax wasn't as adept at reading faces. Seth didn't want Jax to think he was skeptical of him. Thankfully, Jax had turned to unhitch the first horse and lead him forward to introduce him to Seth and Caden.

"Now, let me start out by telling you that choosing horses for children isn't something I do a lot of. I usually train horses for ranch work or for the rodeo circuit and I've recently been working with some mustangs over at Faith Duggan's rescue ranch. I think I've got some good options for you, but I won't be offended if you want to look around at other places, get a sense of your options."

"Wes said there was no better man in the area when it came to evaluating horses," Seth said, a little surprised. He wasn't making *any* purchase until he was absolutely certain it was the right horse for Caden. "If Wes trusts you, then so do I."

"I appreciate that," Jax affirmed with a nod.

"These horses look big for such a little guy," Rachel said, verbally expressing the concern at the top of Seth's list. He squeezed her hand in gratitude and slowly released the breath he'd been holding.

Jax tipped back his hat and grinned. "Well, I figured you'd be wanting a horse Caden can grow with. You don't want his feet dragging the ground next time he has a growth spurt."

Seth chuckled, but it sounded dry even to his own ears. Caden gave a squeak of protest and wiggled in his arms and Seth realized he was holding him too tight. He made a conscious effort to relax his muscles.

Jax shifted his gaze to Seth. "Maybe you were expecting a pony?"

Seth didn't answer. He didn't want to look ill informed, especially not with Rachel standing right there. He'd been doing enough of that on his own lately without adding ponies to the list.

To his relief, Rachel spoke up. "I know I was. One of those cute little ones with the long manes. What are they called? Shetland ponies?"

Jax barked out a laugh. "Those 'cute little ones' are often the orneriest things you'll ever see. Trust me. You want a nice, steady quarter horse for Caden."

Seth did trust Jax, but when it came to his little Caden, a child who had already suffered so much in his short life, Seth was overprotective and not ashamed to admit it.

"Can I pet it?" Zooey asked, waiting for Jax's nod before running her hand down the dapple gray's neck.

"This is Monty. He's a seven-year-old gelding and as

gentle as the day is long. Patient, too. You'll get a lot of good years out of him."

Rachel approached a palomino mare and stroked her muzzle.

"That's Fancy. She's a real sweetheart. Calm as can be. Very aware of her rider."

The third horse was a stunning black with four white socks and a sizzle of white lightning down his muzzle.

"We call that one Storm," Jax said as Seth approached and Caden reached out to tangle his fingers in the gelding's dark mane. "For obvious reasons. I'll admit it was probably not the most original name I've ever come up with."

"But it fits," said Seth, tracing his fingers along the white slash on the horse's face.

"In looks, yes," Jax agreed. "But in temperament, not so much. You'll never find a steadier, more tranquil horse than Storm here."

Caden was mesmerized by the black. Seth had been worried that Caden might get too excited and frighten the horses with his quick movements, but even when the toddler leaned over and hugged Storm's neck, the horse didn't so much as toss his head or skitter to the side. Instead, to Seth's amazement, Storm bowed his head toward the little boy. It almost looked like Caden was getting a horsey hug in return.

"It looks like we might have a match," Jax said, moving to Storm's side and tightening the cinch on the saddle. "Do you want to give him a go-round?"

Caden was clearly enthralled, but Seth didn't think the boy was ready to sit in the saddle on his own.

He hesitated, looking first at Jax and then at Rachel, who was still standing by the palomino's side.

"Come on over here, buddy." Jax held out his arms to Caden and the boy immediately responded, barreling into Jax's chest. Caden was really becoming an outgoing child, easily interacting with everyone he met. It had been only a few weeks, but Seth suspected Rachel had a lot to do with his new social skills.

"Seth, you go ahead and mount first," Jax instructed, "and then I'll put this little guy up in front of you."

Seth mounted Storm with no problems. He shifted his weight in the saddle and gathered the reins. He was glad he'd been practicing with the horses at the Bar H ranch so that now he looked more comfortable with Storm than he actually was.

Jax grinned as he propped Caden up in front of Seth and told him to walk the horse around the corral a few times.

"Get up, Storm," Seth said, nudging the horse into a comfortable walk.

"Storm," Caden repeated excitedly, leaning forward to pat the horse's neck. Seth drew the boy back and readjusted his hold around the toddler's waist.

"I think you found your perfect match," Rachel said with a chuckle that Seth joined in on.

"Looks like."

"For a while, this is how you'll want to teach Caden to ride," Jax instructed. "Stay in the saddle with him and let him get used to the horse's movements at different gaits. You'll know when he is ready to try sitting on the saddle on his own. Caden has long legs, but you'll probably want to invest in a children's saddle so you can adjust the stirrups to his height.

"When you make this transition, start by leading him around for a while rather than giving him control of the reins. Before you know it, he'll be a regular little cowboy, galloping across the fields and herding cattle."

"Cowboy! Cowboy!" Caden flapped his feet against the leather, both hands on the saddle horn. "Storm!"

"That settles that, then," Seth said with a laugh. "Storm is our match. How much do I owe you?"

Jax ignored the question for the moment and turned his attention to Rachel and Zooey.

"Monty and Fancy are both saddled and eager to go. Why don't you two mount up and take them for a spin?"

Seth almost laughed out loud at the dismayed expression on Rachel's face, but he had too much sympathy. Riding might be something he already knew how to do, but when it came to other tasks, he'd been thrown in over his head plenty of times in the past month. As for horseback riding, it was harder than it looked, and the sheer size of horses could feel intimidating to a new rider.

Jax tightened the cinch on Monty, and Zooey mounted with surprising ease, waiting with an excited smile as Jax adjusted the stirrups for her. Seth suspected it was not her first time on a horse.

Rachel, on the other hand—

"Um, yeah," she said, clearly flustered. "I don't really do horses."

"No?" Jax adjusted Fancy's cinch and laced his fingers in order to help Rachel mount. "There's a first time for everything, right? Just put your foot right here and I'll boost you into the saddle."

"You have the boots for riding," Seth pointed out, thoroughly enjoying not being the one completely out of his element for a change.

"Oh, all right." Rachel planted her boot in the cup of Jax's hands and he hoisted her into the saddle.

She sat as straight as a board, clinging to the saddle horn for all she was worth. Jax adjusted the stirrups to fit her height and handed her the reins, but Rachel looked as if she thought the horse was going to bolt off at a dead run.

Seth drew Storm up by her side. She'd encouraged him a lot during the past few weeks. The least he could do was try to repay the kindness.

"Relax. It's sort of like driving a car."

The look she shot him could have started a forest fire.

"Sitting on this horse is *nothing* like driving a car."

"Seriously. You've got to try to relax. Fancy can feel your tension. It will make her nervous."

"Fantastic. Good to know," she said acerbically. "Freaked-out rider on a nervous horse."

"Okay, now for the directions," Jax instructed. "Gently tug the left rein, the horse goes left. Tug right for right. A gentle tug with both reins means stop, and a soft nudge of your heels will get her in gear."

Zooey giggled as she trotted Monty past Rachel and made her way around the corral for the fourth time.

"Come on, Mom. This is fun."

"You have lived in a ranching town for the last fifteen years," Seth said. "I can't believe you've never ridden a horse before."

"You're one to talk. You weren't exactly an expert when you moved back to Serendipity."

"Point taken," he said with a nod. "I rode a little with Luke when we were kids, but I had to relearn a lot when I returned from the army. Happily, it's like the old cliché about riding a bike. It didn't take me long to remember what I was doing, although I got a little bit saddle sore. The first few days I spent my evenings sitting on ice."

She laughed. "Is that supposed to encourage me?"

He tightened his arm around Caden's waist and urged Storm into a trot.

"Maybe not, but my progress ought to," he called back to her. "I may not have remembered how to ride a horse when I first got back to Serendipity, but, sweetheart, look at me now."

Chapter Seven

Rachel was looking.

It was hard not to—an attractive cowboy teaching his son how to ride a horse. Caden laughing. Seth grinning with the same glow in his blue eyes as when she'd seen him on the auction block performing his beloved parkour for a crowd of people.

And the casual way he'd inserted a term of endearment into the conversation—making it almost a cliché but not quite.

Just enough to throw her for a loop.

It probably meant nothing. Likely, he'd simply misquoted the old saying.

Baby. Sweetheart.

She could see how they could get mixed up.

But his words sent a tremor of awareness down her spine nonetheless.

She closed her eyes, struggling to counteract those thoughts and feelings by reminding herself not to take them seriously. Seth loved to tease. Even if he had meant what he'd said, it was only in good fun, and that was how Rachel was going to take it.

It was the *only* way she would take it.

She ought to be concentrating on staying on Fancy's back, not on analyzing a handsome cowboy's word choice, especially now that Jax had left them for a few minutes to go check on his twin baby girls.

And anyway, that was the shocking thing in this whole situation—she actually *was* staying on the horse. She'd made a few circuits of the corral, and she hadn't slipped off the saddle. This was amazing. Pride welled in Rachel's chest.

She was riding a horse.

Riding a horse!

She couldn't believe where this day had gone. She'd had no intention of riding when she'd come out earlier.

Who knew she would be on a horse, enjoying a relaxed walk around the corral like a regular horsewoman? She was starting to get used to Fancy's slow, rocking rhythm and was adapting to it. She wasn't even clinging to the saddle horn anymore.

She wasn't trotting like Seth and Zooey were, but she counted the fact that she was staying in the saddle at *all* as a win.

"Storm's the one for Caden," Seth said definitively. "Now, what about Fancy and Monty?"

Rachel narrowed her gaze. Caden needed only one horse. But Seth had a sparkle in his eyes that she couldn't quite read.

"What about them?"

"I was just thinking," he said mildly, "that there you are, doing well on Fancy, and Zooey on Monty. You both have good matches, too, right?"

She could see where he was going with this.

Kind of.

He had to be teasing, right? Seth with his typical enthusiastic shortsightedness. A horse was an enormous investment, never mind two. And it wasn't as if she were going to become a regular rider.

Zooey was already beaming in anticipation.

Rachel caught Seth's eye and shook her head. This was *so* not a done deal.

"I have a cat. Myst wouldn't like sharing the house with a couple of horses."

"Mom," Zooey pleaded. "I'll throw in all the allowance I've saved up."

She met Zooey's gaze. "You don't have enough allowance to buy a horse. You used it bidding on Seth, remember?"

"There's plenty of room in the Bar H stable," Seth added. "You two can come out to ride anytime you want, borrowing our saddles and bridles. You don't even need to call first."

There were so many things wrong with this scenario, starting with the fact that she was being ganged up on. She had two sets of puppy-dog eyes on her, pleading for her to give in. That was hardly fair.

"We don't have the money to buy two horses on a whim, never mind paying for the upkeep. Zooey, you can't spend all the money you've saved on a horse."

"But Monty is *my* horse. Can't you see that? I'll do anything. Get a part-time job. Help Seth take care of the horses every evening."

"You have to finish summer school. When are you going to find time for a part-time job? Besides, honey, you're going off to college in two years' time. I'm fairly certain they don't allow horses in dorm rooms."

Zooey's downcast expression nearly shattered Rachel's heart. She hated to have to be the one to douse her daughter's hopes and dreams. She felt worse than when Zooey was eight and she wanted a kitty.

Rachel had lasted two whole days before she'd broken down and they'd visited the local cat rescue to adopt Myst.

She couldn't break down now. This wasn't a cat. It was horses, completely impractical on every level—the biggest being counting on Seth to help shoulder the burden when he wouldn't need her in his life forever.

She might be visiting the Bar H often now, but there would be a time, maybe in the not so far-off future, when Seth would find his foundation as a parent.

He might think he needed her right now, and maybe he did, but eventually he would adjust to life as a single father, and she was sure it wouldn't be long before he found a nice young woman to settle down with— someone without the kind of baggage she carried. Then how would it look for her to show up at the ranch unannounced in order to ride a horse?

Seth looked disappointed, but he nodded, respecting her wishes.

"Just Storm, then. And I'll pick up a children's saddle from Emerson's. I can't wait to teach Caden to ride."

"He's a fast learner," Rachel commented. "I have a feeling he'll be galloping across the fields in no time."

Seth's eyes widened and his Adam's apple bobbed as he swallowed. She could tell he was picturing the scene in his mind, going through every parent's personal crisis of imagining everything that could go wrong.

"In time, of course," she added to quell the flicker of worry in his eyes. "I meant when he is older."

They rode for another half hour before Jax helped

them all dismount and led the horses back to the stable, promising to deliver Storm to the Bar H ranch within the week. Zooey lingered over Monty, feeding him a carrot and stroking his rich dappled mane.

With every turn around the corral, Rachel found it harder and harder not to want to find a way to purchase the horses.

Maybe Jax would take an installment plan. Or she could donate plasma every week for the next year.

She could picture it now, feel it, the lure of true country life, of riding off into the sunset on an amazing animal, perhaps with an equally amazing man.

She might even make it to a trot, eventually.

But her life was too complicated right now to consider adding any kind of change, especially one as large as a horse.

And Zooey had her own set of troubles to worry about. She didn't need any extra distractions.

And as for Rachel, she needed to be concentrating all her time and attention on navigating Zooey through the rough waters of adolescence.

A cat would have to do for now.

And when Zooey moved out and got on with her life, Rachel just might make it a dozen.

She'd be the youngest cat lady ever.

"Earth to Rachel," Seth teased as they drove back to her house. "Man, you were really out there in the ozone somewhere. Care to share? A penny for your thoughts, and all that. Or are we up to a dollar because of inflation?"

What?

He wanted her to tell him that he was looking at a future cat lady?

She didn't think so.

"It's nothing." Because really, it wasn't. "I think I'm just tired from all the excitement of the day."

"You rode a horse."

"I did."

"That's a pretty amazing accomplishment. And trust me. It grows on you."

It certainly seemed to have agreed with Seth. He was getting there, starting to look more at home with his role as rancher. And father.

Really getting there.

But she wouldn't grow to love horseback riding, because she was unlikely to ever do it again.

"You didn't answer my question," he said.

Question?

"Sorry. I must have missed it. What did you say?"

"I asked if you wanted to join me for the town's Fourth of July celebration. Picnic and fireworks. Caden is going to love it. My whole family can't wait to spend quality time with the little guy."

Rachel's heart leaped into her throat and then plunged back down again, lodging in an uncomfortable hard lump in her gut.

Was she hearing right?

Seth was asking her out?

Zooey, who was seated in the backseat of the dual cab next to Caden, stopped tickling and teasing the toddler in order to hear Rachel's response.

Even Caden went still.

The silence was deafening and painful. Seth mostly kept his eyes on the road, but he occasionally glanced in Rachel's direction. She couldn't help but notice the way his fists clenched and unclenched on the steering wheel.

He actually looked nervous.

She thought about simply telling him that she wasn't planning to attend the community event—and then follow through by staying at home.

But she hadn't missed the Fourth of July celebration since the first year she'd moved to Serendipity, when Zooey was just a toddler. And Zooey had been talking about spending time just the two of them for a week now—Rachel didn't want to disappoint her.

Oh, who was she kidding? With the way Zooey had been matchmaking, Rachel knew her daughter would be thrilled to cancel their plans so that Rachel could go out with Seth. But Rachel didn't want to cancel the time with her daughter just so she could pretend for an evening that she had a chance at a romantic relationship that she was certain would never work out. There was no future for her and Seth—and only a small window of time left that she could spend with her daughter before Zooey was off living her own life. She needed to make the most of it.

After that, she'd have the rest of her life to be alone.

"Thank you for the invitation," she said at last.

Seth's grip on the steering wheel immediately relaxed and he grinned.

"Great. Do you want me to pick you up?"

"Let me finish. I appreciate your offer—"

"But?"

"But Zooey and I have special family traditions on the Fourth of July. And besides, you'll be really busy with Caden and your family."

"Mom," Zooey protested, but Rachel held up a hand to stop her from arguing.

"I see." Seth's smile faded and his lips pressed into

a hard, straight line as his jaw tightened and a tick of strain appeared in the corner.

"But again," she repeated, "I do appreciate the offer. It was very kind."

"Mmm." Seth nodded.

The rest of the ride home passed in an uncomfortable, heavy silence. Seth wasn't his usual talkative self and Rachel didn't know what to say. Zooey was curled up, fuming, in the backseat, her earphones in her ears, and Caden had fallen asleep, probably from all of the excitement.

The only thing Rachel could think of to talk about was Caden's new horse, but the conversation had taken a turn so far past that that she thought it would be awkward to return to it.

She was relieved when Seth pulled up in front of her house and she was able to remove herself from the tense situation.

Seth was pleasant enough with his goodbye, so much so that she wondered if she'd imagined the awkwardness between them.

But even if everything was fine between her and Seth, there was another relationship that was on rocky ground. And the outburst started the moment Seth's truck rounded the corner out of sight.

Zooey turned on her, her face red with fury.

"Mom. How could you?"

"How could I what?"

"Seth asked you out—and you turned him down."

"Yes, I did."

"But why? Seth is a great guy. I could tell he was really upset when you said you wouldn't go with him."

"I know."

"Then why? I know you like him."

"I think we've already established that he is a nice man."

"No, Mom. I mean, you *like* him, like him. You should call him or text him or something and let him know you made a mistake and you want to go out with him."

"I don't *like* like anyone. I'm not in high school anymore," Rachel snapped, and then instantly regretted it. "I'm sorry, Zooey. I didn't mean to be short with you or minimize your opinion. It's just— Well, it's a lot more complicated than that now that I'm an adult. I can't just consider how I do or do not feel about him."

"Why is it when adults don't want to face something, they say *it's complicated*? Everything in life is complicated. What advice would you give me if I was the one in your circumstances?"

Rachel sighed. "To follow your heart and not let anything get in the way of your dreams."

"Exactly. So look in the mirror when you say that and ask yourself, why aren't you?"

"Because you still have two years of school left." Rachel grasped at the first excuse that entered her head.

Zooey's eyes went big. "What does dating Seth have to do with me?"

"Everything. You're the most important person in my life. I want to make sure I'm always there for you, to help you navigate through the rough waters that are ahead of you—if and when you need my help, I mean. That's where my attention should be—not on some man I barely know. Besides, I'm busy with the day care."

"But not too busy to help Seth with Caden."

"That's different."

"*How* is that different? You're spending all of your

spare time with Seth anyway. Why not make one of those times an official date?"

Because...because...

She was scared to death.

"You're right. I enjoy helping Seth with Caden, and I love how much you and Caden have bonded. But what if I date Seth and we end up breaking up? It won't just be my heart that is broken. Our relationship would affect you and Caden, as well. Can you imagine the awkwardness we'd all feel when Seth brought Caden to day care?"

Rachel was speaking the truth from experience. In the past, the few times she'd been in a relationship she felt was serious enough to bring Zooey into the picture, it had always resulted in disasters. It took a lot for her to trust a man enough to even introduce him to her daughter.

And when it didn't work out?

She couldn't just hide out and nurse her broken heart—it would upset Zooey if she saw that Rachel was depressed. So she had to be cheerful and upbeat while explaining why her ex-boyfriend would no longer be coming around. There were no easy answers.

"So you've already brought yourself all the way from the beginning of a relationship to a breakup in one fell swoop, when you haven't even gone out with him once. Nice, Mom."

"I'm just being practical."

"No. You're not. You're concealing yourself behind excuses so you won't have to deal with the possibility of failure. You can't live your life that way. Don't hide behind me, Mom, or make me a justification for why you aren't living your own life, chasing your own dreams. That's not fair to me or to you. Two years is going to pass in a heartbeat. Even right now, I've got my own life to live. School to attend. Friends to hang out with. I love you, Mom, but it's time for you to go start living for *you*. I want the best for you, just like you always have for me. And trust me on this—Seth is the best."

They hugged for a long time and then Zooey kissed Rachel's cheek before racing inside and upstairs to her room.

Rachel stood in the middle of the front lawn for a long time. She felt as if someone had replaced the blood that ran through her veins with lead.

She'd raised an amazing young lady.

Was it true, what Zooey was saying?

That she was making excuses, hiding behind her daughter so she didn't have to expose her heart and risk being hurt?

She might be protecting herself from pain by putting up walls around her heart, but she was also keeping other emotions out—and keeping other people at arm's length. Special people who could potentially change her life for the better.

Maybe she should call Seth and tell him she'd made a mistake. Maybe she should give the two of them a chance.

She pulled out her cell phone, stared at it a moment and then promptly replaced it in the back pocket of her jeans.

She felt her chest squeeze the breath out of her lungs just thinking about trying to move forward with her life.

Did she really dare open her heart again?

The Fourth of July dawned bright and clear without a cloud in the sky. A wonderful day for a picnic and an ideal sky for the spectacular grand fireworks finale.

For Seth, though, this morning wasn't sunshine and roses. His mood was closer to cloudy with a chance of rain and nothing he did helped snap him out of it.

At first Seth hadn't understood why Rachel turned him down. After all the time they'd been spending together recently, he'd thought Rachel and Zooey would enjoy spending the Fourth of July celebration with him and Caden, and with his family—the Howells and the Davenports.

He had to admit he was disappointed. And his ego had taken a direct hit.

He was eager for his sister, Samantha, and brother-in-law, Will, as well as his parents to get better acquainted with Rachel, the woman who'd helped him so much in his transition from bachelor to single dad.

He'd analyzed the conversation over and over again in his mind before he finally realized the truth of what had happened.

Rachel had thought he was asking her out on a date. And that was why she'd said no.

Wow.

Ouch.

And here he thought his ego had taken a hit when he believed she was turning down a family get-together.

If he was right in his conclusion, Rachel had turned *him* down.

Personally.

She was willing to help him when it came to Caden, but that was as far as it went. She didn't want to spend time with him socially.

And the worst part was, now that the notion of asking Rachel out on a date had entered his thick head, it wouldn't leave him alone.

He *should* have asked her out on a date for the town festivities.

Of course, she would have turned him down anyway. But he should have asked, with those intentions in mind.

Yes, they both had their fair share of responsibilities that would make pursuing a relationship challenging—and risky. It made his gut tighten just thinking about the possibility of failure. But when had he ever given up just because something was hard to do?

He wouldn't have succeeded as a soldier if he'd quit when the going got tough.

He was attracted to Rachel. He couldn't help but admire her giving, caring, empathetic heart. When she committed herself to something or someone, she went all in. The way she'd stepped in to help him with Caden was the perfect example of that.

He and Rachel got along well. They'd become good friends. And Caden and Zooey had bonded in a special way.

So what was it about him that had caused her to balk?

They had physical chemistry. At times, when their eyes met, electricity crackled between them.

It couldn't be one-sided. He knew she felt it, too.

So, why, then?

He still hadn't come up with a satisfactory answer when he met with his family on the community green later that afternoon.

Even with his thoughts heavily on Rachel, he was looking forward to attending the first Fourth of July picnic with his family since he'd returned to Serendipity. The last time he'd had the pleasure, he'd been a senior in high school.

Man, how things had changed since then.

Seth wasn't the same man he'd been when he left town. The army had forced him to start the process of growing up, but it was accepting the guardianship of Caden, and the weeks that had followed as he learned how to be a father, that had really made him a man. With his newfound maturity, he could look at a celebration like this and really appreciate all that went into it—and what it meant to be part of such a terrific community. He could hardly believe that just a month ago, he'd been intent on leaving this all behind.

Serendipity was where he belonged. Especially on a day like today, when there was so much to enjoy.

He was particularly looking forward to partaking of his mother's homemade country cooking. Amanda Howell was known far and wide for the bounty she served up at their bed-and-breakfast. He wasn't much of a cook. Straight meat and vegetables, usually grilled.

Sometimes even a fitness nut needed to cheat.

Even more than the food, though, he was highly anticipating the opportunity to spend quality time with his parents and his older sister, Samantha. Sam had married Will Davenport, who had served in the same army unit as Seth and was now not only his brother in arms but his brother-in-law.

And then there were his nieces and nephew—seven-year-old Genevieve and two-year-old twins Charlie and Melody. Even with the slower pace small-town living offered, everyone had busy schedules, and it was precious time when the whole family could be together.

His mom and dad owned and ran the town's only bed-and-breakfast, while Sam and Will took care of Sam's Grocery, which had been passed down through the family for several generations.

Upon arriving at the already-crowded community green, his mother immediately relieved him of Caden, while Sam and Will's twins tackled Seth, anxious to wrestle their "fun uncle" to the ground.

He kept his eye out for Rachel and Zooey but didn't see them in the crowd. He wasn't sure what he was going to do or say when and if he *did* see them.

Approach them and give his invitation a second try?

Honor Rachel's wishes and leave her to enjoy her family day with Zooey?

While the adults set up the food, he entertained all of the children with parkour tricks, teaching the younger ones front somersaults in the grass and crab-walking.

Before he knew it, he had a much larger audience and over a dozen young participants. Everyone, it seemed, wanted to get in on the action. Several of the teenagers were trying different moves—handstands, banking off tree trunks or hanging off branches.

"It looks like you're a hit."

Seth's heart skipped at the sound of Rachel's voice. He hadn't seen her and her daughter approach. Zooey's attention had already been diverted by nearby friends, and she was showing them how to do a banking backflip off a bench. She'd been practicing.

"All in good fun."

"Better than good. You have a gift. Look how the children and teenagers respond to you. You've even got a few teenagers as part of this group who are here from Redemption Ranch." It took him a moment to make the connection, but then he remembered the ministry program he'd heard about from his family in their letters and phone calls while he was overseas. Alexis, a local rancher, brought out teens who'd committed minor criminal offenses and let them work off their court-mandated community service hours on her ranch, where she tried to help them turn their lives around with love, prayer and a good dose of hard work.

Seth hadn't visited the ranch himself, but he figured if there was anyone on earth who could push a bunch of surly teenagers into being better people by sheer force of will, Alexis—one of his sister's best friends and possibly the most determined woman in the world—could do it.

"Alexis will be thrilled to see how excited they are," Rachel continued. "Those kids come from bad situations and need a little tough love. Parkour might be good therapy for them. You ought to think about offering them some classes."

"Exercise is always good therapy, especially for kids."

"True, although some of us don't find quite the joy in it that you do. I like to dance as much as the next woman, but there are still many days when I have to force myself out of bed early so I can stick in my dancing workout DVD before my itty-bitties start showing up for day care."

"I have days like that, too," he admitted, helping Caden somersault forward and backward on the soft grass.

"No way. You're going to college to major in athletic training. Working out is probably the highlight of your day."

"Okay, I'll admit it doesn't happen often. I love being outdoors and stretching my muscles while I take in the fresh air. But I don't think college is in the works for me, at least not right now. I've got the ranch and Caden. That's more than enough to keep me busy."

Rachel dropped onto the lawn next to Caden and he

immediately crawled into her lap. Seth sat cross-legged next to her, and within a minute he had Charlie and Melody, one on each knee.

"I wasn't sure I was going to see you today," he confessed, deciding not to beat around the bush. Rachel was a straight shooter and didn't care to play games, unless they were the fun kind and involved children.

She looked him right in the eye and nodded. "To be honest, I wasn't, either."

"What changed your mind?"

"In part, at least, a conversation I had with Zooey. She made me see I was hiding behind her, using her as an excuse for not living my own life."

Seth's heart welled. "She's a smart young lady."

"Yes, she is. And she's right. I don't want to get to the end of my life and realize I missed out because I was afraid to put myself out there." She shrugged and flashed him a rueful grin. "I don't want to end up a cat lady."

He tried to chuckle and choked instead, then swallowed around the lump that formed in his throat. She still thought he'd asked her out on a date, and yet here she was.

Maybe he ought to leave well enough alone and make the most of this evening, but somehow that didn't feel right.

For one thing, he really did want his family to have the opportunity to spend time with Rachel and see what he saw in her. And then there was Zooey. He wanted her to join in the family gathering, as well.

"The other day, when I asked you to the picnic—"

He paused, trying to choose his words carefully so he didn't screw this up.

"And like an idiot, I turned you down," she said before he could finish.

He grinned. "You're not an idiot. You were protecting yourself, which I respect. That's always a smart thing to do." He cleared his throat. "That said, in full disclosure, I wasn't actually asking you out on a date."

Her gaze widened to epic proportions and she practically gaped at him. He'd definitely caught her off guard with that statement.

"You weren't?"

"What I *was* trying to do—badly, apparently—was to suggest our families celebrate together. My parents have a very high opinion of you, and I thought you might enjoy spending time with my family. I know they'd like to spend time with you. Then again," he said, lifting up his arms so the twins could crawl over him like a jungle gym, "maybe you'd rather have a quiet celebration with your daughter."

"As you can see," she said, gesturing toward Zooey, who was still trying parkour moves with her friends, "my daughter has her own idea of what a fun Fourth of July celebration looks like."

"So you'll stay?"

"Yes. But—I want to be clear about this—it was never a date?"

"Well, no, but— That is, I—" he stammered.

How in the world was he going to explain that while his first thought had been for a family gathering, he now thought the idea of a date between them was spot-on?

Maybe he should have left well enough alone.

"Yes?"

He shook his head. "No. Never mind. I'm glad you and Zooey showed up."

Who was the idiot now?

"Shall I add the food I brought to your family's goodies? I don't cook as well as your mother."

"I'm sure your dishes are just fine. My motto is, the more food, the merrier." He patted his stomach and licked his lips to accentuate his point.

Rachel handed Caden off to Zooey and went to lay her offerings down with the Howells' already-tasty smorgasbord.

Meanwhile, Seth was furiously considering how to get some time alone with Rachel. He didn't know how it was going to happen, or when, but he was determined he'd create some kind of dating atmosphere at some point tonight, and he'd be watching for his moment.

"Soup's on," Rachel called in an animated tone, and everyone gathered to eat and share fellowship.

The picnic dinner was the most enjoyable he'd ever had, surrounded by family and friends and with Rachel by his side and Caden in his lap.

He thought he might get a little ribbing for having invited Rachel to celebrate with them. He was the baby of the family and they liked to give him a hard time.

He was taken aback, however, by how warmly they welcomed Rachel to their meal, as if she'd belonged there all of her life, as if she were already part of the family and not an invited guest.

Even Zooey fit in, dividing her time between conversing with the adults over what her plans were after high school and playing with the children. She had Rachel's nurturing gift with the kids, taking seven-year-old Genevieve under her wing and making her feel special by engaging her in girl talk and getting into a serious, animated discussion about her favorite books.

It wasn't long after everyone had cleaned their plates and what was left of the food had been put away that Seth noticed a couple of teenagers he didn't recognize had joined Zooey.

Rachel, who'd been deep in conversation with Samantha, had noticed, too, and quickly excused herself to head in Zooey's direction.

Seth, who was playing with Caden, followed her.

"Hi, Abigail," Rachel said to a tall, thin auburn-haired girl. "My, it's been a long time since I've seen you. I remember when you were just a little tyke. Now you've grown up into a pretty young woman."

The girl blushed, her pinkened cheeks clashing with the color of her hair.

Rachel's gaze shifted to the teenage boy standing with them. He was a clean-cut kid, dressed in khaki Bermuda shorts and a bright green polo shirt, with well-trimmed blond hair combed back off his forehead.

Before Rachel could say a word, the young man reached out to shake her hand.

"Hello, Ms. Perez. My name is Dawson McAllister, ma'am. My mom and I just moved into town."

"Glad to meet you, Dawson."

Rachel had told Seth about the questionable friends Zooey had made during summer school, teenagers she'd been afraid might influence Zooey into dangerous behavior.

Seth briefly wondered if these might be the kids she'd meant, but he immediately decided that wasn't the case.

These two were far too polite to be trouble, and he could see from Rachel's relaxed smile that she was genuinely happy to see the girl and meet the boy. Both teenagers were wholesome looking and respectful to the adults.

"His mom is a single parent like you and Seth," Zooey added excitedly. "But she has the flu and can't make it to the fireworks tonight."

"I'm sorry to hear that," said Seth. "You'll have to introduce us later."

"Mom, is it okay if we hang out for a while?" Zooey asked. "I promise we'll stay on the green."

"Just be sure to find us right after the fireworks display is finished," Rachel said.

As soon as the teenagers were out of hearing distance, Rachel turned to Seth with an amused smile. "I overheard a conversation between Zooey and Abigail the other day on the phone. Dawson is the new guy in town, and I think Zooey might be crushing on him."

Seth laughed. "I'm no judge of looks, but I like his character. They both look pretty respectable to me."

"They are good kids. I'm so thankful to God that she's found better friends."

Seth was getting used to Rachel attributing all of the circumstances in her life to God's care.

When there was good, like Zooey's new friends, she praised God. When she bumped up against trials and tribulations—and she'd had many—she had faith that the Lord would see her through.

Had God brought Rachel into his life?

The thought stunned him, shifting his view entirely.

Rachel had always been there, in the exact right times and places, precisely when he needed her. There were too many factors involved for it to be a mere coincidence that she'd come into his life when she had.

For the first time in a very long time he saw God's hand at work in his life. The Lord wasn't far off somewhere in the high heavens, too busy to care for His creations.

He was here. Now. Watching over His people and blessing them.

Seth had only to look around him to realize the number of blessings he had to be thankful for—his family, his friends, and most of all, Rachel and Caden, and even Zooey.

"Who is that?" Rachel asked, nodding toward a thin woman with platinum-blond hair crossing the green. "I don't recognize her. Maybe she's Dawson's mom and she decided to come out for the fireworks."

Seth shrugged. Whoever she was, she stuck out like a sore thumb, wobbling along in four-inch spiked heels and wearing a skirt cut well above her knees. He knew zilch about purses, but he suspected the giant one she carried in the crook of her elbow cost more than he made in the army in a month. Her short, stylish hair and heavily applied makeup completed the odd picture.

It wasn't that she looked unattractive; her outfit just seemed overdone and out of place in this relaxed community gathering. This woman was definitely not from the country.

He watched as she stopped and spoke to Jo and Frank Spencer. They exchanged an animated dialogue—Jo was always animated, but this time it seemed to Seth that she was especially vivacious.

But then Jo pointed directly at him and waved.

His skin prickled and the hair stood up on the back of his neck as he apprehensively returned her wave.

He didn't know why his pulse ratcheted up and his lungs suddenly felt as if he were breathing lead.

It was probably Dawson's mom, he reminded himself as the woman started toward him. Who else could it be?

"Seth?" Rachel threaded her hand in the crook of his arm. Her gaze was also on the woman crossing the green, and her tone was wary. He sensed she was experiencing the same disquiet he was.

"Seth Howell?" The woman's ice-blue eyes bore right through him, making his insides feel frosty.

"Who's asking?"

Rachel squeezed his arm.

Maybe he did sound a little short with her. He tried to smile.

The woman didn't answer him. Instead, she glanced around their picnic area, and suddenly her face broke out into what Seth thought was the fakest smile he'd ever seen.

She made a beeline for Charlie but stopped short before him, leaning down and barely patting him on the head, as if she was afraid he might get dirt on her fancy outfit.

No chance of that—Charlie hunched back and looked for his father, instinctively not trusting the woman. When he made a sudden movement and she snatched her hand back in alarm, he rushed into Will's outstretched arms.

The stranger definitely had everyone's attention in their little group now.

"How cute my little nephew is," she crowed, awkwardly dropping her hand to her side.

"Nephew?" Will repeated, his brow lowering.

"Ma'am, I think you must be mistaking us for someone else. How can we help you?" Seth asked, trying to remain polite and ignoring the fact that it seemed she'd asked Jo specifically for him and the question of what that might mean.

"No, no. That redheaded old lady over there said this is where I'd find him."

"Find your nephew?" Rachel clarified.

The blonde nodded.

"I'm afraid you're mistaken. This is Charlie, Samantha and Will Davenport's son."

"Oh, I—" she stammered, looking confused for a moment. "No, no. Not Charlie."

She looked around and Seth's heart stopped beating when her gaze landed on Caden, who was playing with Genevieve and was unaware of what was going on around him.

"Why, there he is," she said, as if she hadn't first accosted Charlie with the same intentions.

Her false smile returned in spades and it was all Seth could do not to race forward and snatch his son away before she could get to him.

He moved closer but at a slower pace, ready at a moment's notice to go with his original plan.

"It's my little nephew. *Caden.*"

Chapter Eight

Rachel's heart plummeted at the words. This woman could be none other than Tracy's sister, Trish.

What was she doing in Serendipity?

Seth had said she hadn't had anything to do with Luke and Tracy in the past. She'd completely alienated herself from her sister. She hadn't even shown up for Tracy's funeral and had sent a lawyer in her stead for the reading of Luke and Tracy's will.

If she remembered correctly, Seth had said Trish had never seen Caden in person, not even as an infant. She certainly didn't have a clue who he was now. She'd scared poor Charlie half to death with her inept approach.

"Trish?" Seth asked, clearly having come to the same conclusion. "Trish Ward?"

When the woman's gaze shifted from Caden to Seth, Rachel used the opportunity to steal Caden into her arms, which she hoped would offer the boy a sense of security in what was looking to be a confusing mess.

Caden was an intelligent, sensitive child and she knew he would perceive the undercurrent of tension that was already crackling between Trish and the Howells, who had gathered around Seth, presenting a united—and slightly intimidating—front before the woman.

"That's right. I'm Trish. Caden's auntie. And I've traveled a long way to see the child, so I would appreciate your cooperation in the matter."

She sounded as if she were brokering some kind of business deal, not asking to visit her nephew.

For a moment, Seth's expression appeared torn, but then he straightened his shoulders decisively and reached to take Caden from Rachel's arms.

She closed ranks, standing side by side with Seth, her hand on his shoulder to let him know she was there for him and offer him silent reassurance and support.

"This is Caden," he said cautiously.

Trish studied Caden for a second but made no move to reach out and take him.

Which was good for her, because Rachel was fighting against a profound protective urge to step between Trish and Caden and hold her arms out to imitate a physical wall.

She wasn't sure what it was about Trish that set off all of Rachel's internal alarms, but she knew she wasn't the only one feeling it. Every adult in the vicinity, including Seth, had the same expression on their faces.

Perhaps it was that Trish looked so out of place among the country people. Maybe it was that she was so awkward with children. Then there was the fact that she hadn't made the least effort to see Caden in the past when Tracy was alive.

She hadn't even gone to her own sister's funeral.

And now she was standing in the middle of Serendipity's community green during a traditional celebration, dressed in outlandishly inappropriate clothing and asking after Caden because—

Why *was* she here?

"I've traveled a long way to get here," Trish said, sounding annoyed. "A ridiculously long plane ride, not to mention the time it took to get to this podunk town in the middle of Nowhere, Texas. My limo driver said it wasn't even on the map."

"You should have rented a car," Amanda Howell suggested, with only the tiniest trace of sarcasm in her tone. "It would have been much cheaper."

Trish sniffed. "I won't be staying long."

Well, that was a relief, anyway. Perhaps she'd just had a touch of conscience and thought she ought to check in on her nephew. Now that the woman had seen that Caden was happy and healthy, well cared for and loved by everyone, maybe she would leave it at that.

And just plain *leave.*

"Why *are* you here?" Seth asked, pulling Caden even tighter against his chest.

"I have a perfect right to see my nephew."

"True," Seth agreed, his tone flat. "I'm not questioning that. I guess what I am wondering is why you're here *now.* Let's be honest, Trish. You haven't shown much interest in Caden in the past, so I have to ask myself what changed that brought you here?"

Rachel bristled. Trish hadn't shown *any* interest in Caden in the past. And now all of a sudden she was so concerned about her nephew?

Rachel didn't think so.

The real question was—what was in it for her?

Then again, maybe she wasn't being fair to Trish.

Rachel was in no position to judge anyone. Technically, she wasn't involved in this situation at all.

Except she was.

She had somehow become personally invested in Seth and Caden. She cared what happened to them.

She cared about *them*.

And though Trish hadn't said as much, Rachel suspected she was a threat to them in some way. It only remained for her to figure out how.

And in the meantime, to try to show patience. And grace. The Lord could have worked on Trish's conscience. No one was beyond His help. Granted, she didn't know how to act around children, but that didn't mean she was here out of anything but the best intentions and not the selfishness Rachel had automatically attributed to her.

Rachel decided to take a wait-and-see attitude.

Trish shrugged and flashed a not-quite-sincere smile. "Well, of course I want to see how my nephew is getting on, especially now that Tracy's gone and Caden has a new—"

Trish paused and gave Seth an appreciative once-over that sent a chill down Rachel's spine.

"—guardian," Trish finished, her alto voice thick and humming with pleasure.

Apparently, the woman was much more adept at interacting with adult males than she was with toddlers. What she probably didn't know was that not every single man walking the planet was susceptible to her charms.

Rachel felt Seth's muscles stiffen and his jaw ticked with strain. She could tell that he didn't enjoy Trish's flirtatious manner with him any more than Charlie had cared for her disingenuous pat on the head.

"As you can see, I've got my whole family here celebrating the Fourth of July. Would you like to join us? We've got plenty of food left over," Seth said, with far more grace than Rachel imagined she could have mustered.

Trish's cool blue gaze flicked over the family and she pursed her lips.

"No, I don't think so," she said abruptly. "I have the limo driver waiting for me. If you will direct me to the nearest hotel—preferably five stars—I will get out of your way so you can have your family time. Seth, you and I will meet to discuss Caden later—in *private*."

Rachel seethed at the way Trish ordered Seth around. Despite her resolve to keep an open mind, that clinched Rachel's opinion of her. Trish didn't really want to interact with Caden or see how he was faring, and she most definitely didn't want to have anything to do with Caden's new extended family.

Trish wouldn't mind spending time with *Seth*, maybe, but Rachel was equally as sure he didn't want to have a thing to do with Trish.

"I'm sorry to say we don't have a hotel here in Serendipity," Samantha said, not sounding particularly sorry at all. "If that's what you need, you'll have to ask your limo driver to take you into one of the larger cities. Amarillo has some nice hotels."

"Or you could stay with us," Samuel offered. "We're no five-star resort, but we run a nice little bed-and-breakfast down by the stream. You'll have your own private cabin with heat and indoor plumbing, and my Amanda here is well-known for her homemade country cooking."

He paused and tossed Amanda an affectionate grin

before returning his gaze to Trish. "You'll be quite comfortable. We even have Wi-Fi in the main lodge."

Trish looked aghast, as if the thought of spending the night in a country cabin was akin to camping out in a tent in the middle of a rugged mountain terrain.

With bears.

And coyotes.

With or without Wi-Fi.

"I think not," Trish said, not even bothering to thank Samuel for the offer.

Rachel didn't think she'd ever met anyone quite as rude and arrogant as Trish Ward.

"That is a very sweet offer, Samuel," Rachel said, feeling like she needed to cover for Trish's glaring lapse in good manners.

Trish appeared to take the hint.

"Yes, yes. Of course. Thank you, Samuel, but I think I'd prefer to find a hotel. Amarillo, did you say?"

Samantha nodded, a satisfied smile creeping up her lips.

When Trish wasn't looking, Samantha caught Rachel's eyes and mouthed, *Or Mars.*

It was all Rachel could do to withhold her laughter. This was the wrong time and place for that.

Trish fished around in her enormous designer purse for a moment before withdrawing her cell phone.

"Punch in your number for me, will you, Seth?" Her smile became so syrupy sweet it turned Rachel's stomach.

Seth's jaw was still set and pulsing as he put in his number.

"I'll call you later so we can get together when you're not so...*busy* with other people."

"You do that," Seth said, although it was evident from his tone that he hoped she would not.

Rachel hoped she would not, although she knew better than to hope they'd seen the last of Trish. For whatever reason—and it very obviously wasn't to visit Caden—Trish Ward had traveled clear across the country to Serendipity.

And she wasn't going away.

Seth thought he might be sick as he watched Trish Ward with her ridiculous platinum hair wobble her way off the community green. Several people tried to engage her in conversation, but she just lifted her chin and ignored them.

Not even a polite nod toward the friendly folks who were just trying to welcome a stranger in their midst.

He didn't know how people acted where she came from, but in his part of the country, her behavior was considered just plain rude.

And wasn't it wonderful that she was Caden's aunt—by blood. He didn't even want to think about the possible implications of that fact.

He pulled Caden tight to him and breathed in his little-boy scent—something that two months ago he never would have imagined as being so sweet and comforting. Caden had become completely vital to his existence.

The toddler wasn't merely a responsibility in his life anymore, or a sacrifice he had to make for the sake of his deceased friends.

Caden was his baby blessing.

The toddler objected to being held so closely and squirmed and wiggled until Seth set him down. Seth let him go.

The boy was safe for now, anyway.

There were still times when Seth woke up late at night in a cold sweat, wondering why God had allowed the sniper to take Luke and not him. But he'd finally come to accept that, for whatever reason, he and Caden now had an inseparable bond together—one that went beyond blood and straight to Seth's heart.

But Trish?

She *was* related to Caden by blood. Seth had Luke and Tracy's will naming him Caden's legal guardian, but what if Trish was here to make trouble and try to claim custody for herself?

"Hey." Rachel's voice was gentle as she laid a hand on his arm. "Are you okay?"

Seth took a deep, cleansing breath and slowly let it out, then picked off his hat and raked his fingers through his hair. He was getting a killer headache.

"Honestly? I don't know." He shook his head. "To tell the truth, I'm not sure of anything anymore."

"Don't second-guess yourself. Luke and Tracy knew what they were doing when they wrote their will and asked you to be Caden's guardian. I'm sure they made sure that it's completely ironclad. That's what they wanted for Caden—*you*. Whatever Trish wants or thinks she's entitled to, don't forget that *you* are Caden's daddy now, and nothing Trish does or says can change that."

His heart warmed. It meant a lot that he had Rachel's trust and support. He wished he had the words to express how grateful he was to have her near him, but his throat closed and he got all tongue-tied.

Samantha approached, holding Caden's hand as he toddled around on the grass.

"You look like you're about to jump out of your skin, little brother."

He replaced his hat and stood to his full height, towering over Samantha.

"I haven't been your *little* brother in years."

Samantha jerked the brim of his hat down so it covered his eyes. "Maybe, but I'm still smarter than you are."

"You wish."

He might not have lost his sense of humor, but stress was still rolling off him in waves, and he knew Samantha was just trying to cheer him up.

"No, seriously, I came to tell you that Mom and I want to spend some quality time with Caden," Samantha said. "I don't think there's any concern about Trish returning this evening. Why don't you and Rachel take a walk around the green—to clear your big head."

"You two are terrible." Rachel chuckled at the back-and-forth interchange between the siblings.

Samantha snorted. "You should have seen us when we were little tykes."

"Yeah," Seth agreed. "She could outwrestle me until I hit my adolescent growth spurt."

"You'd better believe it," Samantha crowed.

"She'd start it, and then when Mom and Dad would come in, she'd blame it on me and I'd be the one who got in trouble. Dad said I wasn't supposed to wrestle girls, but Samantha isn't a girl. She's my sister."

Samantha snickered.

"And worse, she still pinches me when she doesn't get her way."

Samantha demonstrated, pinching Seth's cheeks like

she would a toddler's. "Isn't he just the cutest little thing you've ever seen?"

"Cut it out." Heat filled his cheeks, and not because his sister had been pinching them. He wasn't sure he wanted to know Rachel's answer to that question. What if it was another ego-deflating reply? He swatted Samantha's hand away.

Rachel's chuckle turned into outright laughter. "I never had a brother or sister to spar with, and Zooey is an only child. Seeing you two together makes me wish she could have had a sibling."

"Zooey's really good with children," Samantha observed. "I saw her playing with Caden earlier and he just adores her."

"Like mother, like daughter," Seth agreed, feeling oddly proud about the statement.

"Speaking of Zooey—where is she?" Samantha asked. "I can keep an eye on her, too, if you want."

"Off with her friends," Rachel answered. "I told her to be back right after the fireworks display is finished."

"Great. Then there is no reason for you two not to take that walk I mentioned."

Samantha winked and mouthed the words *Be good* to him. The heat in his face turned to a burning open flame. Thankfully, she hadn't voiced her comment aloud, and Rachel didn't appear to have noticed.

Otherwise, he would have had to string his sister up by her ears.

He still might.

He mock-scowled at her and took Rachel's hand.

"Come on. Let's get out of here before Samantha finds something else to embarrass me about."

He didn't realize that he was practically running off

the green until Rachel pulled him up, her breath coming in short gasps.

"Look, I know you want to put some distance between yourself and your mischievous sister, but if you don't slow your pace, you're going to be dragging deadweight here in a second. I'm about to pass out. You may be a marathon runner, but me, not so much."

He laughed. "Sorry. Do you want to sit for a moment?" He gestured to a nearby bench.

"Just for a minute, if you don't mind. It won't take me long to catch my breath."

He led her to the bench and sat down beside her, never once letting go of her hand.

She didn't seem to mind—and he needed the human contact right now just to ground him after that confrontation with Trish.

Rachel stared at their clasped hands, and for a moment he thought she might pull away, but instead she threaded her fingers through his and gave his hand a light squeeze.

"I'm sorry Trish had to show up and ruin your family get-together," she said softly. Regretfully.

"Yeah. What is *with* that?"

"I don't know. She's a strange cookie. I just don't understand why she's suddenly shown up in Serendipity, pretending to be interested in Caden."

"You got that, too, that she's just pretending to be interested in Caden, huh?"

"It was kind of hard to miss. I think she frightened poor Charlie half to death. As someone who works with children on a regular basis, I can tell you definitively that that woman has never been around a child in her life."

"Which makes me wonder…"

"Why she's here now," Rachel finished for him. "Because it can't be for Caden's sake."

"Exactly." He put his other hand over their threaded fingers and gently stroked the inside of her wrist with his thumb.

They were both silent for a moment before he shared what was on his mind.

"Do you think—" He inhaled deeply and plunged on. "Is it possible she's just here to meet her nephew? That she suddenly realized she was making a mistake to alienate her family, and she wants to make amends now?"

"It's possible," Rachel said, quietly and deliberately. "But not probable. Nothing I saw or heard today made me think she was really here because she cares for Caden in any way—except that I had the oddest feeling she wanted something from him."

He cringed, and Rachel tightened her grip on his hand.

"I agree. I want to think the best of her. She's Tracy's sister. And even though they were estranged, I know Tracy loved her and always wanted to reconcile. But something about Trish rubs me the wrong way. She doesn't seem…sincere."

"Which leads us back to square one," Rachel said with a sigh. "Why is the woman here, and what does she want with Caden?"

"Nothing good, I don't imagine. Honestly, I'm afraid even to speculate."

"I understand how you feel. The magnitude of possibilities are frightening, to say the least. But I think if we talk through it, you'll be better prepared when you meet with her."

"My gut turns over every time I think about having

to see her again. I don't want to hear anything she has to say, and I don't know why she's so adamant about meeting with me alone."

"Don't you?"

Rachel could have been teasing him, but Seth doubted it. Her tone was dead serious, and he knew she was thinking the same thing he was—that Tracy was after him romantically.

"Well, if that's what she's looking for, she's barking up the wrong tree."

"I think finding out that Caden's guardian is a handsome single man is just frosting on the cake for her."

"I'm no one's frosting." Despite the seriousness of their conversation, one side of his mouth kicked up.

Rachel had just said she thought he was handsome.

Well, she'd said she imagined *Trish* thought he was handsome, but wasn't that the same thing?

Too bad thinking about the coming meeting with Trish had to spoil the moment for him. He wasn't able to revel in Rachel's attention.

"What I don't get is why she was asking about Caden when she clearly had no interest in spending time with him. I'll tell you this—I'm not inclined to let her anywhere near my child."

"I think she wants something from him."

"What could Caden possibly give her? He's only two, for crying out loud."

She shook her head. "I don't know. Maybe there was something in the will."

"She wasn't at the reading of the will—she sent a lawyer in her stead."

"Did they leave Trish anything that might somehow be misconstrued to be connected with Caden?"

Seth furrowed his brow. "I don't think so. I have to admit I don't really remember the details. I was pretty broken up having Tracy die so soon after Luke. And I was trying to wrap my mind around the reality that I'd just become the legal guardian of their son. Everything from that time is really foggy. I assume Trish was left something. I think the lawyers met together afterward. If there were any concerns, wouldn't the lawyers have brought it up then? I never heard that she was contesting the will or anything."

As soon as the words were out of his mouth, the air left his lungs in a whoosh, as if he'd been sucker punched.

"Could she really do that, do you think?" he asked, his voice ragged.

"Contest the will? I don't know. Maybe. But why would she *want* to do that? There's no doubt in my mind that she has no interest in raising Caden herself."

"I don't know." He inhaled sharply and then shoved out a breath. "I just don't know."

"I don't, either, but if that's what she has in mind, we'll contest it."

She caught what she'd said, and even in the dark of twilight, Seth could see the blush that slashed across her cheeks. He didn't know what she had to be embarrassed about. He was glad she was by his side, supporting him.

"I mean *you* will contest any claim that she makes to challenge the will. It seems to me that it's all straightforward, right? In black and white. And you know Luke and Tracy would have made it airtight."

"Well, if it comes to that, and I pray it doesn't, I'll make an appointment with the lawyer who executed Luke and Tracy's will. But frankly, I have to say I'm concerned. Trish seems a little off-kilter to me. I don't know how to deal with that. Plus, she came in a limo and insisted on staying in a five-star hotel. I'm guessing she has way more money than me—enough to hire a fancy lawyer. What if they find a way around my guardianship?"

Rachel grimaced. "Okay, it was my idea to speculate, and now I'm going to say we ought to stop. I'm sorry, Seth. All I've managed to do here is stress you out even more than you already were, and that was the last thing I wanted to do. We don't know anything yet. Let's wait and see how it plays out. I'm certain Samantha wanted me to help you calm down when she suggested we take a walk together."

Seth choked on his breath and it was his turn to blush. "What do you mean?"

Maybe she had seen Samantha's wink and the teasingly mouthed words after all. But Rachel only looked confused by his question.

"She knows we've become close friends. I figure she thought I could be a sounding board for you to work through your worries and settle a little bit—not rile you up as I've apparently done."

"Close friends," he repeated, unlacing his fingers from hers and putting his arm across the back of the bench so he could turn her way and hopefully read her emotions in her eyes.

She touched his face, skimming her fingers across the line of his stubbled jaw.

"You've been clenching your teeth since the moment Trish appeared on the green."

"Have I?" He leaned in closer, inhaling the coconut

scent of her shampoo. Why was it that that particular smell was suddenly so incredibly enticing?

"Seth, I... I hope you know you can always count on me. I want to be there for you, whenever and wherever you need me. I know you already finished with the playhouse, and you're doing great with Caden, so there's no reason you need to call on me. But if you want to, I'm offering my friendship, with no obligations attached."

"Whenever?" he repeated, his voice a ragged whisper. "Wherever?"

It wasn't that his problems with Trish and his fears about Caden disappeared, exactly. Rather, they melded with the dozens of other emotions rising to fill his chest. He desperately craved human touch, but not just anyone's.

He wanted to feel that connection with Rachel, and it was unlike any feeling he'd ever before experienced. His chest warmed and his skin tingled as his gaze dropped to her lips.

They'd been through a lot together these past few weeks. He trusted Rachel completely. With her by his side, and aided by prayer, they could face this new challenge.

Together.

"Whenever?" he asked again softly, close to her ear. Her warm breath fanned his cheek. "Wherever?"

At the audible catch in her breath, he slid his arm down around her shoulders.

"How about here? Now?"

He saw the answer in her deep brown eyes, luminescent in the moonlight.

"Thank you," he said, softly brushing his lips over hers. "For being there for me. And for Caden." Each phrase was followed by a kiss, and with each kiss he lingered just a little bit longer on her soft, full lips.

She was oh, so sweet.

Rachel wrapped her arms around his neck and he removed his hat as he slanted his head to deepen the kiss.

He was beyond speaking. He could only feel, not only the gentle press of her lips against his, but all the emotions behind them.

The whiz and pop of fireworks sounded in the distance, but Seth was too absorbed in Rachel, in making fireworks of their own, to even notice the vibrant colors lighting up the sky.

Chapter Nine

The next morning, Rachel awoke to the sound of a lawn mower directly outside her window, the growl of its engine too close to be that of a neighbor's.

She really didn't want to be pulled from her dreams—the ones where she was kissing Seth under the magnificent glow of fireworks.

But when she came fully awake—well, as awake as a person could be before her mandatory two cups of coffee—she realized it wasn't a dream at all.

Seth *had* kissed her last night, and it was one of the most wonderful moments of her life, second only to the first time she'd held Zooey in her arms.

With semiwakefulness also came the doubts and fears, sneaking up on her before she had the ability to keep them at bay.

Yes, Seth had kissed her—but why? Was it the result of true emotions, those that had slowly grown over the time they'd spent together the past few weeks? Her response to him came from exactly that.

But afterward, she realized he could merely have been reacting to the shock of Trish's arrival, needing the feel of one heart connecting to another in order to ground and reassure him, all precipitated by the day's events.

What if his kiss had meant nothing at all?

She couldn't blame him for seeking comfort during such emotional upheaval. It was a very human thing to do. And the truth was, she was more than ready to give him whatever emotional support he needed.

Even if it left her own heart in peril.

She was beginning to care for Seth in a way that went far beyond the solid friendship they had developed, and that put her in a precarious position, totally open and vulnerable to being hurt.

She could very well end up with a broken heart.

She'd had other relationships in the past, but none that compared to what she had with Seth—the bond of friendship that was the foundation of other deeper emotions she'd never experienced before.

But there was so much more to consider than just how *she* felt, even if Seth felt the same way about her.

A relationship with Seth might not even be in *Seth's* best interest. Seth had his hands full to overflowing learning to be Caden's father and a single parent. And a ranch owner.

And now there was Trish.

Even if pursuing a relationship had been a remote possibility before, this would be the worst of all times to do so. Seth needed to keep his head on straight, not be distracted by the staggering emotions a new relationship invariably brought.

Finally, what about Zooey? And Caden? Yes, Zooey had encouraged her to try for this relationship, but she knew her daughter would still be hurt in the end if things went bad. And Caden—that precious toddler had become so much a part of her life that she couldn't imagine no longer being in his world. If they broke up, Seth might even remove him from day care. What then?

She scoffed at herself. She was borrowing a load of trouble where, at least for the moment, there was none.

And there *was* none because there was still time for Rachel to apply the brakes and avoid this potential train wreck altogether.

Whoa, Nellie.

She was shaken from her reverie by an engine cutting out and starting again. Now she was certain there was no doubt about it. There really *was* someone mowing her front yard.

Curious, she peeked out through the curtain and was surprised to find Seth plowing straight, neat rows across her grass, Caden happily strapped in a backpack and enjoying the ride.

What on earth?

Wrapped in a plush cotton robe, she tiptoed up the stairs to see if Zooey had been wakened by the noise, but in typical teenage fashion, the girl was sound asleep.

Rachel took a moment to tuck Zooey's comforter around her shoulders and then she brushed her daughter's hair back and planted a soft kiss on her forehead, just as she used to do when Zooey was around Caden's age.

She quietly closed the door to Zooey's bedroom and returned to her own room to throw on jeans and a T-shirt and run a brush through her bedhead hair.

She didn't think about makeup until she was already out the door and Seth had spotted her. He waved and killed the engine on the lawn mower.

She must look a mess.

Too late now.

Blame it on lack of coffee.

"Why are you mowing my lawn?" she asked bluntly as he jogged up to her.

Again, that lack of coffee…

"Because it needed to be mowed."

"Yes, that's true, but my question is, why are *you* mowing my lawn? It's seven o'clock in the morning on a Saturday. No one gets up at seven o'clock in the morning on a Saturday to mow someone else's lawn."

"I do. I've already eaten a good breakfast and have been for my run. Bright eyed and bushy tailed," he said with a cheesy grin.

"So I see," she said wryly.

"I borrowed your lawn mower out of your shed. I hope you don't mind."

"Why should I mind? Mow away to your heart's content. That's one more thing I can scratch from my list of things to do before the inspector comes."

He nodded. "That's the plan. I know the inspector is coming to evaluate your day care on Monday, so I thought I'd do a little more spiffing up so your place really shines."

Tears sprang to her eyes before her emotions even caught up with her.

"You remembered."

Seth reached up and gently wiped away her tears. "Of course I remembered, sweetheart. If it's important to you, it's important to me."

It was an intimate, caring gesture, made even more so by the kindness in his eyes. Apparently, he was prepared to embrace what had happened between them the evening before and move forward with their relationship.

And she wanted that, too—wanted it so much it terrified her. She'd never been a runner before, but she felt like running. As far and as fast as she could.

She barely stopped herself from scurrying backward. She was an adult and should act like it, but she might as well have been an angst-ridden teenager, as discombobulated as her mind and body were acting.

She wanted to throw away every reason why being with Seth was a bad idea and just *do* it, follow her heart for maybe the first time in her life.

But she would not follow those inclinations, because she couldn't. Because too many people depended on her to keep her head on straight.

"That's so sweet," she told Seth, and meant it with all of her heart.

"I think the inspector is going to be happy with this place, especially when she sees how much your kids adore you."

Rachel laughed. "That will be the one day they all decide to act up. Anyway, it's not the children she'll be examining. She'll be checking off a list of standards every in-home day care in the state must adhere to. Thanks to you and my beautiful new play set, I have high hopes that I'll pass with flying colors."

His hand moved from her face to her fingers, which he squeezed lightly.

"You will. And if for some reason they find something that needs fixing, I'm your man."

I'm your man.

He said it so casually and yet so genuinely, accompanied by a grin that could charm the wrapper off a lollipop, that his words slipped straight through the cracks of the walls she'd so carefully put up and plunged right into her heart.

She might know in her head what was best for all involved, but her wayward heart didn't care to listen to what her mind had to say.

"If you want, I can come over tomorrow and—" Seth started, but he was interrupted by the ring of his cell phone.

He pulled it out of his pocket, checked the number and scowled deeply.

"It's her," he confirmed. "Who would have thought that she was an early riser? I pictured her as the type who stayed up until all hours of the night and then slept until noon."

Rachel had reached pretty much the same conclusions about the woman. She chuckled and nodded toward the still-ringing phone. "Are you planning to answer that?"

"If I ignore her, do you think she'll go away?"

"Doubtful."

He sighed and answered the phone.

"This is Seth... No, you didn't wake me. I was up." He paused as Trish spoke on the other end of the line. "All right. Where do you want to meet?"

Again, a pause. Seth's jaw tightened, and Rachel slid her hand into his free one.

"No, that's probably not going to work. Listen, I have a better idea. There's a café called Cup O' Jo's on the end of Main Street. You probably saw it when you drove in—er, came into town in your limo. You can't miss it. There's a hitching post and water trough out in front of it."

He rolled his eyes and covered the receiver. "She just called Serendipity a hick town," he mouthed.

"Actually, people often ride their horses to the café, so the hitching post gets a lot of use," he informed her.

Rachel covered her mouth so Trish couldn't hear her snickering in the background.

While it was true that Cup O' Jo's occasionally saw a horse hitched to its post, it wasn't exactly a regular occurrence the way Seth was painting it, gently mocking Trish's closed-minded perceptions of the town. Trish probably thought she'd stepped back in time by at least a century.

"All right. I'll see you at two."

Seth hung up and half groaned, half growled from deep in his throat.

"This is one meeting I'm definitely not looking forward to," he said.

"I know. I've been praying for you since the moment Trish showed up yesterday."

"And I appreciate that. It means a lot. But can I ask you for another favor? It's a big one, and I won't blame you if you say no. But I'm really uncomfortable with the idea of meeting Trish alone, even if it's in the middle of Jo's café."

"I don't blame you. She was trying to get you to meet in a private place, wasn't she?"

"As if I'd even consider that."

"That woman has an agenda you know nothing about—and she seems to have a thing for you, too. It's wise to meet her in a public place. Plus, you know Jo will be watching over you, with *your* best interests at heart."

"Right. That was my thought when I suggested the café. I know Jo will subtly—or not so subtly—keep an ear on the conversation and break in if she thinks she needs to. She's not shy about that. But I would really

like it if—" he took a deep breath and plunged on "—
if you would agree to come along with me for moral
support. I'd feel so much more comfortable with you
watching my six."

"If you ask me, I'd better watch your three and nine,
too, with that woman."

Seth chuckled, but it was a dry sound nearly devoid
of amusement, and Rachel knew why.

Seth was right. Whatever Trish had planned, it would
be a lot more difficult for her to accomplish with Rachel sitting at the table with them, even if she didn't
say a word.

Ha! As if she would be able to hold her tongue with
that woman. If she tried to threaten Seth, or Caden's
well-being, Rachel would not be held responsible for
what happened after that.

Yes. Rachel had every reason in the world to go—
even if she was bolting forward when she'd just this
morning once again resolved to pull back.

Just this one time, she promised herself.

Seth needed a friend, someone who understood his
situation. She could be that friend for him. She would
go with him to meet Trish, and then afterward, if things
went well, she'd have to talk to Seth about what had
happened on the Fourth of July and how it should never
happen again. She wasn't looking forward to that conversation, but she knew it needed to take place.

Or if things went badly, she would wait until an ap-
propriate moment at a later time and offer him whatever
kind of support he needed to deal with Trish.

"Of course I'll go," she said, putting a hand on his
arm. "You couldn't keep me away."

He visibly relaxed at hearing that.

"Thank you," he said simply, though the words were profound. "Now I'd better finish mowing so we can impress that inspector of yours with your world-class landscaping."

"You mean *your* world-class landscaping."

He grinned. "I say we both take credit for it."

Seth mowed the front and back lawns of Rachel's house, trimmed her bushes and cut back her roses, snipping a few stems to present to Rachel as an impromptu bouquet.

It might have come straight from her own flower bed, but Rachel reacted as if he'd purchased an enormous bouquet of exotic flowers and had it sent by special courier, instead of given her a half-dozen thorn-ridden roses.

"Careful," he said as he transferred the small bouquet into her hands. "These roses aren't the hotbed kind. They have thorns."

"I'm not sorry the roses have thorns," she replied. "I'm just happy that the thorns have roses." She chuckled. "See? You've been rubbing off on me. I'm looking at the bright side of the world instead of dwelling on the overcast."

They'd evidently switched places, because he was seeing clouds all over the place.

"I have a feeling it's going to be difficult to keep a positive attitude today," he admitted. He glanced at his watch. "Speaking of which—I guess it's time for me to face the dragon."

Rachel laughed. "Oh, Seth. You crack me up sometimes. Does that make you Saint George?"

"Don't I wish."

They arrived at Cup O' Jo's about five minutes early,

but Seth knew Trish was already there, given the ridic-ulous-looking stretch limo parked on the other side of the street, taking up practically half a block of parking spaces.

He reached for Rachel's hand and gave it a squeeze as he blew out an unsteady breath.

"Let's do this thing." He straightened his cowboy hat, stretched his neck muscles both ways and tried to relax his shoulders.

Trish was seated in a far corner booth. Her eyes lit up when she spotted Seth, but her lips drooped into a pouty frown when she realized Rachel was with him.

"I thought we were going to meet privately," Trish argued as they approached the table.

"You said that, not me," he said. "Besides, anything you can say to me, you can say to Rachel."

"Why? Is she your fiancée? Your girlfriend?"

The question threw Seth for a moment.

After last night's kiss, he didn't know *what* they were—somewhere in the indefinable space between being close friends and something more. He knew what he wanted them to be, but he wasn't going to go an-nouncing his intentions to Trish before he'd discussed them with Rachel.

"I'm a friend," Rachel said firmly, taking a seat in the booth across from Trish and scooting to the farside so Seth could sit beside her.

A friend?

Was that how she saw him?

"Whatever," said Trish with a dismissive wave. "Seth, it's you I need to speak with."

"About what?" he asked cautiously as Jo set steaming mugs of coffee in front of the three of them.

Trish took one look at the contents of her mug and pushed it aside. "I don't do coffee. Bring me some chai tea."

If Jo was thrown by the woman's rudeness, she didn't show it. She merely picked up the mug Trish had shoved away and smiled at Seth and Rachel.

"Enjoy your coffee," she said with a pert grin.

Trish turned her attention back to Seth. "I'm here to talk about Caden, of course," she said, as if it was obvious.

And it was.

He'd known from the beginning that Caden played into this somehow; he just didn't know the details yet.

But the very thought of Caden being caught in the middle of some tug-of-war made him bristle, even after he'd promised himself he was going to remain calm and composed.

Rachel reached for his hand under the table and linked his fingers with hers.

"What about Caden? Why don't you get right to the point and tell me why you've flown clear across the country to visit a child you've shown absolutely no interest in before this week?"

"Well, he is my nephew," Trish stated, pressing her crossed forearms onto the table and leaning forward. "As his auntie, of course I'm worried about his welfare. He has no one to care for him now."

"He has me."

"Yes, well, that's what my lawyer told me after he attended the reading of Tracy's will. His understanding was that Tracy and Luke were very specific that Caden's guardianship should go to you."

"Exactly," Rachel said.

Where was this leading? Had Trish really expected to inherit Caden's guardianship after she'd completely alienated her family?

Why would she even want it?

She turned the question on him.

"You're a good-looking single man. Why would you want to be burdened with a baby?"

"Caden is *not* a burden," Seth replied through gritted teeth. Despite his determination to be civil, this woman was really poking at his sore spots.

He didn't like where this conversation was going.

Not at all.

"If you ask me," she said, although no one *had* asked, "it doesn't make any sense at all for you to have him. I mean, let's face it. If you adopt Caden, you'll be a single father. Why would you want to do that to yourself? Forget having any time for yourself. Forget dating. No woman wants a man burdened down with a child."

Trish slid a sidelong glance at Rachel and sniffed, as if she didn't like what she saw.

He didn't know if Rachel was aware of how hard she was squeezing his hand at Trish's scrutiny, but he could tell Trish's words bothered her. He unlaced their fingers and made a big production of putting his arm around her shoulders.

What did Trish know, anyway?

When Seth looked at Rachel, he saw the most beautiful woman in the world—not only on the outside, although in his eyes she was that, but on the inside, because he'd seen her heart.

He'd thought his action would reassure Rachel, but if anything, her shoulders tightened even more and she curled down in the booth.

Trish's expression changed as she narrowed her eyes on the two of them.

"You will also have to ditch other things you probably enjoy, like live sports games," Trish added. "You won't be able to play poker or go out with the boys to hit the bars."

Seth raised his eyebrows.

Wow.

Trish was really shooting in the dark here, trying to guess what he considered to be a priority in his life, and she was missing by miles.

Well, maybe not the live-sports part, but that was a small sacrifice to make for Caden's sake. He could watch his favorite teams on his big-screen television. Not to mention the fact that he had loads of relatives who would be all too happy to take Caden for the day if Seth somehow happened to score some prime tickets.

Even better, it wouldn't be long before he could take his *son* to live games with him—teach him all the ins and outs of every sport. Teach him to throw a football and catch a baseball in his little mitt. Seth could coach Little League. And he would definitely show Caden more parkour moves. The kid was already somersaulting forward and backward like a pro.

Seth was actually excited over the prospect as he saw it, which he expected wasn't the outcome Trish anticipated when she'd made the comment.

Despite his anxiety, he experienced a moment of true joy. Trish had no idea how much he'd come to love Caden. And that love was going to be what saved the day.

He wasn't going to be a good father.

He was going to be a *great* father.

"You can see where I'm going with this," Trish continued, tapping her fingers on the table.

"No, not really," he said, hoping what he was thinking was wrong.

It just had to be.

"It's just not right for my sister to hand off her kid to a perfect stranger instead of a relative."

"I wasn't a stranger to Tracy. I was very close friends with both her and Luke. In fact, Luke was my closest friend growing up. I was best man at their wedding."

"Maybe that explains their poor decision making," Trish said.

"I'm sorry. What?"

Seth had had enough. At this point, he just wanted to get up and walk away. There was nothing Trish had to say that he wanted to hear.

He was preparing to do just that when Trish spoke again, freezing him in his tracks.

"Let's not bring lawyers into this, okay? I think we're both reasonable adults and can work it out right here between us."

"Work what out?" Rachel asked.

He was glad she spoke, because in his anger, he had completely lost the ability to form words.

"The details," Trish said.

She made a dismissive gesture as if none of that mattered.

"For me to take Caden off your hands."

Chapter Ten

Rachel was worried about Seth. After Trish had made her bold proclamation regarding Caden, which both Rachel and Seth had feared, Seth got up and stomped out of the café, not even bothering to pay for his coffee.

Jo had stopped by their table to ask if everything was all right, but of course it wasn't. Trish didn't care to speak to Rachel, and Rachel couldn't speak for fear of bursting into furious tears.

Jo had graciously said the coffee—and the *tea*, with emphasis—were on the house. Rachel had thanked her. Trish had not.

Rachel had gone searching after Seth, but no one had seen him. He wasn't at the ranch. Samantha was still watching Caden and hadn't heard from Seth at all. Neither had his parents.

Eventually, Rachel returned to her own house and waited, assuming Seth would call or come over when he'd cooled down and was ready to talk.

They had a lot to go over, to work through, in order to eliminate any possibility of Trish making good on her threats to try to take her nephew away. Caden would stay with Seth, if Rachel had to dump her entire life savings into paying a good lawyer to make sure of it.

It was all she could do to pull herself together, but she wanted to appear composed so she could give Seth the support she knew he would need when he sought her out.

Seth was a strong man, but even the strongest men sometimes needed a shoulder to lean on.

She was determined to be that shoulder.

Except he never came.

She'd waited until after midnight to go to bed and woke early for church, hoping he would be there.

He wasn't, and neither were any of the rest of the Howells and Davenports.

Rachel assumed they were with Seth, helping him come up with the best solutions to use to fight against Trish. If she was being honest, it hurt her feelings that Seth hadn't included her in his plan making. After all, she'd been there when he'd met with Trish. She knew better than anyone what he was up against.

But, she told herself every time those thoughts rose, he was with his family, which was where he should be. Those were the people Seth would be counting on to keep Caden safe.

They were Caden's family.

She was just a friend.

When Monday morning came, Rachel had no choice but to switch her thoughts and attention to the upcoming inspection of her day care.

She didn't expect Seth to bring Caden by. Not under the current circumstances. It was understandable that he would want to keep Caden by his side. If the whole family had missed church on Seth and Caden's behalf, she doubted that he'd drop Caden off at a day care and leave him there, even if that day care was hers.

Everything inside the house was spick-and-span and in perfect order, thanks mostly to Zooey, who had offered up her Saturday to do a deep cleaning. Seth had taken care of everything on the outside. Both the front and back lawns and the flower beds were as neat as she had ever seen them. And the new play set was the triumph of them all.

She was nervous, as she always was before an inspection, even though she knew everything was up to standards and she'd done all she could do to see that it went well. She'd been doing in-home day care in this house for long enough that she would have thought she'd be completely confident in the outcome, but there was still that slight little niggling doubt that she had overlooked something important and she would lose her life's work and ability to care for her family.

The day-care kids started trickling in and she set everyone up at the craft table to make puppets out of paper bags. Zooey didn't have summer school on Mondays, so she was crouched at the preschool-sized table, helping the kids cut funny mouths out of colorful construction paper with blunt-edged child safety scissors and paste googly eyes on their projects.

When the doorbell rang at just after ten, Rachel was as ready as she would ever be. She took a deep breath and opened the door.

"Seth," she said in surprise, ushering him and Caden inside. "What are you doing here?"

"Sorry we're late," he said, placing Caden on the floor so he could run and join his friends at the craft table.

"Is everything okay?"

A shot of anxiety passed through Seth's gaze and then it was gone, as quickly as it had come.

"I didn't miss the inspector, did I?"

"No. Actually, when the doorbell rang, I thought it was her."

Rachel's home inspection wasn't what she wanted to talk about, but she respected Seth's unspoken wishes and remained on the topic he had introduced.

"Awesome. I want to be here when she gets her first look at the playhouse."

"Which is no doubt the pièce de résistance of the entire day care. You outdid yourself."

"It was for a worthwhile cause."

"The senior center?" she asked, thinking back to the day of the auction, when Zooey had won the bid on Seth on her behalf.

How much had changed since then. Now she couldn't imagine her life without Seth and Caden in it, even if it was merely in passing when Seth dropped Caden off for day care and picked him up again. At least she'd still be able to spend a big part of her days with that precious little boy who had stolen her heart just as thoroughly as his new daddy.

Which was why it was so crucial that Caden stay with Seth.

Those two special characters had changed her life for the better.

"Not the senior center," Seth said softly, shaking his head. "You."

Her.

Not the senior center. Not even the day care.

Her.

She didn't have time to reflect on what that might mean, because the inspector chose that moment to arrive.

The *she* turned out to be a *he*, and he was very impressed with the work Seth had done on the play set. A weekend hobbyist and do-it-yourselfer, he blatantly admired Seth's skill and workmanship.

The kids came out to play and crawled all over the new equipment. Seth got sidetracked helping a couple of the preschoolers across the monkey bars. The inspector formally approved her day care.

Rachel was relieved that there was one less thing to worry about, but as she called the kids inside for carpet time and out-loud reading time, her mind turned back to the situation of Seth and Caden.

Seth lingered as she read the kids a story and then read the same one again as an encore. The little ones liked the repetition.

She fed them a snack and then it was nap time.

"Coffee?" she asked Seth, who was standing in the middle of the indoor imagination center, pushing a toy truck back and forth with the toe of his boot.

"Sounds good," he whispered, so as not to wake the children.

She gestured toward the kitchen and he followed her inside, where he sat down across from her at the table after she'd served him coffee.

"I was worried about you when you took off that way," she said bluntly. They had only forty-five minutes to talk before nap time was over, and she didn't want to waste even one second on trivialities.

"Yeah. Sorry about that. I needed some time and space to clear my head. But I should have called or texted you or something to let you know I was okay."

His hand curled into a fist around his coffee mug, so tightly that Rachel was afraid the cup might shatter in his grip.

"Where did you go? I checked the ranch and spoke with Samantha and your mother. No one knew where you were."

"I went to one of my mom and dad's cabins. They didn't even know I was there until the next day. Samantha took care of Caden for me."

He paused and swept in a breath.

"I was so angry and was feeling so panicked that I was afraid I might frighten Caden if I picked him up from Samantha's in that state. I don't ever want Caden to feel like Daddy's angry."

"It happens. Everyone needs to step back and cool off sometimes."

"What happened after I left? Sorry I stuck you with the check."

"You didn't miss much. Jo stopped by the table and absolved us of our bill. Trish didn't have the least interest in speaking to me, so she took off right after you did. I stayed and ate a piece of Phoebe's famous pie."

"Apple?" One side of his mouth kicked up.

"Cherry." She raised her hand and waved it. "Guilty. Emotional eater here."

"Nothing wrong with pie."

For one beat the tension lightened, but then it came crackling back and they both instantly sobered.

"Have you heard any more from Trish?"

He shook his head. "No, but I don't know whether I should be relieved or worried that she hasn't tried to contact me."

"Maybe she changed her mind," Rachel said hopefully, even though she knew better.

"Or else she's revving up to go full-court press on me."

Rachel deduced that it was a sports reference, but she didn't know which sport. Not that it mattered. She understood the gist of it.

"I've been thinking and praying about this ever since we met with her," Rachel said.

"Yeah. Me, too. I've been kicking thoughts around with my family, but we haven't come up with much."

"I have a few ideas," she ventured.

"I thought about calling you, but frankly, I didn't want you there."

"Oh." She was confused and hurt and felt like he'd just stabbed her in the heart with a steak knife.

"Look. I was ashamed of myself. I didn't want you to see me after I'd acted that way."

"What way?"

"Angry. Frustrated. Panicking. It was bad enough having to have my family there to see me all unwound, and they've known me their whole lives."

"I guess I understand where you're coming from, but I want you to know there is no possible condition I could see you in that would change my perception of you," she said, putting her whole heart into her words.

"That's what my mom said. My sister, too. They said I didn't put enough confidence in you, that you were a stronger woman than I gave you credit for. They told me I was stupid for walking out of that café without you. And I guess I was."

It was silly, but she was beyond relieved that he'd shut her out because of his focus on maintaining her positive image of him and not because of anything she'd done—although that nonsense had to stop right now.

So Seth was human. He got angry. Didn't everyone?

He was being far too hard on himself. He had good reason to be upset. Trish had managed to rattle the status quo in his life, and he had every right to be thrown by it.

Even Rachel felt as though she were precariously balancing on a precipice.

"Did you come up with any good ideas? What do you plan to say to Trish when you see her?"

"That I'm getting a lawyer, I suppose, despite Trish saying she doesn't want to go that direction. I put in a call to the lawyer who executed Luke and Tracy's will, but he hasn't gotten back to me yet."

"I've been thinking about it also, and I'm not sure you're going to need a lawyer to fix this problem."

"Why? Just because Trish said not to bring them in? I'm going to need all the backup I can get."

"That much is true. But as far as Trish saying she doesn't want lawyers involved—I think she's showing her hand. A lot of her story doesn't add up. Her not getting her lawyer involved is just the start of it—a major clue."

"How so?"

"Don't you think it's odd that she wants to challenge the will but doesn't want to bring lawyers into this? She's pressuring you into thinking that giving Caden to her would be the best thing for you, giving you all these silly reasons that don't make any sense. And yet she expects you'll just hand the baby over to her and be done with it. I think she doesn't want you going to lawyers because she knows she doesn't have a legal case. She's hoping you'll just decide to give him up."

"That's not going to happen."

"No. And we'll fight to keep Caden to our last penny if necessary. But think about it. If she believed she had a legal foot to stand on, don't you think she'd have brought her lawyer front and center? She has the money and the resources, obviously. Why come herself?"

"I don't know."

"Me neither. I can't think of a single rational reason. It seems to me to be the move of a desperate woman."

"A *crazy* woman," Seth agreed.

Rachel brushed a lock of hair off her shoulder.

"She didn't even go to her sister's funeral, never mind the reading of the will. She sent her *lawyer* to represent her. It was completely impersonal. And now she's going face-to-face with you, trying to act like the loving auntie, implying that she'd be a better parent for Caden. Do you see where I'm going with this?"

"Keep talking."

"I think her lawyer came back from verifying Luke and Tracy's will and told her she *had* no real inheritance. I think she feels ripped off—upset that Caden got everything and she got nothing."

"It's true. Caden was the major beneficiary of the will, which makes perfect sense, since he's their only son. I'm sure Tracy left her sister some keepsakes or something."

"No doubt. But I don't think keepsakes are what Trish is after."

"You think she's after cash?"

"It makes sense, doesn't it? She clearly doesn't care for Caden, so she's after something else, something she thinks Caden can give her."

Seth scoffed and shook his head. "But it's not like

Caden's inheritance is a big stash of money sitting in a bank. They had a little in savings and a college fund they'd started for Caden, but everything else Luke and Tracy had was wrapped up in the land. I can't imagine Trish being any more interested in cattle than she is in toddlers."

"I don't think she's interested in the land, unless she wants to liquidate it."

"Which she can't do. The land is in trust as Caden's legacy. As his guardian, I'm supposed to keep the ranch running for his benefit. I couldn't sell it if I wanted to, not without permission from the trustee."

"Good. That's one less reason she has to pursue this madhouse scheme. Honestly, I don't even think she's given a thought to the ranch."

One corner of Seth's lip quirked in amusement. "No, I am guessing not."

"Is there any way she'd be able to get her hands on Caden's college fund?"

"Absolutely not. No one can touch that money until Caden is old enough to attend college. Not even me. That's all done by a trustee at the bank." He shook his head. "But I still don't get it. Why would she come out here thinking to take Caden for the money? Raising a child is a huge responsibility, not to mention a money drain. I can't imagine why Trish would really want to take him on. And why would she need to if it's money she's after? She seems to already have more money than she knows what to do with. I'm no connoisseur on such things, but it looks to me like she dresses in some pretty fancy, high-priced clothes. And she rode into town in a stretch limo, for crying out loud. She's got to be loaded."

"Maybe," Rachel agreed. "But looks can be deceiving. She's clearly desperate, and if it has nothing to do with Caden's well-being, then it almost has to be about money. She hasn't thought this all the way through, because I can't imagine her wanting to be saddled with a baby, even to get her hands on his trust fund. Maybe she just wants to make a point and then threaten you into giving her what she wants without the baby changing hands."

"What she wants? You mean like a bribe?"

"I don't know. Maybe. I can't think of any reason why she would make the effort to fly across the country and try to settle with you on her own other than something to do with the almighty dollar. It could be that the rich just want to get richer, although it's strange that she'd go to all this trouble if she's already loaded."

"Wow. You really have thought it through. One thing I admire about you—you have a special sense about people. You're empathetic. I think you may have hit the nail on the head about Trish coming out here trying to wrest Caden's trust fund from him."

"If that's the case, then she's following a dead-end trail and she doesn't even know it," Rachel pointed out. "What we have to do now is make her realize that on her own. I don't think talking to her is going to be good enough to get it through that thick head of hers, especially when she thinks she has a bargaining chip in being Caden's blood aunt."

He clicked his tongue against his teeth and chuckled. "Why do I have the feeling you've already got an idea formed in that wonderful, brilliant mind of yours?"

"I might," she said, teasing him. "But I have to prepare snacks before I get the kids up from their naps and things are going to get kind of hectic from this point on.

Do you think we could meet with your family tonight, say about seven o'clock, at your folks' lodge? I'll explain my plan in detail then and we can get everyone's take on it. If I'm right, Trish may decide to turn tail and head back to the big city on her own."

"And good riddance. But you're not going to give me any hints?"

She smiled mischievously. "Not a one."

"Fine. Dangle the carrot and then make me wait. That's cruel and unusual punishment, you know."

She laughed and bobbed her eyebrows. "It'll be worth the wait, I promise you."

"I believe you, sweetheart. I'll see you tonight."

Seth paced back and forth across the polished oak hardwood floor in the main lodge of his parents' bed-and-breakfast, eager for the family meeting to start.

He'd teased Rachel about dangling a carrot, and it had seemed funny at the time, but now it was driving him stir-crazy knowing she had an idea about how to keep Trish from taking Caden away but not knowing what it was.

It was raining cats and dogs outside, but, ignoring both the storm and the mud that caked to his shoes, he'd already taken a long run down one of the nearby trails.

Twice.

Will and Samantha and the children were playing a board game in one corner of the guest lobby, while his parents puttered around with the never-ending projects that made their bed-and-breakfast such a big hit in the local area and beyond.

He was debating setting off on a third run when Rachel appeared at the door, wiping her feet on the mat before removing her rain boots and folding her umbrella.

"Finally," he said, rushing up to her and taking her by the elbow. "My mom has snacks set up at their kitchen table. Everyone is anxious to hear what you have in mind."

And by *everyone*, he meant himself.

Rachel chuckled and pulled back. "At least let me take off my raincoat first."

He assisted her, gentleman that he was, and hung the coat on the rack, then ushered her into the kitchen, where the rest of the adults gathered, leaving the kids to play together.

"As you all know, we've been dialoguing on the situation with Trish," Seth said by way of opening. "In short, we both see clues that lead us to believe she isn't quite who she says she is."

"She's not really Caden's aunt?" Will asked, his eyes widening in surprise. "I thought that was a given."

"No, no. She's unquestionably Tracy's sister," Seth said.

"When we met with her," Rachel said, jumping in before the conversation went offtrack, "she tried several different tacks to persuade Seth that he didn't really want the responsibility of Caden's guardianship and that he should simply hand Caden over to her."

"Which I told her in no uncertain terms was never going to happen. I wouldn't give Caden up for anything."

"Not even the chance to go see more live sports games, which truly is impressive," Rachel teased, winking at Seth. His family laughed.

"She made all of these really lame arguments in favor

of me retaining my bachelor status," Seth explained, "but I shut her down, at least at first."

"And then came a really strange stipulation," Rachel said, picking up the thread again. "She expected that Seth would buy into her arguments about Caden and that he'd want to hand over his guardianship of the boy, but she didn't want to get any lawyers involved."

"Well, that's ridiculous," said Samuel, shaking his head. "Impossible. Seth is Caden's legal guardian. Even if he wanted to, he couldn't just pass Caden off to her like a football."

"Which I don't," Seth grumbled.

Amanda put her hand on Seth's shoulder. "We know you love Caden, son. You don't have to keep reminding us."

"I know. I just get riled up every time I think about some of the things that woman said."

"Back to the lawyers?" Samantha suggested.

"It seemed an odd request for Trish to make," Rachel continued. "If she thought she could contest the will through the court system and win, she would have sent along one of her high-priced lawyers. I'm guessing the lawyer she sent to the reading of Tracy's will has already told her that Caden's guardianship is securely locked up in Seth."

"Which is why she flew across the country to do this herself." Seth scoffed. "I believe she honestly thought, at least at first, that I could be easily talked out of caring for Caden."

Samantha snorted. "As if that woman has any interest at all in Caden's well-being."

"None of us believe that she does," said Amanda.

Rachel nodded. "So Seth and I asked ourselves—if

her interest doesn't really lie with Caden, then why is she here?"

"The answer is money," Seth said. "We think she wants to try to claim Caden's inheritance."

"Preposterous," Samuel said with a huff of breath.

"Why would she need money?" Samantha asked. "Her purse alone is worth more than I make in a month at the grocery store."

"This is the part we're a little iffy on," Rachel admitted. "All we can do at this point is make an educated guess. Maybe it's just a grudge, because she thinks the will was unfair? In her view, she got nothing from Tracy, and Caden got everything."

"Of course he got everything," Amanda said, appalled. "He's their son."

"Obviously, we don't know what her financial situation is like," Rachel said. "It could be that she's just greedy and wants everything for herself. It could also be that she's not as well-to-do as she would have everyone believe."

"We all know that Caden's inheritance is tied up in Hollister ranch land," Seth said. "I'm pretty sure she doesn't want to have anything to do with cows. And if she's looking at Caden's trust fund, she'll have to look elsewhere, because that money belongs to him. No one can touch it. Not even his guardian."

"So basically what you're saying is she's going on a wild-goose chase," Samuel said. "Taking on Caden's guardianship is a financial liability."

"Not to me," said Seth. "But to her? Yeah."

"So—you think if she is in possession of the full picture, she won't try to take Caden from you?" Amanda asked.

"It might take a little more coercing than that," Rachel suggested. "I'm not sure simply talking to Trish is going to do any good. But I thought maybe if we *showed* her, she might be less inclined to pursue this current line of reasoning."

"And now Rachel is going to tell us how we are going to do that," Seth said, hoping she truly had a solution up her sleeve. Because he agreed with her that talking to Trish would get them nowhere.

"I say we give her a little taste of what her future would look like should she take over Caden's guardianship. There's a little risk involved, but I think it's our best play."

"This isn't a Hail Mary, is it?" Seth said, his throat closing around his breath.

He didn't even *like* the word *risk*. Not when Caden was involved.

"I don't know what that is, but I'm guessing you're not talking about a prayer, are you?"

Samantha laughed. "Leave it to my baby brother to couch his sentences in football terms."

Rachel smiled and shrugged. "Sorry, not my game."

Seth rolled his eyes. "Rachel doesn't have a game."

"But she has *game*, which is far more important, right, Rachel?"

"I should think so," Rachel said. "Now, what's a Hail Mary?"

"Sometimes in the last few seconds of play, if a team is losing but could potentially win with a touchdown and they are too far downfield to execute a normal play, then the quarterback—that's the guy who throws the ball— throws it as hard and as far as he can and hopes that one of his receivers can get upfield fast enough to catch the ball and make a touchdown," Seth explained. "Needless to say, that doesn't work very often."

"So you're asking if my plan is basically a shot in the dark?" Rachel competently condensed his drawn-out explanation.

Samantha laughed. "That's the short version. I like yours better."

"Can something go wrong? Maybe. But I don't think we're looking at a wing and a prayer. We don't actually have what Trish wants. At the end of the day, Trish can't take something we're legally unable to give her. She won't listen if we try to explain it to her, but if we show her what she would really be signing up for, I don't think she'll be so quick to pick up that pen. More than likely, she'll scurry back to where she came from."

"How are we going to show her?" Seth asked, interested but not thoroughly convinced.

If it could happen, if they could make Trish go away, he could look forward to his future—a future with his custody of Caden secure...and hopefully Rachel by his side. It would be a whole new world for all of them, and he wouldn't take it for granted. He would thank God every day for all His blessings.

Rachel grinned, and Seth thought he might have seen a bit of a puckish gleam in her eyes.

"I'm glad you asked. That is where you all come in. We have to think of ways to help her visualize what her life might be like if she were to take over Caden's guardianship. If we make it real enough to her, she won't be coming back, even with a lawyer."

She pulled open the notebook she'd brought with her and clicked on the pen.

"Put your thinking caps on, ladies and gentlemen, and let's get creative."

Chapter Eleven

Rachel couldn't help but laugh as she surreptitiously watched Trish pick her way across the dirt to Seth's office at the Hollister ranch. The limo had had to stop halfway down the driveway or risk getting permanently stuck in the mud, so Trish had to make it the rest of the way on foot.

In heels.

Spiky ones.

At least the woman was predictable.

Trish scrunched up her face in disgust as she carefully dodged the many cow pies littering the area. Rachel suspected her distress was as much from the pungent smell as it was from trying not to land an expensive shoe in a pile of pucky.

Someone *may* have let ten head of cattle onto that ground earlier in the day, and Seth certainly hadn't had time to remove the droppings.

No—he was too busy riding the range and herding cows. He wasn't going to have time to shower, so he was bound to come in dusty and smelling of horse.

The copy of the legal document outlining the terms

of Caden's trust—twenty pages of legalese on a blue background—was propped neatly on the desk, waiting for Trish's perusal.

Most important of all, Caden was sitting on Zooey's lap on a blanket in one corner, quietly playing with a set of toy cars.

Everything was in place.

Now it was up to Trish to show her hand and admit to the real reason she was here.

Rachel glanced once again at Caden and Zooey, so sweetly interacting together. Her heart clenched in her throat when she considered that this evening might be the last time they were together like this.

After tonight, when they'd effectively banished Trish from Seth and Caden's life, Rachel and Seth would have no more reasons to seek each other out. She wasn't even sure Seth would keep Caden in her day care once she was finally able to speak with him.

Was she crazy, talking herself out of the opportunity to be in a relationship with the best man she'd ever known?

The man she was in love with?

The answer was an unquestionable yes, and though her heart was breaking into terribly painful shards, it was best for everyone to end things now—before their lives got more complicated.

But oh, how it hurt.

As it was, Zooey had already bonded with Caden in a special way, and he clearly adored her. That alone was reason enough to be steadfast in her decision. A failed relationship would be far too damaging for everyone involved, not just Rachel and Seth.

She couldn't go there. She couldn't risk hurting the children.

"Oh, it's you," Trish said when she walked in the door and slammed it behind her with an annoyed huff of breath. "When Seth asked me to meet him in his office, I assumed he meant a nice professional building—not some run-down add-on in the middle of a *barn*."

"Come on in, Trish, and make yourself at home," Rachel said with a smile. "You'll find this place is quite cozy. Seth runs all of the Bar H ranch business from here. If you're serious about taking up Caden's guardianship, you'll be spending quite a lot of time here."

"But it smells." Trish cupped her palm over her nose and mouth. "Like cows."

"Yes, that's generally the primary aroma on a cattle ranch, although you'll probably get a nice whiff of horses, pigs and chickens as well, when you take a full tour of the place. Don't worry—you'll get used to it."

"What do you mean, *I'll* get used to it?"

On cue, Seth stepped through the door. Rachel almost cheered at how he had outdone himself. She was honestly impressed. She didn't know what he'd done to make himself look quite so…dirty. It looked rather as if he'd rolled in the pigsty.

Maybe he had. He smelled bad enough, and there were streaks of mud on both cheeks and all down the front of him. If he'd wrestled with the pigs, he'd lost.

But to Rachel, he had never looked better.

What was wrong with her?

Trish gaped as Seth flashed her his most charming grin and then removed his hat and slapped it against his thigh. Clouds of dust burst forth and then slowly settled on the ground at his feet.

"Long day riding," he said by way of apology. "Do you know how to ride a horse, Trish?"

She shook her head violently. "I haven't been on horseback since I was a child. The closest I've ever been to a horse in twenty years is a carriage ride through Central Park."

"Oh, well, no matter. I was out of practice when I started, too. It's easy enough to pick back up if you put some real effort into it."

"What are you talking about?" she demanded.

Seth raised a brow. "I thought Rachel would have told you. The Bar H ranch comes with Caden. They're a package deal."

She looked alarmed for a moment and then nodded as an idea hit her. Rachel knew exactly what she was thinking. She could almost see the dollar signs in Trish's eyes.

"Okay. I can live with that. How much money do you think I can make selling it off? Do you know someone who might want to commercialize the land, or am I better off trying to sell it as is?"

"Yeah, well, that's just it," Seth said smugly, and then paused for dramatic effect.

Rachel didn't know if Trish was holding her breath, but Rachel was, just waiting for the punch line.

"You can't sell the ranch."

"What?" Trish squeaked. "I thought you just said the ranch comes with Caden."

"Oh, it does. It's his legacy, written into the will, which you would know if you had been at Tracy's funeral. You can't sell the ranch. If you take over Caden's custody, then you have to see that the ranch prospers for the next twenty years so Caden can take it over when he reaches manhood."

Trish grabbed the nearest chair and sat down. Rachel could tell the wheels in her brain were spinning, trying to make this new piece of information work into her plan.

"It's hard, physical work, but it's quite fulfilling, I assure you," Seth continued. "I never thought I'd want to be a cowboy, but actually, it kind of fits my style."

And it did, more even than Seth probably recognized.

"I am not leaving New York City to come live on a ranch," Trish protested. "I was born on a ranch and I promised myself I would never go back."

"Hmm," said Rachel. "That's unfortunate. I mean, you can talk to Wes, the ranch manager, but there are a lot of day-to-day decisions that will have to be made by you. I don't think you can do that long-distance—at least not if you want the ranch to thrive, for Caden's sake."

"She means make money," Seth clarified.

Trish already looked overwhelmed.

Now for part two.

"I assumed you'd want to look at the paperwork for Caden's trust fund."

Rachel scooped it off the desk and handed it to Trish. The type was so small Rachel couldn't even make it out with her reading glasses on. Not that it would have mattered. She didn't understand half of what the paper said anyway, and she doubted Trish would be able to, either.

Trish scanned the paperwork with a frown, but her eyes lit up when she spotted the figure with the dollar sign and several zeroes after it.

"That's the value of all the assets being held in trust, including the dollar value for the ranch," Seth pointed out. "There's some cash in savings, true, but it's for his college education," Seth explained before Trish exploded with joy.

"But he'll be getting the ranch. A cowboy doesn't need a college education."

"And there's where you're wrong," Seth said, leaning his hip against the desk and crossing his arms. "A ranch owner needs a good business education. I've just signed up to start taking online business classes on the GI Bill. Trust me, there is much more to cattle ranching than herding stock from pasture to pasture. Accounting, for one. How are you with numbers?"

He winked at Rachel. She was still trying to absorb the new information Seth had just shared. She had no idea he'd signed up for an online college. She was proud of him for his foresight. He'd really embraced his role as guardian of the ranch as well as little Caden.

He'd taken the curveballs that life had thrown him and used them—not to give up on his dreams, but to alter them into something better.

Just as she'd had to do when she was sixteen, pregnant and alone.

Trish set the legal papers back on the desk—upside down, as if she didn't want to look at them.

"It doesn't matter," she said. "Caden is two. He won't be in college for years. I can borrow the money and then pay it back when it's time for him to go to school."

"Actually, you can't," Seth said smoothly.

"And why not? It would be my—er, Caden's—money."

"*Just* Caden's money," Rachel replied. "Locked in until he turns eighteen and earning good interest."

"*Locked* in?" Tracy sounded appalled—and a little discouraged.

"The trust fund is run by a trustee from the bank. Not even Caden's guardian, whoever that might be, can touch it."

"So there's no money there, either."

Trish was thinking hard. Rachel could tell their plan was working. Now all that was left to cinch the deal was the grand finale.

Caden.

This was the part of the plan Seth was most nervous about. Everything else had gone off without a hitch. He was pretty sure Trish was doubting herself right now— trying to figure out how she was going to come out on the winning side of things and starting to realize there *was* no winning side. Or rather, no way to win if you wanted just the benefits without the responsibilities. Responsibilities that had frightened Seth at first, but that he was now happy to embrace. He was starting to feel at home in his role as rancher, and he loved being Caden's daddy. His heart ached at even the thought of giving that up.

But whether he liked it or not, Caden was the crux of this entire matter. They had given Trish a lot to think about. Hopefully, she had seen by now that trying to get guardianship of Caden was a losing proposition—

Not in *her* best interest.

And there was one way to prove it.

He met Rachel's eyes and she nodded briefly.

It was time.

He walked over to the corner and gently lifted his son into his arms, giving him a soft, reassuring kiss on the cheek before turning to Trish and carefully settling the toddler in her lap.

She sat frozen to the spot, stiff and unyielding. She didn't try to engage with Caden. Trish looked like she thought if she moved, Caden might bite.

Fortunately for her, Caden wasn't a biter.

Much.

Seth took a deep breath and plunged in, even though his gut was churning and he wanted to snatch his son back out of that woman's arms.

"If you really want guardianship of Caden, I imagine you'll want to get to know him better."

"I…er…yes, okay," she said, looking around nervously at anything but Caden.

"I'm sure you've thought a lot about how you'll take care of him. It will take careful management of the ranch to continue to make a real profit. You'll probably have to invest your own money into covering your expenses. What is it you said you do in New York?"

Trish didn't answer. She'd clasped her hands around Caden and was rubbing them together, one over the other.

"Well, you'll have to focus on learning ranching for now," Seth said. "It's a full-time job, so you'll want to find a decent day-care provider for Caden. You'll be in the area, so I recommend Rachel here. She runs the best day care in the county. No—that's not right. In all of Texas."

"My facility is just a small home-run operation. I'm sure you'll want him in one of those high-end preschools," Rachel added. "Pretty pricey, and it's going to be a long commute each way, but entirely worth it if you want all the bells and whistles the top-tier preschools offer—foreign-language lessons, musical training, the works. Caden is a smart kid. He's already showing potential in several areas. I'm very impressed by his early learning skills."

Trish looked as if she were choking.

"Were you thinking of a private school?" Seth asked. "He'll need to be in a heavily academic school if he wants to get into an Ivy League college. Oh—and you'll want to make sure he plays sports. Whatever interests him."

Not that Seth felt that there was any need to send Caden to an Ivy League school, unless that was what he wanted. There were plenty of good colleges and universities out there, and the important thing was getting a solid education that would prepare Caden for the life he wanted to lead. Maybe an expensive private school would have the best program for that—maybe not. It would be Caden's decision, either way.

But with her designer-label lifestyle, Trish seemed the type to assume more expensive automatically meant better. Even if that involved pulling Caden from Rachel's day care, where he was loved and appreciated, and dumping him into some high-pressure day care that crammed the kids full to bursting with education and discipline but probably skimped on individual care, affection and fun.

"And since the money for his education can't be touched until he's ready for college, that means the tuition costs before that will have to come from you."

He couldn't believe he was saying this—talking about Trish's role in Caden's upbringing as if it were really going to happen. As if there were even the slightest possibility that he would hand off his guardianship to this woman.

He wouldn't. Not in a million years.

No worries, he reminded himself. They were talking her *out* of guardianship, not into it.

And it was working.

"Aside from school," Rachel said, "children are a persistent drain on your bank account. Clothes, food, diapers. Although obviously, you don't have to worry about money."

Rachel had phrased the sentence as a given, but in truth, Seth knew she was trying to ferret out the real answer.

And Trish was turning green. And red. And purple. A whole rainbow of colors.

"I don't have any money," she mumbled, almost too low to hear.

"I'm sorry, what was that?" Rachel asked.

"That's why I came here. I work as a fashion buyer's assistant. I planned to go to school, but that never worked out. I'm a glorified secretary. I don't make much money, and living in New York is expensive."

Now that Trish had started talking, the whole story poured out of her.

"I was too ashamed to go to Tracy's funeral and let everyone see what a failure I am, so I sent a lawyer. I really had to scrape to put that together. I thought I'd get some kind of inheritance that would allow me to finally go to school. But when the lawyer came back, he said all of Luke and Tracy's money was tied up in Caden's trust."

"Meaning land," Seth said.

"Yes," Trish agreed with a rueful chuckle. "I got that message loud and clear."

Telling her story was apparently cathartic to her. As she relaxed, so did Caden, so much so that he fell asleep in her arms. She stroked his silky hair, the first time she had really touched him.

"He is a sweetheart, isn't he?" Trish murmured.

"Yeah," Seth said, his voice cracking with emotion. "He is."

Trish sighed. "Obviously, I didn't think this thing all the way through. I wasn't going to neglect him," she assured them. "I just had this vague notion that once I got Caden's guardianship, I wouldn't have to worry about money. I was going to get a live-in nanny. I know nothing about children. I thought I could raise him without really interacting with him."

She paused and sighed again. "But now I realize what a mistake that would have been. I was thinking about what I wanted—not what Caden requires or deserves. Caden needs love and attention, and that's what you two give him."

Seth's heart warmed toward Trish. And he didn't try to correct her about his relationship with Rachel. They might not be officially in a relationship yet, but he intended to fix that as soon as possible.

"Believe it or not, I was raised in a very close-knit family," Trish continued. "Tracy and I were best friends. She loved the ranch, but my passion was sewing and designing clothes. I got it in my head that I was going to take off and make a big-name label for myself." She scoffed. "Not so much, huh?"

"But what about your clothes? The limo?" Rachel asked, her voice now gentle and empathetic.

Trish's eyes filled with tears. "I wanted you all to think I was a big success so giving me Caden's guardianship would seem like the right thing to do. The clothes were easy—I have access to a lot of samples through my work. As for the rest…in reality, I've maxed out my credit cards. I've got nothing left."

"Then send the limo away," Seth said. If someone had told him two hours ago that he would be feeling compassion for Trish, he would have laughed in that person's face. But now—

"I know Serendipity is not New York, but we've got a strong community here that will help you get back on your feet. You can stay in one of my parents' cabins until you get settled."

Her eyes brightened for a moment, but then hope once again faded. Seth knew the feeling of saying goodbye to your dreams. But he also knew the blessing of embracing new ones.

Better ones.

"Let me talk with my best friend, Lizzie," Rachel added. "Her family owns Emerson's Hardware. I think maybe we can find a position for you there."

"You want me to work in a *hardware store*?" Trish asked, surprised. "I know even less about hardware than I do about ranching."

Rachel laughed. "Emerson's is a catchall in a town as small as this. If you want clothing, you go to Emerson's. It's all Western wear, but I imagine they'd be open to suggestions on how to spruce up their offerings. They may even take to the idea of you producing your own line, if you can come up with something that fits the style around here."

For the first time since he'd met her, Trish was glowing with enthusiasm. Her expression turned the hard, obnoxious woman into a real live human being. Who knew that under all that brass was a person who was hurting, who was secretly waiting for someone to reach out to her with kindness?

"You would do that for me? After the way I treated you?" A tear slipped down her cheek.

Rachel laid a hand on her shoulder. "Absolutely. We'll help you however we can to get you back on your feet."

"And another benefit of staying right here in Serendipity is that you'll be able to see your nephew whenever you want and really get to know him," Seth added.

Trish smiled softly, a real, genuine smile, then sniffled and tried to wipe her tears with her shoulder.

"You'd better take Caden," she told Rachel. "I don't want him to get soaked when I start bawling."

"So you'll stay?" Seth asked as Rachel settled Caden on the blanket in the corner, where Zooey was lying on her back. The teenager smiled and slipped earphones into her ears before cuddling with the toddler.

"No hard feelings?" she pressed.

"None," he assured her. "Now, if you'd like, I'll help you get settled with my parents for tonight. You can send for your suitcases tomorrow."

Seth was gone for maybe half an hour, and he was anxious to get back to Rachel, who'd stayed behind to watch the kids.

"I can't believe how great this all worked out," he announced as he entered the office. "Can you believe after all the kerfuffle that Trish was just a mixed-up woman in need of help? I'm so relieved that I'm shaking. This is awesome."

Rachel held a finger to her lips.

"Shh. The kids are both sleeping. Zooey's just as conked out as Caden is. I thought she was just listening to her music until I heard her snore."

He grinned. "They look good together, don't they? Like brother and sister?"

Rachel gasped.

He reached for her waist and turned her around to face him, but she didn't quite meet his gaze. He put a finger under her chin and tipped her head up until their eyes met.

"What? What's wrong?"

He'd thought he'd be coming back to celebrate, to whirl her around and kiss her silly. As far as he was concerned, the night couldn't have turned out any better.

His *life* couldn't be any better. But—

"Rachel, talk to me."

"We can't do this, Seth. You know we can't."

He frowned, his eyebrows lowering. His gut tightened until it hurt. He didn't want to hear what was coming next, but he had to ask.

"Do what?"

"Be together. You. Me. We've got to stop this now, while we're still able to."

He didn't know about her, but he was well past being able to stop his emotions. He was flat-out in love with her.

"What if I don't want to stop?"

She laid her forehead against his shoulder and groaned softly.

"You're not making this easy. I don't want to stop, either. I… I…care for you. Very deeply. But it's not just about us."

Her coconut shampoo assaulted his senses as he pulled her close. He wanted to kiss her until she realized that there was no way for them to be apart.

He didn't want to live his life without her. He loved

her. Caden loved her. Caden already looked up to Zooey like a sister, and he suspected Zooey wouldn't object to the news that her mom and Seth were a couple.

She pulled in a breath and leaned back. This time, she looked him straight in the eye.

"Say we did get together, start a real relationship. What if we break up? Zooey and Caden have grown so close to each other over the past few weeks. And she thinks *you* hung the moon."

She pulled in a raspy breath. "So what happens when we are no longer together? It won't just be our lives that are ripped apart, but theirs. I can't risk doing that to Zooey, or to Caden. I just can't. You've got to understand, Seth."

He tensed and let go of her, afraid he'd hold her too tight. Because he never wanted to let her go. He wouldn't prevent her from walking away if that was what she was determined to do—but he was nowhere near done trying to convince her to stay.

"No, I don't have to understand. You've already got us breaking up when what I see is a wonderful future in front of us. What about that, Rachel? What if we could be happy together? If you're going to take a risk, why not risk that, huh?"

"I'm sorry," she said, her voice cracking with strain. "I've thought this through and I've made up my mind."

She'd hit him right where it hurt.

His heart.

"So that's it, then. We stop seeing each other?"

"We can still be friends."

"Friends. Right. Like that ever happens."

"It could."

Seth couldn't let it go. He couldn't let *her* go. But he saw no way to convince her, unless—

"Okay, then. I agree. Friends. But as a *friend*," he said, emphasizing the word, "I would like to invite you and Zooey to my parents' place for Caden's third birthday party two weeks from Saturday. I think he would be really upset if you missed it."

"I wouldn't think of it."

"Of going?" He was so frustrated he wanted to run for miles. Just not away from her.

"No. Of missing it. Zooey and I will be there. What time is the party?"

"Three o'clock."

She leaned over to shake Zooey awake. The teen stumbled to her feet, muttering something about hard floors.

"Three o'clock it is, then," Rachel said, starting to walk past him. "Good night."

He reached for her elbow and gently pulled her back to him, brushing his lips over her cheek.

"Good night, Rachel."

She didn't respond to his kiss but just kept walking. Out the door, and apparently, right out of his life.

Chapter Twelve

The day of Caden's birthday arrived, sunny and warm, the perfect day for an outdoor party at the Howells' bed-and-breakfast. The whole family would be there, and Seth had invited Trish—all information that Rachel had obtained from Trish herself. She and Trish had spoken several times over the week and were fast becoming friends.

But as far as *other* friends went, Rachel wasn't talking to Seth at all. Samantha had been dropping Caden off at day care, and though she was friendly with Rachel, they never spoke of Seth. She hadn't seen him since that night in the office, and she wasn't certain she was prepared to see him today.

If he looked at her the way he had that night in the office—the love in his eyes, followed by pain and confusion—she didn't know if she could stand it.

Friends.

They could be friends.

She just had to buck up and stuff all her emotions somewhere deep inside, where they wouldn't interfere with Caden's birthday celebration.

Zooey had come down early, for Zooey. A typical teenager, she usually slept past noon on a Saturday. But this Saturday was important to her. She hadn't quite hit coming downstairs early enough for breakfast time, but they had an early lunch before they wrapped Caden's gifts and headed off to the bed-and-breakfast.

Rachel dragged her feet, forgetting this and that and remembering something else she had to do, until she had completely annoyed Zooey.

"Mom, you're always on time," Zooey complained.

"On time is late," Rachel quipped.

"Then why is it three fifteen and we still haven't left the house? What's up?"

Rachel shook her head. Her daughter was far too perceptive. She was going to have to play this carefully.

"I'm just a little scatterbrained today."

Zooey shot her a look that told her she didn't buy it, but she didn't push the subject, thankfully.

They were the last to arrive at the party. Rachel recognized most of the kids toddling around as children from her day care. Trish was helping Amanda bring out dishes piled with food. They were chatting amicably, and Trish looked the best she had since she'd arrived in Serendipity—heavy makeup washed off, fashionable clothes put aside for jeans and a colorful top, frowning displeasure replaced with a bright smile, like a load had been taken off her shoulders.

Rachel supposed it had, although it would still be a steady climb for Trish to get back on her feet.

Now it was Rachel with the load on her shoulders, but she wouldn't let anyone see that.

Not on Caden's birthday.

Rachel laughed when Zooey caught sight of Dawson.

Apparently, he had a little sister who'd been invited to the party and he was the chaperone. It wasn't long before he wandered over and started talking to Zooey. Rachel was glad Zooey wasn't the only teenager at the event, but seeing her daughter so happy with Dawson made her heart ache.

Rachel had never known young love, and the only real love she'd ever had—

She cut that thought off without finishing it.

Seth was playing horseshoes with Samuel and didn't notice she'd arrived, or else he simply didn't acknowledge her.

Which was fine.

She sat down at a picnic table where Will and Samantha were in a heated match of cribbage. Rachel was content just to watch the interplay between the married couple, but envy sneaked up on her. The green monster was really on her heels today.

Soon it was time for cake and the birthday song. They took pictures while Caden grabbed a fistful of chocolate cake with white icing and smashed it on his face, mostly missing his mouth.

Rachel's heart welled with affection for the little boy. They'd been through so much together that Rachel didn't think that special place in her heart reserved for Caden would ever go away.

But then again, neither would that Seth-sized hole.

Her heart must look like Swiss cheese.

After cake came presents. Zooey was super excited for Caden to open her present, a stick horse that made neighing sounds when he pushed its ear. Caden loved it, and after all the gifts were unwrapped, he charged off to play cowboys and cowgirls with his friends.

The adults pulled out a board game and nearly everyone joined in—Trish, Amanda and Samuel and a few parents who were chaperoning their children at the party. Even Dawson and Zooey participated.

Pretty much everyone was there except Seth, who had disappeared.

He hadn't spoken to her once since she'd arrived at the party, and she was respecting his space. He was probably angry with her for the way she'd left things, and she couldn't blame him for that.

But someone had needed to say the words. She hated that it had had to be her.

Soon she was caught up in the game, belting out answers and receiving a marker for each right guess. The first person to get six markers won the game.

Rachel wasn't particularly competitive, but it kept her mind off Seth, so she threw herself into the game, and before she knew it, she had five markers and her next turn had arrived.

Samantha was reading off the question on the card.

"This one's for the win," Samantha reminded everyone. "Okay, Rachel, are you ready?"

Rachel laughed and nodded.

"The topic is sports."

She groaned. "Well, I'm not winning this turn. I know zilch about sports."

Samantha grinned. "Don't be so sure about that. Now here we go. In the game of football, what is it called when a quarterback launches the ball upfield during the last seconds of the game in the hope of a touchdown?"

"Are you kidding me right now?" Rachel asked.

"No. Seriously. That's the question. I read it word for word. And I know you know the answer to it."

"Unbelievable. The one and only sports question I can answer. It's called a Hail Mary."

The adults around the table clapped, and Zooey hooted.

"Way to go, Mom!"

"Aaaand she's in for the win," Samantha announced excitedly. "Way to go, sis."

Wait, what?

Had Samantha just called her *sis*?

"Thank you for ruining the surprise for me," came Seth's smooth tenor voice from behind her.

She stood up from the picnic table so fast that she bumped her elbow. Seth reached out to steady her.

"That had to hurt. Are you okay? Do you need a bandage with a cartoon on it and someone to kiss your owie better? I'm getting pretty good at that."

Rachel laughed, although she'd never been so confused in her life.

"I think I'll live."

"Good to know," said Seth. "Because I kind of want you around. For a long time. Like the rest of my life."

Rachel had lost her voice. This was nothing like what they'd decided together that night at the office. He was looking at her with such love in his eyes that there was no possible way anyone in the vicinity could miss it.

What had happened to being just friends?

"I thought a lot about what you said the other night. About being friends. About not wanting to hurt anyone, especially the children. And you are right about that."

She leaned forward to whisper in his ear. "Is this really a conversation we should be having in front of other people—especially your family?"

He chuckled. "I should think so. I want everyone to hear what I'm about to tell you."

He reached into the pocket of his red chambray shirt and retrieved a small black velvet box.

Rachel's breath caught in her throat and for the life of her she couldn't dislodge it. And her heart—

Her heart was swelling until it hurt.

"Like I said, I've been thinking about the talk we had. And I realized what part of the equation was missing." He grinned. "I solved for X."

He went down on one knee and opened the velvet box to display a beautiful square diamond solitaire with tiny diamonds lining it all around. It was the most beautiful ring she'd ever seen, from the most wonderful man she'd ever known.

"I love you, and I think I have for some time now, but I realized after talking to you that love is not enough. I want you to be able to see the future with me and Caden and believe in it. You've had people leave you behind before, and I understand that you're scared it might happen again. But I am pledging my permanent commitment to you, and to the kids, before God and all these witnesses. I promise to guard your heart always. Zooey and Caden will have a stable home with two parents who love them—and each other."

He stopped and cleared his emotion-clogged throat. "Because I do love you, Rachel. So much. Will you be my wife?"

Tears flowed freely down Rachel's face as she reached out her hand. Seth stood and placed the ring on her left finger. He framed her face in his hands and smiled down at her.

"God was answering our prayers when we weren't

even looking," he murmured huskily. "I love you, Rachel, with my whole heart."

"And I love you." Those were the only words she could manage, but she knew the rest of what she wanted to say was in her eyes.

His lips came down on hers just as the applause started. She vaguely heard the hooting and hollering.

"Way to go, *new sis*."

"Welcome to the family."

"Yay, Mom. I knew he was the right guy for you. I told you so."

Seth kissed her until she couldn't breathe and then he kissed her some more. Her head was spinning by the time he lifted his lips from hers, and that was only enough for him to whisper one word close to her ear.

"Awesomesauce."

* * * * *

HER UNEXPECTED COWBOY

Debra Clopton

This book is dedicated to all those making a new, fresh start with their lives. May God bless you and keep you as you make a change in your life.

Put your heart right, Job. Reach out to God....
Then face the world again, firm and courageous.
Then all your troubles will fade from your memory,
like floods that are past and remembered no more.
—*Job* 11:13, 15–16

Chapter One

Rowdy McDermott closed the door of his truck and scanned the ranch house that had seen better days. Carrying the casserole he'd been sent to deliver, he strode toward the rambling, low-slung residence. He'd always liked this old place and the big weathered barn behind it—liked the rustic appearance of the buildings that seemed cut from the hillside sloping down on one side before sweeping wide in a sunny meadow. There was peace here in this valley, and it radiated from it like the glow of the sun bouncing off the distant stream cutting a path across the meadow.

This beautiful three-hundred-acre valley was connected to his family's ranch. Rowdy had hoped one day to make this place his own, but the owner wouldn't sell. Not even when he'd moved to a retirement home several years ago and Rowdy had made him a good offer. He'd told Rowdy he had plans for the place after he died.

Four days ago his "plan" had arrived in the form of the owner's niece, so Rowdy's grandmother had informed him, at the same time she'd volunteered him to be her delivery boy.

He knocked on the green front door, whose paint was peeling with age. Getting no answer, he strode to the back of the house, taking in the overgrown bushes and landscaping as he went. Years of neglect were visible everywhere.

A black Dodge Ram sat in the drive with an enclosed trailer hitched to the back of it. He'd just stepped onto the back porch when a loud banging sound came from the barn, followed by a crash and a high-pitched scream.

Rowdy set the dish on the steps and raced across the yard. The double doors of the barn were open and he skidded through them. A tiny woman clung to the edge of the loft about fifteen feet from the ground.

"Help," she cried, as she lost her grip—

Rushing forward, Rowdy swooped low. "Gotcha," he grunted, catching her just in the nick of time. He managed to stay on his feet as his momentum forced him to plunge forward.

They would have been okay if there hadn't been an obstacle course's worth of stuff scattered on the barn floor.

Rowdy leaped over cans of paint and dodged a wheelbarrow only to trip over a pitchfork— They went flying and landed with a thud on a pile of musty hay.

The woman in his arms landed on top of him, strands of her silky, honey-colored hair splayed across her face.

Not bad. Not bad at all.

She blinked at him through huge protective goggles, her pale blue eyes wide as she swept the hair away. A piece of hay perched on top of her head like a crown.

"You *saved* me," she gasped, breathing hard. "I can't believe it. Thank you."

"Anytime," Rowdy said with a slow drawl, forcing

a grin despite feeling as if he'd just lost a battle with a bronc. The fact that there was a female as cute as this one sitting on his chest numbed the pain substantially.

Those amazing blue eyes widened behind the goggles. "I'm sorry, what am I thinking sitting on you like this?" She scrambled off and knelt beside him. "Can you move? Let me help you up." Without waiting for his reply, she grasped his arm, tugging on him. "That had to have hurt you."

He sat up and rolled his shoulder. "Hitting the ground from the loft would have been a harder fall. What were you doing, anyway?"

Leaning back on her heels, she yanked off the goggles.

Whoa— Rowdy's pulse kicked like a bull as he looked into her sparkling eyes.

"I was knocking a wall out with a sledgehammer. It was a *splendid* feeling—until the main beam gave way and I *flew* over the edge like a ninny." A nice blush fanned across her cheeks. "Talk about feeling silly— that'll sure do it. But I am so grateful you were here. For a short person like me, that was a long drop. And that you got to me so *quick*. How fast are you, anyway?"

She talked with the speed of light and Rowdy had a hard time keeping up. "Fast enough, but clearly not as fast as you talk." He chuckled.

"*Ha,* it's a curse! I do tend to rattle on when I've been saved from sure disaster." She stood up—which wasn't all that much farther from the ground.

Rowdy wasn't real sure she was even five foot, and knew she wasn't when he stood up and looked down at her. At only six feet himself, he towered over her by a good twelve inches…which would make hugging a little awkward, but hey, he could overcome.

"I'm Lucy Calvert." She stared up at him and held out her hand.

Lucy. He liked it. Liked more the tingle of awareness that sparked the moment he took her small hand in his. When her eyes flared, as if she felt the same spark, his mind went blank.

"Rowdy. Rowdy McDermott, at your service," he said as his pulse kicked up like a stampede of wild horses.

"Rowdy." She slipped her hand free and tugged the edge of her collared shirt closed. Her smile faltered. "I think I may have heard my uncle mention you—I think he said your name fit you."

The disapproval he detected in her voice snapped him out of his infatuated fog as regret of the life he'd led twisted inside his gut. What exactly had his old neighbor said about him?

"It fits, but in all honesty, I'm trying hard to mend my ways."

"Oh." Her blue eyes dug deep. "What were you here for before I literally threw myself at you?"

"Food," he said, feeling off balance by the way she studied him. "My, um, my grandmother made you a casserole and I'm the delivery boy."

"How sweet of her." She laid her hand on his arm and his pulse kicked again. "And of you for bringing it over."

Rowdy wasn't sure he'd ever been called sweet. He looked down at her hand on his arm as that same buzz of electricity took his breath away. She turned, hips swaying and arms pumping as she headed toward the exit and left him in her dust.

"Tell her thank you for me," she called over her shoulder, keeping her steps lively without looking back.

Rowdy followed.

"Can I ask what you were doing up there knocking out walls in your barn?"

They'd made it into the sunshine, and what had appeared to be her dark blond hair glistened like gold in the sun. She was getting better by the minute.

"I'm starting my remodel job. I'm making an art studio up there and a wall was in my way."

"So you knocked it down. Do you do that with everything that gets in your way?" That got him the smile he was looking for. Trying to put her more at ease, he tucked his fingers into the pockets of his jeans and assumed a relaxed stance, putting his weight on one leg.

"I like to hope I do."

"Really?"

Her brows leveled over suddenly serious eyes. "*Really.* That happens to be my new life motto."

"Sounds kind of drastic, don't you think?"

"Nope. Sounds good to me. It felt quite pleasant actually—" she scowled "—until I flew over the edge of the loft."

"The little woman has anger issues," he teased.

"This little woman has a *lot* of anger issues."

Rowdy knew a lot about anger issues, but would rather not discuss them. Trying to figure out a change-of-topic comeback, he caught a movement out of the corner of his eye.

"Uh-oh," he groaned, looking where he'd left the casserole. The oversize yellow cat had ripped through the foil and was face-first in the Cowboy Goulash. "Nana isn't going to be happy about that." Even so, Rowdy was grateful for the distraction from the conversation as Lucy raced toward the cat, arms waving.

He owed the hulking orange cat big-time.

"No!" Lucy yelled, tearing across the yard with the troubling cowboy on her heels. She was not happy with her reactions to the magnetic man. Not only had he saved her, he'd taken her breath away. And she didn't like the air being sucked out of her. Nope. Not at all.

What was more, the fact that he—that any man—could do that to her was shocking.

"Bad kitty," she admonished Moose when she reached him. The cat had adopted Lucy four days ago when she'd arrived. Now the moose of a cat—thus his name—looked up at her with a goulash-orange smile, then promptly buried his head in the noodles again. "Hey, how much can a hairy beast like you eat?" Lucy asked, pulling him away from the pan as his claws dug in, clinging to the wood.

"Shame on you. Shame, shame." Lucy was so embarrassed. "Honest, I feed him. I really do."

Rowdy chuckled. "In the cat's defense, Nana's food is pretty irresistible."

Lucy's gaze met his and her insides did that crazy thing they'd been doing since the moment she'd found herself in his arms.

"I would have loved to find that out for myself," she snapped.

He gave a lazy, attractive grin. "Don't worry, Nana will be coming by soon to invite you over for dinner. She figures you need to feel welcomed, but also she wants to introduce you to our wild bunch over at Sunrise Ranch. We can be a little overwhelming for some."

His odd statement stirred her curiosity. "And how's that?"

"So you don't *know*. You're living next door to a boys' ranch."

"A boys' ranch—what do you mean exactly?" Envisioning a bunch of delinquents, Lucy felt her spirits plummet.

"No, no, I didn't mean to make you worry. They're good kids. We have a foster program of sorts. There are sixteen boys ranging from eight to eighteen who call our family ranch home. They've just had some hard knocks in their lives and we're providing a stable place for them to grow up. Speaking of which, I need to run, they're waiting on me." Grinning, he started backing away. "No more flying, okay?"

Lucy laughed despite feeling off-kilter and uneasy. "I'll keep that in mind," she said, and then he was gone. The unease didn't leave with him.

After the betrayal and nightmare she'd been through with her ex-husband, she was stunned by the buzz of attraction she'd felt toward her new neighbor.

Especially since he'd admitted being a reformed rowdy cowboy. *Reformed*—that alone was all the deterrent she needed to keep her distance. Fuzzy warm feelings or thoughts of cozying up to cute cowboys hadn't crossed her mind. Even to feel attraction at all was startling to her. Then again, the man had swooped in and saved her from breaking her neck—maybe that explained away the attraction.

The thought had Lucy breathing a little easier. She'd come here to find the joy again. Joy in her life and in her painting: things she'd lost and desperately needed to find again. She was praying that God would help her and show her the way. What she wasn't praying for was romance, relationships or attraction. She'd learned the hard way that there was no joy to be found there.

None at all. Nope, this ole girl was just fine on her own, swan diving out of the hayloft and all.

The day after he'd caught her falling out of the hayloft, Rowdy drove up Lucy's driveway again as Toby Keith played on the radio. He had a ranch to run and horses that needed training, so what was he doing back here?

Making sure she wasn't dangling from the roof. He chuckled as the thought flashed through his mind.

Stepping out of his truck, he looked up at the eaves just to make sure she wasn't doing just that.

All clear; nothing but a rooster weather vane creaking in the breeze.

Looking around, the first thing he noticed was a large pile of barn wood a few yards from the barn. It was after five and, by the looks of the pile, she'd been busy.

He had work to do, but he hadn't been able to get his new neighbor off his mind. True, he couldn't get those pretty eyes out of his head or that cute figure he sensed beneath that oversize shirt she'd been wearing, but mostly he hadn't been able to stop thinking about her over here ripping her property apart all by herself.

He shouldn't have left the day before without offering to help, and that he'd done just that had bugged him all night. He'd been taught better by his nana; buying the property for himself had vanished with Lucy showing up. And though he hated that, he didn't hold it against his new neighbor— Well, maybe a bit. But that shouldn't have stopped him from helping her.

He was headed toward the barn when Lucy came out of the back door carrying an armload of Sheetrock pieces. She wore her protective goggles again and another long-sleeved work shirt. Her jeans were tucked into a pair of low-heeled brown boots. How could a woman look that good in that get-up? He must be losing his mind.

Tucking a thumb in his waistband, he gave her a skeptical look. "So I'm thinkin' you have something against walls."

"Yup." She chuckled as she strode past him to toss the load in her arms on the pile with the other discards. "I like open space. Don't you?"

"Yeah, but you do know a house has to have some walls inside it to hold the roof up?"

She paused. "I've left a few."

"But have you left the right ones? Maybe you should hire some help. I know some contractors who could do this for you. Safely."

She stared at him for a moment, a wrinkle forming above her goggles. It suddenly hit him that she didn't look like she was in a good mood.

"Did you have a reason for stopping by?"

So he was right. "I just dropped by to check on you. Make sure you weren't dangling from high places."

The crease above her goggles deepened. "Actually, I've managed a whole day without mishap. Of course, there was a tense moment when I climbed up on the roof and lost my balance walking the peak."

His blood pressure spiked even as he recognized she was teasing him—so maybe she wasn't in a bad mood after all. "I'm glad you're teasing me."

"Had you there for a moment, though."

"Yes, you did."

She smiled sweetly. "The thing is, Rowdy, I just met you yesterday, and while I am very grateful that you saved my neck, I really don't know you. And that being the case… Well, you get what I'm saying?"

Get out of my business. Okay, so maybe she was in a bad mood—twinkling eyes and all. He was losing his touch reading women. That was an understatement. He hadn't read Liz right at all. Not until her husband had shown up and punched him in the nose had he suspected he'd gotten involved with a married woman. His stomach soured just thinking about it.

Looking at Lucy, he held his hands up. "You are absolutely right." He planned to leave it at that, get in his truck and hit the road; after all, it wasn't any of his business. The problem: Rowdy was known for not always doing what he was supposed to do. He'd suffered from the ailment all of his life.

"But you don't know what you're doing."

The words were out of his mouth before he could edit them.

Lucy's eyes flashed fire his way before she spun on her boot heels and strode back into the house, leaving him standing just off the porch.

Clearly the woman did not want to hear what he had to say. Any man with good sense would get in his truck and head home to tend to his own business. There was sure no shortage of it and that work was what he'd promised himself and the Lord he was going to do for the next year.

But what did he do?

He followed her. That's what.

Right through her back door and in the direction of

a sledgehammer beating the stuffing out of a hunk of wood somewhere inside the house.

All the while telling himself he needed to mind his own business. He had a well-thought-out plan for his life—he was done jumping off into relationships impulsively. He'd given himself at least a year to be completely single. He'd made the deal with the Lord—no attachments—and he'd almost made it.

So what are you doing?

Chapter Two

Leave it to her to get a nosy, *arrogant* cowboy for a neighbor!

What was his problem? Who was he to come here and question her intelligence? Did he really think she'd be stupid enough to knock out the walls that held her house together?

Lucy swung the sledgehammer and took unusual pleasure when it hit the two-by-four stud exactly where she'd aimed—where it connected to the wood on the bottom of the frame.

She'd been startled to walk outside and find him standing there looking all masculine and intriguing… Why did she keep thinking of him like that? Since the fire—since Tim's betrayal—she'd been around men, some even more handsome than Rowdy McDermott. But she'd not given them a second thought, other than to acknowledge that she was done with men. When a woman learned she'd been married to the poster boy for extramarital affairs, those scars weren't easy to heal.

Why, then, had she thought about her new neighbor off and on ever since he'd left the day before?

Maddeningly, he'd been the last thought she'd had going to bed and the first upon waking. Swearing off men had suited her. She swung the sledgehammer again, feeling the point of impact with a deep satisfaction. God forgive her, but she knew visualizing Tim every time she swung was not a good thing. Yet it was the best satisfaction she'd had since that woman had walked into her hospital room and exposed the lie Lucy's life had been.

Lucy swung again, harder this time. Her hands hurt with the jarring impact as the hammerhead met the solid stud.

No. She did not appreciate the cowboy showing up and causing her to realize just how much she longed to be able to trust someone. And why was it exactly that Rowdy McDermott had her thinking about trust?

She would never trust a man again.

"Well, I guess that answers my question."

Lucy jumped, so caught up in her thoughts that she hadn't heard Rowdy come into the room.

The humor in his voice was unmistakable.

"What is that supposed to mean?" she snapped. She hadn't really expected walking away from him would make him leave. So it really didn't surprise her that he'd followed her inside. After all, he had already proved he was nosy.

"You don't like walls. And you need help."

Of all the nerve. "If you must know, I planned to hire help." She yanked off her protective eyewear with one hand and set the sledgehammer against the wall—getting the thing out of her hand might be the smartest thing. "And again, *if* you must know, I was enjoying myself too much to do it."

He'd stopped smiling at her angry outburst, looking a little shocked. Now that infuriatingly cocky grin spread again across his features, like a man who knows he's charming.

Well, he wasn't to her.

"Stop that," she blurted out. His grin deepened and his eyes crinkled at the edges. He was fighting off laughter—*at her!*

"So you're angry with someone, and knocking out walls satisfies a need inside of you. I get it now. For a little thing, you really do have a lot of anger issues."

Her jaw dropped and she gasped. "Of all the—"

"How about if I help you out?"

"Do *what?*" The man had pegged her motives somewhat correctly at first guess. Yet if he only knew of the anger issues buried so far back inside her, he would not be grinning at her like that.

"Hire me—I'm cheap and will work just to watch the fireworks. You put on one entertainingly explosive show."

"This is outrageous," she huffed. Crossing her arms, she shot daggers at him—he'd think explosive. "I bet you don't get many dates, do you?"

He chuckled deep in his chest and her insides curled like a kitten in response. "We aren't talking about my love life. We're talking about me helping you out."

Lucy could not get her foot out of her mouth. She should never have mentioned anything to do with dating. Talk about getting into someone's business!

"Well," she faltered, still stuck on that chuckle.

"Look, like I said yesterday," Rowdy continued, "my nana is going to have you over to dinner next week and if she finds out you need help and I didn't do the neighborly thing and help you, believe me, it won't be pretty. So help a fella out and put me to work."

Despite everything, Lucy found herself wanting to smile. But the past reared its ugly face—this was so like Tim.

How many times had he cajoled her into doing something he wanted? *Too many.* The fist of mistrust knotted beneath her ribs.

"I'll think about it," she said, having meant to tell him no. She repositioned her goggles.

He frowned. "Fine. I'll let you get back to your work, then."

Irritation had his shoulders stiff as she watched him leave. She almost called out to him, but didn't. She'd given in to Tim too many times in her life. Why did men believe women were supposed to just stop thinking for themselves whenever they were in the picture?

Lucy wasn't going down that road again. The screen door slammed in the other room, and a few seconds later she heard his truck's engine rumble to life. Drawn to the window, she watched him back out onto the hardtop. But he didn't leave immediately. Instead, he sat with his arm hooked over the steering wheel, staring at the house. Though he couldn't see her, she felt as if he were looking straight at her.

She stepped back and he drove off. Her heart thumped erratically as she watched him disappear in the distance.

It's better this way.

It certainly was.

Then why did she suddenly feel so lonely she could scream?

"Women," Rowdy growled, driving away. "They drive me crazy." She could just knock her whole house down for all he cared. He had things to do and places to be and being the Good Samaritan was obviously not his calling. It was his own fault—he should have minded his stinkin' business.

After only a short drive down the blacktop road, he turned onto the ranch, spinning gravel as he drove beneath the thick log entrance with the Sunrise Ranch logo overhead.

Dust flying behind him, he sped toward the ranch house in the distance, its roof peeking up over the hill that hid the majority of the ranch compound from the road.

The compound of Sunset Ranch had been divided into sections. The first section was the main house, the ranch office and the Chow Hall, where his grandmother, Ruby Ann "Nana" McDermott, ruled the roost. For sixteen boys ranging in age from eight to eighteen the Chow Hall was the heart of the ranch. But Nana was actually the heart.

Across the gravel parking area, the hundred-year-old horse stable stretched out. Most every horse he'd ever trained had been born in the red, wooden building since the day his grandfather had bought the place years ago. Beside the horse stable stood the silver metal barn and the large corral and riding pens. Making up the last section was the three-room private school the ranch provided for the kids. It sat out from the rest of the compound, within easy walking distance, to give the kids space from school life. This was home.

Rowdy pulled the truck to a stop beside the barn. He slammed the door with the rest of the disgust he was feeling just as his brother Morgan walked out of the barn.

"What bee's in your bonnet?" Morgan asked.

Rowdy scowled. "Funny."

"Obviously something is wrong."

All the McDermott brothers were dark headed, square chinned and sported the McDermott navy eyes, but Morgan was the brother who most resembled their dad—steadfast. Respectable.

Rowdy had always lived up to his more reckless looks—good-time Rowdy. That had been him. But he'd turned a corner and was trying hard to be more than a "good time." And that misconception irritated him the most about Lucy turning down his offer to help. It was almost as if she saw his past and chose to bypass trouble. As if she'd decided in that moment she couldn't trust him.

The thought pricked. Stung like a wasp, to be honest.

If she couldn't trust the man who caught her swan diving off the hayloft, then who could she trust?

And why did he care?

Morgan crossed his arms and studied him. "Nana tells me you met our new neighbor yesterday. Does this have something to do with her?"

"No. Maybe. Yeah."

"So what did you do?"

"I saved her from breaking her neck falling out of her hayloft, Morg. And I offered to help her do a little remodeling."

"I see. So that'd mean she must be good-looking."

"Yeah, she is," he growled.

"Then why are you so agitated? She's single, from what Nana said."

"She turned me down."

Morgan blinked in disbelief. "Turned *you* down. You?"

It was embarrassing in more ways than one.

"I don't think that's ever happened before." Morgan started grinning. "And did you actually save her from falling out of the hayloft?"

"Stop enjoying this so much, and yes, I did, and it's not like I asked her out." He knew Morgan was just giving him a hard time. That was what brothers did. He'd never missed an opportunity where Morgan and Tucker were concerned. So much so that he was due a lot of payback from both brothers. He gave a quick rundown of catching Lucy the day before. Morgan's grin spread as wide as Texas.

"So you really didn't ask her out?"

"Are you kidding? No."

Morgan cocked his head to the side, leveling disbelieving eyes on him. "Are you feeling okay?"

"Crazy, isn't it? I'm not saying I'm not going to. But my days of rushing into relationships are done. I told you that."

"Yeah you did, but it's been over nine months."

Rowdy wanted on a horse. Needed to expel the restless energy that suddenly filled him. "I wasn't kidding when I said I was done with women for at least a year. I'm trying to be a role model for the guys."

It was true. Rowdy might not have known he'd gotten involved with a married woman, but then he hadn't really asked enough questions, and he sure hadn't been any kind of role model. After this last fiasco, God had convinced him that he needed to change his life.

"You're doing it, too. What you need is to find a woman like Jolie, who has her priorities straight," Morgan added.

"True, but I'm not ready right now. And besides, if

Lucy won't let me help knock out some walls, she's most definitely not going to say yes to dinner and a movie."

"True," Morgan agreed, clapping him on the shoulder. "Speaking of dates, Tucker's here helping out with practice because I've got a date. And Jolie is a whole lot prettier than you."

"Tell that beautiful lady of yours I said hello," he called, then headed into the stable. He breathed in and the scents of fresh hay and leather filled him. Horses nickered as he passed by.

He grabbed a saddle and entered the stall of the black quarter horse he was working with. He spoke gently to Maverick as he saddled him. Just the motions of preparing to ride calmed him and helped him think.

Lucy said she had anger issues. It didn't fit, but she'd said it. He hadn't seen anger, though. When their eyes locked, he saw fireworks. And there lay the problem.

He had a fondness for fireworks—even though the fondness had gotten him into more trouble than he needed. Thus the reason he was trying to mend his ways.

Fireworks burned—he'd learned that the hard way.

Leading Maverick out of the stable, he headed toward the corral and the sound of whoops of laughter. His behavior hadn't been anything to be proud of and certainly nothing for these boys to look up to. Rowdy was changing that. No one had said it would be easy.

And living his lifestyle down was going to be the hardest of all, he suspected. The boys' laughter rose on the breeze out in the arena as he approached. This was what he needed to concentrate on. These boys and the ranch.

"What's up, Rowdy? Thought you'd skipped out on

us." Eighteen years old, Wes gave him his wolfish smile as he rode his horse over to the arena fence.

"Nope, just running late." Rowdy hooked his arms on the top rail and surveyed the action. "Did I miss much?"

"There was a runaway wagon a few minutes ago when Caleb lost his grip on the reins and the horses took over." Wes chuckled, his blue eyes sparkling with mischief. He was one of the natural leaders of the group. Stocky and blond, he always looked as though he was ready to have a good time. Too good. He had a reck-lessness about him that reminded Rowdy of himself. All the more reason for Rowdy to make a good impres-sion on the teen.

Rowdy had a suspicion Wes had been sneaking around riding bulls behind everyone's back. Bulls were the one rodeo event that was off-limits for the ranch kids to participate in. And purely Rowdy's fault from when he'd been a teen. Because of his many close calls with bull riding, his dad had set the rule—no bull riding at Sunrise Ranch.

"By the glint in your eyes, I'm assuming it was pretty entertaining."

"It was awesome." Wes hooted. "I never knew your brother could ride like that. Tucker did some pony tricks getting the horses to stop."

The sheriff of Dew Drop, Tucker didn't spend as much time on the ranch with the boys as Rowdy, Mor-gan and their dad, Randolph. But when it came to rid-ing, Tucker could hold his own.

"I'm glad Caleb was okay." He glanced out into the arena and saw Tucker talking to a group of the younger kids.

"He's fine. Didn't even shake him up." Wes spit a sunflower seed in the dirt and continued grinning.

Rowdy suddenly had an idea. It might not be a good idea, but that was yet to be seen. "Wes, I need you and Joseph to help me with something in the morning. Can you do it?"

"Sure thing. What are we going to do?"

More than likely make Lucy madder than a hornet. "We're going to do a little yard work and y'all can make a little pocket change."

"*Sweet.* When do we start?"

"Sunup."

"Sounds like a plan to me." A group of the boys over by the chutes called for Wes. "Showtime. I'll tell Joseph." Giving his horse a nudge, they raced off at a thundering gallop.

Rowdy watched him and the horse fly across the arena as one. When it came to riding, Wes was the best. He was a natural. Rowdy had a feeling the kid would ride a bull just as well. Though it was against the rules, Rowdy hesitated to say anything until he knew for certain. Wes was courting trouble…but then so was Rowdy if he went through with his plan in the morning.

What was he thinking, anyway?

The woman didn't want his help. She needed it, though, and for reasons he didn't quite understand he felt compelled to follow through—despite knowing he needed to steer clear of her.

He had a feeling he was about to see some major fireworks tomorrow…but he'd rather take that chance than do nothing at all.

Chapter Three

The morning light was just crawling across her bedroom floor when Lucy opened her eyes. She'd been dead
to the world from the moment she'd fallen into bed late
last night, and she stared at the ceiling for a moment,
disoriented.

The ache in her arms brought clarity quickly.

And no wonder with all the manual labor she'd been
doing for the past week. The muscle soreness had finally
caught up with her last night. Caught up with her back,
too. She'd always had a weak lower back and sometimes
after a lot of stooping and heavy lifting, it rebelled on
her. That moment had happened when she'd taken her
last swing at the long wall in her living room—a muscle
spasm had struck her like a sledgehammer.

It had been so painful she'd been forced to stretch out
on the floor and stare at the ceiling until it had eased up
enough for her to make it upstairs to bed.

She'd had plenty of time to contemplate her situation and the fact that she really had no timeline to finish
her remodel. She could take all the time in the world if

she wanted to. Uncle Harvey, bless his soul, had made sure of that.

He was actually her grandfather's brother, whom she'd lost as a young girl. He had been in bad health when her world had fallen apart, and hadn't lived on the ranch for a couple of years. But he'd told her this was where she needed be. And he'd been right. She'd known it the moment she'd arrived. She was making the place her own and searching for her new footing at the same time.

And yet, things had changed when Rowdy McDermott had offered to help her. She watched him drive off, and her conscience had plucked away at her.

To prove that she'd made the right decision turning him away, she'd gone at her work with extra zeal…but the pleasure she'd felt had disappeared. Drat the man—he'd messed up her process.

He'd had no right trying to take over her work. *He was only being a good neighbor.* The voice of reason she'd been steadily ignoring yesterday was louder this morning. Had she judged him wrong? She didn't like this distrust that ruled her life these days.

Sitting up, she had no control of the groan that escaped her grimacing lips. "Hot shower, really hot shower." She eased off the bed and walked stiffly toward the bathroom.

She'd wash the cobwebs out of her mind, the dust out of her hair and the pain out of her muscles. Then maybe she could figure out what she needed to do about the problems her good-looking neighbor was causing her.

She'd told him she would think about his offer. But did she really want him here? And he'd already shown that he thought his way was the best way. Did she want to fight that? Because she wasn't giving up control of anything.

The niggling admission that she might be in over her head and needed help on this simmered in her thoughts. The realization that she was allowing distrust of men— all men—color her need for real help bothered her.

Shower, now! She needed a clear head to sort this out.

Twenty minutes later, feeling better, she padded down to the kitchen. The shower had helped her spirits, but she knew that today her back was going to give her fits if she did anything too strenuous. It needed a break. Her mind needed a break, too. She couldn't shut it off....

When a gal wasn't quite five feet tall, she grew used to people assuming she was helpless because of her size. Too weak to swing a sledgehammer.

It was maddening. More so now—since her husband's betrayal had left her feeling so pathetically blind and weak-minded.

Too weak to realize my husband was cheating on me.

The humiliating thought slipped into her head like the goad of an enemy. Not the best way to start her day. She was going to miss not knocking out a wall—and the satisfaction it gave her.

People's lack of faith always made her all the more determined to do whatever it was they assumed she couldn't do.

Glancing down at her wrists, she could see the puckered skin peeking out from the edge of her long-sleeved T-shirt. She knew those scars looked twisted and savage as they covered her arm and much of her body beneath her clothing. The puckered burn scars on her neck itched, reminding her how close she'd come to having her face disfigured…reminding her of her blessings amid the tragedy that had become her life two years ago.

She hadn't felt blessed then, when she'd nearly died in the fire that had killed her husband.

And learned the truth she hadn't seen before.

Reaching for the coffeepot, her fingers trembled. There had been days during the year she'd spent in the burn center that she'd wished she hadn't survived. But it was the internal scars from Tim's betrayal that were the worst.

Those scars weren't as easy to heal. But they made knocking walls out a piece of cake. She'd just overdone it. Easy to do when there was enough anger inside her 105-pound frame to knock walls down for years.

Each swing made her feel stronger. She might have lost control of her life two years ago, but thanks to her dear uncle thinking about her in his will, she was here in Dew Drop, Texas, determined to regain control.

On her terms.

And knocking out walls was just the beginning. Just as Uncle Harvey had intended. He'd recognized that she was struggling emotionally and floundering to find meaning in it all after finally being released from the hospital.

Walking to the sink, she flipped on the cold water and looked out the window as she stuck the pot under the spray. Two young men were carrying fallen tree branches to her burn pile!

Lucy jumped at the unexpected sight and sloshed water on herself. Setting the pot down, she grabbed a dishrag and wiped her hands as she headed for the door. *What is going on?*

She stormed out onto her back porch and caught her breath when Rowdy stepped around the corner.

"You," she gasped. "I should have known. What is going on here?" This was what she was talking about—control. "Just because you saved me doesn't give you the right to just disregard my wishes—"

"Look, I knew you needed help. I just brought the fellas over to pick up a few limbs for you."

Teens, not men, watching them from the burn pile, clearly uncertain whether to come near or not. They could probably see steam shooting out of her ears.

"They've cleaned up a lot. We've been at it since about six."

"Six!" It was eight-thirty now. How had she not heard them?

"We tried to be quiet so we wouldn't wake you."

Her mouth fell open. What did he think he was doing?

"You were quiet because you didn't want me to know you were here."

His eyes flashed briefly. "I wanted to surprise you."

"You just can't take no for an answer."

He stared at her, his jaw tensed, and a sense of guilt overcame her. Guilt. He was the one who should be guilty.

Right?

She was glaring at him when his gaze drifted to her neck and it was only then that she realized she hadn't pulled on her work shirt yet over her long-sleeved T-shirt.

He was staring at the scar. It licked up from the back of her neck, out from the protection of her hair, and curled around, stopping jaggedly just below her jawline.

"You've been burned." There was shock in his voice.

"Yes." Turning, she went back into the house to get the work shirt draped over the kitchen chair. Her hands shook as she slipped it on. Rowdy barreled inside behind her.

"Lucy, I'm sorry we startled you like we did. You have every right to be angry."

Angry? She could barely think, she was so embarrassed. Striding to the living room, she grabbed for her sledgehammer, and without putting on her goggles she took a swing at the wall. Her back and shoulders lashed out at her, forcing her to set the hammer down immediately. She was being ridiculous and she knew it. Why was she so afraid to let Rowdy help her?

The man was obstinate, that was why. Arrogant even, by showing up here to work anyway.

"I'm sorry about that burn. It looks like it must have been terribly painful."

She met his gaze and gave him a quick nod. Her scars were something she didn't talk about. Especially the ones on the inside. "It's fine now," she said bluntly. She hoped he'd take the hint and not continue this line of talk.

"Look—" he shifted from boot to boot and scrubbed the back of his neck in a show of frustration "—you need help and you know it. You said yesterday that you would think about it. I was just trying to let you see that the guys were good kids and hard workers. They could whip this yard into shape for you in no time. And they'll do it for free. C'mon, give them a chance. Give *me* a chance."

As aggravating as it was to admit—the man had charm. And there was no way to deny that she needed help. She couldn't go through life shunning all men. That was unrealistic. The fact he'd seen a portion of her scars ate into her confidence, and that was maddening. It did not matter what the cowboy thought of her.

It didn't.

"Why not?" she heard herself saying. "It looks like you're going to be over here every day bothering me anyway. But just for a few days. And I'll pay you." *Lucy! What are you doing?*

A slow smile spread across his face. "There you go. That wasn't so hard after all, was it?" he said, reaching for her sledgehammer. "No pay needed for me, but if you want to pay the boys, that's fine. I was going to pay them for today myself."

"I'll pay them for today."

"No, I said I would—"

"Look, Rowdy," Lucy said, in her sternest voice. "If they are going to be over here, then I'm paying them. It's either that or this deal is off." They stared at each other and she got the distinct impression that he didn't "get" her in the same way that she didn't get him. But she was taking back control of this situation, or she wasn't having any part of it.

"Okay, have it your way."

"Good."

"All righty, then, stand back," he warned.

Lucy felt her body automatically obey, and watched him swing the heavy sledgehammer as if it was a plastic toy. The muscles in his forearms strained with the strength he put behind the swing. The hammer met the same spot her swing had barely dented and instantly the wood cracked beneath it.

She brought her hand up and touched the base of her throat where her heartbeat raced.

After three more swings along the base of the studded wall, it broke free. It would have taken her all day to do that!

"I see what attracts you to this." He looked over his shoulder at her with a teasing light in his eyes. "I kinda like it myself."

"Yeah, it does kill a bad mood, doesn't it?"

He laughed at that and they stared at each other. Tension radiated between them.

"Okay," she said at last. "Thank you for helping me. I did need it."

"No need to thank me." His smile widened. "You're the one helping me. Saving me from the wrath of Nana is a good thing. If there is one thing she prides above all else, it's that her boys are gentlemen. And I have to admit I have sometimes been her wayward child."

"Say it ain't so," Lucy mocked.

"Yeah, but I'm gonna make points when she finds out about this. So I guess that means I'm still the wayward child, since I'm really doing this for myself. Does that make you feel any better about letting me swing away?"

"Much better. I'd hate for you to actually admit that you're doing it because you're a nice guy." And he might be, even if he was a little nosy. But that didn't stop her from being wary...not so much of him, but of the way she reacted to him.

"Me, a nice guy." He looked skeptical, and that grin played across his face. "I don't know about that."

The man's personality sparkled and drew her like his eyes and his smile, stunning her once again.

Had she truly thought she was going to go the rest of her life not finding a man attractive?

Of course not.

That her neighbor just happened to have qualities that,

regrettably, reminded her that she was still a woman, meant nothing. Absolutely nothing.

She was still telling herself that when Ruby Ann McDermott, Rowdy's grandmother, showed up at her house midmorning bearing welcome-to-Dew-Drop gifts: a basket loaded with homemade fig and strawberry preserves and green tomato relish, along with several small loaves of banana-nut bread to freeze and take out as needed, she informed Lucy.

Ruby Ann had long silver hair pulled back in a ponytail and strong features like Rowdy, along with those deep blue eyes the color of a twilight sky. She held her tall frame ramrod straight, with an elegance about the way she moved.

Two friends came along with her. The first of them, Ms. Jo, owned the Spotted Cow Café in town. Lucy had met her the day she'd first arrived. She'd had supper at the cute café after spending the day unpacking. Ms. Jo's piercing hazel eyes seemed to take everything in from behind her wire-rimmed glasses. She wore her slate-gray hair in a soft cap of curls. Lucy felt a kindred spirit, not just from the fact that they were close to the same height. She liked the older lady's spunk and hoped her own personality would be similar when she was nearing seventy.

Ms. Jo brought along a coconut pie that looked so mouthwateringly delicious Lucy could barely keep from diving in the instant Ms. Jo placed it in her hands.

Mabel Tilsbee, the other member of the welcoming committee, owned the Dew Drop Inn. The towering, large-boned woman with shoulder-length black hair spiced with just a few strands of gray handed over a tray of cookies that were clearly overdone. "There's no need in me even pretending to be the best in the kitchen when the county's best are both standing here beside me. I gave it a whirl, though." She winked. "I got distracted and baked these a little too long. But, if you like coffee, they're real good dunkers."

Lucy laughed and felt instantly at home with these ladies. "Thank you all so much for coming by," she said, leading them into the kitchen. They eyed where a wall had obviously just been knocked out.

Ruby Ann's hand fluttered at the construction area. "Rowdy told me at breakfast this morning that he helped you do this. And that he and some of the boys will be helping you out for a little while."

"Yes, ma'am, he did." It was all Lucy could do not to smile at the thought of Rowdy's brownie points. She decided to help him out. "He's doing a great job. I worked almost two days knocking a wall out of the hayloft and half the morning just getting this wall to budge. He had it down within an hour. It was quite humiliating."

That got a chuckle from everyone.

"All my boys are strong and know how to work," Ruby Ann said.

"That's the truth." Ms. Jo's eyes sparkled with mischief. "Handsome, too, wouldn't you say?"

"Yes, he is." She couldn't deny the obvious. "I was just about to have a coffee break when y'all drove up. Please join me. I suddenly have lots of great food to choose from."

"You know, hon—" Mabel gave her a nudge with her elbow "—that's a *great* idea. I'll slice the pie."

Lucy headed for the cups. This move was getting better by the day.

Mabel took the knife she handed her and sliced the pie and one of the loaves of banana-nut bread, instantly filling Lucy's kitchen with mouthwatering aromas.

She filled four mugs with coffee and in a matter of minutes they were all gathered around her kitchen table laughing and talking between bites.

An hour later, with an official invitation to dinner the next evening, she waved goodbye and was smiling as she watched her new friends drive away.

Her mother called this Nowhere, U.S.A., but to Lucy, this small town felt like home.

Turning back, she surveyed the low-slung ranch house. Three days ago, overgrown shrubs had threatened to obscure it, and one of the shutters had needed to be straightened. Not so since Wes, Joseph and Rowdy had stepped in.

Ever since she'd awakened in the hospital to discover the truth about her life, she'd been adrift and searching for something. Only her faith that God was beside her had gotten her through. And her God-given stubbornness.

From his perch on the porch railing, Moose purred, and even that from the ornery tomcat felt like a welcome—after all, he'd picked her.

"Yes, big fellow," Lucy murmured, lifting him up and hugging him, "I do believe us two strays have found our home."

Rowdy McDermott's image plopped right back into her contented thoughts, settling in like a sticker poking through a sock.

Pushing the irritating worry aside, she headed inside to reread her home-repair guide on plastering a wall.

She might have trust issues by the wagonload, but she was not a chicken.

She would not allow her fears to send her running.

She'd taken her first step toward starting over, and this was where she was making her stand.

Dew Drop was where Lucy Calvert took control of her life again.

Chapter Four

"Excuse me, ma'am. But you want me to do what?"

Rowdy's lips twitched as he watched tall, lanky Joseph staring down at Lucy with a look of complete confusion. Always ready to please, the kid usually wore an affable grin, but right now he looked almost in shock. On Saturday Lucy had talked to them in-depth about what she wanted the yard to look like and they'd done a fantastic job. But they hadn't been inside the house.

For example, they didn't know until now that Lucy had a thing about walls. That the only good wall to her was a torn-out wall. He tugged on his ear and watched the show, enjoying every minute of it.

"I want you to take this sledgehammer," Lucy said, "and I want you to take a whack at this wall. It's fun! Believe me. It's freedom in a swing."

"Oh, I believe you," Joseph said. "It's just you already knocked out that wall over there, and I wasn't sure I was hearing you right. I mean, this one's a perfectly good wall and all."

Wes was champing at the bit to swing the sledgehammer. "Knock that dude down, bro. Or I'll do it."

Lucy chuckled. "I want this house opened up. It's too closed in. I like big airy rooms with lots of light. And, fellas, I've got to tell you that your Texas manners are perfect. Y'all have about ma'amed me to death. But you can call me Lucy from here on out. Got it?"

"Yes, ma'am—I mean, Lucy," Joseph complied, taking the sledgehammer and grinning as he looked from it to the blue wall. "I guess I can give this a go."

"Oh, yeah." Wes rubbed his palms together gleefully. "Swing away, Joe."

Rowdy's shoulders shook in silent laughter as Joseph pulled his protective eyewear down, then reared back and swung. A large hole busted through one side of the Sheetrock into the next room. It didn't take any more encouragement after that. The two teens started taking turns whacking away at the long wall that separated the living room from the den. The wall Rowdy had knocked out had been the divider for the kitchen and living room. What had once been three small dark rooms was now going to be one large space. He had to admit it was going to look good when it was all over with.

If she didn't knock *all* the walls out. The thought had him smiling and he almost said something to set her off, even though he knew she was leaving the load-bearing wall.

"Those have got to be the sweetest boys," she said, walking over to him. "Thank you for suggesting they come help me out. I think Joseph thought I had a few screws loose or something."

"He's on board now, though." Rowdy was curious about Lucy. She was an artist, though he'd yet to see any sign of art anywhere. He suddenly wondered about that. Her house was still loaded down with boxes and the walls were bare. Probably a good thing while she was stirring up all this dust. But was there more to it? His brothers had always called him the curious one. And his curiosity was working double time on Lucy.

As if sensing he was watching her, she turned her head and met his gaze with eyes that held a hint of wariness. She looked at him often like that and it added to his curiosity. Why?

She lifted her hand to her collar and tugged it close. He'd noticed she'd done this several times before, as if self-conscious about the burn scar on her neck.

He'd wondered about the scar and what had caused it. It was obvious that whatever had happened had been painful.

Being self-conscious about anything was at odds with his image of Lucy.

"Your grandmother came by this morning with her friends. They're a great group." She waved toward the counter loaded with pie and cookies. "I have all kinds of goodies in there left over if you and the guys want to take a break."

That made him laugh. In the background the pounding grew steadily, and then something crashed and the boys' whoops rang joyfully through the house. "As you can hear, I'm not doing anything, so if you mean there's pie in there from Ms. Jo, then I'm all in."

She'd started smiling when the boys started whooping. She was one gorgeous woman.

"There's pie. And, by the way, I put in a good word for you."

She headed into the kitchen and he followed. She wore another of those oversize shirts, hot pink today, and he began to think it was an artist quirk or something.

The collar brushed her jaw and the sleeves covered half her hands, they were so long. And still, as dwarfed as she was in all that cloth, he remembered the feel of her in his arms that first day.

She might be small, but Lucy Calvert was all woman.

She turned suddenly and he almost ran over her. Automatically, he wrapped his arms around her, lifting her instead of mowing her down.

"Sorry about that." He set her on her feet and she immediately put distance between them.

She gave a shaky laugh. "I'm so short it's easy to miss me."

"Hardly. No one would miss you." His frank assessment of her appeal had her swinging away from him to reach for a pie. She lifted the cover, her shoulders stiff as she did so, and he realized she didn't like him flirting with her. "I just wasn't watching where I was going," he added, trying to ease the tension that had sprung between them.

She'd started slicing pie with a vengeance. "Will you ask the boys what they'd like to drink with their pie, please?" she asked, as if he hadn't spoken.

He stared at her back for a few minutes, confused by her reaction. "Sure," he said, and went to get the guys.

What had just happened?

Lucy arrived at Sunrise Ranch with the pit of her stomach churning. She knew a lot about the ranch now, since working with Wes and Joseph. The teens had been fun to be around and had worked really hard. She'd been glad she hired them and got to watch their excitement over being destructive. And they'd been so polite doing it.

Even now the thought made her smile.

If it hadn't been for their constant exuberance, she didn't know what she'd have done when she'd found herself in Rowdy's arms once more—one minute she'd been fine and the next his muscled arms had swept her off her feet and his heartbeat was tangoing with her own.

She'd overreacted. Panicked. She'd forgotten how wonderful it felt to be held by a man.

Forgotten the feel of another heart beating against hers.

What she *hadn't* forgotten was how complete betrayal felt and that had driven her, shaken and babbling, out of his arms and across the room.

He probably thought she was crazy. Well, that made two of them.

Letting the excitement of meeting her neighbors take over, she parked beside the house like Ruby Ann had instructed her to do.

Kids were everywhere. There were several across the way in the arena riding horses, including Joseph and Wes. Three younger boys were taking turns trying to throw their ropes around the horns on a roping dummy in front of the barn. They stopped to watch as she got out of her truck and immediately, ropes dragging, they headed her way.

"You must be Lucy," the smallest boy said, arms pumping from side to side as he raced to beat his buddies. His plump cheeks were pink and dampness suffused his face. Obviously he'd been outside for a while and his oversize wide-rimmed cowboy hat hadn't completely shaded him from the sunlight.

"Yes, I am. How did you guess?"

"I heard Rowdy say you were kinda short. And you ain't much taller than me."

Ha! "True. I can't deny that you are almost as tall as me."

"I'm B.J., by the way. I'm the youngest one here, so I'm supposed to be short."

The other two crowded close. Almost the same size, one had brown hair and brown eyes, and the other was blond haired with blue eyes. They looked around nine years old and were almost her height.

"I'm Sammy and this here is Caleb," the brown-haired one said. "We heard you let Wes and Joseph knock down walls in your house. We been thinking it would be mighty fun to do. We're pretty strong. Show her your muscles, Caleb."

Immediately all arms cocked to show small bumps that would one day be muscles and truly did have some definition to them despite their young ages.

Vitality radiated from the three of them in their oversize hats, jeans, boots and B.J. with his leather vest. They could easily go on the cover of a greeting card.

"So how's the roping going?"

"Good, you wanna come try?" B.J. asked, taking her hand in his damp, slightly sticky one. "It's real fun. I ain't got it all figured out, but Caleb here, he's pretty good."

"I am, too," Sammy said, looking put out that B.J. hadn't said so. "I might be the newest kid here, but I been working real hard and almost got Caleb caught."

Lucy laughed at the competitiveness as she allowed B.J. to pull her across the gravel to the metal roping dummy. "I'll try it. But I'm not promising much."

Wes and Joseph rode up to the fence with a slightly

younger kid with coal-black hair, blue eyes and a crooked grin. The skinny teen looked amazingly like a younger version of Elvis Presley, whose old movies she'd loved as a kid, watching with her mother. It was one good memory she had of time spent with her mother.

"You made it," Wes called over the rail.

"Your house didn't cave in yet, did it?" Joseph's soft-spoken teasing made her smile. He had been so skeptical about taking a swing at the wall, but in the end he'd been a wall-knocking maniac just like Wes. It was easy to see Wes lived on the edge—much like she'd picture Rowdy at that age. But Joseph, he was a gentle soul.

"No, it's still standing. At least when I left."

"We want to help, too, please," Sammy said, reiterating what B.J. had said earlier. "Wes was telling us about how you just told them to beat that wall to smithereens and we all want to take a whack at it."

Everyone started talking at once, and Lucy found herself in the midst of a huge discussion on why the younger boys should get the chance to come knock out her walls.

"Whoa, guys." She called a time-out with her hands. "I have no problem with more help. We'll set it up with Rowdy. How does that sound?"

It wasn't long before Rowdy rode up on a horse with a couple of other men—one was an older cowboy with snow-white hair introduced as Pepper, the horse foreman, and the other was Chet, the Sunrise Ranch top hand. She'd learned from Nana's visit that Rowdy was the cattle-operation manager and quarter horse trainer. It was easy to see that Rowdy was a hands-on kind of cowboy, dusty from whatever he'd been doing out there on his horse. Lucy's fingers itched with the desire to paint him and his friends as they'd looked riding in from the open range.

She'd been struck by the Old West look of Rowdy in his chaps and spurs. And those deep blue, dangerous eyes as they glinted in the sunlight.

Chet and Pepper led their horses into the barn and he dismounted.

"I see the boys are making you feel at home."

"Very. They're a great bunch."

They all began talking at once and she loved it. Their excitement was contagious.

"What are y'all practicing for?" she asked them.

"The ranch rodeo. We got to get good so we can help our teams," B.J. said, holding his coiled rope in the air like a trophy.

As she was not sure what the difference was between a ranch rodeo and a regular rodeo, the kids explained that at a ranch rodeo there were events done with teams. The younger ones began telling her about their roping skills and asking if she'd ever mugged, or roped, a calf. Their questions were coming faster than paintballs from a paintball gun and she was barely keeping up.

Rowdy had crossed his arms, grinning at her as he rocked back on his boots, enjoying her induction into his world.

"Lucy," Ruby Ann called from the back porch of the house across the parking lot. When Lucy turned her way, she waved. "Could you come here and give me a hand?"

"Sure, I'll be right there." She smiled at the boys and realized a couple of extras had appeared from somewhere, maybe from inside the barn. There were boys of all heights and sizes everywhere. It was going to be a test of her memory skills just to get them all connected with their names. "If you'll all excuse me, I'll see you soon."

"We've got to wash up and put horses away, and then we'll be joining you," Rowdy explained. "Nana gave the house parents a date-night pass, so you get to hang with all sixteen boys and the rest of the family tonight."

Lucy did not miss that he was including the boys in the "family." It touched her deeply. As much as she was struggling with certain aspects of being around him, this was one more glaring declaration of his being a nice guy.

Ruby Ann held the door open for her and smiled as she entered. "It's so good to have you here. Met the crew, I see." She enveloped Lucy in a welcoming hug, then led the way down the hall past the mudroom and into the expansive kitchen.

"Did I ever! I'm in love."

"I know, they'll just twist your heart and hook you in an instant, won't they?"

"They're amazing."

The scrumptious scent of baked bread and pot roast filled the house, if her nose was correct. The tantalizing scents had her stomach growling. These scents were similar to those of her grandmother's home back when she'd been alive.

"Dinner smells amazing, Ruby Ann."

"Thank you. Now take a seat, and, for goodness' sake, call me Nana. You're going to hear it chanted all through the evening by my boys."

"Nana it is." It felt comfortable and right to call her Nana. She loved that Nana called them her boys. "Is there something I can help you with?"

"I love a woman who pitches in. You can peel these grapes for the fruit salad, if you don't mind."

"Peel the grapes? Sure," she said, shocked at the request. She'd never even thought about someone peeling grapes, much less doing it herself.

Nana chuckled. "I'm just teasing. I've already peeled the grapes. But you can slice up these strawberries for me if you don't mind."

Relieved that Nana had been teasing, she sat down and took the knife Nana held out to her.

There was food everywhere. "This is amazing. How did you ever learn to cook for a group this large?"

Waving the spoon she'd been stirring cheese into a mountain of mashed potatoes with, she chuckled. "I talked to a caterer and she gave me some formulas. Now it just comes naturally. Kind of like I expect painting comes to you. Right?"

Lucy remembered the first time she'd walked into a local art studio and picked up a paintbrush. She'd been ten, and her mother had wanted to encourage her drawing ability. Lucy had loved the scents that filled the studio, linseed oil and turpentine, and the instant she'd held that brush, everything in the world had seemed suddenly right.

It had been a long time since she'd had that feeling. She smiled. "Yes, you're right. My painting is from instinct, though I had some formal training when I was young."

"I read about you, you know. Looked you up on the Net." Nana's wise eyes settled on her as she spoke.

Lucy knew if that were the case, then she knew about the fire. "You did?" she asked, trying to keep her voice steady.

Nana studied her. "You had a hard time of it. I'm sorry. How are you doing now?"

"I'm okay," she said, trying to figure out where to direct the conversation. It wasn't as if she hadn't thought that someone could check her out online. After all, she was an artist with a bit of success. A rush of sound broke into their conversation as the back door opened and one after the other of the boys streamed down the hall and through the kitchen. She wasn't sure how all of them would fit in the house.

As if reading her mind, Nana said, "We usually eat in the Chow Hall, but tonight is special, we're having a guest. So it may be a tight squeeze."

Laughter and banter filled the room as Rowdy ushered the boys into the den. His brother Morgan and his wife, Jolie, arrived and Rowdy introduced them. Not that she'd needed the introduction—their resemblance was too similar. Morgan, like Rowdy, had Nana's direct navy eyes.

"Morgan and my dad run the business side of the foster program and the ranch. Jolie has been our schoolteacher since the beginning of the year."

"I can't wait to see some of your work." Jolie's wide smile reminded Lucy instantly of Julia Roberts, especially with her auburn hair and her expressive eyes. "I envy an artist their abilities. I'm a klutz with a brush in my hand."

"I won't believe that until I see it." Lucy had the distinct impression that this lady could do anything she set her mind to. And quickly she learned it was true when Morgan told her Jolie was a champion kayaker. It was easy to see his pride in her accomplishments. Tim had always seemed threatened by her success. His greatest wish had been for her to give up her work.

Lucy was so thankful that she hadn't done that.

Looking at Morgan and Jolie, she had to admit that she envied the bond between them. Their mutual respect spoke volumes.

They all talked about her work some—that it was in galleries and that she also sold prints. She wasn't Thomas Kinkaid or Norman Rockwell, but she was blessed to have some recognition, giving her the ability to paint full-time.

It wasn't long before they were all helping carry the large platters of food to the huge table in the dining area. There were so many of them that card tables had been set up to help accommodate them all.

While they were setting the table, Rowdy's brother Tucker showed up. Introductions were made and she knew before they told her that he had been in the Special Forces. There was just something about the way he carried himself. He still wore a very close-cropped haircut she could see when he removed his Stetson and hung it on the hat rack. Rowdy's hair was more touchable, run-your-fingers-through-it type. Where both Morgan and Tucker had serious edges to their expressions, Rowdy's was more open, and—she searched for the right word—*light* was all that came to mind. Rowdy's eyes twinkled as he wrestled on the couch with B.J. and Sammy. His infectious laughter had Lucy wanting to join in.

She brought her thoughts up short, realizing that she was comparing Rowdy's attributes with his brothers'. She had no reason to do that.

No reason and no want to.

Frustrated by her thoughts, Lucy marched back to the kitchen in search of a plate of food to carry. She needed something constructive to do. What was wrong with her, anyway?

Chapter Five

Dinner was a loud affair. But with that many boys crammed beneath one roof, it was to be expected. Rowdy enjoyed watching Lucy's reactions to the wild bunch. She handled herself pretty well for a newcomer. Then again, how he was handling himself *was* the question, as he found himself sitting next to her.

He could tell Nana had her eagle eyes trained on them and wondered if she sensed the undercurrent.

He tried to hide his acute interest in Lucy. After all, he'd sworn off women for a while. And she was sorely putting that commitment to the test. What was that verse that kept popping into his mind—"Test me, oh Lord, and try me." The Lord was doing a bang-up good job of it, and that was for certain. When he got home he was going to find out what the rest of the verse was so he could figure out a nice way to tell the Lord He could lay off. Lucy sitting next to him, at a crowded table, their elbows practically rubbing together, and smelling of something fresh and sweet— Refusing temptation had never been his strong point. He had always gotten low marks.

His dad said the blessing, having come in just before the meal was ready, and Rowdy talked to the Lord and expressed his concerns. When he opened his eyes and glanced to his left, Lucy was looking at him—and for a second he got the feeling she'd been talking to the Lord just as fervently as he had about being forced to sit with him.

"You're an artist," Randolph said, after he finished blessing the food. It was more a statement than a question. "And you're tearing out and making a studio. How's that going?"

Rowdy had the feeling she'd been trying hard not to look at him up to this point.

"I'm getting all the ripping out done first before I start the rebuilding, though."

"Hopefully she's gonna leave some walls, but it sure is fun knocking them out," Wes called from his seat at the card table with Joseph and Tony.

"I'm leaving the major walls," she chuckled, and the sound had him fighting not to lean in closer to her.

"What do you paint?" Caleb asked, his big blue eyes full of curiosity.

"Well, I paint whatever catches my eye—people, flowers, whatever. But I'm known for roads and landscapes."

"You paint those yellow lines on the roads?" B.J. asked excitedly, and Rowdy was pretty certain the little kid thought that would be the greatest job in the world. Eight-year-olds saw the world in their own way.

"Not exactly. You see, I paint a road in a landscape." When it was clear he didn't understand, she added, "You know the gravel road that cuts through the pasture at the entrance of the ranch? Well, I'd paint something like that, when the bluebonnets are in bloom. Or the doves lined up on the telephone lines."

His brows crinkled up and Rowdy had to hide a chuckle.

"Why would you want to paint a road like that?"

She smiled, making Rowdy want to smile, too, because he was enjoying listening to her.

"Because I'm infatuated with them. I love roads and love pictures of roads that make people want to know where the road leads."

"But we know the one in the pasture leads here to the ranch," Sammy interjected, sitting up in his chair.

"But the first time you came here, did you know what was just over the hill? I mean, you could see the roof of this house, but didn't you wonder what the rest was going to look like? Weren't you curious what you would see once the car reached the top of the hill? Wasn't there a sense of wonder?"

"Yeah," Wes said, his voice trailing low. "I was hoping there would be a horse and, sure enough, there was one tied to the arena saddled and ready when the social worker stopped the car. It was awesome."

Lucy placed her elbows on the table and leaned closer. "Yes. That's what I love about a picture of a road—it lets the person viewing it dream their own story. Everyone who looks at a picture of a road sees and feels something different."

Rowdy got it, and his curiosity was ramped up to view her paintings. He liked the way her mind worked.

"I was hoping I'd find a place where I wouldn't be sent away." Tony's words rang through the silent room.

"And you found that, didn't you?"

His expression eased. "I found my family."

"And we are so glad you did." Nana said what everyone else was thinking.

"I think it would be neat to paint a picture," Sammy said. "Can we see some of yours sometime?"

"Sure. I'd love to show you when I get some unpacked. I don't really have much, though. What I've painted recently is at the galleries. But I've got to get busy because they are waiting on me to turn new work in. There's an important show coming up and I need something in it."

"I'd like to see some myself," Rowdy said, more than ever wanting to see her work.

"Sure," she said, their eyes meeting. Tearing his eyes away from hers, he gave his undivided attention to his pot roast. He liked his neighbor, it was true, but he had horses to train, boys to coach for the upcoming ranch-rodeo benefit and a cattle business to run at the same time. He had committed to helping sassy Lucy Calvert do a little remodeling, but that was it.

For now, anyway. He'd had the tendency to date women who were drama queens—partly because they were usually really good-looking and that seemed to be his downfall—not that he was proud of any of it, but he couldn't deny it. Maybe this attraction he was feeling toward Lucy was because she seemed to be the complete opposite of that.

He'd made a commitment to himself and the Lord. Women were off-limits. Until the Lord showed him the right woman, he wasn't making a move. No matter what.

"Lucy, I've been sitting here thinking and I've just had this crazy idea," Jolie said, leaning close to the table in her excitement and taking the heat off of Rowdy.

"Would you consider teaching the boys a brief art class? Just a class or maybe two a week for five or six weeks?"

Startled by his sister-in-law's proposal, Rowdy swung his head to the side and saw that Lucy was just as startled. Then her eyes lit up as if she'd just been plugged into an electric outlet.

"I'd love to do that!" she exclaimed.

He held in a groan and knew right then and there that he was in trouble. "But you have your hands full of projects," he protested before he could stop himself. Every eye at the table slammed into him and he knew he should have kept his stinkin' mouth shut.

Test me, oh Lord—there was no denying it. None at all. God obviously got a real kick out of giving exams.

What had she just done? Lucy toyed with the collar of her shirt. She'd just committed to teaching the boys of Sunrise Ranch art lessons. The very idea sent shock through her, but excitement at the same time. She was going to teach an art class. And she was going to do it for these boys. It hit her suddenly that maybe this was what she was looking for. What she needed right now, a way to make her feel as if she was making a difference—her way of giving something back. Of paying it forward, so to speak.

This was her shot. It would be great!

"Whoa, there, you mean we're going to have to *paint* pictures?" The shock on Wes's face equaled that of being told he was going to participate in a ballet and it brought her excitement up short.

Cowboys obviously didn't do ballet or painting.

Joseph's eyes widened with worry, too. And with the two obvious leaders of the group balking at the idea, looks of excitement began giving way to looks of skepticism.

"Some of the greatest artists in the world are men," Lucy assured them, suddenly really wanting to do this. "Western art is a fantastic art form and I'd love to see if we have any future talent in this room with me."

Jolie jumped in to help. "Fellas, you'll have fun with this. Lucy and I will figure out projects you will enjoy. I promise."

Wes got a twinkle in his eyes. "I think if we have to paint, then Lucy needs to have to help us in the wild-cow-milking competition."

Excited chatter and agreements erupted about the room. Rowdy joined in the laughter beside her.

Well, she could have a good time, too. "Sure, I'd do that. I can learn to milk a cow."

Nana had been fairly quiet during the conversation, clearly enjoying listening, but now she chuckled. "Lucy, you're a good sport and true Sunrise Ranch material. But, to be fair, I think someone needs to explain the whole concept to you before you commit."

"That might be a good idea," Morgan agreed from across the table. "Jolie loves this sort of thing, but not all women do."

Instantly the competitive side of Lucy lit up. She might not be as tall and athletically built as Jolie, but she was certain that she could milk a cow. How hard could it be? "I'm sure it will be fun," she said.

"It is," Jolie told her. "Still, Wes, maybe you should explain this since it was your idea."

"It's a blast," the blond mischief maker said. "There's a team of five and one of them is the 'milker' and one is the roper. While the other team members catch and control the wild cow, the milker gets the milk, then runs it to the finish line. It's a hoot and a half."

"Yeah, a hoot and a half," B.J. echoed. "You gonna do it?" His big dark eyes were wide with wonder and expectation.

Though Lucy had sudden qualms about the wild-cow part, she swallowed her trepidation and nodded. "Sure I am. I'm game for anything."

From the end of the table, Randolph joined the conversation. "For safety's sake, I'm going to venture in here and require you to have some experience under your belt before you jump out there and try it. Rowdy can be in charge of that. What do you say, Rowdy?"

Lucy's spirits sank like the *Titanic*. Suddenly she wasn't so sure about this great idea. She'd already allowed Rowdy to help with her construction. She'd realized tonight that she wasn't comfortable being in his company overly much. The man made her nervous—he affected her in ways that she'd rather not think about. Now this....

"Sure," Rowdy said beside her. "We'll figure something out."

It hit her that he didn't sound all that enthusiastic about the idea, either. As she turned to him, her arm brushed his. Tingles of awareness like an expanding spiderweb etched across her body.

"Good," Randolph said. "In that case, I'll look forward to seeing you in the competition."

"Sure." Lucy's voice was as weak as the smile she mustered up.

How had this happened?

B.J. tugged at her sleeve and she turned to him, glad

to have a distraction from Rowdy. "We're gonna have fun." He dragged the word *fun* out for miles.

Lucy liked his positive thinking, but she wasn't so sure about that anymore.

Chapter Six

She'd awakened thinking of the man as if she had nothing else on her mind. She padded barefooted straight to the kitchen and the strong pot of coffee that she'd set to automatically brew this morning.

Yawning, she grabbed an oversize red cup from the cabinet and filled it almost to the brim. Taking a sip of the strong black brew, she let the warmth seep through her, then loaded it with three teaspoons of sugar—one more than usual for the extra shot of energy she would need before attempting to plaster a wall today. She took another sip, sighed then headed outside to drink it on the porch. She loved the quiet of the morning.

She'd come here to clear the air and move on with her life. Knocking walls out and spending her afternoons carrying the wood to a burn pile had empowered her. True, her back ached—and she'd had a very near miss with disaster—but since arriving in Dew Drop, she'd had a blast. And now she'd found something else to do that would be fulfilling—something she needed so badly.

Still, she knew it would take time away from her own painting, which she really should get busy on as soon

as she finished renovating. But she would make time
for the art classes. They might actually help her regain
that spark of enthusiasm she'd come here searching for.

She needed inspiration desperately.

Needed something to motivate her to pick her brushes
back up.

She'd come here determined that if she got her studio just right, the joy would return. And she was still
trusting that it would.

What about the cowboy?

There he was again, the big white elephant in the
room. What about him?

Her cell phone rang, saving her for the moment.

Digging it out of her pocket, she glanced at the caller
ID. So maybe she was wrong, she'd rather deal with the
cowboy than her mom. Bracing for drama, she pushed
the touch screen to accept the call.

"Hi, Mom."

"Have you lost your *mind*?"

"Not the last time I checked." Lucy concentrated on
keeping her tone light, having long ago grown numb to
the melodrama.

"Then why are you living at that dump in the middle of nowhere? You've come a long way, Lucy, after
what that jerk did to you." Lucy held back a retort. Her
mother had no room to call names, having put Lucy's
father through basically the same thing that Tim had put
Lucy through, only her mother had been an open book.
But Nicole didn't see the two as the same thing; everything she did felt justified in her mind.

"Mom, we've been through this. I want to be here.
I'm loving it."

"Your father should have stopped this—"

"I'm twenty-six years old and plenty old enough to make my own choices." *Without being dragged through guilt trips and hysterics.*

There was a long, exaggerated sigh on the other end of the line. "I never said you weren't capable of making your own choices." Nicole's voice dripped with emotion. "But what if *I* need you?"

And there was the whole gist of the conversation. Lucy fought off her own exaggerated sigh. "Mother, you are forty-seven years old—"

"Forty-four," her mother corrected.

Nicole had shaved off three years of her age a few years back. Just knocked them off and somehow didn't think anyone would notice. It wasn't worth arguing over. "The thing is, Mom, I moved here to start fresh. I am going to be fine and so are you. After all, you have Alberto."

"There you go again not paying attention to me. His name is Alonzo and no, I don't have him anymore."

Her mother was destined for unhappiness. The one good man she'd ever married had been Lucy's dad, and Nicole had kicked him to the curb years ago. And when Lucy's dad had had the audacity to fall in love and remarry—and be *happy*—Nicole had made it her life goal to try to make his life miserable.

Lucy had been the pawn her mother used most of the time in that quest. As a girl Lucy had suffered because of it and trusted no one with her heart until Tim. A bad move on her part—he and her mother were two of a kind.

"Mom, did you have a reason for this call?" Lucy asked, not happy about being reminded of what she wanted so much to escape.

She was ready to get to work and be done with this bad start to a good day.

"There you go being negative. Can't a mother just call to check on her child?"

Sure she could, but then Nicole wasn't a normal mother. There was always a reason for her call.

"Yes, she can." Lucy waited.

"Well, there is one thing," Nicole said, as if suddenly thinking of something. "Now that I've got you on the line. You still have your condo in Plano, right?"

"Yes." She hadn't put her condo on the market yet, wanting to make certain she wanted to stay here in Dew Drop.

"Great, then I'm sure you won't mind if I stay at your place for a while. I've moved out of Alonzo's place and…"

So that was it. "Yes, Mother. That will be fine. You know where the key is." And that was that.

Her mother made a quick ending to the call after she'd gotten what she wanted. Lucy held the phone for a minute, staring at it as she realized her bond with her mother was as blank as the screen. There was a time when she'd longed for more, but then she'd faced facts and knew it would never be more than it was now.

Standing, she looked about her new property. Her sweet uncle had wanted her to find that missing link here on this property and among the folks of Dew Drop. And maybe with her neighbors at Sunrise Ranch. He always had been a perceptive man.

Breathing in the fresh air, Lucy headed toward the barn to find her sledgehammer—the hunk of metal had become her new best friend and she was smiling as she walked along.

Moose appeared, weaving between her feet and arching his back as he rubbed his furry orange body against her leg.

"You and me, Moose," she said, bending to tickle him between his ears. She had things to do. There was no time to waste on areas of her life she had no intention of opening up again.

Here she might have to figure out how to maneuver around her new neighbor, but her mother had just reminded her of the circus her life could be back home and what her uncle had known or hoped she would find on this property.

She could deal with a certain happy-go-lucky cowboy if she must in order to keep her feeling of contentment. Her mother could have Lucy's condo for all she cared.

What had he been thinking?

Stalking to the burn pile, Rowdy carried the guts of yet another wall that Lucy had decided needed to bite the dust. At this point he'd begun to really worry about the woman's brain. This wall wasn't connected to the living room/kitchen area or he would have put his foot down. This wall happened to be on the upper floor of the house between two small bedrooms that she'd decided needed to be one larger room. There was no doubt in anyone's mind that the woman liked open space.

Or, he had begun to wonder, perhaps she really did just love to knock out walls. Maybe it was a disorder of some kind.

"Calamity Lucy's at it again," Wes said as he walked up. "I'm thinking we're going to have to talk her into leaving something standing in there or her house is gonna fall right on top of her."

"He might be right, Rowdy. Aren't you worried?" Joseph asked. "I mean, that's three walls. And I think she has her eye on the one beside her bedroom downstairs. I think I heard her muttering something about closet space."

Rowdy tossed his armload on the pile, stripped off his gloves and rested his hands on his hips. "I know it seems crazy, but it is her house, fellas. And to her credit, she hasn't knocked a wall out yet that would cause the house to cave in." For that he was grateful. He didn't tell the guys, but at the rate she was going it was only a matter of time before those were the only walls left, and then…who knew?

Wes rubbed his neck and squinted at Rowdy in the sun. "I guess it's good we're here to talk her off the ledge if she decides to get really crazy with the sledgehammer."

The kid had been ambling around nursing what looked to be a sore hip and a sore neck. Rowdy wondered again about whether he was bull riding. He'd asked about the hip and Wes had said he'd had a run-in with a steer. Logical answer…and maybe not the lie Rowdy suspected it was.

If his dad or his brothers suspected anything, none of them were saying. Maybe it would be better just to turn his head the other way and leave it be. As soon as the school year ended in six weeks, the kid was free to do as he pleased per the state. In all truth, he could do it now, but thankfully college was in Wes's plans.

Sunrise Ranch didn't cut the foster kids loose when the state did. Once they were here at the ranch, they were family and treated as such. Wes and Joseph were both graduating with scholarships to college. Joseph was heading off to become a vet and Wes was looking at an education in agriculture.

Rowdy pushed the thoughts away. He was probably worried about nothing. Looking at his watch, he saw it was nearing time for rodeo practice. "Hey, why don't y'all head back now? I'll go see if Lucy is ready to start practice tonight and be there soon. Tell Morg for me, okay?"

"Sure thing, Rowdy." Joseph nodded toward the house. "I think she might be a little worried about it."

Rowdy gave the kindhearted teen a smile. "I'll make sure she knows we're all going to take good care of her."

"I have a feeling she's tougher than she looks," Wes said. "Did either of you glimpse that burn on her neck?"

So they'd seen it, too. Since he'd seen it the other day, he was aware of it. He'd caught glimpses of it when she was busy working and forgot to tug her collar tight.

"I wondered if y'all had noticed," he said.

Joseph nodded. "I don't think she wants people to see it, though. Kind of like Tony not wanting to go without his shirt."

It was true. Tony had been badly mistreated by his parents before the state took him away from them and brought him to the ranch. His background was like nothing any kid should have to go through and he had scars to prove it. Bad scars that made Rowdy's stomach curl thinking about them.

"Maybe we can keep this between us, then," he said, immediately getting agreement from them. "I appreciate it, guys."

They headed toward the ranch truck as he headed toward the house. When he heard the distinct whack of a sledgehammer, he picked up his pace.

What could she be tearing out now?

Wes and Joseph's laughter followed him as he took the porch steps in a single stride and pulled open the screen door. Calamity Lucy they were calling her—he had to agree at this point. The woman had to stop. Getting her out of this house and involved in something else, even if it was wild-cow milking, was just the thing she needed.

Chapter Seven

"Okay, that does it. Put the sledgehammer down."

Lucy spun at Rowdy's irritated growl. "What do you think you're doing?" she gasped when he grabbed the tool. She hung on to the handle with all she had.

"I'm stopping you from destroying your house. Do you realize this is the *fourth* wall you've knocked out? Five, if you count the one in the barn."

"I can count, you know," she snapped. "And it's *my* house," she added indignantly, yanking hard on the sledgehammer. The irritating man yanked right back, slamming Lucy up against him with only the hammer between them.

"Let go, Lucy."

She glared up at him. "I will not!" The man had been working for her all afternoon and she'd been trying not to think about how every time he looked at her she forgot all about not wanting a man in her life.

Holding the handle with one hand, he covered her hands with the other. The work-roughened feel of them caused goose bumps on her arms.

His lip twitched at the corners as he stared down at

her. "You sure are pretty when your eyes are shooting fireworks. I'm kinda growing fond of it."

She couldn't breathe. She couldn't move. What had this man done to her?

One minute they were staring at each other, and then he lowered his head and kissed her. How dare he....

Goodness... The dreamy chant began ringing through her head as his lips melded with hers.

You're a fool, a fool, a fool, the small voice of sanity began to scream. Tearing her lips away from his, she put footage between them. "Why did you do that?"

His brows had crinkled together over teasing eyes. "I've been wanting to do it from the first day you dropped into my arms. And you know it. I've seen you looking at me, too."

Her jaw dropped. "You don't have a clue what I want. Or don't want." That he had her pegged did not make her feel good. "I don't want a man. I don't need a man. And certainly not one who kisses me right out of the blue like that." *Well, it had been nice*— She told the voice in her head to take a hike!

Rowdy stared at her as if she'd grown two heads or something. "Look," he said at last. "I kissed you. I'm sorry. I told you I was trying to mend my ways and you're right, I went and kissed you and I shouldn't have."

"Aha! So you freely admit that kissing women is a regular pastime for you. It just goes to show you that men are all despicable." The words just flowed out in a rush. "And another thing," she flung at him when suddenly it hit her that he was still looking at her as though she'd clearly lost her marbles.

She swallowed hard and prayed for the floor to open up and swallow her. How horribly embarrassing.

The clock on the wall in the next room could be heard in the silence that stretched between them.

"Are you okay?" Rowdy asked gently.

She couldn't look at him as she nodded.

"I'm really sorry. I overstepped myself and you're right. I was way out of line. It won't happen again."

He was actually apologizing to her. What a concept. When had Tim ever done that? Only when he'd wanted something…or when she'd figured out he'd done something he hadn't wanted her to find out about. The sleaze.

"Look." Rowdy held up his hands in surrender. "I'm not sure what your problem is, but if it will make you feel better, I'll leave." He turned to go and it was then that she realized she'd been glaring at him the whole time.

The man had to think she was a complete loon.

Stomach churning, she ran after him and caught him on the porch. The sun hung low on the horizon behind him. "Rowdy, wait. I might have overreacted."

At her quiet words he halted and turned back to her. "Maybe. But, hey, if my kiss drove you to it, then I guess that's a good thing. Only I get the feeling what's going on here goes a whole lot deeper than my kissing. Right?"

She owed him, so she nodded. "It's a long story."

"Look, I have a feeling you're not comfortable sharing whatever it is with me. Especially now. But how about getting out of the house to practice for the rodeo?"

She had to shut down the sudden impulse to spill everything to him. Working with him was one thing— confessing to him was another. But she had made him feel terribly bad—at least it seemed that way—and she had signed on for this wild-cow milking. "Okay, that sounds like a plan," she said.

He waved a hand toward his truck. "In that case, your

chariot awaits you. And I promise to stay on my side of the truck, behind the steering wheel."

Feeling more foolish than ever, Lucy pushed her hair behind her ear, contemplated changing her mind and then followed him to his truck.

"First things first. Do you know how to milk a cow?"

Lucy blinked blankly at him, and Rowdy took that as a no even before she confirmed what he'd figured out.

"Um, I can't say that I've ever had the need to know how to milk a cow."

Rowdy was having trouble concentrating. He shouldn't have kissed her. Hadn't meant to. He was a yahoo, a buffoon, an idiot. That was for certain. He'd swallowed the woman up as if she was sweet tea on a hot afternoon, and then he'd lost his mind in the process. He just didn't think straight around her.

He knew that now.

The thing was, he liked Lucy and he couldn't seem to do anything but want to get to know her better. But if he'd thought there was something bothering her before, he knew it was true now. Not that he was God's gift to women or anything, but she'd responded to him and then shoved him away as though he was Jack the Ripper.

What was her story? Something had happened to cause this leeriness.

She had a mistrust of men. And he wanted to know why.

The best way to do that was to get to know her, and teaching her to milk a cow was one more way to do that.

"So this isn't a milk cow." It wasn't a question but an observation on her part. She bit her lip—he fought to focus—and she studied the mama cow in the holding pen. "Aren't mama cows dangerous?"

"Yes, they are when their calf is around. They're not to be toyed with, and you need to know what you're doing so you can get in there and get out. Okay?"

She rolled her gorgeous eyes. "I'm thinking this is the craziest stunt I've ever agreed to."

He chuckled. "I hope so, because it is kind of crazy."

"Then why are you allowing the kids to do it?"

"They're ranch kids. Other kids skateboard on rails and jump bikes over holes and ramps. Ranch kids get in the arena with cattle."

She crossed her arms tight and glared at the cow that stood contently in the pen. He knew as well as she did when she started after the cow's udder things would change in an instant.

"Look, I don't want you to get hurt. The thing is the older teens know what they're doing. This isn't for little kids. You have to remember, one will have her head, and one will control her tail and one will be helping the boy holding the head. I'll be helping you get to the udder. They'll have her stretched out and it won't be as dangerous as it could be. You just have to look out for her feet, and I mean it. Watch them. Now I'm going to call the boys over and we're going to demonstrate."

"Fine. You do that."

He almost chuckled at the way she was fighting her fear. He'd learned that she wasn't one to back down.

Rowdy liked that. Respected it.

"Okay, you need to hold your hand like this, like you are going to shake my hand."

Lucy watched Rowdy hold his hand out with his fingers together and his thumb slightly separated from them. She copied him, trying hard not to think about the kiss. But it was a little bit distracting— Okay, it was a lot distracting.

She held her hand as he was and then looked skeptically at him. "Then what?"

"Then you grab here at the top," he explained. "No pulling like you see in the movies. Just clamp it between the fingers and push gently upward. Milk will come. Remember, in the competition, you need a few drops."

How hard could it be?

"And then you run."

She glared at him. "Thanks. Thanks for letting me get myself into this. If the boys don't want to paint, then I wonder why I'm doing this?"

"Sometimes even if a boy is curious about trying new things, he needs an excuse to do it. Painting isn't the most macho thing for these guys to do, so you getting in the ring with this cow gives them the excuse because you called their bluff. Get it?"

She did, actually. "Yes. So now I know." And she couldn't back down even if everything in her warned her to run now. As she looked at Rowdy, her stomach felt off-kilter and she wondered if the warning was for her to run from him instead.

"So do we have a regular milk cow somewhere that I can practice on?"

He chuckled. "Sorry, we're not in the milk-cow business. You're going to have to test it out on Betsy Lou here."

"Why does this not surprise me?"

"Hey, Wes, Joseph, y'all come on over." He'd sent the boys to practice with Morgan on the other end of the arena and now, at his call, the entire group came running. It looked as though she was about to be the show for the day.

Morgan rode his horse over behind the boys. She liked Morgan—he seemed to be a rock, and as steadfast as they came. She had a feeling—just from all the responsibility that he carried on his shoulders—that if a man could be trusted, Morgan McDermott would be that man. Rowdy's boyish grin tickled her memory.

Could Rowdy be trusted?

No. He was too reckless. Too good-time Rowdy. Not that anyone had told her this, but she knew in her heart that he was. Tim had had that same look. His smile came too easily and it teased too often.

The boys who weren't on the team climbed to the top of the arena rails. They looked so cute sitting up there. Wes, Joseph and Tony climbed between the rungs and sauntered her way.

"We'll take care of the cow," Wes said, looking cocky, and Lucy believed he would.

"We're going to let you learn here in the small pen. So I won't have to rope her, the boys will just grab her and then I'll move into place and tell you when to make your move."

She nodded. "Gotcha."

"Okay, then, let's get this party started. Fellas, it's all yours."

They whooped like she'd learned they were prone to do, then dived at the cow so fast it didn't have time to make a break for it. Wes grabbed the head and Tony joined him. Joseph grabbed the cow's tail. They all grinned at her as the cow let out a "Maaawwww" that sounded like a battle cry.

"Let's go. Follow my lead and watch out for the back leg. I'll get the milk first, so watch closely."

Was he kidding? She kept him squarely between her and the cow as she crept behind him. He whipped out the jar that was supposed to hold the milk, and as she watched he raced into the danger zone and reached for an udder.

It was *udderly* unbelievable. *Funny, Lucy, you're a real riot.*

"You do it like this," he called, bending toward the moving target. The boys were holding the cow, but she was bigger than them and not standing still. Rowdy displayed the milk in the clear jar as he moved back beside her.

"Piece of cake. You can do it."

"Yeah, go for it, Lucy!" the kids called from the fence.

Praying she didn't lose her lunch, she was so nervous, Lucy grabbed the jar and headed toward the cow with Rowdy beside her. "Piece of cake, my foot," she quipped, making herself smile for the kids. Hunching down, she reached toward the udder. When she slipped her hand in, the cow moved as she grabbed hold and milk shot her in the face.

Spitting and blinking, she scrambled to hang on. The cow bellowed and sidestepped, taking the boys with her. Lucy didn't let go, but lost her balance and fell forward, hitting the cow in the belly before planting herself face-first in the dirt! The cow bucked, kicked its leg out then stepped on her arm. Then her shoulder. Pain seared through her and Lucy would have screamed but her face was plastered two inches deep in smelly arena dirt.

Chapter Eight

This was not how it was supposed to go. Rowdy put himself between Lucy and the cow. The boys let the animal go and it sped to a corner at the far edge of the pen. Rowdy knelt down just as Lucy lifted her face out of the dirt and spat.

"This is *disgusting,*" she croaked.

"Yeah, you're right. Sorr—" Rowdy's words stuck in his throat. The sleeve of her shirt was ripped and flapped open as she sat up, exposing her arm. The skin, as far down as he could see, was puckered and angry, disfigured terribly in spots. His gaze locked on her burn scar and he couldn't tear his eyes away. Suddenly seeing him looking, she snapped a hand to her arm and pulled the material closed the best she could.

Beside them, Tony stood stock-still, staring at her arm. Even though she now had it covered, it was clear Tony had glimpsed what lay beneath the cloth.

Rowdy moved to her side and helped her as she tried to stand up, not at all sure what to say. Her collar hung loose at her neck and the other scar was visible beneath. Without thinking of his actions, he reached and gently tugged the collar close to her neck like he'd seen her do so many times. Her eyes met his and there was no missing the pain shimmering in their depths.

"Thank you."

He nodded, his voice still lodged in his throat with the knot from his stomach. "Hey, guys, I think Lucy's been a good sport about this. We're going to call it even. Right?"

"R-right," Wes said. His blond brows dipped together and his expression revealed that he, too, had glimpsed the gruesome burn on Lucy's arm. "You just tell us where to show up for art class and we'll paint a road that no one will be able to forget."

That got a smile from Lucy. "We're going to start painting tomorrow. I talked to Jolie yesterday. But—" she grimaced, clearly in pain as she continued to grip her arm "—I'm going to compete in the rodeo just like I promised, so don't think I'm not going to hold up my part of the agreement. But right now I need to go home."

Rowdy shot Morgan a glance. "I'll be back."

"Don't worry about us. Make sure she's okay," Morgan said, frowning with concern.

"Yeah." Rowdy jogged after Lucy, who was already almost to his truck. He barely made it there before she did and pulled open the door for her. Without a word, she climbed in and stared straight ahead as he went around to his side. "See you fellas later," he called to the younger ones who were craning their necks from their perches, clearly worried.

"Tell Lucy she done good," B.J. called.

"I'll do that." Rowdy hopped behind the wheel and had them heading back toward her place within seconds.

She continued to stare straight ahead. When he

glanced worriedly at her the second time, she swallowed hard and he wondered if she was fighting tears. If so, what did he say?

"Are you hurt? Those burns on your neck and arm look like they were painful." What an idiot. Clearly they'd been painful.

"They're well now. I think my shoulder is going to have a good-size bruise."

Her voice was soft. He had never been so glad to get to a house in all his days. He practically spun gravel turning into her driveway. He was out and around to her side of the truck before she had time to even think about opening the door herself.

"I'll see you tomorrow," she said, and headed toward her house, still holding her shoulder.

"Hey, I don't know what kind of men you're used to being around, but I'm not just going to drop you off alone after I got you stomped by a stinkin' cow."

She spun around. "I'm fine. I don't need your help."

What was with this woman?

"Of all the stubborn—" Rowdy stared at her, then marched past her to her front door. Yanking it open, he held it as she glared at him. "After you."

"Fine," she snapped, storming past him and through the door. "I'm going to wash my face and change my shirt—if that's okay with you?" Her eyes were like spikes.

"Fine with me. I'll be right here when you get back, and then we're going to talk."

Her brow shot up to her hairline. "Fine."

"Fine," he snapped, too, and watched her storm away. All the while his head was about to bust imagining all the different things that could have caused such a burn on her neck and arm.

Every one of those scenarios was too painful to think about.

They'd seen her arm. The look of horror on Tony's face had cut to her core. The kid had almost looked as if he could feel her pain.

Drats and more drats. Her scars made people uncomfortable.

She stared at herself in the mirror. It had taken a while for her to be able to do it without cringing, herself, so how did she expect others to not react the same way?

The brutal burn ran ugly and twisted from her neck down her right arm and torso. It wrapped around her rib cage and covered the majority of her stomach. The memory of the house caving in on her swept over her, and the scent of burning flesh made her nauseated. Reaching for the clean shirt, she pulled it on. The traumatic memory faded as she buttoned the buttons with shaky fingers.

Rowdy had seen the scar before and not said anything. Today, he'd looked into her eyes and pulled her shirt closed so no one else would see it. He'd saved her from the curious stares of the kids for the most part. Tony, and maybe Wes and Joseph, had seen her arm. He'd kept them from seeing more.

She had the feeling that this time he was going to ask questions.

Not sure if she was going to answer his questions she walked from her room and rounded the corner into the kitchen/construction site. Rowdy was leaning against the counter with his back to the sink and his scuffed boots crossed in front of him as he stared at the spot where she would be when she rounded the corner. She stopped. Her stomach felt unsteady…or maybe that was her feet. And her arm throbbed like a fifteen-hundred-pound cow had stepped on it.

As soon as he saw her he pushed away from the counter and yanked a chair from the table. "Here, have a seat."

She sat because she needed to.

He reached for a bottle of pain relievers that he'd obviously dug from her cabinet. Popping the top off he poured two into his hand and held them out to her. "You're going to need these."

She took them, because he was right. Then she accepted the water he held out to her.

Once she'd washed them down, he took her glass and set it on the counter, where he resumed his original pose leaning against it. His deep blue eyes rested on her.

The man really made her nervous.

"You were a good sport out there."

Not what she'd been expecting. "I still think y'all are crazy, but I'm going to do it."

"You don't have to. In the boys' book, getting out there and trying was all they needed."

"A deal is a deal."

They stared at each other and the clock ticked on the wall over the stove. "I guess you're wondering about my scars."

"I am. But if you want to tell me it's none of my business, I understand. You just seemed sort of—" He raked his hat from his head and ran his fingers through his straight dark hair. She could tell he was struggling with the right words. He didn't know that there weren't any.

She wanted to tell him it was none of his business

but…he'd seen her arm. And her neck. Still, accepting them was one thing, but for her to talk about them was an entirely different one.

"Our house burned down. We were sleeping and didn't realize it until it was almost too late." Her heart rate kicked up and she rubbed her sweating palms on her jeans, while trying to control her breathing like the therapist had taught her. "The fire was hot and the smoke was so thick when we woke. Tim shook me awake, and we were crawling to the window when the roof caved in and burning wood rained down on top of us…" She hadn't told this much of the story to anyone but her therapist. "It was— I woke up in the hospital and they told me Tim hadn't made it."

She hadn't been able to talk about the moments of pain before she'd lost consciousness. Blinking back tears, she rubbed those that had escaped and were rolling down her cheeks. "I didn't know anything about Tim's affairs then," she almost blurted out, but didn't. She'd believed he'd died loving her. Even after she knew that was a lie, she wouldn't have wished death on him.

"I'm sorry." Rowdy came and pulled a chair out so he could sit facing her. He clasped her hands with his and squeezed gently. "That's tragic. All of it."

She nodded, closing her eyes. "Yeah, especially knowing I killed him."

Chapter Nine

"You killed him? I don't believe that," Rowdy blurted in reflex. He didn't know her well, but she hadn't killed her husband. No way.

She looked away, toward the window that could be seen past the breakfast bar in the front room. "It's true. The fire started in my studio with some oily rags."

Guilt was etched in her features when she turned back to him. "That may be the case, but you didn't start the fire. Things happen. I'm sorry you lost him that way." He could tell she took what he said with a grain of salt. She looked to be around twenty-five or twenty-six. About his age.

She'd been through a lot for her age. He didn't know a lot about art, but he thought he knew making money in the art world was almost impossible. So there was one more thing to be curious about.

"You must have loved him very much." His heart ached for her—having lost his mother at a young age, he knew the pain that went with losing someone you loved.

She lifted a shoulder in a slight shrug. She stood suddenly. "Hey, thanks for bringing me home. But I need to get some things unpacked for art class tomorrow."

"Sure," he said, knowing a dismissal when he heard it. "You're sure you're okay? Do you need anything?"

She shook her head. "Nope. Really. I'm good." She had begun walking toward the door the moment she'd started speaking. He followed like a puppy being sent outside. She opened the door and held it for him. He ignored the urge to touch her as he walked past. He'd been pretty harsh earlier, and now he felt like a heel.

She didn't follow him onto the porch.

"Take another couple of those painkillers before you go to bed," he said, as if the woman didn't know how to take care of sore muscles.

"I'll do that. Good night."

Before he got his good-night out, she'd already closed the door. He stared at it, stunned. Something tugged in his chest. And he wondered for the umpteenth time what had happened to Lucy Calvert. There was more to this story. He felt it to his core.

He didn't feel right leaving. He raised his hand to knock but let it hover just in front of the door before pulling back. Turning away, he strode to his truck and left.

Lucy had a right to her privacy.

Lucy couldn't believe she'd opened up to Rowdy about the fire. She'd had to catch herself before she said too much. And yet she'd admitted the part that tormented her. Yes, she was angry at Tim for what he'd done. But to know that she was responsible for a person losing his life… It was unthinkable.

And then there was the scene at the burn center. His

girlfriend blaming her and the horrible things she'd learned that day.

Lucy poured herself a glass of iced tea and drank half the glass, suddenly feeling parched as a desert. Then, forcing the thoughts away, she headed to the back room where she'd stored her canvas and paint supplies. It was time to think about something positive. Teaching the boys to paint appealed to her. She'd never thought of teaching before, but with this wild bunch, she was certain it was going to be an adventure.

And that was exactly what she needed.

Did it matter that they'd seen her scars? She would see tomorrow. Tony would have time to let the shock of seeing them ease and they'd move on. No big deal.

No big deal.

Rowdy's soft gaze touching hers as he'd pulled her collar closed slipped into her thoughts. The man had been nothing but kind to her since she'd arrived—bossy and nosy, too, but kind. Her lips lifted thinking about him. Why was a guy like him still single? The question startled her.

She had come here so angry at Tim. At herself. And here was this handsome cowboy who wouldn't go away. Of course, she could say he was just being neighborly… but that kiss had nothing neighborly written in it. Tracing a finger along the edge of an unfinished canvas, she remembered his kiss, and the feel of it came surging back and almost took her breath away.

No, neighborly was not what she'd call that kiss.

Chemistry, yes. Very much so.

And it had been a very long time since she'd felt anything like that. For two years her life had been full of pain, inside and out. Her extensive burns hadn't been a simple fix.

God had been good to her during that time. She didn't think she could have made it through without Him, but God hadn't been able to fix the anger inside of her. He hadn't been able to fix the mistrust that ate at her.

But tonight, she'd talked to Rowdy. Opened up to him in a way she hadn't been able to do with anyone since she woke in the hospital, other than her therapist at the burn center.

She'd trusted Rowdy enough to do that.

The very idea was a breakthrough for her. Maybe God had brought her here for that reason.

Taking a deep breath, she began assessing supplies she would need tomorrow. Jolie had taken the list of paints she'd need to the art store in the larger town eighty miles away and had promised to pick up some canvases, too. Despite feeling nervous about tomorrow after all that had happened today, she went to work gathering the rest of the things she would need.

So far life here at her new home hadn't been anything like she expected, not quiet time spent alone rehabbing her house and her soul— Nope, not that at all.

Rowdy, she had to admit, was the most unexpected. Trepidation filled her again when she thought about having opened up to him. She hadn't told him about the scars on her body. Had let him think the scars on her arm and neck were all there was. Why had she done that?

She knew why she hadn't said anything about Tim's cheating for so long. It was embarrassing. But was that why she'd kept silent about the scars?

"Tony, dude, you saw how bad they were, didn't you?" Wes, Tony and Joseph were sitting out under the crooked tree back behind the schoolhouse. They'd agreed to meet there after practice, after seeing the scars on Lucy's arm. The younger boys hadn't been close enough to see them.

Tony nodded. "They were bad. Like angry welts."

"Like yours," Joseph said, looking sad.

Wes knew Joe had a tender heart. It was one of the reasons he was going to make a good veterinarian. Wes wasn't as tenderhearted. He got plenty mad when he thought about his life, but he stuffed it deep inside of him and for the most part enjoyed his life here on the ranch. He felt lucky to be here. Looking at Tony, he knew his life could have been rougher. At least his parents had just left him on the steps of the welfare office. They hadn't tortured him like Tony's parents had.

They hadn't tossed gas on him and struck a match.

"Yeah, like mine. I wonder what happened to her?"

"I don't know, but she's hiding them," Wes said.

Tony looked down, rubbed his hand on his thigh. "It's easier that way," he said, real quiet. "People look at you funny. Y'all know it. Y'all've seen the look on people's faces the first time they see my back. It ain't worth it. I totally get why Lucy covers hers up."

Wes did, too. It was true what Tony said about people getting all shocked and horrified at the sight of his back. His back looked like roadkill. He didn't hardly ever go without his shirt.

They were all quiet for a few minutes. It was hard to say anything after something like that.

"I'm just glad you didn't die from it." Joseph was the one to speak.

"Yeah." Tony took a deep breath. "Truth is, till I came here to Sunrise Ranch, I kinda wished it had…you know.

Killed me." He swallowed hard and chucked the rock he'd been holding as far as it would go.

Wes figured he had it good compared to Tony, but then he still didn't get why a kid had to go through all the junk the world had to offer sometimes.

Tony smiled and changed the subject. "Did—" He started to say something, then stopped. "Did you see the way Rowdy looked at her?"

"You mean with the goo-goo eyes?" Wes grinned.

"I saw it," Joseph said. "It's pretty clear he's into her. I mean, I could tell that when we were working at her place."

"Yeah, I know," Tony said. "But did you see how he didn't care about the burns?"

Wes shot Joseph a glance. They stopped grinning.

"Not everybody's going to freak over your burns, either, Tony," Wes said, hoping he was saying the right thing.

"Yeah, maybe." Tony shrugged, looking as though he didn't believe it.

Wes's fist knotted up and he had to knock the anger back in its dark hole. "You hold your head up, dude. It'll happen."

"Yes, it will," Joseph added.

Wes sure hoped so. He wondered if Lucy had the same thoughts as Tony. "Maybe Rowdy will fall in love with Lucy, you think?"

A grin spread across Joseph's and Tony's faces.

Yup, that would be the cool...and it might make Tony feel better about himself. That would be the coolest of all.

"Y'all did great today," Lucy called, forcing her voice to sound upbeat as the kids streamed through the schoolhouse door like a herd of wild mustangs. Several shot thanks over their shoulders, but nearly pushed the others down clamoring to get away.

Lucy sighed, watching the last one escape. Her shoulders drooped; it had not exactly been the day she'd planned.

"They love working cattle, so don't let their stampede out of here get you down," Jolie said, coming up beside her. "You did great, and I think they enjoyed themselves."

"Like a trip to the dentist."

Jolie chuckled. "It wasn't that bad. And remember, they're boys. When you get more to the actual painting part of the class things will get better."

"Well, at least there's hope." It was true that today she had to spend time teaching a little theory. Not much, but she had to explain the different art forms, the brushes and mixing the paint, etcetera.

"I'm pleased. They need a little Art 101 and it's just a wonderful thing that you showed up right here beside us. God just works everything out. It's a wonderful thing to watch."

It was Lucy's turn to chuckle. "I'm not so sure the fellas would agree."

"They don't have a clue what's good for them." Jolie winked and then began straightening desks. Lucy did the same. "So how's the remodel going?"

"Pretty good. I think we've got all the walls knocked out that I can possibly knock out."

"Well that's a good thing. I overheard something about Calamity Lucy the other day. We're studying women of the West right now and so they have heard stories of Calamity Jane. I think they were beginning to fear the house was going to fall in on you."

She shook her head. "Crazy guys. I do admit that I kind of fell in love with certain aspects of swinging that sledgehammer. There's a lot of clearing of the head that goes into that swing."

Jolie sat on the edge of the desk as her smile bloomed wide. "Speaking of Rowdy, how's that going?"

Had they been speaking of Rowdy? She thought they'd been speaking of her house and clearing her head. Suddenly uncomfortable with the conversation, Lucy bluffed. "What do you mean?"

"C'mon. There's something there. I saw it the other night. It's okay. I can tell you he's a good guy."

"First of all, I'm not looking for any kind of guy right now. Just so you know. But also, he told me he's trying to mend his ways. That's a red flag to me. I bet he's very popular." *With the ladies* went unsaid.

"And I'll be one of the first to say he needs to mend his ways. Especially after..." Jolie's words trailed off and her eyes dimmed.

Lucy didn't want to pry, but couldn't help herself. "What? After what?"

Jolie bit her lip. "I shouldn't have said that. Rowdy is a great guy. I've known him since I came here at age ten, when my parents were house parents. He didn't take his mother's death well. He got into all kinds of trouble—reckless stuff. My mom used to say it was as if his mother dying young made him think his life was going to end early, too, so he might as well live fast and furiously. He almost got killed trying to ride a bull that the best bull riders in the country had trouble riding. It stomped him—it was terrible. It scared Randolph to death." Jolie shook her head. "Anyway, I know we all want the best for him."

Jolie had changed what she'd been about to say, but hearing about Rowdy as a grieving boy tugged at Lucy's heart. Still, why had Jolie thrown out the "especially after" comment, then backpedalled like an Olympian?

Whatever it was, she'd already figured out it couldn't be good or Jolie would have had no reason to withhold from her.

"Rowdy just needs someone who can help mend the heart of that boy he once was. By the way, I want to say how sorry I am. I read the article about the fire." Her eyes softened. "I'm sorry you lost your husband and were so badly burned. A terrible thing. I guess me pushing you about an interest in Rowdy is probably way off base right now. Forget I said anything. I'm just glad you're here and agreed to teach art to the guys. Working with them will bless your soul."

Lucy tried to figure out what to say, but in the end she said nothing. Just that the boys already were getting to her in a good way, and then she'd gotten out of there as fast as she could.

She had very nearly let her defenses down where Rowdy was concerned. The thought plagued her all the way home.

There was something behind Jolie's remark. And it had a big red stop sign painted all over it. And yet, she thought about that boy who lost his mother and dealt with it by living hard and recklessly, and her heart ached for him.

Chapter Ten

Driving back from Bandera a few days after Lucy had told him about her husband, Rowdy had a lot of time to think. He'd been unable to get her off his mind. He'd had to make the almost four-hour trip to hill country on the spur of the moment to finalize the buying of a horse he'd been working on for weeks. The trip had turned into a two-day affair and he was anxious to get home.

Morgan had relayed to him that the first two art classes had been exactly as they'd all thought they'd be—met with strong opposition.

"If it had been us being forced to lift a brush at that age, we'd have been moaning just as loud," he'd told Morgan.

"You'd probably have skipped out and found you someplace to hide out there holed up under the stars where you always used to run," Morgan had accused, and been right on target.

Still, that being said, he hoped the boys weren't making Lucy feel too bad.

He had to admit that after hearing her story—or at least part of what he suspected was a story with more to it—he was glad Jolie had asked her to teach the art class. It opened up a reason for her to be at the ranch some. He knew that what he and the boys could do at her house was not going to last much longer. They'd already knocked out every wall that could be knocked out and the hedges were all trimmed and the yard cleaned up. He enjoyed being around Lucy. He couldn't deny it.

He was supposed to be cooling his jets, and here he had gone and kissed the first woman since "the bad move of the century." The only good thing he could say about that—other than the fact that he'd enjoyed it more than any kiss he'd ever experienced in his entire life—was that at least he'd kissed a good woman. A really good woman.

Not that every woman he'd ever dated had been bad—they were just not what he was looking for anymore. He was digging himself deeper and deeper. He was a shallow jerk.

It was as much his problem as it had been theirs. Until Liz.

Liz was in a realm all her own, and if there was one good thing he could say for her, it was that at least knowing her had set him on a different course. He still felt for her family and what she'd put them through. And he knew that when and if he ever married, he was taking no chances on a woman like Liz standing across from him saying "I do."

Like his dad had said, there was always a positive to every situation. You could learn from the bad ones and if you didn't, then the blame for that sat squarely on your own shoulders.

Rowdy had learned and learned well.

His dad had also told him once that living hard

wouldn't bring back his mother. Wouldn't right the wrong he'd felt done to him when she died. They'd created the ranch as a haven for lost boys, boys who had no one and yet Randolph sometimes worried that Rowdy was the most lost and alone of all the boys who'd come to the ranch. Rowdy couldn't do anything more than just look at his dad that day, because he'd felt his words were true.

Staring at the night flashing by, Rowdy wasn't sure why his thoughts had gone there. He didn't like excuses, didn't like thinking that he had been unable to deal with the feelings of loss that had coiled inside of him for so long. He'd been angry on the inside—hiding it as best he could—finding relief in his reckless ways.

Much as he suspected Wes was doing. For Rowdy, everything had come to a jolting halt when he'd been confronted by Liz's husband. It was as if icy cold water had been poured over him, startling him awake.

He'd known then he wanted to change. He'd gone down on his knees and asked the Lord to forgive him. To change him. And that change was in process.

He just hadn't refined the process yet. Bad habits were hard to break. Especially when a gal like Lucy fell into his arms.

He smiled thinking about that first meeting. She'd surprised him from the beginning, and every day he wanted to know more about her.

Not far to go until he'd be driving past her place. It was late, but if her lights were on, he might stop in.

Once again, maybe he was getting ahead of himself.

Patience had never been a strong suit of his.

So he'd play it by ear. It was eleven o'clock, anyway.

She was probably snug in bed with the lights off. The best thing he could do was drive on by and let her be.

Lucy stared at the sketch she'd just finished of how she wanted the studio to look. The barn was sturdy and the concrete slab made it all the more workable to have an art studio here in the loft. Sitting on the edge of the loft with her legs hanging over instead of her body this time, she studied the floor below. There were possibilities for that space, too…if what she'd heard at the Spotted Cow Café today had been any sign. Both Mabel and Jo had voiced a desire to learn to paint. They'd said they had a lot of friends who would enjoy an art class one night a week—maybe even two.

Possibilities. She let her imagination open and saw the loft as her personal studio with the first floor set up as an art classroom. The idea wasn't something she'd even thought about until Jolie had asked her to teach the boys. What a disaster that was on the verge of being. But if she was actually offering art classes to people who wanted to take them, and were excited about it— Well, that was really appealing to her.

As far as the guys, she was feeling like a failure, despite Jolie assuring her they'd come around.

Ha!

The crunch of tires, then headlights flashing across the open barn doors, alerted her that someone was pulling into her driveway. She glanced at her watch. It was after eleven-thirty.

Who would be coming to her house at this late hour?

And what was she doing out in the barn this late alone? Her door was even unlocked and every light in the house was on. *Hello—*

She'd not realized how late it was. She'd gotten lost in her drawing. Pulling her legs back from the edge, she stood and went to the window to peek out and see who was out there.

Rowdy!

What was he doing here so late?

She'd been relieved when he hadn't shown up to work two days ago. The boys had relayed the message that he'd had ranch business out of town. It hadn't made her happy that her first reaction had been to feel let down that he was gone. She'd kicked that out the door in an instant and been more than happy not to have to see him for a few days. It gave her time to think. Time to take control of her circumstances again.

She'd called a contractor and set up a meeting for tomorrow.

Rowdy got out of his truck, stretched and then, looking better than she wished he did, he strode to her back door and knocked on the screen-door frame.

Drats!

He waited, looked at his watch then turned and glanced toward the barn. She knew he couldn't see her and she didn't move. But then she realized that maybe since it was so late, there was an important reason he was out there.

"Rowdy," she called, pushing the window open and waving. "I'm up here. Is everything all right?"

"Lucy! What are you doing out there at this time of night?"

Okay, so maybe she should have let him stand out there all night. "I'm working. What are you doing?"

"Looking for you?" He was steadily heading toward

her. The barn's spotlight showcased him all the way. He looked up as he got closer. "Mind if I come up?"

Yes. "No," she said instead. Walking over, she sat back down on the edge of the loft and let her legs dangle as she watched him stomp up the stairs.

When he made it to the floor he came and sat down beside her. Too close for comfort, his shoulder brushed hers. Butterflies came out of nowhere and attacked her stomach. There were just some things she was finding out that she couldn't control. Butterflies were one of them.

Drat and double drat!

God had been having an excellent day when He'd created Lucy Calvert. Yessiree, it was true. He'd also been on a let's-torture-Rowdy kick.

He'd missed her.

There, he admitted it. Staring into those amazing eyes, he knew there was no use trying to deny it.

"What did you say you were out here doing? Working?" he asked as the sounds of the night settled in the stillness between them. Through the open barn doors, crickets chirped and he could hear the coyotes in the distance, so far off their lonesome call almost blended with the night.

She nodded, picking up a sketch pad on the floor beside her. She handed it to him. His fingers brushed hers as he took it. "This your studio?" he asked, trying not to send any signals that would put a wall up between them.

She'd had her hands folded together in her lap, and now she just nodded. This had been a bad idea on his part. But to be true to the path he'd committed to with the Lord, he was keeping his distance.

Looking into her eyes, he knew he was a fickle soul. That had always been his problem where women were concerned. But if he didn't want to run Lucy off, then he now understood he would have to move slowly. She was different than any woman he'd ever known.

He yanked his gaze away from hers and stared at the drawing. He sent up a prayer for help.

Because he did have good intentions.

"Yes. I drew it up and kind of lost track of time. The contractor starts on Monday."

She'd hired a contractor. He'd known this was coming, had thought as much earlier, but he knew that meant his time here was done. He hadn't realized it was going to hit so hard. "So you're kicking me and the boys out?"

"Y'all have been wonderful, but a girl can't wear out her welcome. You have a job to do and the guys have enough on their hands with school, ranch work and preparing for the rodeo."

It was true.

"Besides, I only agreed to let y'all help for a short term. And my agent really needs me to get busy."

True again.

"You're sure this doesn't have anything to do with me grabbing you like a jerk and kissing you?"

She stared up at the rafters for a moment, engrossed in the moths playing in the lamplight as she stalled for time.

"Maybe some. But you have been nothing but great to me since the moment I moved in here. It's me. There's—" She stopped speaking and took a deep breath.

He waited.

"I didn't tell you the whole story the other day."

You haven't told her the complete story, either. "Look, about that. I need to say something here," he said.

She shook her head. "No. I need to tell you something first. I think you deserve to know so you understand."

His gut burned with the need to come clean. It was as if once he'd realized Lucy deserved to know, he needed to get it out. But ladies go first. "Okay, then you first."

"I've told you that my husband was having an affair when he died. It's hard to think about, much less talk about."

Lucy's expression was so mingled with anger and sorrow he wanted to put his arms around her and comfort her. But he couldn't move.

He caught himself before blurting out that her husband was an idiot. "Who in their right mind would do that to you?" He finally said what he'd been thinking ever since she'd first told him about her husband's cheating.

She wrapped her arms together across her midriff and held his serious gaze with one of her own. "Tim Dean Calvert, that's who."

Tim Dense Calvert. "So were you still together when the fire happened?" he asked, wanting to know more—he'd felt from her first revelation that there was more to this story. She'd said they were asleep. So she'd overlooked the affair. That didn't strike him as the Lucy he knew.

"I didn't know. I found out afterward."

"Afterward. So were you having problems?" What was he pumping her for information for? *Did you love the guy when he died?* The question slammed into him and he held it back.

"Not as far as I knew. Well, some. Things had gotten tense. But you know, that happens." She took a deep breath and stared at the clouds as if seeking her next words. "I woke up and found I was in a burn center and my husband was dead. I was grieving when…the next day a woman came to my room."

He didn't like the way this story was going at all.

Her eyes glittered. "She was bitter and blamed me for the fire that had killed the man she was in love with. She told me about the affair and that Tim had planned to leave me for her. I mean, honestly, how could I have been so blind?" She took a deep breath but he couldn't find words.

"Once I got out of the hospital, several friends came to me and told me they'd known of Tim's infidelities. *Infidelities.* As in more than this woman. But they hadn't known how to tell me…so they'd said nothing."

Rowdy started to speak but she picked back up as if once she'd started talking she couldn't stop.

"I haven't looked at anything the same since. So many things came to light about the real Tim that I had to take a good hard look at my life. I think I knew deep in my heart something wasn't right, but I just hadn't wanted to face it."

The look on her face told him she'd begun to question herself in that time. He couldn't even imagine how horrible that had been for her. Burned as bad as her neck and arm were, and the pain she must have been in both physically and emotionally. And that was before being confronted by the other woman.

"Unbelievable," he said at last. "That explains the walls." It all made perfect sense now.

And he was toast.

She shivered though it wasn't cold. "Yes, it's been two

years and I'm still angry. But coming here has been good for me. And those walls, though great therapy, haven't been completely satisfactory in ridding me of the anger. Or my other issues."

"Other issues?" *Please, Lord, don't let her have gone through something else.*

She looked almost apologetic. "You've been nothing but nice to me, but I can't get past the broken trust. I don't know that I'll ever trust a man to get close to me…ever. I think you should know that since I reacted so badly the other day."

Burned toast. Rowdy rubbed his jaw, completely understanding Liz's husband trying to break it with his fist. Rowdy would have found great satisfaction in breaking Tim *Dense* Calvert's jaw.

"And now that you know, you'll understand why I'd like you to not kiss me again."

His blood was rushing in his head so fast he was dizzy. "Sure," he managed. Any chance he might have thought he had with Lucy was gone. Period. If she found out about what he'd done, she'd probably hold it against him.

"Now, what were you going to tell me?"

"Aah, I… It's not important." God forgive him but he couldn't tell her. Not right now. She suddenly looked tired, defeated and he just couldn't add more on top of that—at least that was his excuse to keep his mouth shut.

"Then I think I'll call it a night."

"Yeah, me, too." He needed to get out of there.

He stood up and took her hand, tugging her up and away from the edge, not taking any chances she was going to tip over. There was that same electrical voltage sparking from her to him but he played cool, letting go the minute she was safe.

They walked one behind the other down the steps and across the yard. His mind was racing and guilt kept trying to suffocate him. "I'll see you later," he said, stopping at his truck.

She turned and walked backward a few steps. "Yes. Later. Good night."

And then she spun around, hurried up the steps and disappeared through the door without another glance.

Toast. How had he ever been so stupid? He had a horrible feeling that the best thing that had ever happened to him had just walked out of his life.

Chapter Eleven

The music was already playing when Lucy walked into the side door of the church—a rustic-looking building set on a hill overlooking the town. She'd been planning to visit ever since she'd arrived, but had found herself dragging her feet. Today she knew she needed to be here. Dew Drop had a couple of churches, but Nana had told her this was where they worshipped, and so she'd come to visit. She'd stayed home the first couple of Sundays in town, settling in. It was a lame excuse, she knew, but since her life had turned upside down, she'd only gone to church sporadically. She'd had anger issues to deal with. She wasn't angry with God, but with Tim. She was determined to put that all behind her. She prayed that God would ease the knot that had buried deep in her heart.

The interior of the church was different from most, also rustic looking with concrete floors and cedar walls.

Mabel and Ms. Jo were the first to greet her.

"Lucy, it is good to see you here." Mabel hunched down and engulfed Lucy in a hug. The overpowering scent of magnolias clung to Lucy even after Mabel let go of her.

"You'll learn to run when you see her coming," Ms. Jo said, eye to eye since they were both less than five foot. "Mabel, she's blue. Do you see that? One of these days you're gonna let loose of someone and they're gonna already have gone to their heavenly reward."

Lucy chuckled, trying to breathe past the magnolia fumes stuck to the white blouse she was wearing with her slacks. "I'll live, so rest easy that it won't be me," she said, tugging her collar close, making sure it was in place. "I'm glad to see y'all." It was so true. They'd been so nice coming out to the house and welcoming her.

"Then come on over here and sit with us." Mabel locked her arm through Lucy's and started walking her toward the pews that were set in rows. Lucy almost had to run to keep up with Mabel's long strides.

"Dragging the poor girl around like a rag doll," she heard Ms. Jo grunt.

Mabel ignored her as the band of men with guitars up on the platform stood and began strumming. "We've been hearing good things from Ruby Ann, haven't we, Jo?" Mabel pulled Lucy into a pew in the middle section.

"Said Rowdy's become a regular over at your place." Ms. Jo pushed her round glasses up on her pert nose, her intelligent eyes seeing right through Lucy—or at least that was how it felt.

"That's what she said, all right. He's a wild one, but worth taming, if you know what I mean."

Lucy wasn't sure she wanted to know. And she was about to say there was nothing personal between them when the band let loose with a foot-stompin' version of "I'll Fly Away."

Ms. Jo went to clapping and Mabel did, too—thankfully she'd let go of Lucy's arm. Now that she was settled, she realized that the band consisted of Mr. Drewbaker Mackintosh playing a guitar. His pal Mr. Chili Crump was getting after it on a fiddle. There were a couple of other young cowboys playing guitars that she didn't recognize. The lead singer, though, she thought worked for Sunrise Ranch.

With Mabel and Ms. Jo settled in enjoying the music, Lucy relaxed. She looked around and saw the boys lined up in two rows. B.J. was sitting beside Rowdy, looking at her. He lifted his hand and gave her a small wave.

She smiled at him, then went back to watching the band. She didn't want Rowdy to catch her looking at him. The last thing she needed was for him to think she was staring at him. He sure did look nice in his crisp burgundy shirt and starched jeans. Her gaze wandered back to his direction when the band started playing George Strait's "I Saw God Today."

Ms. Jo caught her looking and grinned. "Don't you just love Cowboy Church? A little traditional mixed with our cowboy culture. That George is telling the truth in this song. All you have to do is look around to see God's working miracles everywhere."

Lucy did not know exactly what to think of that statement. She had a feeling she was talking about more than the song itself.

When the band ended and the preacher stepped up to the podium, she had to force herself to concentrate and not let her mind wander across the aisle to Rowdy.

She'd opened up to him about Tim. It wasn't something she talked about. But once she'd started telling him the whole ugly story, she couldn't stop. Maybe it was simply because she'd made him think the kissing freakout she'd had was his fault, when she'd known it really wasn't. And maybe it was because she was attracted to him and he was attracted to her and he needed to know the boundaries. It was only fair.

She was facing things straight on now, or at least looking at life with her eyes wide-open. No more sleeping on the job for her. She did not need a man in her life. She didn't need the headache of always looking over her shoulder. She had Tim to thank for that.

Her gaze slid to Rowdy again. His dark hair lay smooth at the nape of his neck and almost touched his collar— *What was she doing?*

Lucy yanked her gaze away and stared at the preacher. She concentrated on what he was saying.

"…Psalm 147 says, 'He heals the brokenhearted and binds up their wounds.'"

Lucy couldn't move; the words were so relevant for her. As if the Lord had been listening to her heart.

But it wasn't that easy for wounds to heal.

Beating down walls was far easier than letting go. Her gaze shifted back to Rowdy, who had yet to glance her way as far as she could tell. She'd told him to leave her alone when it came to a relationship. Made it perfectly clear and he'd agreed on the spot. Her wounds were too deep to completely heal.

Just too deep…

Sunday after church, the arena was full as the boys practiced for the ranch rodeo. He wasn't sure if Lucy would show up, given that she'd been kicked during the first practice and then there was the uncomfortable situation he'd put them in with the kiss. And then there was his past and her past and the fact that there was not going to be any meeting in the middle.

Their situation ate at him. He hadn't been able to get the fact that there seemed no solution to help their relationship out of his mind. He'd gotten up before daylight and started riding the new horse just because riding and thinking went hand in hand for him.

But it hadn't helped him much this morning. Lucy was a hard woman to figure out, and she'd been through more than any woman should have to go through.

He let her have her space at church that morning. He was glad she was there. When the service was over, he'd stopped by where she was talking to the boys and reminded her of practice in case she wanted to come. He'd had to force himself to look at her. After the preacher's sermon about wounds and how God could mend the brokenhearted, he'd started praying that He would do this for Lucy. But he knew it would take time. And even then with his past, there was no hope.

They'd been practicing for about thirty minutes and there was no sign of her. He hated it, that he'd made her uncomfortable…that he'd messed his life up and that the consequences of his past stood between them like a mountain.

"Lucy's coming!" Sammy called, riding his horse over to the fence and waving his coiled rope in the air as Lucy's black Dodge pulled to a stop beside the arena.

Rowdy's chest felt like a steel band had just clamped down around it, and he forced himself to hold back. Morgan rode up beside him.

"Looks like it's your lucky day," he said, smiling.

"Yeah, I wish. She's out of my league, bro."

"Well, that's true, but sometimes that doesn't matter. Jolie picked me."

He knew Morgan was trying to make him feel better, but Morgan hadn't done the things he'd done. Morgan had always been a hardworking class act—yeah, he'd been irritating as all get-out growing up, but it was true. Rowdy had been the wild child, living recklessly and choosing unwisely. He was just thankful that God hadn't let go of him through all of his prodigal-son days.

Regret was a hard companion, though, and despite having his life on track, it trailed him like a bloodhound.

Lucy was smiling and kidding with the boys as she climbed to the top rail of the arena. She wore her long-sleeved shirt and her stiff collar. Her beautiful hair cascaded around her shoulders. Her smile was contagious.

Feeling like a stack of horseshoes was stuck in his throat, he rode over and forced a grin. He might not have a future with her, but he could be her friend.

"So are you here to watch or are we going to have another go at it?" Okay, not the best word choice.

"I'm here to milk a wild cow." There was challenge in her eyes. "That was the bargain I made with the fellas."

"We don't want you gettin' hurt." Wes came out of a holding pen where he'd been helping B.J. learn to wrestle a small calf. "Ain't that right, little dude?" he asked, scrubbing B.J.'s head with his knuckles. B.J. grinned and twisted away, laughing as he ran over and climbed up the fence to Lucy.

"We don't want you to get hurt, but if I can learn, I know you can, too. It's fun. You shoulda just seen me take that calf over there down. I mean, I locked him in a headlock like Wes just done me, and that dude came right off his feet. You should try that."

Lucy had started smiling halfway through the boy's excited words. He was standing on the rungs with his hands on the rail behind him, grinning at her. She smoothed his hair out of his eyes and Rowdy's admiration of her went up yet another notch. She got that these boys craved love from the adults around them. The small kids especially needed the attention of the women who were in their lives.

That he was jealous of her gentle touch was understandable. Only a fool wouldn't want to get close to Lucy, so at least he recognized that he had grown smarter over the past little while.

"You know," he said, a thought hitting him. "B.J. has a good idea. Learning to wrestle a calf would be good for you. It would help you with your reflexes and make you more comfortable being around the cattle."

She looked at him for the first time. He felt the spark of electricity that arched between them all the way to the tips of his boots.

"I'll do whatever you cowboys think I should. You may make a cowgirl out of me yet."

"It won't be hard," Joseph said, grinning affably. "If you just change your sledgehammer skills over to cowboy'n, you'll leave us in your dust."

That got hoots, and she made a cute face at them all.

"Then let's get to it," Rowdy said, needing action rather than sitting in the saddle mooning over what he couldn't have.

Climbing from the top rail, Lucy felt glad. Sitting there trying not to stare at Rowdy had been hard. But the boys were so sweet and she was determined to make them proud of her.

Wrestling a calf sounded perfect. At the moment, she had so much pent-up frustration about the entire situation that her life was in she could probably milk a wild cow and wrestle a bull at the same time.

Of course, she thought a little late, after she was already in the pen with the calf and Rowdy, that she was doomed. Goodness, her senses were in overdrive standing there beside him.

"Okay, I'm going to hold him. What you need to do is lock your elbow like this." He held his arm crooked to illustrate.

"Like Wes had me," B.J. called. "You just don't give the calf a knuckle to his noggin."

Lucy laughed despite her nerves. "Okay, I'll remember that."

"Once you have him like that, lean back and he'll flip with you. A bigger calf is going to be harder but if you put your determination into the elbow lock and twist he's going to do just what you ask."

Looking up, she got lost in his eyes. Her throat cramped and she couldn't speak. She nodded instead and ripped her gaze from his and back to the calf.

"I can do this," she said, accepting the challenge. Wanting the challenge. "I don't need you to hold him."

"Show him you're the boss."

A roar of agreement went up from the boys gathered tight around the pen.

She laughed hesitantly and shot Rowdy a glare. It was his fault after all. The man smelled of leather and something so tantalizing she wanted to lock him in a neck hold. What was she thinking? "I've got this."

He grinned and waved an arm. "Go for it," he said, backing out of the way to lean against the fence panel, arms crossed and a too-cute-for-words expression on his face.

She took a step toward the calf and suddenly there was no standing still. The animal bolted toward the fence, faked left then turned right. She went left and landed in the dirt. A roar of laughter erupted behind her. Gritting her teeth, she was up in a second. The animal might be small but it was quick. Something bigger might have been easier than this. But she was not going to let it get the better of her.

It raced past her again and she grabbed its head, tripped and was suddenly being dragged around like a rag doll. How embarrassing was that?

Letting go, she was once more on the ground looking at the underbelly of the calf as it jumped over her. Rolling over, Lucy managed to grab its tail as it flew past and off they went. Hanging on, her ears ringing, her teeth chattering, she spat dirt as she sought to pull her feet around and get them back under her. She almost had her feet under her when the calf kicked a hoof back— Lucy let go in reflex and the foot missed her by a breath.

"It's okay, Lucy. You got nothing to be ashamed of."

She glanced at Sammy with his skinny face and big brown eyes. "Honest. I didn't know how to do that, either, 'bout six months ago."

"Thanks, kiddo," she grunted, pushing up from the dirt. Rowdy reached down and took her elbow, helping her up.

He was grinning. "You've got gumption, that's for sure."

"Is that what it is?"

"Yup. It's a respect builder. And you've just earned some stripes." He winked at her and suddenly Lucy felt ten feet tall.

As she looked around at the fence Wes and Joseph

gave her a thumbs-up. Tony followed and then all the boys copied all the older guys.

Taking a deep breath, she pushed her hair out of her face. "I guess Rome wasn't built in a day."

"Nope." Rowdy let go of her elbow, his hand coming to cup her chin. Her heart kicked. "You have dirt—" He gently brushed his fingers beneath her right eye.

All the air in the universe stalled at his touch. "Thanks," she said breathlessly.

He let his hand drop, looking suddenly as if he'd just been caught stealing money from the benevolence fund. "Sorry. I forgot," he said for her ears only, and stepped away.

Forgot what? Oh…*that.*

So had she!

Chapter Twelve

The diner was crowded Monday morning as Rowdy and Morgan made their way inside.

He'd come to town to pick up feed and met Morgan coming out of the post office. They'd decided to stop for a piece of pie—it was hard to pass up and Rowdy needed to talk to Morgan anyway.

Weaving their way to a table, they shook hands with several regulars as they went. Drewbaker and Chili were sitting at the first booth. They had the *Dew Drop News* spread open over their coffee mugs.

"Hey, hey, McDermotts," Drewbaker said, pointing at his plate of pie with his fork. "Try the chocolate. It's extra nice today. Jo was feeling particularly generous with the cocoa when she whipped these together."

Chili nodded as he stuffed a forkful of it into his mouth. "Good stuff," he mumbled.

"I'm convinced." Morgan chuckled.

Rowdy looked back at Chili as they slid into the booth at the back. "Don't choke on that." The older man hiked a brow and plopped another forkful into his mouth in answer.

"So what's your poison?" Edwina the waitress asked, coming to stand beside their table. "Food or dessert first?" Edwina had the coarse voice of gravel in a grinder and the dry humor to match.

"No 'how do you do' or anything?" Rowdy teased. "My feelings are hurt."

"As they should be. This smile of mine has been known to cause men to faint," she drawled. "I finally understand why all three of my ex-husbands just lay around the house during our years of matrimonial torture—they'd passed out from my smile. And all that time I mistakenly called them lazy no 'counts."

Morgan and Rowdy both grinned. Edwina hadn't had the best record with men. At least she could joke about it.

"You're probably right. No need to smile on our 'counts," Morgan said.

"Yeah, I've got horses to ride when I get home," Rowdy added. "No time for passing out, so it's just as well you keep your frown firmly planted downhill."

She tugged her pencil from the crease of her ear. "You two always were the smarter ones— Well, I take that back. Rowdy, you've still got some catching up to do. But I'll tell you what. If I decide to tag a fourth husband to my belt, I'll give you first shot. How's that sound? And Tucker already turned me down, just so you know."

"Well, Ed, that sounds like a plan. In the meantime I'll have coffee and a piece of the chocolate pie the boys recommended. And I'm wounded that you made the offer to Tucker first."

"Hey, he's the law around these parts. It was just smart thinkin' on my end. But he's passin' on my beauty. Morgan, what about you?"

"Ed, are we still talking marriage or pie?"

She gave her lopsided grin that took up most of one side of her face. "You're taken already, so we're talking pie."

"Then I'll have the same as Rowdy."

"Back in a jiffy."

When she was gone Morgan asked, "So what's the story with you and Lucy? If I had just suspected something was going on, it was made perfectly clear in the pen with the calf yesterday."

Rowdy leaned in. "I messed up. I kissed her."

There was a heavy pause as Morgan let the words sink in. "So that's it. It's plain you two have a connection."

"It was a stupid thing to do. She's had it rough and—" he shifted uncomfortably "—with my past, when she learns of it, I won't be her fondest friend. As it is, she's had it so rough that trusting a man is the last thing she's going to do and one who just hauls off and kisses her? Big mistake." He kept his voice low. There was no way he wanted anyone else hearing what he had to say. Talking about this in the diner was a mistake.

"I'm impressed."

Rowdy was not in the mood for jokes, and the glare he shot Morgan said as much.

"Hey, I'm serious. You obviously have some good emotions going on for Lucy if you're this concerned. That's a good thing."

"I'm not so sure about that. I'm supposed to be changed—to be moving slowly where women are concerned—and here I up and kissed her."

Edwina walked up with their pie and he leaned back again and tried to look relaxed.

She gave him the eagle eye as she placed the plate

and his coffee in front of him. "You look like you ate a porcupine while I was gone."

"You got that right," he said, giving her a halfhearted smile.

"Eat this pie and all your troubles will disappear. If they don't, take it up with Ms. Jo." She shook her head and walked away to bring words of wisdom to the next table.

Rowdy cut a big bite of the chocolate pie and let the rich flavor give him some comfort as he mulled over the situation.

Morgan did the same. After a few minutes, Morgan said, "Don't beat yourself up. Women are just hard to read sometimes. But there's something going on here, or it wouldn't matter to either one of you. Give it time. You're making progress, and don't forget that."

Rowdy drank his coffee, his mind tumbling over itself thinking about Morgan's words. Progress. Was he?

He hoped so.

But there were some things even progress couldn't help.

The contractor had started working on her studio and had informed her that the barn had good sturdy bones. He'd have the loft finished in a couple of weeks.

Wonderful!

Or at least it should be, but she wasn't in the best of moods. Lucy hopped to her feet. She had to get outside; a walk would do her good.

There was only a mild breeze blowing across the endless pastures as she started walking. Moose pranced behind her, stalking grasshoppers along the way.

The sky was a gorgeous cerulean-blue, the clouds

perfect for painting. Despite her foul mood, the walk seemed to clear out some of the negativity and she was not quite as down as she made her way back up the hill thirty minutes later.

To her surprise, Tony was sitting on her back porch playing with Moose, who'd abandoned her not long after she'd started the walk. When he saw her, Tony jerked to his feet.

"Hi, Lucy."

"Hey, yourself," she said, feeling better just seeing him.

He looked nervous, she realized. "Is something wrong, Tony?"

He sat back down on the porch and Moose curled against his side. "Can I ask you something?"

"Sure." Lucy sat down on the other side of Moose.

"I saw your scars the other day."

Lucy took a long breath. She'd never talked to him and Wes and Joseph about seeing her scars. "I thought so."

"You know I have them, too."

The words took her by surprise. "I'm sorry, I didn't know."

He was such a handsome kid and he now pinned serious eyes on her. Pain was shining in them. "My parents… Anyway, I've been thinking about it and watching you. And I figured out you're not comfortable with them. Me, either, just so you know."

She didn't know what to make of this. Why had he come? She looked around to see how he'd gotten there and spotted a horse tied to the fence. It was almost hidden by a huge oak tree.

"It's been bugging me, and I had to come make sure you knew you weren't alone."

Lucy blinked back the threat of tears. Tony was concerned for her. How bad were his scars? she wondered. And she was afraid to know how he got them, realizing that he'd almost said something about his parents. Surely not from them?

"Thank you for your concern. I'm so sorry you've suffered, too. And you're right that I'm shy about them. They—" She started to say they made people uncomfortable, but how could she say that without telling him his scars did the same? The thought of this kid being handicapped by the fear of others seeing his scars just didn't sit well with her. She couldn't do it, so she changed her words. "I was burned two years ago."

"I was ten—when I came here and it stopped."

Lucy's stomach turned. *It stopped*. What did that mean?

He stood up. "Anyway, just came by to say that I enjoyed your classes."

Lucy's heart clutched. "You did?"

He nodded and gave her a half grin. "Don't tell the fellas, though. You know—" he shrugged "—I was thinking it might be cool to paint something on the ranch. There's some pretty places here. I figure some of the others might like that, too."

She smiled and suddenly felt like crying with happiness. "Thanks for telling me, Tony. About everything. And I think I can get us to paint a ranch scene."

He nodded, ducked his head and headed for his horse, and within moments was riding across the pasture toward the ranch.

Lucy watched him go. "Moose," she whispered. "I have an art class to prepare for."

And she had questions that needed answering.

Hopping in her truck, she headed down the road toward Sunrise Ranch, feeling so sorry for Tony but also like the sun had just risen. She knew how to get the boys' attention now. Classes were going on over at the school; Jolie's cranberry-colored Jeep sat out beside the building. Lucy parked her truck in front of the Chow Hall and met Randolph coming out the door.

"Hi, Lucy. Everything going good?"

"Hi, I was looking for Nana. Is she around?"

Randolph looked apologetic. "Sorry, she went grocery shopping. Is there anything I can help you with?"

Rowdy's dad was a handsome man with a great smile, like him. He had silver temples and coal-black hair otherwise. From what she'd learned of him, his wife had passed away before her dream of opening the ranch up as a foster home became reality. Randolph and Nana had worked hard to make her dream happen and, all these years later, he was still devoting his life to better the lives of all the boys who had come and gone. And he'd never remarried. For all the trust issues she had, she couldn't help but admire him.

"I bet you can. I'm sure you've heard that art class could be better, but I have an idea about that. I need some places on the ranch where we can take the guys and let them paint in the open. Something really great to hold their attention. Can you give me some suggestions?"

"I think that's a great idea." He looked thoughtful for a moment. "But the man for this job is Rowdy. Why don't you head over there through the stable to the round pen? He's working a horse. Rowdy knows this ranch better than all of us. He can show you some spots and then you can go from there."

It was inevitable—once again Rowdy was the answer. And besides, she needed to talk to him about Tony.

She'd tried for the past few days, since the roping, to not think about him but she hadn't succeeded. He'd snuck into her thoughts every time she let her guard down.

"Thanks, I'll head over there now."

"He'll fix you up," Randolph said, and headed toward his truck.

Lucy crossed the yard and walked into the stable.

"Hi, Lucy," Walter Pepper called from inside a stall where he was brushing down a black horse.

"Hi, Mr. Pepper. I'm looking for Rowdy," she said. He grinned and pointed toward the doors on the other end. "Thanks."

The scents of hay and feed tickled her nose as she went, and the anticipation of seeing Rowdy tickled her stomach.

The round pen was just out the back with Rowdy inside astride a beautiful horse. Tan with a black mane, the animal was as handsome as the cowboy riding him.

As he concentrated, Rowdy was at an angle to her, and while she could see his face in profile she knew that he hadn't seen her. She leaned against the side of the stables and watched, mesmerized.

The horse made a quick maneuver forward, then cut left, then right. The movements would have tossed Lucy out of the saddle and straight into the dirt. But Rowdy was almost like a part of the horse, and not only stayed in the saddle but in control.

Lucy knew enough about quarter horses to know in

a real-life situation there would be a calf or cow breaking for freedom. The horse was trained to cut in front
of it and get it to go where he wanted it to.

She knew Rowdy had made a name for himself in a
competition setting with several of the ranch's quarter
horses. Unable to help herself, she'd looked him up on
the internet and had been stunned to see how successful he was.

He'd never mentioned that. Never said anything other
than that he ran the cattle operation of the ranch.

She wasn't sure how long she watched him before
he saw her. And her heart betrayed her when it jumped
the instant his gaze touched hers across the round pen
railing.

Beefing up her determination, she gave him a small
wave. "Hey."

He walked the horse over to where she stood. "This
is a surprise. I hadn't expected to see you."

"Yes, well, I need your help." *Keep it about the boys.
This doesn't have to be personal.* "I need you to show me
some places you think the boys would like to try to paint."

He just stared at her for a minute. "Okay," he said at
last. "Give me a minute and then we'll load up."

The butterflies that had been hibernating since she'd
last seen Rowdy came alive—and the way her pulse was
pounding it felt as though each one of them was working a sledgehammer.

"Sure, sounds good." She managed to hold her voice
steady despite the construction site her insides had suddenly become.

Truth was, turning around and running back to her
place sounded much better. Much safer.

Much, much safer.

* * *

Sunrise Ranch was made up of ten thousand acres, and they leased another ten thousand from surrounding landowners. It wasn't the King Ranch by any means, but it was a manageable size and a beauty.

He'd offered several options when he and Lucy had first climbed into his truck. The river, the valleys— What did she have in mind? She'd said for him to show her his favorite places because places that touched one person would touch others.

There was nothing personal in her voice when she said the words. It was business. Sure. At least she was speaking to him. That was a positive. She might not want him to kiss her, but she didn't seem to mind being around him. That was good for now. He didn't know how long that would last.

"There will be lots of things to see on the way to the spots I've got in mind," he'd said. "So if you see something you like, just let me know and we'll stop and check it out."

She had a camera with her. And a sketch pad. She'd nodded and they'd been on their way. Neither had said much since then and it had been a good twenty minutes. He was afraid of opening his mouth too soon and her telling him to take her back to her truck. At least this far out it was a safe bet that she'd not want to try walking when he made her mad.

Not that he was going to do that intentionally. Nope, he was keeping this conversation as nonrisky as possible.

She'd been sitting over there hugging the door, as rigid as a T-post. But now her shoulders had relaxed and she had settled back into the seat a bit. It was hard not to relax when driving across the ranch. The ranch had always given him a sense of peace. Even when he was at his most reckless, after he was in his teens and the anger at his mother's death had steeped for a few years, riding the ranch had been the place where he could think. Where he could almost feel God's touch.

It was that peace and beauty that his mother had loved. That she'd wanted to share with less-fortunate kids. He knew that was why he'd found comfort roaming the land his mother had loved. The kids… Back then they had been a major issue for him. He'd been a kid who'd lost his mother, and then suddenly he was forced to share his beloved ranch with other kids. At first he'd had trouble. Thankfully, he'd gotten over that within a year.

"This is gorgeous."

He almost jumped when she spoke. "Yeah, I think so."

"This is a great time, too—all these spring flowers in bloom. After the drought two years ago, I love seeing them again."

"Me, too." The drought had not only stressed the ranch out financially with the lack of grass but had also forced a sell-off of livestock in order to trim expenses down to a minimum. But the damage it had done to the land had been hard to stomach. Thankfully this year there had been a decent amount of rain and the wildflowers were a sign that things were on the mend.

"Stop!" she exclaimed as they rounded a curve on the barely visible ruts they called a road. In front of them, the road made a wide arch and then disappeared over the ridge. Wildflowers of a variety of colors with vivid splashes of pink and yellow jumped out at them.

Overhead, an eagle soared.

"You have eagles." She scrambled from the truck and started shooting photos in rapid fire.

Rowdy stayed watching her as she moved in front of the truck, then across to the side, taking shot after shot.

He wished he had a camera. Then, remembering he did, he grabbed his cell phone and started snapping pictures of her.

When the eagle soared over the ridge and finally disappeared she turned, smiling as wide as the eagle's wingspan, and came back to the truck and climbed in.

Rowdy's heart hammered like the staccato of a horse racing across a wooden bridge. She was beautiful.

Whoa, boy!

"Yeah," he said, his voice tight. "Let's get over that ridge and see what you say."

"I say that's a wonderful plan. I'm dying to know where this road goes."

Roads. Right. She painted roads.... He knew what was on the other side of the ridge, but for a moment he wondered where this road led, too. The one he and Lucy were on together. Maybe there wasn't any hope for him, but like Morgan said, he was making progress. Their road led somewhere.

"I love this spot," Lucy said a few minutes later, as she looked out over the rugged terrain. Once they'd topped the ridge, the wildflowers had diminished but the road turned into gravel, and the soft pink of buttercups and wild lavender verbena trailed through the scattered rocks along the road that sloped downhill to the base of a rocky ravine. Like a wall before them, the ravine rose up, and at the top a gorgeous, huge dogwood was in full bloom. Mid-April was the perfect time of year, and the dogwood wouldn't last long. Beauty was fleeting. But not for Lucy; he knew her beauty, her goodness, radiated from the inside.

He wondered if she even realized how beautiful she was. He wondered if she worried about her scars. He wished he could help her see that they didn't matter.

"It is breathtaking and manly. It might appeal to the boys. Can we transport art class out here tomorrow?"

He jerked his mind back to what she was saying. "Sure. Whatever you want."

"This is just to encourage them. We'll start out with background and slowly build from there with each lesson."

"Sounds good to me. I can't say I've ever painted, so I don't have a clue."

"Then you should join us."

He relaxed against the fender of his truck, watching her, and shook his head. "I'm not an artist. I want to see your work, not mine."

"You might surprise yourself. There could be a masterpiece or two inside of you."

He grinned. "I don't think so. My place is on the back of a horse."

"And you do a beautiful job of that. I enjoyed watching you work with that horse earlier."

That she'd said that pleased him. "Thanks."

She smiled, gave a nod and then, as if realizing suddenly they were staring at each other, she looked up at the dogwood. "I love what a dogwood stands for," she said. "God's love is so deep. My grandmother used to always tell me that the white color represented Jesus's purity. The four leaves represented His hands and feet and the burgundy indents on each leaf represented the blood He shed for us." She looked at him then, strong yet gentle.

"My mom used to tell me something similar. I think that's one reason this is the perfect place for the boys to paint."

She smiled. "They need every reminder we can give them that they are not only loved by us, but by God."

Rowdy's heart was banging again. This time it was because she got it. She got everything about Sunrise Ranch and the mission of it. "Yes. Exactly."

She sobered suddenly. "Rowdy, Tony came to see me this morning. I don't know if he skipped class, but if he did, I hope he didn't get into trouble. He needed to tell me something."

"He's a good kid. If he felt compelled to come see you, I know it was for a good reason. He won't be in trouble."

"Good. He—he came and told me he was burned, too. He told me he didn't want me to feel alone." She shook her head and swiped a tear from her cheek. "How could parents hurt their child like that?"

Rowdy wanted to hug her so badly he could barely stand it. "It happens every day," he said, his voice gruff. "It makes me furious, but I've come to realize that here on this ranch we can help heal their hearts. This is where *I* can make a difference. And that helps me. You're making a difference, too. Tony doesn't talk about his past much. So I know your scars are tough for you…but God just used them to touch a kid."

Her eyes filled with tears and she shook her head. "No, God used that beautiful, brave kid to touch me, too."

Chapter Thirteen

Using a few two-by-fours nailed together, the men constructed several easels for the kids' canvases, and Lucy watched as they loaded them in the back of the truck. Rowdy had hooked a trailer to the truck and threw some hay bales on it, and the boys were ready for a hayride across the ranch.

Lucy was pleased that the boys seemed more excited about the whole process.

"You mean I'm gonna get to paint a rock today. Not a flower?" B.J. asked the question with the serious eyes of an eight-year-old. As if painting a flower would give him cooties.

Jolie and Lucy both laughed at his seriousness. A rock rated very highly on his radar.

Lucy couldn't help reaching out to tousle his hair. "Yes, you will be able to look at the landscape I've chosen and focus on a rock if that's what you'd like to paint the most."

"All right!" he yelled, doing a jump and running off to grab Sammy's arm and give him the great news.

Jolie reached for another canvas to load on the trailer. "Kids—the funniest things make them happy."

"I know," Lucy agreed, carrying the case with the paint to the trailer. "I'm thrilled this outing is making them more excited."

"They just love being outside. And besides, they really were worried about you after you got kicked by that heifer. And then when you came back and held your own with that calf, you should have heard them talking about how you wouldn't give up. They like you, Calamity Lucy."

Lucy rolled her eyes. "They're really calling me that?"

"Just in teasing," Wes said, overhearing her comment. He was helping Rowdy load a cooler full of drinks. "Your house just barely missed imploding. One more wall and poof, down it would have come."

"I have to agree," Rowdy said. "The boys were thinking of confiscating the sledgehammer."

Lucy rolled her eyes. "Y'all are crazy. Jolie, they knocked out five walls. There are at least five still standing." She laughed.

Nana came out of the Chow Hall, followed by Joseph and Tony carrying another large ice chest. They'd already loaded one just as big.

"There's enough food in those two chests to serve an army, so you should be okay. And the third one Wes and Rowdy brought out is packed full of water and sodas."

Lucy went over and gave her a hug. "Thanks, this is going to be a good day."

"Me and the girls are champing at the bit to do this. Have you thought any more about offering us old fogies art classes?"

"I have, and the contractor started yesterday. The

place is going to be finished very quickly. It's nothing elaborate, more a rustic-cottage style. And if y'all are really interested, then I'd love to start a class and see how it goes."

"Wonderful! I'll tell the gals. They are going to be excited."

"I'd be interested, too," Jolie said. "It would be a great girls' night out."

Lucy was touched. "I'm getting more excited by the minute."

"Okay, load up," Rowdy called.

Morgan and Randolph had come out of the office.

"Have a good time," Morgan called to the boys. He slipped his arm around Jolie's waist and hugged her to his side. "This was a very good idea."

"Yes, I think so. Lucy's a gem for doing it."

"My pleasure."

Randolph had been talking to the boys who'd rushed the hay wagon. "Settle down when the trailer is in motion. I don't want any of you falling off and getting hurt."

Every one of the boys listened to him and stopped their good-natured pushing and shoving.

Rowdy grinned. "That's more like it. Okay, let's go paint us a rock." He shot a wink at B.J., who giggled and pumped his arm in the air.

Jolie and Lucy climbed in the truck with Rowdy and, since Jolie beat Lucy to the truck and claimed the backseat first, that left Lucy in the front seat with Rowdy.

Thoughts of him had hovered in the background of her thoughts since yesterday, and she wasn't pleased about that.

He'd agreed not to kiss her anymore and clearly had taken his hands-off promise seriously. But yesterday when she had gotten emotional talking about Tony, she'd wished he had folded her in those strong arms of his and held her close. Instead, he'd remained firmly where he was, and though his words were comforting, his arms had stayed locked tightly across his chest.

What was wrong with her? She'd gotten what she wanted, so she should be relieved.

But she wasn't. So far today he'd stayed on the fringes as they'd gotten everything loaded up. She thought he'd say he was dropping them off and coming back later to pick them up. But that wasn't so. Jolie had wanted one man out there with them since they were going to be a good distance from the compound. With this many crazy boys, they needed a man along.

Lucy was in agreement, but had half hoped Morgan would be the one to go. Or one of the many cowboys who worked at the ranch. But no, it was Rowdy and she was stuck.

Stuck in the middle of so many conflicting emotions, she felt dizzy.

She didn't want to put herself out there. She didn't want to put herself at risk again in a relationship. No matter how much she was beginning to wish she could each time she looked at Rowdy McDermott.

"It looks like a fat tick sitting on a pile of mud," Wes said, standing back and staring critically at his painting.

Rowdy had to agree with the kid. He hid a grin.

"Now, Wes," Lucy said, coming to stand beside the teen. "You've actually got some very good undertones in this. Now you need some variation of tones. Listen, guys. Brown is not simply made up of brown. If you'll look over there at that rock cluster for a minute, I'll explain again. See the way the sun glints off it? It looks lighter in that spot, right?"

Wes grunted what Rowdy took as a yes. And others agreed.

"To get that take your brush and dip it in the light ochre color, that's the yellowish color that I had you place on your palette. Then add it onto the rock like this." She demonstrated a quick dash on the rock and suddenly there was a little definition to Wes's tick.

"Hey, that's weird how it looks better."

Lucy chuckled, looking up at Wes. "It's really fun to see how different colors create what most people look at and see as a single color. That rock is made of lots of tones. Now you try it. Wipe your brush and add another tone. Mix a couple of tones together to make a completely new shade. Go have a close-up look at mine and see the various strokes."

Excited calls for help had her moving to the next kid, and she gave him her undivided attention. Rowdy enjoyed watching her in action.

Lucy was kind, and her goodness came across when she was dealing with the kids. He still couldn't understand her husband. How could a man do that to such a wonderful woman? It went against everything Rowdy believed in. He might not have dated wisely before but he could honestly say he believed in marriage. When he married, he'd be committing for life. And he was going to be looking for a woman of good character when he fell in love.

"You sure are in deep thought," Jolie said, coming to stand beside him.

"Hey, Pest, I'm a deep thinker. Haven't you figured that out after all this time?" He nudged her arm playfully. Jolie had grown up with them ever since she was about ten. And he'd been calling her Pest from day one.

"I totally have. So you like her a lot, huh?" She always had been too perceptive.

"What's not to like? But I'm afraid my past might be too much for her to handle. And with good reason. Some mistakes aren't fixable."

"Everyone deserves a second chance. You certainly do."

He slid a skeptical eyebrow up. "I don't know. Maybe, but it may not be something Lucy can accept. After hearing her story, I get it."

"You're all right, brother-in-law. Maybe time can merge your stories." She started to walk away, then turned. "She told you her story and that counts for something. Don't forget that. She shared some things about her past that she doesn't just share with anyone, so that's a good thing. Remember anything worth having is worth being patient for."

Patience. It was going to kill him.

Lucy was happy that the day was going so well. At noon they paused, and she and Jolie opened the ice chest and pulled out the lunch that Nana had so carefully created. The woman knew how to feed the masses, that was for certain. There were thick roast turkey sandwiches, sandwich bags full of homemade brownies and pound cake, plus chips and dips and cut vegetables. The woman thought of everything. And no telling how many hours she'd spent preparing the fare for "her boys," as she called them all.

"Your grandmother is amazing," Lucy said, when

Rowdy came to stand by her and watch as the boys raided the open ice chest like ants.

"Tell me something I don't know. She loves it. Lives for it actually." He looked thoughtful. "It's kind of weird, but this was my mother's dream, and when my dad took up the flag and carried it, Nana just took to it like it had been her destiny all along. God has a plan, doesn't He?"

Lucy stared at him, dumbfounded. "Yes, He does."

He looked a little uncomfortable. "Do you want to take a walk over there and eat on the trailer?"

The boys were sitting around on the ground with Jolie and asking her some questions about kayaking. The trailer was empty. "Sure," Lucy agreed.

He grabbed a couple of sandwiches and a couple of waters, then handing one each to her, they walked over to the trailer.

They both concentrated on opening their sandwiches and taking their first bite.

"Delicious." Nana could cook. The sandwich nearly melted in her mouth, it was so tender and juicy.

He just nodded and took a bite himself.

After a few minutes spent enjoying half the sandwiches, he nodded toward the paint setup. "This is good for them. Jolie had a great idea. Thanks for doing it."

She took a deep breath, studying the boys, then turned to him again. "They are so funny. And I'm loving it. You know, what you do is wonderful, also. Teaching them to work cattle and have fun at the same time. It's a good thing, Rowdy. You said the other day that this was where you could make a difference and it's true. You are." She meant it, too. Rowdy's attitude, his ability to lift the boys up with his teasing banter and his ability to be one of them was a gift.

He didn't say anything for a moment, just looked at her thoughtfully, and she wondered what he was thinking. "Thanks, that means a lot."

She thought for a moment he was going to say something else, but then his lip quirked up on one side and moved into a tight smile as he rose. "I guess we'd better join the group. They look like they're getting restless."

It was true, Sammy had just slipped a handful of dirt down Caleb's shirt and a dirt fight was in the making. "Yup, you definitely need to step in on that," she said, and followed him as he strode toward the "fun" breaking loose.

He'd been about to say something before duty called—and as she followed him she couldn't help wondering what it had been. There was more to Rowdy than met the eye—more than the good-time cowboy— and she was certain of that.

Not that it changed anything.

Over the next week Lucy spent time getting the house cleaned up. She had the floor people come out and look at the floors that needed replacing because she'd ripped the walls out, and they were coming back at the end of the week to lay the new floors. Thankfully the contractor had come into the house and spent one day finishing the wall openings that she'd made. Her house was coming together.

Sitting at the breakfast bar and sipping a cup of coffee, she had her computer opened and was studying the photos she had taken of the ranch. She had a problem— she needed to find new places to paint. Her fingers were finally itching to work. It felt so right—like a long-lost friend returning.

The gloom that had hung over her past few paintings

had disappeared and the sun had finally come back out for her.

Pausing on one of the photos she'd taken, she saw that she'd captured Rowdy's contagious come-play-with-me smile. The man just oozed charisma. She didn't even remember snapping the picture, but she'd been shooting rapid-fire clicks and there he was. She took a sip of her coffee and studied the photo.

Instantly, her pulse skittered. When he looked at her, Lucy couldn't explain the feelings that swept through her.

Sunshine.

Warmth, and excitement. Not to mention that she lost her train of thought and her good sense at the same time.

The small voice in the back of her mind warned that he—that men—couldn't be trusted. And yet he'd done nothing to make her think otherwise. In fact, she'd moved to the outskirts of Dew Drop and found herself immersed in a male-dominant area. Men were everywhere, and if they weren't men they were boys, teens and nearly men.

And they were all good to her.

How could she hold Tim's sins against them?

Her finger tapped rapidly on the counter beside the computer as frustration set in. She couldn't help the fear that gripped her when thinking about letting a man have the power to hurt her like that again.

Standing, she snapped off the computer and walked outside. Moose was sitting on the corner of the porch railing cleaning his paws with his tongue. He stopped and stared at her with green eyes as if assessing her.

"Hey, Moose, don't judge me," Lucy snapped, and headed out to see the progress of her studio. It had only been a week, and yet the contractor was making good time. His crew of four guys worked like ants, each with a job to do, and they were getting it done. Which was great because Margo, her agent, had been leaving messages. She had to have something new soon. The art show of the year was coming up and she needed to have something in it. True, but until now she'd not wanted to think about it.

Mac stuck his head out of the large window that they'd already installed on the side of the loft. "Hey, Lucy, got a second to come up here?"

"On my way." Taking a big breath, she headed to the studio and banished thoughts of Rowdy right out of her mind.

Walking into the barn, she stared toward the loft area that only extended out over half the ground floor. The wall was almost finished that would close it off from the downstairs except for a large window that would enable her to look out over the first floor. Hurrying up the stairs, she pushed open the door and stepped into her new studio.

"What do you think?" Mac asked. He was a large man with a jovial smile. "Give me a couple more days and she's all yours."

"Are you kidding me? It's only been a week."

"We buckled down and since I brought the men in from the other job that stalled out on us, we were able to double up on the work. You'll be painting in here next week. If that's okay with you."

"It's more than okay. I can hardly wait."

The floors were white pinewood planks they'd laid then stained and sealed. Overhead they'd left the rafters open. The focal point was the large window on the outer wall of the barn, allowing her a gorgeous view of the house and valley. It let the much-needed light stream into the room. On the back wall was a cabinet with storage for her supplies. And then there was the wall space for showcasing her work as it was being finished.

"This is fantastic." She gave the man a hug and he blushed.

"I'm going to have to see some of your work. I may want to buy my wife a present."

"I need to get crackin' and get some subject matter."

"Boy, you live near some of the prettiest country in these parts."

"I know. I've been exploring some." She told him about teaching the boys art lessons and he was impressed.

"You've got the best showing you the place. Rowdy was always exploring growing up. He spent days at a time camping all over that ranch. He knows every nook and cranny, that's for sure."

A few minutes later Lucy was in her car heading to the ranch. If Rowdy was the best to help her find the unique beauty of the ranch, then she was going to ask him to show her around some more. After all, they were neighbors, and they were just going to have to put this thing between them aside.

He was doing his part. She had to do hers and stop thinking about him all the time.

Maybe the more they got used to being around each other, the easier it would be.

Sure it would. She was ready to try, anyway. And the need to paint gave her incentive to overcome anything.

Even Rowdy.

* * *

Rowdy was mounting his horse when Lucy drove into the yard. Mixed emotions slammed into him at the same time. He was glad to see her, but at the same time seeing her sure made it hard on a guy who was trying keep her off his mind.

"Hi," she said, hopping out of her truck.

He tugged on the cinch of his horse. He knew good and well it was just fine, but it gave him something to do. Lucy wore large black shades that hid her eyes and he regretted the loss, but at the same time not seeing those eyes helped him.

"No art class or wrestling class today." He hadn't meant his words to sound negative. "What's got you out and about?"

"I need more scenes. Places that inspire me to paint. And I was wondering if I could impose on you again and ask you to show me around some more?"

He concentrated on his saddle. Patience and progress. She was torturing him.

"Sure," he said, finally looking at her. She and God were determined to make this hard on him. "I'm riding over to check on the branding and you're welcome to ride, too. There's some places not too far that I could show you. Plus, I don't know if you're into a Western branding scene, but you'll sure see one."

She tugged her shades off, exposing those killer eyes. "That sounds great. But I'm not the best rider in the world. I've done it a few times but that's it."

"Cupcake will work great for you." She was going riding with him. The idea had him smiling even if he was going to have to be on his best behavior. "I'll go saddle her up and be right back."

"I'll get my stuff together."

"Stuff?"

"My camera."

He nodded. "Oh, right. Be back in a minute."

He had Cupcake saddled and ready in a flash and led the old horse out of the stable. Lucy stared at the big horse.

"She's big."

"And easygoing. This is a beginner horse. You'll be fine. I promise."

She nodded and he wondered if she was going to trust him. When she touched Cupcake's soft neck and spoke sweetly to the horse, he knew everything would be all right. Everything but him.

Lucy had to have Rowdy help her get into the saddle. She was far too short to get her leg up in the stirrup. He lifted her effortlessly and she grabbed the saddle horn and threw her other leg over the saddle. Rowdy had to give her a little shove so she could get up there and sit straight. Otherwise she'd have been hanging off to the side.

"Thanks," she murmured once she was settled. Hanging on to the saddle horn, she tried to look more confident than she felt. It had been a very long time. He looked up at her, his hand resting on her leg.

"You sure you're okay?"

"Uh-huh," she said, seeing something deep in the depths of his eyes that touched a dark corner of her heart. It shook her. "I'm fine."

He nodded, pulled his hand away and headed to his horse. In a graceful, fluid movement he stepped into the stirrup and swung his leg over the horse's back. He settled into the saddle as though it was as comfortable to him as sitting down or standing up.

Lucy would have gone home if she could have gotten off the horse by herself. What had she been thinking? It was as if the man was irresistible to her. How could that be?

"Okay, let's go." He and his horse took off as she took her reins. She tugged on them, then clicked her tennis shoes on Cupcake's sides to try to get the horse to follow Rowdy, who was already turning the corner at the arena.

"Come on, Cupcake. Don't make me look like an idiot." When the horse didn't move, she started making clicking noises and gently urging the horse with her heels again. "Yah," she said. "Giddyap."

Rowdy rode back to her. "You haven't done this much?"

"That's what I told you," she said irritably.

"Behave, Cupcake," he scolded the horse, and gave a gentle slap to the horse's rump. Cupcake started walking. Rowdy walked his horse beside them as they slowly started moving.

Lucy could feel the sting of embarrassment on her cheeks. She was probably as red as the horse stable.

They rode across the pasture in silence and over the incline. In the distance she could see a large group of cattle and a lot of horses and cowboys. There was a group bent down, working the branding irons, but from this distance she didn't recognize any of them. She wasn't sure if they let the boys out of school for something like this or not.

"Are the boys down there?" she asked at last.

"Yeah, they love to help with the branding. Jolie works with them to get their assignments done in a situation like this. Working on the ranch is a little different. We feel it gives the boys a sense of pride to join in and these boys need all of that they can get. Some are really beat down when they get to us. Their self-esteem is in the cellar and this helps boost them up."

"I think it's great. The entire situation is so inspiring. It makes me want to paint them."

He gave her a sidelong glance. "I think that's a good thing. Speaking of, when are you going to show me some of your work?"

He seemed insistent on seeing her work; she fought the smile that nearly burst to her lips. "My studio is almost done. Mac pulled in some extra help and cut the process in half. I'll have some paintings up then. Not that I keep many hanging around. Most are in the gallery in Austin and the gallery on the River Walk in San Antonio."

"I'll see what you have and maybe when I'm near I'll stop in at one of the galleries." He smiled, and she smiled back.

"You don't have to do that."

"I know, but I want to."

She didn't know what to say and suddenly looked as if he'd said something wrong.

"Hey, Mac is a good guy. I knew he'd do a good job for you. He's spent a lot of time out here," he said, suddenly wiping away the personal direction the conversation had taken.

She realized she didn't like the wall between them but she'd asked for it. "He told me. He also said the same thing your dad did, that you were the guy to show me the ranch."

"I'm your man. When it comes to seeing the ranch,"

he added quickly. "I tended to spend a lot of my rebel years camping out here alone any chance I got…and sometimes when I should have been in school."

They'd almost reached where the branding was in progress and she regretted it.

"So you came out here to be alone?" she asked over the lowing of fifty or so cattle.

"Yeah, I didn't take my mom's death all that well and then I had trouble sharing the ranch, at first, with a bunch of kids I didn't know or want to know."

So he'd been angry. "Life isn't always fair, is it?"

"Nope, but you would know all about that, wouldn't you? I got nothing on you. Or these boys here."

"Lucy!"

Lucy tugged her gaze away from his and searched for who was calling out to her. She spotted little B.J. waving from where he was carrying a branding iron to the calf a couple of cowboys were holding down.

"Watch me," he shouted. And then he branded the calf.

"He looks ten feet tall," she gasped. "You're a regular cowpoke," she called to him.

His smile was wider than he was. "I got the *moooves*," he mooed, making Lucy laugh.

"That kid blesses my soul."

Rowdy chuckled. "Yeah, he does that."

"I need to take pictures. Will I be in the way?"

"I'd rather you try to do it from the horse—unless you get the hankering to come down and help with the branding."

"I'll stay right here and, now that Cupcake has warmed up to me, I'll move around a little, too. Thanks for bringing me."

"Any time," he said, tipping his hat as he headed over to where the action was.

Reaching for her camera hanging from around her neck, she started snapping shots. She couldn't stop herself from letting the first shot be of Rowdy.

After all, he had brought her out here.

Chapter Fourteen

"I see you brought your friend," Tucker said, tugging his aviators down to let Rowdy see the questions in his McDermott-blue eyes.

Rowdy squinted through the haze at him, since the sun was over Tucker's shoulder and he hadn't worn his shades. "She's taking pictures—looking for subject matter for her artwork."

"That's why she just snapped your picture."

Rowdy's brother liked to kid. "Yeah, right."

"I'm serious. She pointed that camera straight at you as you rode off. Believe what you want, but the pretty lady got you on that camera of hers."

It was all he could do not to look over his shoulder. Or not to let the pleasure show from knowing Lucy had taken a picture of him. Maybe she wasn't as immune to him as she wanted to be. The idea gave him a shot of hope. One he knew he wanted more than anything he'd wanted in a long time.

Lucy was having a great time. She had quickly realized that cattle branding made for great photo opportunities. She had Cupcake trotting on the outskirts of the group so that she could get different angles and different facial expressions of the boys' faces as they worked. It was wonderful. One minute their faces were serious with concentration, then they were throwing their heads back and hooting with laughter at some joke someone told—usually that someone being Rowdy. The man was like a lightbulb even in the bright sunlight. He was so good with the boys.

Lucy's heart thrilled at the thought of capturing these images on canvas. It was a very welcome feeling, one she'd missed greatly.

Wes's cockiness reminded her of Rowdy. Joseph was so soft-spoken yet tenacious and Tony, the quiet one, shot her shy looks when he thought she wasn't watching him. And then there were the younger ones, so many of them so thrilled with being a working cowboy. All of the boys looked up to Morgan, Tucker and Rowdy.

They'd been working for about two hours when Rowdy pulled his hat from his head and slapped it across the front of his jeans. Dust rose about him and, just as he looked her way grinning, she snapped a shot that captured the pure essence of the man.

Her heart was thudding, and she lowered the camera, grabbed the reins and urged Cupcake to move on. She didn't need to look at Rowdy anymore—he made her stumble.

Made her stop thinking straight.

She decided it was time to head back to the barn and let Cupcake be free and, since they were all busy, she didn't bother them as she headed back toward the barn. But Cupcake had different ideas. Halfway to the crest, the goofy horse took off at a teeth-jarring trot, heading for the open range.

What was wrong?

"St-stop," Lucy chattered, bouncing on the saddle like a ball bearing on corrugated tin—through her jostling she saw bees. Cupcake, having seen them, too, or felt them, made an awful whinny noise and went from a jaw-breaking trot to a gallop.

Lucy didn't even have time to yell. Off they went toward the horizon, with Lucy leaning forward, clinging to the saddle horn. Her camera swung from around her neck, slapping the poor horse on the side and probably making matters worse by scaring the poor animal.

She didn't know much about a horse, but she knew the huge horse must have been stung by the bees—or had decided it was getting away, and quicker than Lucy wanted. Miraculously, Lucy was managing to hang on, but she didn't know how long that was going to last.

Rowdy had already taken off after Lucy when she'd started back toward the stable. He hadn't meant to stay at the branding so long, but she'd been busy taking pictures, so he had lost track of time until he'd caught her riding off. The instant Cupcake had started trotting, he'd known something was up. He knew the old horse was in distress about something. He'd urged his horse into a gallop immediately.

He'd shortened the distance, only to see Cupcake shoot to a gallop, with Lucy clinging to the saddle horn as they disappeared over the horizon.

Praying and riding hard as he topped the hill, he was not sure what he'd find on the other side. Lucy was still in the saddle.

She might be small, but she'd managed somehow not to fall off, though she'd slid so far to the right, he didn't think she'd last much longer. He finally rode up beside her and could reach out for her.

The minute his arm started round her, she turned her head. "Rowdy!" Her eyes were wide with fear.

"Let go. I've got you."

Without hesitating, she did as he asked and he swept her onto the saddle with him. She turned instantly and threw her arms around him, clinging to him as he pulled his horse to a halt.

"It's okay. I've got you," he said into her silky hair, breathing in the scent of her and feeling her heart thundering against his.

She nodded her head against his neck but didn't let up on her hold on him—and in that instant he knew he didn't want her to. He knew with all his heart that if it were up to him, he would never let her go.

Rubbing her hair gently with his hand, he just let the moment be. In the distance, Cupcake continued galloping.

"B-bees," Lucy mumbled, answering his question about what had come over the gentle horse.

"They'll do that. But you're okay now."

He half expected someone to ride up behind him, but when no one did, he knew that she'd been out of their sight range when the horse had acted up. He was glad he'd been watching and gone after her, or she very well could have been in trouble and no one would have known.

He sent up a prayer of thanks to the Man Upstairs.

Lifting her head, she gave a shaky smile. "Thanks,

cowboy." Her voice was as shaky as her smile. "I thought I was done for—or heading to the border."

He chuckled. "You've got skills, Lucy Calvert. You held on longer than I expected. Might be some Calamity Jane in you after all."

"Ha, only by the grace of God."

"True. But I didn't want to say so."

They laughed and it felt as if they were the only two people in the world. Rowdy had to do everything in his power not to kiss her—or even appear as though he was thinking about it. But, boy, was he.

He cared for Lucy. More than he'd ever cared for a woman. And he wasn't sure what he was going to do about it. When she found out what he'd done…she wouldn't have anything to do with him. She'd never, ever trust him.

His heart started thundering.

Lucy's gaze feathered over his face like a caress— she probably wasn't even aware how she was looking at him or what it was doing to him. When her eyes stopped on his lips he bit back a need to crush her to him and kiss her, to feel the softness of her lips against his. He halted his thinking.

He had to be honorable.

If he wanted even the most remote shot at a future with Lucy—and he did—then he had to step carefully and move slowly. He could not mess up again. Lucy had to trust him before he ever thought about kissing her again.

Then tell her about what you did!

"I'd better get you home," he said. He couldn't tell her. Not now, not until the time was right.

When is the time going to be right?

His horse stirred beneath them, reminding him they weren't moving. There was a creek not too far away and he saw Cupcake halt on the bank and begin drinking water.

Wrapping an arm around Lucy, he held her lightly as he urged his horse forward. The sky was darkening ahead of them, but he figured the rain would hold off for a couple of hours.

"Where are we going?" Lucy shifted and studied the pasture ahead of them.

"To that line of trees up ahead. There's a stream there. I thought you might want to see it."

She nodded, but didn't say anything. Within minutes they were there.

"Oh," she gasped. "This is beautiful."

He pointed. "When the setting sun is filtering through those trees, it takes on a golden hue."

As if on cue, the dark clouds parted and the sun broke free for a few seconds. Light streaked through the trees and the creek came alive with a lively glow.

Automatically his arm tightened around Lucy's waist.

She turned to look at him and he knew it was time to get off the horse.

It was either that or he was going to kiss her, no doubt about it.

Weak-kneed when her feet touched the ground, Lucy tried not to wobble as she headed toward the water's edge, putting distance between her and Rowdy. The knowledge that she trusted him swept over her like the warm glow that had just burst through the dark clouds.

That trust changed everything about her since waking up in that burn center, alone, scared and scarred.

When her heart had been closed up tightly, she hadn't thought much about her body. She'd just been grateful to be alive and that her face and hands had been spared. But now, in an instant of discovery and recovery she'd become aware… What would a man—Rowdy—think of her scarred body?

What would a husband think of the sight of her?

The thought was almost more than she could bear. She wrapped her arms about her waist and prayed for the images to fade away from her mind. For God to give her answers.

She felt exhausted and emotionally drained as Rowdy came up behind her and gently tugged at her hair.

"Penny for your thoughts," he said.

She closed her eyes, but couldn't trust herself to speak.

Rowdy walked down the creek, putting distance between them. He seemed restless—bothered. After a minute he swung back around. "I have to say something."

His tone startled her. "Okay."

"I, um… Look, there is no easy way to say this. I rushed kissing you before because that's what I do. That's what I've always done. If I see something I like, or want, I go for it. No waiting patiently for me. I just go for it. And where women are concerned, that's always been the way I operated." He paused, looking uncomfortable as he tugged at his collar.

She knew he had a wild background. But hearing him talk about his…love life brought the wall back up around her heart. She hadn't even realized it had just fallen down.

"Lucy, I'm changed."

Anger that she'd let her guard down crushed over her.

"You kissed me the other day out of the blue. How is that 'changed'?" The memory of the kiss surged through her as if it had been only a few seconds since he'd planted his lips on hers.

His eyes filled with distress. "I know. But—I honestly went a little crazy when we were fighting over that sledgehammer. And I didn't know your story then. I've tried to prove that to you since you shared your story with me."

She hugged herself tighter. Locking her heart down tight. "Yes. I see that. But—"

He came to stand in front of her. The gurgling stream's soothing song only played the tension that was suddenly between them. How could she have even thought she could trust a man who had been with so many women?

"I'm trying to change. I have changed. I haven't dated…for about a year. I'm working at not just jumping in—I've committed to the Lord not to be that man anymore."

But how could she trust that this was true? Lucy's mind filled with the deceit that Tim had pulled off and she'd never even suspected.

Staring at Rowdy, she didn't think this could get any worse. But she was wrong.…

"You need to know the rest of my story, too," he said, glancing at his boots before meeting her eyes. "I got in trouble about ten months ago when I got mixed up with a married woman—"

Lucy gasped. "A married woman."

"I didn't know."

"How could you not know?" Contempt rang in her

words at his excuse. Lucy couldn't believe what he was saying.

"I didn't know her well enough before I— Well, you know. Before I got involved."

Completely disgusted, she spun toward Cupcake. She wanted out of here. Away from him, and if that meant getting back on that horse then so be it. She'd walk away if she had to she was so mad at him.

"Lucy, I'm changed. I am."

She glared over her shoulder at him. "Ha! You kissed me before."

"Yeah, I know. But—"

"Nope, can't do it." Cupcake looked up from where she'd moved and was now eating grass, but didn't spook as Lucy took the reins in her hand. She stretched to reach up and grab the saddle horn, but Cupcake was too tall for her to do it on her own.

"Hey," Rowdy snapped, coming to stand beside her. "I'm trying to talk to you. To tell you that I'm trying to change. That I'm working at not just jumping in—"

Lucy swung around and jammed a finger in his chest. "Do you even have any compassion for the spouse? For what you put him through?"

"Yeah, even after he busted my nose I felt bad for the guy. But that didn't change anything. And until he showed up, I was clueless."

"Yeah, well, clueless hits both parties and it's not a good feeling."

"Look, I know I'm a jerk. I'm sorry it happened to you but I don't date married women."

"How do you know? If you didn't even take the time to get to know your, your lady friends, then how do you know this was the only one? And besides, I'm sure that excuse made the husband feel okay about the whole incident." She felt tears leak from the edge of her eyes and brushed them away. He looked defeated suddenly and she hardened her heart as he raked his hands through his hair.

"You have a point," he said quietly. "I'll help you up and take you home."

She nodded in agreement, so ready to be gone. Swiping at her face with her fingertips, she turned toward the horse and let Rowdy lift her up so that she could get her foot in the stirrup.

"I can make it back on my own," she said, and turning Cupcake around, they were off at a slow pace. No bees were in sight.

It wouldn't have mattered anyway. She was so numb she wouldn't have felt them even if they'd swarmed her.

Rowdy just stood there and watched Lucy ride away.

Telling her the truth had been a really bad idea. Worst idea of the decade—aside from his involvement with Liz.

He'd known he was doomed the moment the confession came out of his mouth. But regardless of the churning in his gut, he'd known that he had to come clean. And despite the look of accusation that had crept into Lucy's eyes, he'd forced himself to be honest even as he realized it was going to cost him all of Lucy's respect.

It hit him that she probably felt as foolish as he had when she'd learned that her husband hadn't been faithful.

Her tears glistening on her long, dark lashes had finished him off, making him feel every bit the dirt-bag that he was.

Lucy was better off without him. As she disappeared

over the ridge, he knew she deserved so much more than him.

Truth was, if they hadn't had this conversation—or attempted to have this conversation—he might have continued to let himself believe that she could actually have been the one he was waiting on.

Suddenly bone weary, Rowdy walked over and stared at the creek. And he started praying.

Chapter Fifteen

Rowdy McDermott was a womanizer just like Tim had been.

Men could not be trusted.

Oh, they were fine if you just didn't get personal with them. And she'd already gotten far too personal with Rowdy. She'd planned all along to keep him at arm's length, but the man had forced himself into this new life. That was the thing that really had her angry.

It wasn't as if she'd asked him to come around.

No, he'd manipulated her. Toyed with her.

Her worst mistakes seemed destined to repeat themselves on an endless loop.

She was thankful that the ranch appeared deserted when she got back to the barn. Walter Pepper called, "Hello," from the end of the barn when she rode in. Thankfully he seemed busy with a horse. He told her to just tie Cupcake to the stall and he'd take care of her.

Since Lucy had no idea what to do to take care of the horse anyway, she gladly agreed and ran to her truck. She couldn't get home soon enough.

Painting was the answer—she needed to work,

needed the release painting had always been for her up until the aftermath of Tim's betrayal and the fire had stolen it from her. Thank goodness the studio was almost done. Thank goodness she had a renewed passion for the work and the release it offered her.

Whether she was painting anything saleable didn't matter—she was as mad as she'd ever been.

Where had all these problems come from? She'd arrived here with one goal—to get rid of the anger eating up inside. The wall destruction had helped, or so she'd thought. But she knew now that it had only been a temporary fix. The anger was like a living thing eating away inside of her. Hearing Rowdy confess that he, too, was a womanizing fool had relit that fire to a blazing inferno.

Men!

Of course, she knew infidelity wasn't completely limited to men. Women had the same dysfunction. Her mother had proved that—over and over.

Her dad had moved on. He was extremely happy with his new wife and Lucy was happy for him. He deserved to be happy. Still, what her mother had put them through had ended Lucy's childhood.

She was so thankful she and Tim hadn't had children.

At least there was that.

Pulling her paint box from the storage box, she saw the picture album beneath it.

Lucy hadn't realized she'd packed it. She just stared at it in the bottom of the box. Her fingers trembled as she lifted it out. She knew what was inside. Pictures of the lie she'd lived.

If the burn pile had been going, she'd have walked straight out the door and tossed the album in the fire.

Instead, she sat it against the wall. She was moving

forward, not back. And pictures of her and Tim had no place in her future. Whatever good times they'd had were wiped away the day his "female friend" had walked into her room at the burn center and spilled her story.

Funny, Lucy thought it was supposed to be the victim who took revenge. But it had been the opposite way in her story.

Of course in Rowdy's story, it was as it should be. The spouse got the lick in—or she should say the fist.

Good for that guy.

"What's gotten into you?" his dad asked a few days after he and Lucy had had their fight. They were separating calves out to take to the cattle sale and his dad had decided that today would be a good day to get out of the office. Rowdy had a feeling it was to look over his shoulder. His next statement proved him right.

"You've been hard to live with and work with the past few days, so the men have said. What's bothering you?"

Yeah, he was ornery. That was for certain.

Why had he agreed to help Lucy milk a wild heifer?

After they'd parted ways, she'd shown back up for practice because the rodeo was coming up and she was determined to keep her end of the bargain.

"The stubborn woman wants to milk the wild heifer. And I'm afraid she's going to get hurt."

Randolph moved with his horse as it danced to stop a calf from escaping back to the group of cattle they'd just taken it from.

"You'll take care of her. The guys will control the calf."

Rowdy scowled and his dad laughed.

"You and I both know those cows we put in there

aren't range heifers. They are going to be more scared than wild. Wes, Tony and Joseph will have no trouble."

Rowdy stared out across the pasture. His dad was right, but he still didn't like it.

"How deep are you in?"

At his dad's question, Rowdy met his gaze. There was concern etched in the creases around his eyes.

"Deep." There was no use denying what he knew his dad could see. He was in love with Lucy Calvert.

A smile flashed across Randolph's face. "Lucy's a good match for you. Your mother would be pleased."

His heart tightened as he thought about his mother—of all the years he'd longed to make her proud of him. He took a deep breath and held his father's gaze. "It's not that simple. Let's get these in the pen and then I'll tell you about it."

They worked with Chet, their top hand, and the other ranch hands getting the calves into the holding pen. When they were done, Rowdy and his dad loaded their horses up in the trailer and then rode back in the truck together.

"So what's really got you twisted in knots?"

Rowdy raked his hand through his hair and let out a breath before confiding Lucy's background. It wasn't his story to tell, but his father was a man of great integrity.

"You're not going to just walk away from this?" Randolph asked when he was done.

"I don't want to, but Lucy has already been through enough. She doesn't need me and my messed-up background reminding her of what her no-good husband did to her. The man took away her ability to trust. If she stays like she is, she could end up alone for the rest of her life."

"*I'm* alone and managing fine. But I'm twentysome-thing years older than she is, I figure. So I'd hate to see that happen. Are you going to let it happen?"

"What can I do?"

"You can help her learn to trust again. You can start by being there for her."

"She's barely speaking to me now."

"Then what do you have to lose? If you're serious about this new walk with the Lord, then you have to do this because of the man you've become. Not the man you were. You made a mistake. The difference is you've changed and are holding yourself accountable for your actions now. That's all you can do other than keep prov-ing yourself trustworthy."

"You're sure you're ready for this tomorrow night?" Nana asked Lucy. They were in the Spotted Cow Café or, as the men and the boys liked to call it, the Cow Patty Café because of the painted brown spots gone wrong on the concrete floor.

Lucy stared at a dancing-cow figurine sitting on the table. It was one of an abundant cow paraphernalia col-lection that practically hid the walls of the café, there were so many. "I think so. All I have to do is get a drop of milk. The fellas are going to take care of the cow."

"Yeah, but who is gonna take care of you?" Edwina slapped a hand to her hip. "I've seen those cow-milking contests. Grown men fall underneath the animal think-ing for some reason it might be easier to milk the cow lying on their back while getting stomped on." She shook her head. "No, sister, this is not a good idea. And to think I took you for an intelligent sort the first time I saw you."

Lucy chuckled. "Edwina, I am not going to get

stomped on. Rowdy told me not to go for the bag until he gives me the go-ahead. So rest easy, I'm not getting thrown under the cow."

Edwina made a face that clearly said she didn't believe it, and then left to take an order from a herd of cowboys on the far side of the café.

Ms. Jo had come out of the kitchen and heard the last half of the conversation. "Ed get you straightened out?" she asked, sliding into the booth beside Nana.

"No, but she gave it a good try," Lucy said.

The diner door was yanked opened and Mabel came hustling inside. "The Dew Drop Inn's been busier than an ant colony today," she declared, squeezing her large-framed body into the booth seat beside Lucy.

"With all these ranch-rodeo teams arriving, this should be a good weekend for the town."

"Café's been swamped, too." Ms. Jo fanned herself. "The pie baking's been going nonstop."

Jolie came over from the jukebox just as Blake Shelton started singing "Austin." "I love this song. It's an old one but just makes me think of happy endings," she said.

Mabel had taken Jolie's spot, so she pulled up a chair.

"Speaking of happy endings." Mabel turned her full attention toward Lucy. Now, Mabel was a good size bigger than Lucy, and she'd effectively trapped Lucy in the booth. There was nowhere to go.

"Look, I know y'all are all hoping that something happens between Rowdy and me, but it's not going to."

Ms. Jo's eyebrows squeezed together and a V formed above her glasses. "You cannot tell us you don't like that good-looking cowboy."

Everyone started talking at once about how right they were for each other. After they'd all quieted down, she told them her story. She couldn't believe she'd held it in so long.

"Of all the horrible things." Mabel's voice was gentle as she threw an arm around Lucy and gave her a hug. "That brings back memories."

"Tell her, Mabel," Jolie said, and everyone echoed her.

Ms. Jo gave Mabel a nod. "If anyone knows how you feel, it's Mabel. She didn't have a fire, but she got a raw deal."

Lucy was curious now. She knew that Mabel had never been married.

"I was in love once, a long time ago. Paul was a handsome cowboy with a smile that could turn girls' insides to jelly. I knew better than to be foolish enough to fall for the man, but sometimes a heart will do what a heart wants to do and there's nothing you can do about it."

"Tell me about it," Edwina said as she passed by. "I've done fell for three men and not a winner in the bunch." Shaking her head, she kept right on moving toward the kitchen with a new order.

"On this I have to agree with Ed. Paul took my heart and then he decided mine wasn't enough and so he took a few more on the side. Deception is a tough thing to overcome." Her usual jovial good humor was gone. "After I discovered what he'd been doing, I gave him 'what for' every which way I could. That poor man thought his life was in danger. It *was*. But I decided breaking him into pieces wasn't going to help ease my pain any, so I watched him ride away. And I can tell you losing the desire to trust another man like that is a shame."

Lucy wrapped her hand around Mabel's and gave a supportive squeeze. Mabel slipped her hand out and covered Lucy's and continued talking. "There are times when I do regret that I let him take that away from me."

Jolie looked sad; her beautiful green eyes misted. "I almost did that to Morgan, and it is the regret of my life that I hurt him when I chose my career over him and left. God had a plan for us, but if I hadn't come back, there was a very good possibility he might never have married."

Lucy was shocked by both stories. She wasn't sure what to say. "I'm glad it worked out for you and Morgan, Jolie. Mabel, what happened to Paul? Did you ever see him again?"

She tucked her hair behind her ear and shook her head. "Never did. Never wanted to. I've been happy for the most part. I have my mission trips that I'm called to do and I have my Dew Drop Inn and believe me, folks do drop in." Her eyes sparkled. "That place keeps me busy. God's been very good to me. And to be honest, I have no problem with men in general. There are men in this town whom I trust with all my heart. Those Mc-Dermott men are four of them. Don't mean I want to fall in love with any of them, though. There's not anyone I want to fall in love with—I'm too old now anyway. But I'm telling you, girl, you need to think long and hard about letting your heart harden up like you're doing."

"You know, that's right," Nana said at last. "Rowdy is my grandson and I love that boy dearly. And I'm not making excuses for him, but he took his momma's death hard. He has a lot to offer a woman and I think the woman who wins his heart is going to be a very blessed woman."

Lucy suddenly felt as though she was being ganged up on. And she wasn't sure what to think about that. It wasn't as if they were trying to fix her up. They just all thought so much of Rowdy that she felt the pressure tenfold to decide that she was wrong.

"It's something I don't know if I can do. Honestly, I do have feelings for him. I think that's why I'm so mad at him."

At her words all eyes lit up like Christmas lights.

"Hold on. I'm just saying that's why this is so hard. Because he's very lovable. And I am not saying I'm in love. I'm saying— Oh, I don't know what I'm saying! I'm about as confused as a woman can be."

Mabel patted her hand. "There, there. We'll just pray that God's will be done. You just try to keep an open heart."

All the way home, Lucy thought about that. How could she keep an open heart when she was terrified of doing exactly that?

She hadn't told them the truth, either. The whole story. Just like she hadn't told Rowdy. Ever since she'd begun to have these conflicting emotions concerning him, she'd found herself lingering in front of the mirror and staring at the burns that covered her body. It was more than she could ask of any man.

She could barely look at them herself.

Chapter Sixteen

The night of the wild-cow milking had arrived. She'd practiced two more times since she and Rowdy had fought and they'd made it through the practice by communicating with the kids more than each other. It had been awkward for both of them.

But tonight it would be over, and there were just a couple more weeks of art class and after that, they could steer clear of each other.

Was that what she wanted?

One minute. And then the next, no.

All she knew for certain was that tonight she was going to milk a wild cow and not get herself killed. That was her agenda.

The stands were full when she, Wes, Joseph, Tony and Rowdy joined the other wild-cow milkers.

"Go Sunrise Ranch Team!" came yells from the stands, from boys who were screaming at the top of their lungs. Everyone in the group turned to search the stands. Not hard to find, the other thirteen Sunrise Ranch kids stood in the middle, waving and jumping with excitement. Sammy and B.J. held a sign with the word Go painted above a yellow sunrise.

Behind them sat Nana, Mabel, Ms. Jo, Morgan and Jolie.

Tucker, on duty, had wished them luck as they'd passed him on their way into the pens. And Randolph was standing on the other side of the gate at the opening of the arena with some of the ranch hands. She wondered if they were there in case they were needed. That worried her, despite knowing the paramedics were there.

"Y'all've got a cheering section," Rowdy said from where he sat on his horse.

Tony's half grin hitched upward. "All the ranch hands are hanging on to the railing down there, too, with Mr. Randolph. You know they're going to be yelling when it's our turn."

"I'm glad we drew first," Joseph said. "I'd be nervous if we had to wait until the end."

"Me, too," Lucy finally added. She'd been trying to calm the butterflies in her stomach but had finally given up. She was nervous and there wasn't anything that could be done about it.

She met Rowdy's smile with a weak one of her own.

"You'll be fine. Just remember to let us get the cow stopped and then I'll give you the okay to dash in and get the milk."

"She's got it in the bag," Wes said, his confidence sounding far higher than anything Lucy remotely felt.

The PA broadcast the start of the wild-cow milking and Lucy froze. Then to her dismay, the gate opened and they entered the arena. Well, they did, but she almost didn't follow until she forced her feet to move.

From inside the arena, the grandstands looked huge.

The boys were grinning and waving at the crowd as if they'd already won. Wes became a clown. His eyes danced as he whipped his hat from his head and waved it at the crowd. He pumped his hands up and down to get the crowd to roar—it was as if he were born for this. Joseph and Tony just grinned beside him. They were all too cute.

Rowdy looked especially nice tonight in his red shirt, black hat and signature grin. She wished he'd stop flashing that distracting grin around! Of course, him sitting like a champion himself on one of his champion horses, looking ready to shine as he did, was distracting, too. And not just to her. Lucy had no doubt that every female in the stands had absolutely no idea there were three kids and a lady in the arena with him.

He turned his horse and trotted back to her side. "How are you doing?"

That he'd thought of her put a catch in her heart and, looking up at him, she suddenly felt breathless and young and free…as if none of the heavy burdens of her past was hanging over her. "I'm good, thanks for asking."

He leaned down in the saddle, his expression intent. "Good. Now, I'm compelled to remind you—do not get within reach of that heifer's legs until I'm in position between you and her back leg. Is that clear?"

He was worried about her. She nodded. "Clear."

Sitting up, he looked satisfied with her answer. She couldn't grasp what she felt but…watching him, her heart felt full.

Wes turned to her—leaving his adoring fans for a moment and making Lucy smile. "The dude down there on the end standing inside that white circle of lime is who you race to with the milk."

She nodded. After she got at least a drop of milk into the small jar in her hand, she had to run to the man in the circle. The hard work of the team didn't count if she failed in her task. She prayed that she didn't fall down and spill the milk. The boys had done their part painting their pictures; now she had to do her part.

Joseph grinned at her. "Don't be all worried. You're going to do us proud."

"That's right," Tony added, coming to stand beside her. "You look as nervous as me."

She wanted to give him a hug but it would probably have embarrassed him. "Let's do this," she said instead, winking at him. He responded with that grin that had her heart turning over for the kid who'd been so mistreated by the parents who were supposed to love and protect him.

The announcer introduced them as the Sunrise Ranch team, then called out each of their names, and they stepped forward and waved. When their heifer entered the arena, people went wild. A lump lodged in Lucy's throat as the heifer stared at them—clearly wary. Rowdy pulled his rope from the saddle horn and readied it. When the clock started, he rode out toward the animal and the kids followed him into the center of the arena. He twirled the rope above his head, then sent the loop flying. It landed with ease over the heifer's head. Rowdy wrapped the rope around the saddle horn and his horse stepped back as the cow tried to run, but the rope pulled taut and the boys were already on the run. She went right behind them.

The cow dodged one way, but the boys moved with it, anticipating where it would go. Lucy would have gone the opposite direction! Wes dived right in, fearless as he grabbed the cow by the neck and locked his arm around it like she'd been taught on the small calf that day. Joseph grabbed the cow's tail and dug his boots into the ground. Tony moved to help Wes. With the cow sort of under control, Rowdy came off the horse and headed toward the flank. Lucy's adrenaline was revved up and she prayed she could get the milk.

The boys grinned at her, even Wes, though he was gritting his teeth with the effort he was using to keep hold of the animal. Rowdy motioned for her to take her turn. She raced in, or at least she thought she raced in, but the cow chose that moment to try to throw its head up and drag the guys. Wes and Tony held on, Rowdy pushed the animal and Joseph leaned back so far that his seat was also dragging in the dirt as his heels bit into the ground. Lucy looked from Wes to Joseph, not sure what to do, but they got the animal almost still again. Rowdy gave her the nod again as he planted his back against the leg that could potentially lash out and nail her.

Lucy gritted her teeth and dived. She was going to get the milk this time. Holding her hand like she'd been taught, she made contact, and even when the heifer moved back she held on. She pushed, then squeezed. The animal moved. Lucy went down in the dirt but kept milking. From her prone position looking up, she saw a trickle make it into the glass jar.

"I got it," she yelled, excitement overwhelming her. Rowdy was laughing when he reached down and hauled her off the ground and set her on her feet.

"Run, Lucy, run," he said, and she did.

It seemed like miles to the man in the circle, and halfway there she saw the people in the stands in front of her stand up. She made it to the man, winded but with milk in the jar. They'd done it. She spun around but her heart stalled when she saw the heifer run over Tony, trampling him in the dirt.

Cows and steers running over people was a common occurrence in any rodeo; it was part of it. But Lucy hadn't gotten used to it and her stomach dropped and she started running.

Tony didn't jump up and grin. Rowdy was beside him by the time she made it, and the other boys had gathered around. Tony's shirt was ripped wide-open in the back. And to her relief he sat up just as she reached them. She was breathing so hard she thought she might pass out right there in the arena. He grinned at Rowdy.

"Take it easy. Your arm's not looking so good," Rowdy said, seeing a deep gash that was bleeding. Rowdy touched a bruised spot on Tony's lower back, and when he touched it, the boy flinched. But it wasn't the bruise that had Lucy's attention, it was the scars that riddled Tony's body.

Lucy's stomach lurched and it was all she could do not to lose its contents in the dirt right there in front of everyone. Dear Lord, Tony had told her he had scars, but not like this. She hadn't imagined they would be like this.

Hadn't imagined they would be worse than hers.

Her gaze met Rowdy's and he seemed to read everything in her face, because he said, "Hold on." Tony thought he was talking to him and nodded, but Lucy knew he was talking to her. She nodded, too, and couldn't stop nodding. It became compulsive and she had to will her head to stop before the boys realized how shaken she was.

"We're going to take you to the hospital and have this

bruise checked out. I don't want you having an internal problem and us not knowing it."

"Aw, it's okay," Tony said, wincing as Rowdy helped him to his feet. The crowd cheered as Rowdy and Wes helped him out of the arena. The on-site doctor met them at the gate along with Randolph. They had Tony sit down. The paramedic looked him over and agreed with Rowdy that X-rays made sense as a cautionary measure.

"You did it, Lucy," Tony said, grinning up at her from his bench. The kid was tough. Her throat ached with the need to cry.

"I did," she said instead, forcing her voice to hold steady. "But it was because of you fellas. That cow didn't stand a chance."

"Let's get him to the hospital," Randolph said, and they headed out of the gate. Lucy followed close behind.

Morgan and Jolie met them at the waiting room of the small hospital in Dew Drop. Nana and Tucker had stayed back with the ranch kids at the rodeo. It was agreed that the hospital didn't need fifteen rambunctious kids swarming the small waiting room.

They were right, the hospital was very small, but then Dew Drop wasn't a metropolis and they were lucky to have the place.

Randolph, Morgan and Rowdy all went into the emergency room with Tony. Jolie and Lucy sat together and waited.

Jolie watched them disappear through the door. "There is one thing these boys know when they come to Sunrise Ranch—they are loved."

Lucy nodded. She was still shaken about what she'd seen and ashamed that she hadn't realized when she was talking to Tony how badly he'd been injured. "What happened to Tony? I mean, with those burns. He talked to me about them, but I had no idea they were that bad. I talked to Rowdy, who said Tony's parents were responsible, but I didn't realize…" Her voice trailed off.

"I'm sorry." There was compassion in Jolie's voice and she leaned forward. "He had been burned with cigarettes for years and no one noticed. It's horrible to think that. But when his parents tossed gas on him and then a match when he was ten, he was taken away from them. From what I've been told, he had second-and third-degree burns and it took numerous skin grafts. I'm sure with your arm and neck that you understand the pain he went through."

The air had gone out of the room as Jolie spoke. Lucy felt small suddenly. Fury and anguish welled inside of her for what Tony had endured. "How," she rasped, looking down at her hands clenched in her lap, "could parents do such a thing?"

Jolie clasped her hands with her own. "It's a wicked world we live in. I can't understand, either. But Tony is alive and well and loved. And though it's been tough, what he went through, he's been on the ranch from the day he left the hospital almost four years ago. And that has been a blessing. I cried when I read his background, but I've watched him for months now, and he's one of the most well-adjusted kids considering what he's been through. Though, just like you, he doesn't like to show his scars."

Lucy sighed. "We talked about that. It's easier not to let people see them. Easier not to have to answer questions. Or to see pity on their faces."

"That's what Tony has said."

Rowdy and Morgan came out of the room and walked

over to where they were. Both Jolie and Lucy stood the minute they saw them.

"What did they say?" Jolie asked.

"He has a deep bruise, but his organs are all fine, so that's a blessing. Dad's with him finishing up and they'll release him in a few minutes."

Jolie hugged Morgan. "Wonderful!"

Rowdy placed his arm across Lucy's shoulders and gave her a gentle hug. "You okay?"

She was grateful for his touch. "Yes, I'm relieved and happy that Tony wasn't hurt seriously. But I really need to talk to you about something."

"Sure." Concern etched his face. "We'll head out if y'all have it under control from here," he said to his family.

"We do," Morgan said, a rock if there ever was one. "You did good out there tonight, Lucy. I hope this accident didn't shake you up too bad. We try to protect the boys as best we can, but the truth is kids could find a way to fall off the porch and get hurt."

"I know. I get it. Y'all do a great job with the boys."

"Some folks don't understand. But we don't allow them on bulls. Dad draws the line there, so even living the cowboy way has limits at Sunrise Ranch. Much to Wes's dismay."

She'd figured out by small things he'd said that Wes wanted to ride bulls.

She went in and gave Tony a hug, a really gentle but long one, and then left, telling him she would see him back at the ranch. She and Rowdy walked out to the parking lot and he held the door of his truck for her and placed his hand at her elbow as she hoisted herself into the tall truck. Sometimes being short just got old. And then she had to admit that sometimes it had its advantages. His hand on her elbow was one of those times.

After he drove them from the parking lot, he swung through a drive-through and bought them both something to drink. Lucy hadn't even realized how much she needed the sugar in the soda until it hit her system.

He looked at her with kindness in his eyes. "Better? You were wilting on me."

His concern did funny things to her heart.

"Thanks, I did need this. Is there somewhere private we can talk?"

"Sure." He drove out of town and headed toward the ranch and her house. But he continued on past the turn and Lucy watched the scenery go by. She tried to calm the nerves trying to talk her out of what she knew she had to do.

After a while he turned and went through an entrance with the Sunrise Ranch brand.

"This is another entrance to the ranch. It's connected to the original ranch, but would be a long ride as the crow flies on horseback. We usually drive over with horses then unload when we're working cattle." She felt as though his explanation was meant more to fill the dead space floating between them than to inform her of where they were.

The moon shimmered on the white rock road and bathed the countryside with a pale glow.

He stopped beside a pond with the moon reflecting off the water. A huge tree hung out over the water, and there was a narrow pier.

"See the owl, there, sitting in the tree?" He pointed and, sure enough, Lucy saw the owl watching them, his eyes glowing yellow in the headlights.

"You spotted him quickly."

"Out here, you just have to keep your eyes open. This place is alive with animals. But that guy right there has been hunting out of that tree for years."

She smiled at him despite her nerves. She took another sip of her soda. Rowdy rolled down the windows and turned off the engine. Leaning his back against the door, he studied her.

"What did you want to talk about?"

She looked away, toward the water. "I hadn't realized how extensive Tony's burns were."

"I didn't understand that. After we talked…"

"I know you assumed Tony had told me. But he didn't show me. I could not have imagined the extent even if I'd tried."

"I'm sorry. That was why you looked so pale out there."

She nodded. He gripped the steering wheel with one hand and his knuckles grew white in the darkness. "When I saw your burns, I thought of Tony. He feels a bond with you because you have that in common."

Lucy sat her soda in the cup holder and rolled a strand of hair with her fingers, thinking about where to begin.

"I haven't been completely honest with you."

He looked startled. "That's okay."

She shook her head. "No. It's not. I've been hard on you and—" There seemed to be no air in the truck and yet the windows were open. "My burns aren't just on my arms and neck as I've let everyone think. Seeing Tony tonight hit me hard." Her voice cracked and she had to pause to get it back under control. "You see, until now, I've told myself I was okay, blessed that my face had been spared—and I am. I think that's why this is especially hard for me to admit that I'm so ashamed of my body that I haven't told anyone that the burns on my arms extend over most of my torso…" She couldn't say more.

His eyes shadowed and in the moonlight they glistened, and she could almost believe tears were there in their depths. She took a deep breath, torn by whether he was repulsed by what she was telling him or feeling compassion. Her heart of hearts said compassion, but she was uncertain how even that made her feel.

Her throat felt raw.

He looked away and studied the pond; his Adam's apple bobbed. "You—" he started and then stopped. "I can't stand the thought of you suffering like that."

"I didn't suffer long. I was knocked unconscious soon after the ceiling caved in. The recovery was…difficult. So bad I wished at times I hadn't lived."

Rowdy got out of the truck instantly and was at her door within seconds. Without ceremony he yanked it open and pulled her into his arms, crushing her to him.

"I know you'd rather I not touch you—" his voice was muffled in her hair "—but I can't stand the thought of you in so much pain."

He was holding her tightly, her toes barely brushing the ground, and Lucy's arms had somehow locked around his shoulders. She trembled as tears that had long ago dried up tried to break free at his heartfelt words and the earnest way he held her.

The owl's woeful hoot sounded, cutting through the silence. Lucy pulled herself together, very aware of the man embracing her.

He inhaled deeply and then lowered her to the ground and stepped back. Almost as if he had willed himself to do it. Lucy's heart was thundering and, though she wished with all her might that things could be different and that his arms were meant to hold her, she couldn't let herself go there.

"I didn't mean to get personal." He looked almost bashful. "But I didn't kiss you."

She laughed despite the mood over the moment. "You did very well. I needed a hug in the worst way. Thank you."

"You're welcome, anytime. Why did you share that with me?"

His question surprised her. She walked over to the pier, tested it with her foot then walked a few feet onto it. Staring down into the water, she found the moon looking back at her. Rowdy followed her, waiting at the end with a hand on each railing of the narrow pier.

"I'm not sure, really." She turned and leaned against the railing, crossing her arms. "I just saw Tony's scars and suddenly I didn't feel authentic. And I knew that in order to feel like I wasn't being dishonest that I had to be open about my burns."

"It's no one's business."

"True. But, still, I felt like I needed to tell someone… that I needed to tell you."

Lucy wasn't sure why she'd wanted him to know. But suddenly she was afraid. Had she told too much?

Had she shown him too much of her heart?

Chapter Seventeen

It was all Rowdy could do not to blurt out that he loved her. He'd had to hold her when she'd looked so shattered telling him about her burns. He'd known for certain in that instant that what he'd been thinking was true. He'd fallen in love with this beautiful woman and the reality was she would never be able to love him.

Sure, she'd confided in him. That gave him hope, but he knew deep inside that she'd never be able to give her heart to him.

"I'm ashamed of the burns," she whispered, blinking. She held his gaze for a second, and then with a shuddering breath looked away. "I worry—"

"One day you'll fall in love, Lucy. You'll find a man you can love." It wouldn't be him, but someone she could believe in. Someone honorable, and upstanding. "And when you do, your scars won't matter to him. If that's what you're worried about."

They don't matter to me.

She looked lost to him standing there.

"I think I'm ready to call it a night," she said, walking to where he stood. "Thank you for listening."

He followed her to his truck and helped her up into the cab. "Thanks for listening to me," she said again. "I just needed to talk."

"Anytime." What else could he say? He asked himself that all the way back around to his side of the truck. There was a ton of stuff he wanted to say, but nothing he could.

Silence filled the truck as he drove back toward home. "You did good out there, by the way," he finally said.

"You're a good teacher. Not that I'm planning on making a habit of it. That was most likely my last rodeo competition."

He grinned. "Quit while you're on top."

She laughed. "Something like that, anyway."

It felt good to hear her laugh. She amazed him.

When he pulled into her driveway, Moose was sitting on the cab of her truck, watching them.

"No, don't get out," she said when he started to open his door. "I'm fine. Thanks. I fell apart a little, but I feel much better now."

"Lucy, thanks for trusting me with your story. It meant a lot to me that you did that."

She paused before closing the door. "Rowdy, you've been nothing but good to me. I'm so sorry if I've been unfair to you. You said you didn't know that woman was married and I believe you. I admire that you've changed your life."

He watched her go, wanting to go after her. Bowing his head, he prayed that God would help Lucy with the struggles she was trying to face alone.

"You should ask her out."

Rowdy looked over the top of the horse he was brushing down and looked at Wes.

"Seriously, dude. We—" he pointed from himself to Joseph and the fourteen other culprits gathered around "—know you're interested in Lucy. It's plain to see."

"That's right, Rowdy." B.J. stared up at him. "We like Lucy. She done helped me paint a rock and everything. I like her and I know you got to, 'cause you ain't stupid."

Rowdy's jaw dropped and he looked at the older boys, wondering who was responsible for B.J.'s word choice.

Wes fessed up. "Hey, you're not stupid and we all know it."

"We also see you looking all funny when you look at her," Sammy added. "Ain't that right, Caleb?"

Caleb nodded his blond head. "We've seen you do it."

"Yeah," B.J. spoke up again. "It's kinda like you ain't slept in days and days. Your eyelids get droopy."

"Okay, who has been talking to this kid?"

B.J.'s brows scrunched up. "I got eyes, Rowdy. I'm almost nine years old. I know about things."

Wes and Joseph were almost hunched over holding in their laughter on the other side of the horse. Rowdy planned on having a man-to-man talk with them later.

"Look, Rowdy." Tony stepped out of the group, his face a work of concern. "Lucy, well, she's special. And we like you a lot, or we wouldn't be saying this. This is serious stuff. She's new around here and we noticed she doesn't date. She's too young to be sitting at home all the time."

"Hold it. You guys have been listening to Nana."

"True," Tony agreed. "But still. You know you like her and she deserves to go out on a real date. And you used to be gone all the time on dates and you never go now. So it'd be good for both of you."

Rowdy wanted to deny it all, but, truth was, taking Lucy on a date was a great idea.

"You ain't chicken, are you?" B.J. asked.

"No, Short Stuff, I am not chicken."

Tony and the other boys started high-fiving each other and Tony reached across the horse, holding his hand up. Rowdy gave him a high five.

It occurred to him later that the little sneaks had become proficient at getting adults to fall right into their traps.

First Lucy with the cow milking, and now him.

He chuckled, thinking about what easy prey he'd been.

Now the hard part. Getting Lucy to agree.

The smart thing would be to let the boys do their magic.

But this was *his* date. And he'd do the asking.

He just hoped Lucy didn't do the rejecting.

This was heaven on earth. It truly was. Lucy sat on her stool in front of her canvas in the center of her new studio with the awesome light shining through the windows. The painting had come at her fast and furious. Two days she'd been at it almost nonstop. That was how it was with her. When inspiration struck, there was no stopping it. She had to get it out onto the canvas.

Stepping away, she picked up her coffee and walked to the wide windows that overlooked her valley. Her sweet uncle. How had he known this place would be so perfect for her?

Turning back, she stared at the canvas. It was a scene of the calf branding. The colors were vivid, bold. And though there were many in the picture, she hadn't been able to help herself—Rowdy was there, bent on one knee with his hand on B.J.'s shoulder, as the focal point. His features lit up the canvas—the softness in his eyes, the generous spirit coming full force to the scene was what would draw every eye to him. Just like it did in real life.

Lucy wasn't one to brag about her work. There had been a time when she brushed off compliments. But her agent had been the one who pointed out that her ability was a God-given talent and when she belittled it, she was telling God He hadn't done well by her.

Now she recognized it for what it was. And she thanked Him for blessing her with the ability.

Times like this, though, when she looked at a painting and recognized that she couldn't have done it without God's hand on her shoulder, were the moments that she was awestruck. She had feared to never feel that again.

She'd read an interview with an author once who said that there were times when the author would read something she wrote and she would go back and double-check her original manuscript thinking that an editor had switched the words because she couldn't remember writing something so profound. The author would be shocked when she'd realize she had indeed written the words and knew that God had given her the words.

That was how Lucy felt now.

"Lucy."

Rowdy! Like a deer in the headlights, she stared at her painting and then at the stairs. The door was open and his spurs clinked with each step up the stairs.

He'd wanted to see her work. But she hadn't meant for a picture of himself to be the first thing of hers that he saw.

Frantically she set her coffee down and was about to grab the painting and do what? Throw it in the closet?

"Hey," he said, before she could do anything.

"Hey," she said, moving in front of the painting. Like he wasn't going to see the three-foot-by-four-foot canvas behind her.

He looked around appreciatively. "This is great, Lucy."

She couldn't help but smile. The room was long, the walls painted a fresh yellow, the color that inspired her. His attention was snagged by the large painting hanging on the wall closest to him. It was one of her rather stormy days, darker than usual and yet there was something about it that still appealed to Lucy. Most of the others hanging were not her usual signature style. On the wall at the end of the building was the single painting that she had from her days before the fire. It was a pale blue sky with two vivid bluebirds playing chase between the trees as a road curved past the tree and around the bend.

It was to that painting that Rowdy moved. "This is beautiful," he said.

His praise touched her. She moved over beside him and crossed her arms as she looked at the painting. "I painted that years ago—one of my first that I felt was saleable. I gave it to my dad—told him the bluebirds in the picture were to signify bluebirds of happiness. All the joy I wished for him in his life. After the fire, he and my new stepmother brought the painting to me during my recovery and said they wanted me to have it so that the bluebirds would remind me that I would be happy again."

She felt very self-conscious when Rowdy turned to look at her. There was no denying that she had feelings for Rowdy. Lucy had known as she painted him that, though she didn't want to face it, she was falling in love with him. And she didn't know what to do about it.

"You are, aren't you? Happy again?"

Oh, what a loaded question. She nodded. "I am, Rowdy. I have my hang-ups. But I am. And much of that is because of being here." She wanted to say *because of you* but she couldn't. She was confused about her emotions where he was concerned. And yet she knew that if she just released the fear holding her back and gave him a chance…

Her thoughts stalled as he reached suddenly and lifted a strand of hair from her shoulder and rubbed it between his fingers, studying it as if it held the secrets of the universe.

Had he almost touched her cheek? Longing for his touch further confused her.

His eyes met hers, and she prayed he couldn't read the longing in them. His lips curved into a smile. "I'm glad," he said, and let go of her hair.

"Is there a reason you came by?" she asked, wishing her voice didn't sound so breathless. But goodness, the room seemed twenty degrees hotter than it had and her cheeks were burning.

He strode back to the center of the room and the painting she'd been working on. It happened so quickly that she was still standing with her feet anchored to where she stood. From her position she couldn't see the painting, only his face as he viewed it. He studied the painting intently. And then he raised his eyes and looked at her over the top of the canvas.

"This is unbelievable."

The warm rush of satisfaction filled her. "I was inspired."

She didn't say by him. She hoped he didn't realize that he was the focal point of the painting.

"You put me in this painting."

"Yes." She decided to play it cool. "What was going on between you and B.J. in the photo captivated me. I couldn't help myself. You're very paintable." There, she'd taken the personal emphasis off of it and put it in professional terms. He looked back at the painting and she wished she knew what was going through his mind.

"B.J. and the boys will be blown away like I am."

She smiled broadly. "I do love to blow people away. I want them to feel loved, though." The words were out before she could stop them.

"I think they will."

He'd said it casually, not seeming to take her words to mean she wanted him to feel loved, too. And that was a good thing. Right? She didn't want to mislead him. Didn't want him to think she was playing games with him.

He dragged his hat from his head and tugged at his ear as she'd seen him do a few times.

"Okay, time for me to come clean. I came over here because I wanted to see if you'd have dinner and maybe a movie with me this weekend?"

If he'd walked over and kissed her she wouldn't have been more surprised.

"You're asking me on a date?"

He nodded, still holding his hat. She noticed he had a death grip on it, and that simple knowledge got her right in the center of her heart.

"But I—"

"Look, Lucy. Truthfully. I'm just going to lay it out here for you. I don't want to scare you. But I—I care for you. I'm trying to do everything you ask of me, and that includes keeping my distance, but I know that you know in your heart there is something between us. And I'm just asking for a chance. I know I've royally messed up in my past. And I've asked God to forgive me. All I'm asking is for you to give this connection we have a fighting chance."

Her hand came up and she toyed with the collar of her shirt. She was unable to speak or think past the reasons bombarding her that this was a terrible idea. She didn't want to do it. She didn't want to risk her heart. But she knew in her heart of hearts that she wanted so much to give "them" a chance. He'd messed up. But he had respected every boundary she'd put up since the kiss. Didn't he deserve something from her?

"Okay. I would like that."

Chapter Eighteen

"So I hear you have a date."

Lucy blinked in disbelief at Ms. Jo as she dabbed paint on the canvas. This was their first official Gals Night Out Paint Class, as they'd officially called it, and to her surprise she had over half a dozen students. Including Mabel, Ms. Jo, Nana and Jolie. The other three ladies were friends of theirs and just as chatty as they could be. Despite the fact that everything wasn't completely set up, they'd decided to get together anyway.

And it had been a fun night.

They'd had refreshments and she'd walked them through painting their first still life—a beautiful bunch of grapes she'd set on a platter and focused a spotlight on so that there would be shadows and highlights.

No one was painting masterpieces yet, but they were having a great time and Lucy had actually been happy that for a little while she was being distracted from the fact that she'd accepted a date with Rowdy for the next evening.

And now Ms. Jo had just opened her love life up for

group discussion. An internal groan threatened to burst out of her and expose her real fear.

"Yes, I am." She managed to sound calm. Amazing since she was a little bit freaked out about the whole thing.

"Jo, you weren't supposed to say anything about that," Mabel said. It was an odd turnaround that Mabel was getting onto Jo, when it was usually Ms. Jo keeping Mabel in line. "Ruby Ann shared that with us in strictest confidentiality."

Ms. Jo dipped her chin and looked over the rim of her glasses. "It's all over town, Mabel, in case you haven't noticed. I've been sitting here debating if she should be forewarned and decided that yes, it is our duty to let her know."

Nana looked worried. "It wasn't meant to get out. The boys ganged up on Rowdy and gave him the push he needed to ask you out. They convinced him it was the thing to do."

He'd asked her out because the boys talked him into it.

"Now, don't even start thinking he asked you out because the boys wanted him to." Jolie read her mind. "You know as well as all of us that he's been dying to ask you out, but wasn't sure it was the thing to do."

"Well, I heard Drewbaker and Chili discussing it on the bench out by the newspaper office," Vergie Little said, waving her brush.

Sissy Jackson and Bea Norton nodded their heads.

So everybody knew she was going on a date. The room burst into chatter about how nice it was and that she needed a night out and that Rowdy was a changed man.

Jolie didn't say much and Lucy said less. What else was there to say?

If she wanted to, she knew she could use this as an excuse not to go out with Rowdy. She could claim that he shouldn't have told everyone. Different reasons for calling off the date made themselves known to her as she listened to the gals cheer that she was finally going to have a night out like a young woman should.

And the truth was, she agreed. She could let Tim cause her to become a hermit or she could step out and force herself to have a life.

She was not a chicken.

Never had been and never would be. She wouldn't let herself.

And though she'd forgotten it for a while, that meant she had to fight the fear about going out with Rowdy.

She had to fight, to back it down or, like Mabel had reminded her again, the regrets would be hard to live with.

Rowdy deserved for her to give this a chance. Scars and all.

On Saturday evening at six o'clock Rowdy stood outside Lucy's back door, a bouquet of fresh spring flowers gripped in his hand. It had taken him almost thirty minutes at the florist to decide which to buy. He'd wanted all of them but knew that would be a little crazy. But that was how he felt about Lucy.

Rubbing the back of his neck, he took a deep breath and knocked on the door. He hoped she hadn't been looking out a window and saw how nervous he was. He had to be calm, cool and cautious. He could not mess this up.

But ever since he'd realized she'd painted his likeness on that canvas with such detail that even the emotion in his eyes had shown, he knew that Lucy Calvert was not only the most talented artist he'd ever seen, but she also just might care for him deep down. That scared her, and with good reason.

He'd prayed long and hard and he knew that the outcome of this night could very well be the most important of his life.

The door opened and he almost dropped the flowers. "Wow."

She took his breath away. For the first time since he'd known her she didn't have a work shirt on. Though she did have a long-sleeved blouse, it was shimmery silky material in a rich gold tone and she had a colorful scarf draped about her neck. She had hidden her scars without resorting to a bulky work shirt. She had skinny jeans on with strappy high-heeled sandals. She was at least five-two in the heels and it made him smile.

"You look gorgeous," he added to the *wow* he'd blurted out in pure reaction.

She bit her lip then smiled almost shyly. "Thank you. You, too— I mean, not gorgeous—handsome."

They both laughed and his nerves eased with the laughter.

"These are for you." He held the flowers out to her and she took them almost eagerly.

"How lovely. You shouldn't have," she said, but he could tell that he'd chosen right. And that she was pleased.

"Come in, let me put these in water and then I'm ready."

He followed her into the kitchen and watched as she filled a vase from a cupboard, then arranged the flowers, taking time to make them look great. It was amazing what a difference she could make just by pushing and pulling a few flowers here and there. The artist in her was evident in more than her painting.

"Okay," she said, turning to him. "They are beautiful and I'm ready."

But was he? Praying he wouldn't mess up, he held the door for her and they were soon on their way.

It was a lovely evening. The sun was just beginning to set when Rowdy opened the door of his truck for her. He held out his hand and the fiery orange sky lit the world behind him as Lucy took his hand. It felt as explosive as her emotions. His eyes were dark with what she thought was worry. She'd been watching for his arrival. How could she not, with her nerves jingling like they were? And she hadn't missed the hesitancy in his posture and the anxious expression on his face as he'd knocked on the door. He'd been tense since she opened it…other than when he'd almost made her blush by his appreciative appraisal when he first saw her.

He was as uptight about the date as she was.

"I'd better hold on tight or you might topple off those heels of yours," he said, squeezing her fingers gently and eyeing her sandals.

There he was, her happy-go-lucky guy.

Her guy?

"I haven't had any reason to wear heels since I've been here," she said with a smile, suddenly feeling a small semblance of ease between them. "But I'm quite steady on my feet in them."

"Too bad," he said, still holding her hand as he placed his hand on her waist to help her as she stepped up into his truck. "I was hoping you'd need my assistance all evening."

Her heart was fluttering as she sat in the seat, eye level with him and so very near. "I'll probably need it. After saying that I'll probably twist my ankle or something."

"Not on my watch, sweetheart." He tugged her seat belt out and stretched it around her and clamped it in place, meeting her gaze as he leaned over her. "You're safe with me. Heels or no heels."

She could not breathe as he withdrew, closed her door and strode around to slide into the driver's seat. Yup, that sunset didn't even compare to the intense emotions at war inside her as he pulled out onto the blacktop and headed toward wherever…. She didn't even know where they were going and she didn't care. Tonight she felt alive, and beautiful in his eyes—she wasn't allowing herself to think about her scars. Not tonight. Tonight she was a regular woman on a regular date.

Yet she took that back as she looked over at Rowdy's profile. This could never be considered a regular date. Nothing with Rowdy could ever be considered regular. He was special and she knew it.

Rowdy had seriously contemplated where to take Lucy to dinner. It had to be nice. It had to make her feel as special as he thought she was and it had to be romantic. He was going to make sure she knew this wasn't just two friends going out for a burger.

He finally decided on a little Greek place off the beaten path in River Bend. After the hour it took to reach the larger town, they'd both relaxed a little and were talking and laughing about the antics of the boys. The boys were always a safe subject.

The hostess seated them in a quiet corner of the

restaurant at a table for two. Soft music played in the background, candles flickered at tables in the dim light. Lucy's smile of appreciation was all he needed to know he'd chosen right.

"This is nice. I love the atmosphere." She talked about the unique color of deep green on the walls, how the rich hardwood floors combined with it and about the chandeliers hanging overhead made from tree branches. "I think they were going for romance in the outdoors," she said softly. "It's really a neat place, though descriptions would never do it justice."

He chuckled. "You've done a good job. I like the atmosphere, but the food is excellent."

"I would have never taken you for a guy who would eat anything other than steak. Greek. Who would have thought it?"

"Hey, that's stereotyping. Cowboys enjoy things other than steak and potatoes."

"So I see. And I like that very much."

By the time their meal had come and they'd nearly finished, he and Lucy were having a good time. Lucy's eyes sparkled in the candlelight and she'd even flirted with him a few times. It hit him full force that this was who she'd been before her husband had stolen her ability to trust.

When she laughed at something he said about the boys ganging up on him to give him the courage to ask her out, he couldn't help reaching across and tracing the back of her hand with his fingers.

"I'm so glad they convinced me to see if you would accept a date with me," he said, turning serious. "I'd convinced myself there wasn't a chance."

She flipped her hand over so that she was holding

his hand. "I still can't believe I said yes. I am so glad I came."

As she said the words that reached inside him like warmth from a flame, she looked up, distracted. He turned his head to see if the waitress had come back with their check, but his heart went cold when he saw Liz approaching, her gaze locked on him like a target at a shooting range.

Chapter Nineteen

"Rowdy, I saw those amazing shoulders of yours and that black hair and knew instantly it was you."

Lucy had known the woman was coming their way on purpose. Even the distraction of Rowdy's hand holding hers hadn't prevented her from seeing the way this woman zeroed in on Rowdy. She was an amazing creature—tall, willowy, with hair so blond and so shiny it caught every flicker of light as it framed one of the most beautiful faces Lucy had ever seen.

She'd yet to look at Lucy and had eyes for only Rowdy, who, Lucy noted as he'd drawn his hand from hers, looked a little pale beneath his tan. His eyes had darkened with—anger or appreciation? She wasn't sure. But though he didn't say anything, she felt the tension in him even across the table.

The beautiful woman gave a sultry pout that Lucy figured a man might find attractive. She herself would look silly even trying such a move. Lucy decided with a quick judgment that she didn't like this woman.

Something curled inside Lucy as the woman's predatory gaze flickered over Rowdy. At the calculated way she flicked a strand of champagne-colored hair from her shoulder. Even the way she stood was a pose to bring attention to her figure as she crowded Rowdy's personal space.

"I've missed you," she said, perfect hands toying with the silk tie at the low neckline of her blouse.

Lucy sat very still, her gaze shifting to Rowdy. Why was he not saying anything? His gaze was locked on the woman and a muscle in his cheek flinched.

"I have nothing to say to you, Liz," he said at last.

Liz, as he'd called her, gave a soft laugh. "Not so fast, handsome. You need to know I'm divorcing Garret. So no more of that messy situation. I'm a free agent and I'd love to see you sometime. You have my number."

The moment she realized who this was, Lucy went cold inside. Liz turned and walked away, letting her hand slide casually to her back pocket—another calculated move to draw attention as she strolled away. Rowdy didn't watch her leave; instead, he was looking straight at Lucy.

Despite the anxious way Rowdy was eyeing her, she couldn't speak. So many things were running through her mind. This was the kind of woman he'd dated. This was the married woman he'd had the affair with. What a horrible creature she was, and this was the woman— the *type* of woman—that Rowdy had found attractive.

She was beautiful, but— "I'm ready to leave," Lucy said, barely able to look at Rowdy.

He motioned for the waitress, who quickly brought them their check, and within minutes they were out the door and in the truck. It couldn't have been fast enough for Lucy. Her stomach churned and she was almost afraid she was going to be ill.

What had she been thinking? How had she let herself fall into this pit?

Rowdy didn't say much. He was, it seemed, as upset as she was. Halfway home he pulled off the road into someone's pasture entrance and put the truck in Park.

Rubbing the crease that had formed across his forehead, he sighed. "That couldn't have gone more wrong if I'd have written it in a book. Lucy, I know you've got all kinds of bad things going on inside your head right now. I'm sorry that happened. But I'm more sorry I ever got involved with her."

Lucy looked out the window into the darkness. What could she say?

"Talk to me, Lucy."

"About what?" she snapped. Anger that had been coiled inside of her broke loose. "I should never have let this happen. I should never have let my guard down."

"Lucy, I'm not the same stupid guy I used to be. I'm not."

She turned toward him. "It doesn't matter. Don't you see I can't do this—us? *I* can't do this. Please take me home."

Rowdy had died and *not* gone to heaven. That was for certain.

Tucker and Morgan had come out to his house, a small place that he'd taken over after he'd moved out of the big house. It was hidden in the woods, and it worked as a great place to hole up when he wanted to be alone.

And he wanted to be alone.

"What's going on?" Tucker asked, finding him on the back porch where he'd been nursing a strong cup of coffee and a sour mood.

"Now, why would you think there was anything wrong?" he asked, sarcasm thick as the yaupon growing in the woods around them.

Morgan shot him a concerned look. "You didn't show up at church Sunday or work yesterday. And Jolie said that when Lucy came to teach art, she looked about as gloomy as a stormy night."

"The boys noticed, too, and kept asking her how your date went," Tucker added. Even the fact that his brother had driven out here said he was worried, and Rowdy knew it. How many times had his brothers had to come get him out of trouble when he was growing up?

"Oh, yeah, and what did she say when they asked her that?" He had his elbows on his knees and was studying the planks between his boots.

"She told them it went fine. But no one believes her."

"She's not doing fine," he muttered. "I messed up and made her feel bad." Sitting up, he looked at his brothers. He'd never felt as terrible and low as he felt now. He'd spent time praying and venting and wishing he'd taken back ever pushing Lucy to go out with him. And he said as much to his brothers. "Her lousy husband left her with a tremendous amount of emotional scar tissue. The last thing she needed was a man like me thinking there was anything but heartache that I could offer her."

Morgan placed his hand on his shoulder. "Rowdy, you don't need to be talking like that. You have a lot to offer Lucy, or any woman, for that matter. You've made some mistakes, but who of us hasn't one way or the other? You've changed."

"Yes, I have, but I'm no good for Lucy. Lucy needs a man who has been a rock from day one. A solid man she knows she can trust."

Tucker pulled up a chair and sat across from him, looking him square in the eye. "It's not for you to say what kind of man she needs. God knows the man she needs and as far as I can tell He's put you in her life. Now, whether He's put you in her life to be the man she's to end up with, I can't say, brother. But I can tell you that He didn't put you in her life by accident."

Rowdy grunted cynically. But Lucy falling out of the hayloft and into his arms flashed across his mind.

Tucker ignored him. "What you're going through right now is going to come into play one way or another. What I want to know is, are you committed to see it through? When I was in Iraq I didn't need men beside me who were in halfway. I needed commitment even though we had no idea what the outcome was going to be. Do you love her?"

Morgan yanked a chair up and crossed his arms. His hiked brow posed the same question.

Rowdy nodded slowly, mulling over what Tucker had said. Tucker wasn't a man of a lot of words. Rowdy set his coffee on the side table and sat up. "I do," he said aloud. He'd made a commitment to God that he was going to wait for his direction in his life. He'd made more mistakes along the way where Lucy was concerned, but she hadn't just dropped in his arms for nothing.

Rowdy was certain of that.

"Then the question is, are you going to see this through, wherever it goes, even if it's not in your favor?" Morgan finally spoke and Tucker nodded as he talked.

"I've been so caught up in the fact that I wasn't right for Lucy that I never even stopped to consider if God had a different reason for me being here for her." His mind was suddenly churning. He told his brothers about Liz showing up and how it had affected Lucy.

"She barely spoke to me after that. And just wanted to go home. Then she told me she couldn't see me anymore."

"And you gave up, just like that?" Tucker asked. "That's not the guy I know."

"Hey, I changed, remember?"

Morgan shook his head. "Rowdy, just because you changed doesn't mean you roll over and play dead. God's not going to do all the work, you know."

Rowdy scowled at his brothers. "Hey, why are y'all still here, anyway? I've got somewhere to be." He stood up and strode through the house and straight to his truck.

"It's about time," Tucker called after him.

And Morgan's, "We'll be praying for you both," was the last thing he heard before he slammed his truck door closed and revved his engine.

It was time to see his girl....

Lucy couldn't help but worry that she'd hurt Rowdy. She'd been so upset after the date that she'd not said much, and she'd left him in her driveway in a very unkind way.

Just as he had done from the moment she'd told him about Tim and her burns, he'd again done as she wished. He'd not tried to kiss her and he'd kept his hands to himself. He'd been nothing but kind to her. And all that he'd asked of her was to give this, this *thing* between them a chance.

And then this Liz person showed up and made her... what? Jealous? Feel inferior in a physical way?

Liz, as horrible as she was and as much a soul that

Lucy knew needed the Lord in her life, had shown Lucy that Rowdy deserved so much more than either she or Liz could offer him.

By Tuesday morning Lucy knew she had to talk to Rowdy. Pulling up to the ranch, she looked around for Rowdy's truck but she didn't see it. She learned from Jolie and the kids on Monday during afternoon art class that no one had seen him on Sunday and he hadn't shown up at the main ranch compound at all on Monday.

Lucy hadn't shown up for church on Sunday, either, and felt guilty about that, but she had been too upset.

As she looked around now, her spirits plummeted further because she'd felt compelled to talk to him. Not feeling like seeing anyone else, she turned her truck around in the parking lot and headed back home. In her rearview mirror, she caught a glimpse of Tony coming out of the barn, leading his horse. But she didn't stop. She was in no shape to talk to anyone right now. Except Rowdy.

Once she made it back to her house, she slammed out of her truck and walked to the barn. She pulled open the double doors and didn't bother to close them behind her. Her boots clattered on the steps as she jogged up to her studio. She had every intention of trying to paint, but Rowdy stared back at her from his painting and all she could do was stand there and stare back.

She loved him.

It was as clear in the painting as anything she'd ever known in her heart. She'd painted the picture with love and she hadn't even recognized it until now.

Closing her eyes, she let the realization pour over her and she tried to absorb what it meant for her. Nothing.

How long she stood there she wasn't sure, but she tried in every way to convince herself that her falling in love with Rowdy was a blessing sent from God to help her heal. But it wasn't, and there was no use trying to convince herself of the fact.

"Lucy, are you up there?"

Rowdy!

Her heart jumped into her throat and she panicked. He was here! "Yes," she said, stilling herself for a very hard conversation. But it was one that needed to be started and finished. She would not walk away from this again. Rowdy deserved to know her heart.

His steps were quick as he, too, jogged up the stairs. She was startled when she saw him. He hadn't shaved and a five-o'clock shadow roughened his jaw. He stopped inside the doorway for the first few seconds. Lucy fought the need to wrap her arms around him and tell him she was so sorry.

To tell him that she trusted him and that she knew he was a changed man. That everything he'd shown her of his character had been that of a man of integrity.

"Lucy, I've come to say my piece." He crossed to stand just a step away from her. "You're a stubborn woman. And I've realized that I've been letting you have your way just a little too much."

What?

"I'm a changed man. I have messed up and messed up some more and I'll mess up in the future, I can promise you that. But I can promise you that if I give you my word about anything—and I mean anything—I'll come through with it. I'll never lie or cheat on you. I've never done that with anyone, even before I made a commitment to God that I was changing the way I lived. So you can rest assured that with a good woman like you—the woman I love—that I'd be a man of integrity till my dying breath."

Lucy's temper had spiked at the high-handed way he'd started off, but that anger had diffused like a popped balloon.

"I believe you," she said. And it was so true. "You are not Tim. Tim was never the man you are and I've come to realize that as I thought about this for the past few days."

He'd said he loved her.

Lucy closed her eyes and let the bittersweet knowledge seep into the dark places of her heart. Tears threatened and she backed them into a corner knowing this was not the time to cry *or* to be weak. And it was most positively not the time to be selfish.

Touching his cheek, she smiled at him. "I treated you badly, Rowdy. So badly, and I am so very sorry for that. You are so special. But you have this all wrong. I was upset the other night because…" She couldn't tell him she was jealous. "Because I realized when I looked at Liz that you deserve so much more. More than she or I could give you."

His brows met and his head cocked as if in question. He started to speak and she shook her head.

"Please, I need to finish." She pulled her hand away and took a deep breath. "When I said I couldn't do this, I was saying that *I* can't. Not because of anything you've done. I just can't do it. Beneath this shirt is a body so scarred that even I have a hard time looking at it. I don't have it in me to share. As a wife, I'd feel so inferior."

"Don't talk that way," he snapped, letting his eyes fall to her work shirt. "I don't care what your body looks like. Lucy, I love you. The fact that you have scars doesn't matter to me. They would only remind me of the strength and courage you've shown in the face of great adversity. You are beautiful to me, mind, body and soul."

She hardened her heart against what he was saying. She refused to let her guard down. "No, Rowdy. I'm damaged beyond repair in my mind and I can't—" A crash downstairs halted her words. Rowdy spun around and started for the stairs just as the nicker of a horse sounded and then hooves pounded on hard ground.

Running to the window, Lucy felt sick when she saw Tony galloping across the pasture like wolves were chasing him.

"Rowdy, it's Tony. He must have heard what I said."

"Come on." She raced down the stairs and didn't ask questions as she jumped into his truck. She held on as he backed out of the driveway as if they'd been shot out of a cannon.

"Where will he go?"

Rowdy didn't say anything. He turned into a drive a few yards down the road that led into a pasture of the Sunrise Ranch and drove over the cattle guard and into the pasture that stretched between her house and the ranch. Lucy studied his profile as they bounced over that rutted gravel road. They hadn't gone far when he detoured to another road and spun gravel, fishtailing to make the direction change. He was angry.

Everything about him radiated anger as they charged over the pasture in pursuit of Tony.

All she could think about were the scars on Tony's body. And the pain her words must have caused him.

She started praying. In the distance she glimpsed him, riding low as he and the horse practically flew up one hill and disappeared over the other. In the distance she could see the stable.

"He's going home."

"Yes. He's going to the stable," Rowdy said tersely, sounding as though he'd known exactly where Tony would go. "The place he feels safe."

Lucy snapped her head to stare at Rowdy. His curt words had been matter-of-fact. "How do you know that?"

"When he first came to us, that was where we'd find him when things got too hard for him to handle. He'll go into a stall."

When they reached the yard, Lucy was shocked to see the boys climbing out of the arena with looks of concern and curiosity on their faces as they headed toward the stable. Tony's horse was standing alone at the entrance, breathing hard. But Tony was nowhere to be seen.

Rowdy bailed out of the truck in an instant and she followed.

"Stop, guys. Let me go in by myself," he commanded Wes and Joseph, who were almost at the entrance but had stopped when they saw Rowdy.

"He was flying when he rounded the arena and charged through here," Joseph said.

"Flying," Wes echoed, spitting a sunflower seed. "What's wrong with him, Rowdy?"

Lucy walked past them without answering. "Let me, Rowdy. I did this. I need to fix it." Without waiting, she walked into the barn and started down the center of the alley. About halfway down she saw a stall gate slightly ajar. Tugging it open, she stepped inside. Tony was sitting in the corner—his knees drawn up and his arms folded over them with his head down.

After all the pain this kid had suffered, she'd just

caused him more. It was unbearable to her. Foolish, foolish woman.

Swallowing the lump in her throat and praying for the right words—something she'd been sorely lacking of late—she sank down beside him in the soft hay. "Tony. I'm sorry."

"It's nothing but the truth," he said, not looking up. He swiped his face on his shirtsleeve. "I came to tell you that I met a girl." His words were muffled against his arm.

Normally for a kid of fifteen, this would be no big deal, but Tony didn't talk to girls much. He was shy around them and she knew exactly why, just as most of the fellas did. His burns.

"I think that's wonderful," she said, but he shook his head. "I know you worry about your scars."

His head shot up and he glared at her. "I heard what you told Rowdy."

Shame suffused Lucy. *I'm damaged beyond repair in my mind and I can't—* "I was so afraid," she said, aching inside with regret. "Oh, Tony. It's complicated."

"Yeah, it's easy to tell me one thing and believe another. You made me believe God would have a woman out there when I grow up. And for her my scars wouldn't matter."

"Everything she said is true," Rowdy said, entering the stall. "There will be someone out there who won't care. Who will love you with all their heart."

He was talking to Tony, but Lucy knew he was also telling her.

"But the key will be whether you love that woman back. Because that's going to be the tough part, Tony. You'll have to love that person, too, because even if she doesn't have physical scars, she'll have warts of some kind. We all do. She'll have messed up. She won't be perfect. But if you love her enough to trust her with your heart and your scars, and to trust what God has done for you, then you have nothing to worry about."

Tony was looking from Rowdy to Lucy.

"Is that how you feel about Lucy?"

Rowdy gave him a smile that melted her chilled, ashamed heart. He nodded. "I love Lucy, scars and all. Especially with her scars. But the question is, how does she feel about me?"

Tony and Rowdy were both looking at her.

"Don't let your scars stop you, Lucy," Tony said, trying to give her courage. "Do you love him?"

Lucy nodded. How could she not after everything he'd just said? "I do love you, Rowdy."

The words were soft, but they were sure. She held her hand up, and he took it and tugged her to her feet.

"Can you trust me with your heart and your scars? And to love you always?"

She knew she could. "Yes. I already do."

A to-die-for smile flashed across his face and he pulled her into his arms—a sense of home sweet home swept through her at the ironclad strength that wrapped around her.

"Then you'll marry me?" he asked, looking deep into her eyes.

"Yes. Oh, yes, I will," she said, and with the words her heart opened wide. Tony scrambled to his feet behind them and raced from the stall.

"They're gettin' *married!*" he shouted gleefully as he went.

Lucy laughed. "He's going to be okay."

"And so are we," Rowdy said. "You asked me not to kiss you again. But do you think you could make an exception and I could kiss you this once?"

Oh, how she loved this man. Touching his cheek with her palm, she drew his head toward her. "Would you kiss me forever, please?"

And that was all the encouragement he needed as Rowdy's lips met hers with a sigh. "I thought you'd never ask."

"Hubba, hubba! That's what I'm talking about," Wes said, and Lucy and Rowdy jerked apart to find all the boys crammed against the stall railing, peering at them. "Hey, don't stop on our account," the teen said, holding up a hand. "Come on, fellas, let's give these two love-birds some space."

And with that, sixteen smiling faces backed up and followed their leader out of the barn.

"Now, where were we?" Rowdy asked, his eyes twinkling as he slipped an arm beneath her knees and swung her up and into his arms.

Lucy wrapped her arms around his neck. "Right where I've belonged from the first moment I met you," she said.

"There you go, talking some sense now," Rowdy chuckled, and kissed her again. . . .

* * * * *

SPECIAL EXCERPT FROM

⬧HARLEQUIN
SPECIAL EDITION

*When Laurel Hudson is found—alive but with
amnesia—no one is more relieved than Adam Fortune.
He will do whatever it takes to reunite mother and son,
even if it means a road trip in extremely close quarters.
Will the long journey home remind Laurel how much
they truly share?*

*Read on for a sneak preview of the final book in
The Fortunes of Texas: Rambling Rose continuity,*
The Texan's Baby Bombshell *by Allison Leigh.*

He'd been falling for her from the very beginning. But
that kiss had sealed the deal for him.

Now that glossy oak-barrel hair slid over her shoulder
as Laurel's head turned and she looked his way.

His step faltered.

Her eyes were the same stunning shade of blue they'd
always been. Her perfectly heart-shaped face was pale
and delicate looking even without the pink scar on her
forehead between her eyebrows.

Her eyebrows pulled together as their eyes met.

Remember me.

Remember us.

The words—unwanted and unexpected—pulsed
through him, drowning out the splitting headache and the
aching back and the impatience, the relief and the pain.

Then she blinked those incredible eyes of hers and he realized there was a flush on her cheeks and she was chewing at the corner of her lips. In contrast to her delicate features, her lips were just as full and pouty as they'd always been.

Kissing them had been an adventure in and of itself.

He pushed the pointless memory out of his head and then had to shove his hands in the pockets of his jeans because they were actually shaking.

"Hi." Puny first word to say to the woman who'd made a wreck out of him.

Still seated, she looked up at him. "Hi." She sounded breathless. "It's…it's Adam, right?"

The pain sitting in the pit of his stomach then had nothing to do with anything except her. He yanked his right hand from his pocket and held it out. "Adam Fortune."

She looked uncertain, then slowly settled her hand into his.

Unlike Dr. Granger's firm, brief clasp, Laurel's touch felt chilled and tentative. And it lingered. "I'm Lisa."

God help him. He was not strong enough for this.

Don't miss
The Texan's Baby Bombshell *by Allison Leigh,*
available June 2020 wherever
Harlequin Special Edition books and ebooks are sold.

Harlequin.com

HSEEXP0520

Brooklyn K-9 Unit officer Belle Montera glanced back on the shortcut through Cadman Plaza Park, her K-9 partner, Justice, a sleek German shepherd, moving ahead of her as she held tightly to his leash. She had a weird sense she was being followed, but it had to be nothing.

Justice lifted his black nose and sniffed the humid air, then gave a soft woof. He might have seen a squirrel frolicking in the tall oaks, or he could have sensed Belle's agitation. Still on duty, she kept a keen eye on her surroundings.

"No time to go after innocent squirrels," she told Justice. "We're working, remember?"

Her faithful companion gave her a dark-eyed stare, his black K-9 unit protective vest cinched around his firm belly.

They were both on high alert.

"It's okay, boy," she said, giving Justice's shiny black-and-tan coat a soft rub. "Just my overactive imagination getting the best of me."

She had a meeting with a man who could have information regarding the McGregor murders. The DNA match from that case had indicated that US marshal Emmett Gage could be related to the killer.

The team had done a thorough background check on the marshal to eliminate him as a suspect, then Belle had been assigned to meet with him.

Justice lifted his head and sniffed again, his nose in the air. The big dog glanced back. Belle checked over her shoulder.

No one there.

She slowed and listened to hear if any footsteps hit the strip of pavement curving through the path toward the federal courthouse near the park.

Belle heard through the trees what sounded like a motorcycle revving, then nothing but the birds chirping. Minutes passed and then she heard a noise on the path, the crackle of a twig breaking, the slight shift of shoes hitting asphalt, a whiff of stale body odor wafting through the air. The hair on the back of her neck stood up and Belle knew then.

Someone is following me.

Don't miss
Deadly Connection *by Lenora Worth,*
available June 2020 wherever
Love Inspired Suspense books and ebooks are sold.

LoveInspired.com

LISEXP0520